To Steve —
Part of Frack Land!

Mother Fracker

By Larry *Bud* Meyer

Larry Bud Meyer

This is a work of fiction. Names, characters, places and incidents are either the products of the author's imagination or are used fictitiously. Any resemblance to actual events, locales or persons, living or dead, is entirely coincidental.

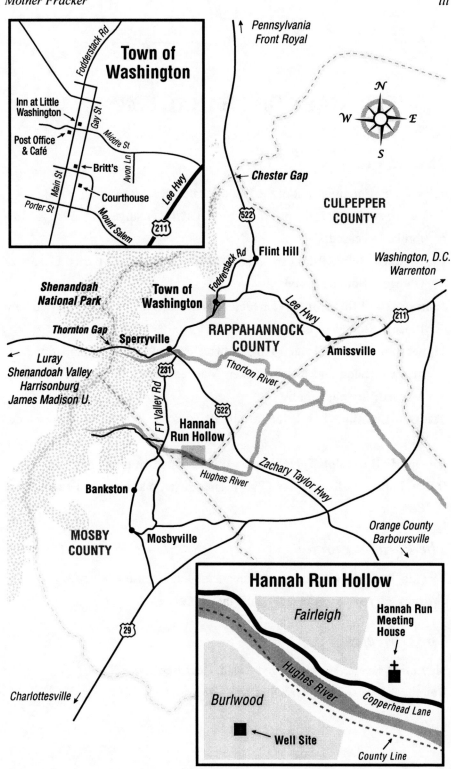

CAST OF CHARACTERS

The Tyler Clan

John Tyler, 10th president of the United States. Deceased.

James Tazewell Tyler, the president's son. Civil War surgeon. Moved to California. Deceased.

Tazewell Randolph Tyler (Taz), the president's grandson. Married Esperanza Obregon. Both deceased.

James Tazwell Randolph Tyler (Jeter), father of Tip and Ting. Married Sara Lincoln. Both deceased.

Tippecanoe Tazwell Tyler (Tip), Pulitzer Prize-winning journalist, gentleman watchdog and brandy maker. Married Rennie O'Keefe (deceased). Married Virginie Paradis.

Madison Lightfoot Lee Tyler (Maddie), Tip's daughter. Foundation executive.

Albemarle Randolph Tyler (Marley), Tip's daughter. Photographer.

Dolley Paine Madison Tyler (Ting), Tip's sister, matriarch of Fairleigh and beet grower.

The Paradis Family

Virginie Paradis (Gini), French bureaucrat and Tip's second wife.

Jacques Paradis, ciderist and Gini's father. Deceased.

The O'Keefes

Slayton O'Keefe, Tip's teenaged friend. Deceased.

Rennie O'Keefe, Tip Tyler's first wife. Deceased.

The Thursday Irregulars

Walker Longwood, a beekeeper.

Provo Starke, a rancher.

Fran McKinney, Rappahannock County sheriff.

Gus Martini, owner of Martini Vineyards.

Tip Tyler.

Green Valley Resources

Roxanna Raye Bleigh (Roxx), engineer. Project manager for Green Valley Resources.

Bill Dinwiddie, department head.

Malcolm X Jones, deputy project manager.

Bob Lock, exploration department.

The Bleighs

Roxx Bleigh.

Capt. Ralph Bleigh, U.S. Army intelligence, father of Roxx.

Barbara Bleigh, mother of Roxx.

The Spinks

Jeremiah Spink, homesteader and builder of original Fairleigh. Deceased.

Gen. Fletcher Spink, Appomattox veteran. Deceased.

Burleson Spink Sr., drilled well at Burlwood. Deceased.

Burleson Spink, older of the Spink brothers.

Woodrow Spink, younger of the Spink brothers.

The Lopez Family

Domingo Lopez (Sunday), long-time farm manager at Fairleigh.

Josefina Lopez, pastry chef at Inn at Kelly's Ford.

Ricardo Lopez, Wakefield student, lacrosse star.

Enrique Lopez, Wakefield student, lacrosse star.

The Ladies Who Lunch

Arva Jones, a former D.C. publicist.

Jaye Holland, co-owner of Holland Emporium.

Britt Schaefer, owner of Britt's on Main restaurant.

Claire Hargadon, artist.

Ellen Martini, co-owner of Martini Vineyards. Wife of Gus.

Ann Schneider, sous chef, Inn at Little Washington.

Heather Mack, the mayor's wife.

Caroline Comer, *The Rappahannock Reporter* columnist.

Beth Hinson, conservationist.

Margaret Prost, the Senator's daughter-in-law.

Ting Tyler.

Fran McKinney.

Marley Tyler.

The Journalists

Paul Schaefer, editor, *The Rappahannock Reporter*.

Andrew Forster, *Reporter* publisher.

Asa Youngblood (Acey), *Reporter* photographer-reporter.

Caroline Comer, *Reporter* columnist.

Harry Warren, VirginiaWatch.

Kelso Arbuckle, editor, *The Mosbyville Monitor*.

Kevin King, *Monitor* photographer.

The Restaurateurs

The Chef, proprietor, Inn at Little Washington.

Big Jim Jay, owner, Country Café.

Michelle, Country Café waitress.

Josefina Lopez, pastry chef, Inn at Kelly's Ford.

Ann Schneider, sous chef, Inn at Little Washington.

Britt Schaefer, owner of Britt's on Main. Wife of editor Paul Schaefer.

The Politicians

Milton V. Smythe, Mosby County supervisor. Publisher of *The Mosbyville Monitor*.

Rep. Robert Morris (R-N.C.).

Rep. Wellington Harm (R-Va.).

The Senator, Evan Prost, retired U.S. senator from Minnesota.

Leroy Jenkins, Rappahannock County supervisor.

Malcolm Martin, Rappahannock County supervisor.

Al German, Rappahannock County administrator.

Dave Walton, commonwealth's attorney.

Others

Cletus Mahan, postmaster, pastor at Hannah Run Meeting House, neighbor.

Melanie Pike-Stanton, public relations executive for the American Petroleum Association.

Miles Massie.

Les Leong, Maddie Tyler's beau, U.S. Undersecretary of Energy.

Lt. Joe Elliot, Rappahannock County Sheriff's Office.

Alvaro Verdeja, president and CEO, Fairfax Grant Foundation.

The Tanker Drivers

Hank Cody. Milton Smythe's nephew.

Jamie Burnham.

PART I

CHAPTER ONE

Tuesday, Oct. 1

In the hour before dusk, sun whitewashed the sycamore branches arching above Copperhead Lane. The Hughes River fell fast and free in a tango with the road's turns. A sprinting cold front refreshed the hollow, trumpeting autumn's first frost.

The brunette driving a battered BMW sped out of Fairleigh's drive and downshifted into the first of the S-curves that gave the gravelly stretch of road its name.

Tip Tyler followed in his pickup with its cargo of produce, windows down, grille blanketed by mud from the sedan. The Dodgers-Cardinals playoff game faded in and out on the tinny speakers of the Studebaker half-ton, but the home team was up, 3-2, top of the third.

In this part of rural Virginia, old pickups were common. Vintage German sedans were rare as celibate priests. Tip's sister Ting, the Beemer's owner, considered the old four-door so essential to a matriarch's life that she'd kept it well past 200,000 miles. Ting Tyler had imported the 5-Series back to Rappahannock County after a rent-to-buy tour of Germany in '93. At first, it was the town car she used to visit her horsey friends in Middleburg. Since then, she'd driven it across every rutted trail at Fairleigh, the Tylers' 200-acre riverfront spread in the county's southernmost corner. These days it took her to the weekly Culpeper farmer's market, bushels of her renowned organic beets in the trunk.

A more customary vehicle for a Piedmont matriarch might be a tree hugger's green Subaru or a soccer mom's Honda Pilot. The ride of choice for most locals living up every hollow would be a rusted red pickup.

She'd dubbed it Silver Cloud. Beneath its gap-toothed front hung a red and white Virginia tag: Farm Use.

Tip trailed, the pickup's shocks creaking with each swerve.

But the driver ahead, home long enough to drop her backpack, had been antsy in his presence.

Her awkward silences on the 78-minute ride home from Dulles that after-noon had removed all doubt about where he stood with her. With *them*. Maybe it was as she'd said: She loathed Northern Virginia's suburban sprawl; couldn't wait to be back amid Blue Ridge rock and oak. Loved sunset. But he knew. No one to blame but himself.

So here she was joyriding up ahead, destination Red Oak Mountain. Both drivers crested a knoll offering a westerly view, close-in hillocks lushly green. Their more distant brethren rose bluish-gray, a chromatic tribute to the pre-served Union's contestants.

The smell of fresh manure wafted into the truck's cab as they passed Fair-leigh's last pasture on the left, occupied by three-dozen Black Angus and their knock-kneed offspring.

"Bases jammed with Dodger Blue," droned Mike Shannon, the Cards' long-time radio voice. Tip remembered him as a hometown rookie back in '62. "Full count on Ramirez."

He saw Silver Cloud hug Copperhead's precarious edge, making way for an oncoming tractor hauling bales on a flatbed. Tip slowed and raised two fingers to Pump Zeigler, chugging to his pasture back up the hollow. Once Tip was clear, the lead car was already out of sight.

He'd spotted her outside of Arrivals, carrying only the backpack. He saw how she'd aged.

He dropped the visor for a look in the mirror, instinctively comparing the fresh reminder of her features with his. Same hazel eyes, though his were get-ting rheumy. She had the olive complexion of her great-grandma Esperanza, Taz Tyler's California treasure. Had her mother's freckled nose, thank good-ness. His own was reddened by hours in the orchard sunshine.

He flipped the visor up as he passed the Hannah Run Meeting House, branches of its majestic Founder's Oak clearing the green tin roof. Too late, Tip waved to Pastor Cletus Mahan riding a mower around the lawn surround-ing the stucco home of local Baptists since 1762.

Tip spotted the Beemer again and snuck a peek over his shoulder. Black-ie had settled between the apples and the beets, nose quivering, tail keeping its own time. She was part Labrador retriever, part breeder's lie; sooty black but for the telltale white paws. His Labradoubt. He'd christened her Arkansas Black after the heritage apple blended in his artisanal brandy.

The sanctifying cirrus promised a classic sunset over the heights of Shenandoah National Park. By dinnertime, there would be no color, no light but for a flicker or three, leaving Rappahannock cloaked in pitch black. When folks 'round here sung the county's praises, they ticked off: no interstates, no fast-food chains, no supermarkets. Oh, and that midnight shroud. Our prized asset.

The BMW zipped into the last hairpin before Sharp Rock Road and disappeared.

CRA-THUMP!

Skidd-dd-dd …

WHAMMM!

Screech of metal. Shatter of glass.

Tip's stomach seized.

The grinding receded into a sickening last crunch as he rounded the bend.

"*GodDAMN*! Not again!"

He braked hard, apples flying, as he spotted the white tail staring from the road. Startled look as always; wide-eyed, haughty. But … a *tic*, a tremor. Blackie leapt out of the truck bed in full pursuit as the fawn bounded to the opposite bank.

"Blackie! Don't!"

In the tangle of roadside brush, Tip saw the dusky doe, prone. Its red-stained forelegs stretched to 11 o'clock; hind legs twisted at 5. A second fawn, motionless. No match for steel belts.

Purple, he thought. *The deer. Purple deer?*

The jagged oak trunk marked the sedan's path. Tip jerked his door open.

"Strike three! Slider, inside corner!"

He peered below. A hundred yards on, the car rested roof-down in the pebbled riverbed, with its mangled grille facing him. Water swirled in the windows.

He scrabbled down the bank.

Where's my daughter?

"MARLEY!!" he boomed. "MARLEY TYLER!! Talk to me!"

CHAPTER TWO

Saturday, Sept. 21, 10 days earlier ...

The Virginia welcome sign loomed, the last of four states Hank Cody would traverse in the refashioned Peterbilt. Highway 522 South finally widened after the molasses two-lane stretch through West Virginia. The LED clock said 1:30 a.m.

Three hours ago, Hank had hopped in the cab fronting the new 4,000-gallon vacuum tank in Mineral Springs, heading toward the infamous Pennsylvania Turnpike. He'd glanced at the mileage: 160,545. The two brother tankers had lined up behind him. Three ships setting sail.

During the pre-trip checkout, he'd wiped clean the RESIDUAL WASTE sign and puzzled over the confusing numbers and the red and green diamonds. He'd spotted signs of age on the rig that its new 305-horsepower Cummins engine couldn't disguise. He'd also caught the whiff of rotten eggs. The last thing his dad's cousin Milton had told him: Don't ask questions if you don't want to know the answers.

Behind them was the knuckle-biting leg of the four-hour trip — the tunnels, twists and inclines of the Keystone State's aging turnpike. So was the nanosecond in western Maryland at the Mason-Dixon Line and the two-lane tedium of West-By-God.

This gig had come just in time for Hank. He'd endured three years without the means to pay rent, feed the family, afford cable. God bless Cousin Milton and the Marcellus Shale Gale.

A quick jog north of Winchester took them to Interstate 81. The speedometer hit 75 for the first time. Signs quickly announced I-66 and the big swing east. Dead ahead, girdled by the Beltway: Washington, D.C. Worst commute in the nation. Not on the itinerary.

All too soon came the exit to Front Royal, again dumping the convoy on 522 — the Zachary Taylor Highway. "Shenandoah River," Hank's GPS indicated. They zigzagged through the small-town surface roads, past '40s and '50s motels still trying to snag visitors headed to Skyline Drive as it starts its meander atop the spine of Shenandoah National Park.

The truckers finally snaked up toward Chester Gap. Hank passed a green highway sign. "Leaving Warren County. Entering Rappahannock County."

Ten minutes later, the convoy entered Flint Hill, slowing to 25. Looks like a nice place, he thought. He whispered the evocative street names: Fodderstack Road. Ben Venue.

Minutes later, the GPS droned instructions. "Right turn in 200 yards on Lee Highway."

The four-lane took him west, passing places speaking to bygone generations: Massie's Corner. Battle Mountain. He passed three exits to a village — "Inn at Little Washington," announced one. St. Peter's Catholic Church sat to the left with its "Choose Life" sign. Directly across the road was the Log Cabin Gun Shop's "HI-CAP MAGS." Just past the gun shop: Kiddie Kare: "A safe place for YOUR tot."

The tanker trio approached Sperryville. Hank turned left to enter the village and immediately rumbled across a narrow bridge. A T intersection came up fast, airbrakes groaning in protest. The headlights framed the Corner Store.

He looked right, began to turn left. A car from the left zipped past *waytooquick.*

"Sonofabitch!"

Hank exhaled and geared up. Two churches and a cemetery later, the tankers turned south on Route 231. A sign with a cheery cardinal said: Scenic Virginia Byway.

And it was, even at night: Processionals of maples, still green in the high beams; rolling hills fronted by neat stone walls safeguarding homes dating to pre-Revolutionary America. Tin-roofed farmhouses squatted amid their dependencies like brood hens. Miles of white fence hinted of stables and moneyed mares secreted behind.

Ten minutes on, just past the turn to Hannah Run Hollow and Old Rag Mountain, Hank saw a new sign: "Leaving Rappahannock County. Entering Mosby County."

The GPS chirped. "Destination approaching."

He couldn't miss the entrance on the right — gilt letters against a white backdrop: Burlwood. He continued past the main entrance a quarter-mile.

"Destination in 100 yards."

The tanker's headlights grabbed a figure in a hardhat standing before a metal farm gate on the right. Hank eased to a stop.

"Turn here," the guard yelled. "Eight-tenths of a mile to the top. Follow the sign."

Hank bounced along the single graveled lane. Not meant for rigs like these.

Another hardhat at the crest of the hill pointed him toward a blaze of lights.

Even now, 2:45 a.m., workers swarmed beneath a towering superstructure surrounded by cranes, dump trucks, stacks of PVC pipes and a scattering of mobile homes.

Hank whistled as he approached a yawning crater lined with new concrete.

"You're late," said another hardhat, this one with a serious-looking clipboard.

Hank blinked. Wisps of blond. *Niiice* chassis, even hidden by the jeans jacket. Lipstick glistened in the overhead light.

"Who are you?" he asked.

"Later, Hank. It is Hank, right? Get this sucker turned around. Back 'er up."

But Hank couldn't miss the smile as she spoke into a headset. "First convoy's arrived."

CHAPTER THREE

Rappahannock Reporter, Thursday, Oct. 3

She blinded me with science

From the moment I returned to Rappahannock seven years ago, the *Reporter* has beseeched me to write local commentaries. I've demurred. Though I got my start here, my journalism days are in the rearview mirror. I don't own a computer. In my day, I reported *facts*, leaving the opinions to others. That said, I sit at my Olivetti Underwood to push back on the misguided proposal detailed on your Sept. 26 front page to teach Creationism in Rappahannock County Schools.

The idea's backers cite their Great Creator as the source of our county's great beauty, waving a mystical wand from His throne in the clouds.

But the fact is, science explains it all. The *sciences*, really. Geology. Chemistry. Biology. Botany. The subjects our schools *should* be teaching.

Allow me to show you the science responsible for the beauty of this place we call home.

Extreme force created our Blue Ridge hollows. Massive tectonic plates collided 1.2 billion years ago, thrusting tortured rock toward the heavens. Old Rag, the highest peak most of us see, gets its humpback from slow-cooling magma that formed nearly impervious rock.

We boast the oldest bedrock in the eastern United States — Precambrian gneisses and granites. Numerous fault lines course deep beneath us. Our backyard peaks are the spine of Shenandoah National Park, making up the western fifth of our

county. From their gnarled tops they plunge, first into ridge-
and-hollow forests, then ease eastward, becoming the Piedmont. Over the mountains lies the grand Shenandoah bowl.

Most of what we sit on started elsewhere when Europe's
mantle up and crashed into Virginia, arriving as volcanic frag-
ments without so much as a visa. The resulting shale deposits
were the first arrivals in Rappahannock. Given the way we
classify ourselves — who's *from*-here and who's *come*-here
— I wish T. rex were around to look down his flaring nose at
all the rest of us.

Beneath us, via a slim (and so far untapped) spur, lies the
Marcellus Shale, one of the planet's largest natural gas fields,
the source of all that drilling just north of us in Pennsylvania.
(Let us be thankful we are spared all that).

What we see gazing at the cerulean blue ridges is a result
of isoprene, a natural hydrocarbon released from our ample
forests.

Only central China rivals this part of southern Appalachia
for biodiversity. Coniferous spruce and firs hug the higher el-
evations. Joining them below are oak, hickory, sycamore, tulip
and black walnut. American bald eagles and red-tailed hawks
patrol the currents above.

Below the canopy, black gum, sassafras, sourwood and
flowering dogwood please our senses. Wild turkey and bob-
white range forest grounds and open meadows. The cardinal,
our state bird, darts between roadside tangles of huckleberry
and mountain laurel. We share our lands with black bear, wild
boar, coons, possums and smaller critters. Sadly, invasives
like coyote and deer — nature's come-heres — are bullying
out red fox and peregrine falcon.

Verdant pastures of bluestem, timothy and alfalfa checker-
board the hills, providing the finish for the grass-fed cattle and
romping grounds for future Triple Crown winners.

More than 2,000 streams keep those lands lush. The Rappahannock's tributaries — the Hazel, Thornton, Rush, Covington and Hughes — have their headwaters high up in the federal parkland before joining the river as it runs southeast toward the Atlantic. Those free-flowing streams complement the aquifer that replenishes the private wells where nine in 10 of us get our water.

All of this took 4.5 billion years to reach its current, *natural* perfection.

Don't make me out to be a tree hugger. I'm a recovering journalist crafting apple brandy. Widower. Father. Brother. Neighbor. Possibly, friend. In three decades of reporting and writing, I witnessed human screwup and breathtaking natural beauty. Science held the answers. Not once could I attribute any of it to a miracle.

I have a one-word definition for Creationism: Hokum. The God you follow may smite me for this, but I offer my nightly thanks to Mother Nature. And when I consider our county's bounteous beauty, I say: You go, Girl!

Tippecanoe T. Tyler
Fairleigh
Hannah Run Hollow

CHAPTER FOUR

Sunday, Sept. 22, 3:15 a.m.

"Eyes here, fellas. Didn't they teach you friggin' tanker jocks any manners in vo-tech?"

Hank Cody and two companions blushed and slowly looked up as the blonde in bright lipstick crossed her arms, clipboard shielding the objects of their stares. Working among male engineers, she was more than accustomed to leers. But this was her first project manager gig, and she meant to establish decorum, even if it meant stifling her use of the F-word.

Behind her was the spanking new containment pond, concrete barely hard.

"Welcome to Burlwood," she said. "THE southernmost frontier of the Marcellus Shale Play."

Three pair of eyes looked anywhere but straight ahead.

"Well, anyway, you fellas will be spending lots of time here on your dump runs. I want you familiar with the place. We're gonna run through our safety — what?"

Hank Cody had raised a sheepish hand.

"What do we call you?"

"I'm Roxx Bleigh, project manager for Green Valley Resources. That's R-O-Double-X. Roxx."

She'd settled on the name, one she felt suitable for a woman in engineering, during the freshman Biology 114 lecture on XX and XY chromosomes. That she was taking a college science class at all had much to do with two primal interests: water and sex.

Her earliest memories were of the pier at Parker Canyon Lake on glaringly cool winter mornings, holding her daddy's hand. Ralph Bleigh taught her to catch sunfish on his R&R weekends away from Fort Huachuca in southwest Arizona. He was on the lowest rung of the ladder for Army intelligence officers, out there among the saguaro and striations. At sunset, Ralph, wife Barb and Roxanna would head in their old '69 VW van to the overlook above the dam impounding the Santa Cruz River. Ralph would put his daughter on his khakied shoulders and explain how the dam turned the thin stream into the mighty blue reservoir, then spin and point to a hill five miles distant where Mexico begins stretching southward.

She hadn't really thought of her own vocational interests until her junior high days in Germany, courtesy of Ralph's tour with the 66th Military Intelligence. The first person to mention the word *career* was Herr Iglesias, guidance counselor and Earth Science teacher at the International School in Wiesbaden.

Ramon Iglesias had strung the 14-year-old along masterfully, offering her extra credit and showering attention during the school year, intriguing her with his Spanish accent. He'd repeatedly offered to show her the rolling hills of the Taunus region on the back of his Vespa. One brilliant May afternoon, days before departing Germany, she'd relented. After their second lusty go at it lying on a cotton blanket in the Spa Park, her tartan uniform skirt bunched at the waist, he'd had the decency to inquire about her scholarly likes and dislikes.

"I don't really know. Math. Science."

Tell 'em what they want to hear.

"And water!" She propped herself up on elbows, engaged. "Rivers. Lakes. Stuff like that. My dad says water's the key to life."

"Sounds like enyeneering," he said.

As it turned out, biology was *kind*a interesting. Cells, dissection, babies. She also liked algebra's challenging equations.

The younger Roxanna had waffled between ambition and lassitude — something about the untethered nature of being an Army brat and the naiveté of being an only child. She fended off the jocks and shrimpers at Key West High after Ralph was transferred to Boca Chica. She befriended the Honor Society guys she towered over, cribbing off their homework. Few of the other sunburned Keys girls aspired to anything more than daiquiris and weed.

Her mom had grown up a Southern belle in Mobile. Barb's femininity was completely out of fashion in Fall-of-the-Wall Germany and the libertine Keys. It was Barb who urged a conflicted Roxanna to enter the Miss Monroe County pageant.

The high school junior mopped up the competition, notably in the swimsuit segment, where the taut burgundy Speedo scarcely contained her physical charms. But Roxanna, representing Stock Island, also impressed judges with a 20-second speech on the fragile water supply serving an island chain that extended 120 miles from the mainland.

Her first and last pageant win was overturned after she and the runner-up, Miss Duck Key, were picked up at 1 a.m. in a weaving Sebring ragtop on the Channel Five Bridge, alcohol levels elevated by a bottle of Cold Duck. It didn't matter that Roxanna was the passenger or that their destination was the Florida Keys Aqueduct Authority to investigate a summer job posting. Chief Warrant Officer Bleigh paid her bail in his full dress uniform and silently drove his daughter home. She was depressed for weeks; she just *hated* disappointing Ralph.

The Duck/Duck irony wouldn't hit her until years later, when she 'fessed up to the underage drinking rap during Green Valley Resource's final interview. A background check had turned up an old police blotter item from *The Keynoter*. The pageant officials had minimized the scandal by offering *The Key West Citizen* a photo of the surprised replacement winner, second runner-up Miss Tavernier.

Fortunately, a new posting in Virginia intervened. Although James Madison U. sits in the middle of the Shenandoah Valley, Harrisonburg was a dump. Her just-above-average high school grades had netted rejections from Virginia Tech and Georgetown, but a call from Ralph had helped land a spot in JMU's freshman class. Her dad's new gig at Langley meant she could see the parentals often. She knew she'd pleased him when she declared engineering as a major.

Roxanna Raye Bleigh, Engineer, she'd inked in cursive loops in the spiral biology notebook.

Gotta look more professional.

Printed letters: R.R. Bleigh, Civil Engineer.

Nope.

Bold block letters: Roxx Bleigh, P.E.

Hmm.

Roxx Bleigh. Just androgynous enough, and it sounded powerful.

With a name like that, the bitchier Tri Delts wondered if Roxx was, *yew knowww*. Behind her back they called her Rosie, as in O'Donnell. Roxx knew they were just jealous of her endowments. At least sorority life as an Alpha Phi had made the mandatory dorms slightly more tolerable. She dated a few guys her age, but most of 'em were from podunks like Peola Mills. They lacked worldliness. She and her sorority sisters roamed the area on the weekends, traveling to Charlottesville and Lexington, where the bars and the guys were more interesting.

She started bearing down and the grades crept up, which pleased Ralph. She bristled when a prof discouraged her from taking 355: The Geochemistry of Natural Waters, saying the class held no appeal for "girls." She took it any-way and got the second highest A in the class. The chemistry classes kicked her butt, what with all those elements, -eses and compounds. She latched on to her Chem TA as her boy toy. Senior year, they blew off a case study (Exxon Valdez and risk) in 478, nicknamed Slip 'n' Slide as it was all about oil and water. Still got a B minus.

Roxx Bleigh. The name helped once she began the master's program at the School of Engineering & Applied Science in Charlottesville. So what if her JMU grades hadn't been *quite* good enough for Virginia Tech's master's program, where Ralph had wanted her to go? At least she got in. The UVA engineering motto: *Git 'Er Done*. As in, complete the job. On time. Under budget. Most famous alum: Larry the Cable Guy.

The name (and her looks) set her apart from the four frumps in her Civ-il Infrastructure Engineering emphasis. The horndog faculty loved having a looker in their seminars and welcomed her to Friday margarita-fests at The Virginian. The tenured associate director of the CE program became her friend with benefits. He orchestrated her election as president of the student chapter of Tau Beta Pi. She got a taste of what it was like to run things.

Roxx had her pick of employers. Firms were jonesing to boost their di-versity numbers. Green Valley, a mom 'n' pop compared to the Chevrons and Schlumbergers, promised management track, offered the fattest bonus and hired her for the Pittsburgh office after a pro forma discussion about risk and responsibility. As far as she was concerned, the buck stopped with the CEO.

That was *sooo* five years ago. Her boss, Bill Dinwiddie, told her Green Valley Resources meant to springboard this Marcellus Shale into the big time. She felt she was ready; she'd been getting 'er done on hydraulic fracturing assignments in the Catskills (well-site exploration) and Youngstown (retrofitting old Ohio wells).

Everyone said the project management road starts in a backwater. Mosby County fit the bill. She was freaked by the hush-hush nature of the assignment and the client's weirdo politics. But now she was on the job at her project, up to here in cowshit and rednecks.

"As I was saying, we take safety seriously here," she said to the truckers. "You're going to be offloading millions of gallons of frackwater — I mean, flowback — and we'll be pumping it down that big old hole over there. And I do mean old. Compressor station, over there. County water supply comes through that pipeline. Offices in those trailers. Finish your load, hit the road Jack, but do come back."

"Now, Malcolm Jones here is my No. 2. He's gonna walk you through the safety procedures."

Then she used her favorite line from grad school.

"Pay attention, fellas. There *will* be a pop quiz."

CHAPTER FIVE

Tuesday, Oct. 1, 8 p.m.

"Room 313?"

The Fauquier Health nurse glanced at the pair of visitors.

"Sorry, hon," she frowned. "Intensive care. Family only."

"We're here for Albemarle Tyler. I'm her father. Mr. Longwood here's her … godfather."

"Oh! I just loved those movies. Why, he looks like that actor. Morgan … whatshisname?"

"Room 313 is …?"

"Freeman! Oh, all right. See those gals through the glass?"

The pair hustled toward a graying matron holding a gardener's hat. Next to her, a brunette GenXer in beige shift and teal scarf. The women looked up as Tip entered.

"How is she?"

Ting Tyler shot him a look. "When did you start to care?" The remark earned her an elbow from the younger woman. "She just fell asleep. About time you graced us with your presence."

"The sheriff needed me. Eyewitness," he said.

He turned to the brunette. "Maddie … I'm … glad you're here."

"Tip."

Always with the Tip. Never Dad or Pop.

"I just got here, too," said Maddie Tyler, twisting the scarf. "Traffic from Old Town to Warrenton was *brutal*."

A beep from the bedside monitor caused the four visitors to turn to the sleeping patient. Marley Tyler's face was a palette of eggplant bruises and butterfly stitches. The dark ponytail rose and fell at her shoulder. An IV fed a vein at her left elbow. The right wrist bore a white cast wrapped in blue gauze.

"She'll be OK," Walker Longwood said to Maddie, hugging her. "You twins are indestructible."

It hadn't quite started that way, thought Tip as he looked at Marley, recalling another hospital bed, another emergency.

Columbia, Missouri. Hot morning. Labor Day weekend, 1975. He'd received the phone call just as he was punching out after the graveyard shift behind the Broadway Diner's grill, shoveling hash browns for drunken Sigma Nus and early-rising State Farm agents. Come quick, their fourth-floor neighbor Allie had said. Something's not right.

He'd raced home on his 10-speed, taking the stairs three at a time, five flights up in the brick Paquin Street apartment building. Halfway up, he heard the approaching siren of the ambulance. His wife, Rennie, lay red and exhausted on the tangled sheets of the two-room flat. Allie held a towel to her forehead.

"She's in labor!" she shouted.

An hour later the twins were born pink and squalling at Boone County Hospital: Maddie first, Marley 10 minutes later.

Maddie and Marley. More formally, Madison Lightfoot Lee Tyler and Albemarle Randolph Tyler. Tip and Rennie, the weight of tradition on their shoulders, picked the names hoping they'd meet with the approval of the twins' grandfather, Jeter.

They did, though the old man thought the new parents were skimping by slapping Marley with just one middle initial. After all, in the land of J.E.B. Stuart, James Tazwell Randolph Tyler, aka Jeter, knew a thing or two of extra nomenclature.

The twins bawled through Tip's final year at the school Walter Williams had founded in 1908 in the audacious belief that the lowly trade of journalism could be taught. The Missouri Method.

That was back when it all still seemed possible, when Woodward and Bernstein brought down presidents, and citizens read newspapers, and the industry was invincible. Back when a career meant spending three decades in Miami covering the Everglades and the Keys and documenting the despicable things man did to the Earth in the name of progress. Back in the era of objectivity, when reporters confirmed facts based on two sources, when larger-than-life editors wrangled and polished and decided, and the readers accepted it all blindly. Back before Tip's after-the-fact Pulitzer, the one with the asterisk.

Pre-Internet, when reporting demanded time, integrity and shoe leather. Back before 140 characters and likes and going viral.

It went south, not just because Craigslist and algorithms and Amazon ushered in the era of red ink and decimated news staffs. The business-side types, lulled by decades of 25 percent operating profit margins, didn't see it coming. Though remaining newsroom denizens may have reinvented themselves by now in the digital age, it ended for Tip by choice in an anticlimactic buyout and self-imposed exile to Fairleigh's cider house.

He'd arrived there in 2006 with baggage. Recrimination. Regret. All because of his treatment of these very girls and their aunt.

"She seems so fragile," said Maddie.

"Don't worry," said Walker, a head taller than the Tylers. "Your daddy pulled her out of that river. Saved her."

Maddie Tyler met her father's eyes with reproach.

"I was worried out of my MIND! I had to hear it from a deputy!"

The frost. Just like her sister at the airport.

"And, Aunt Ting, I left you a gazillion texts!"

"I was at Garden Club," she said. "You know we don't get signals in town. One of the deputies picked me up and gave me a lift."

Ting paused; shook her head. Tip knew she was thinking about Silver Cloud.

Maddie grabbed the chart and flipped through the pages. The words blurred: Contusions. Water inhalation. Abrasions.

"I did talk to Doc Rose Zimmer. They're keeping her overnight," said Ting. "Lungs are clear. A broken wrist's the worst of it."

"That's a relief," Tip said. "Guess she's going to miss the Peace Corps thing."

"How do you get off being so cavalier, brother?" Ting said, hands on hips. "After yet another accident."

"Now wait."

"His Accidency strikes again?" Walker said.

They all stared. Beneath the salted bill of his Stonewall cap, Tip's glazed eyes told them he'd girded for the inquisition. The jinx. The family curse, now falling once again on Tip's shoulders.

In 1840, the Whigs picked William Henry Harrison over Henry Clay. To appease the Great Compromiser, Virginian John Tyler joined a ticket with the Old Injun Fighter in the Battle of Tippecanoe. Harrison won handsomely, bolstered by chants of "Tippecanoe and Tyler too."

His inaugural speech was delivered hatless in a chill March rain. Dead a month later. Pneumonia.

The president's demise thrust the still-fragile democracy into its first succession crisis. Tyler took his own oath and boldly moved into the White House, infuriating friend and foe alike. Detractors, even among his own party, never accepted Tyler's legitimacy. Throughout a checkered administration, he was derided as "His Accidency."

Jeter dressed it up a bit in one of his history quizzes for young Tip.

Quick now. Your illustrious ancestor, boy?

John Tyler, 10th president.

Where was he born?

Virginia, sir.

More exact.

Sherwood Forest.

Same county as ...

President Harrison, sir.

Ol' Tippecanoe, your namesake, all he did was burn Tecumseh's village. But if it weren't for him, boy, nobody'd know the Tyler clan a-tall.

Question, sir?

Go on.

Were they on Robin Hood's side?

"Look, I picked her up at Dulles," Tip sighed. "She didn't say much about what she'd been doing in Colorado. She was eager to get to D.C. to see Peace Corps pals. She said she wanted to catch sunset on Red Oak, and she was upset because she couldn't get online. She insisted on taking Ting's car. I'd forgotten to drop by the Food Bank with the produce, so I followed. Happened just past the Meeting House."

"On Copperhead? Where Walker nailed the 10-pointer last year?" Maddie asked.

"Same spot," said Longwood.

Only road-kill aficionados could be happy with Rappahannock's deer epidemic, a bane to the most cautious motorist. Carcasses littered the region's roadsides. For organic growers like Ting Tyler, it was all-out war.

"Here's the thing," Tip said to Maddie. "She hit *two* deer."

From the bed, a gravelly voice:

"And they were *purple*."

CHAPTER SIX

Thursday, Oct. 3, 6:30 a.m.

"So you heard the whole conversation?" Tip asked Marley as he parked in front of the Country Café's bay window. "Wait, let me get that for you."

"Yeah, they didn't give me much happy juice after the first night," said his daughter as he opened the door. "Two nights in the hospital are quite enough. Thanks for coming so early."

"Least I could do. I'm guessing you're starving."

"You bet. By the way, uhh … Tip. Thanks for pulling me out."

Still with the Tip.

"Call it partial amends," he said, jingling a stack of quarters. "Stay here. I'll get us *The Post* and *The Reporter*."

The brick eatery sat at Main and Middle streets, an intersection busy enough to merit three stop signs. The café shared an ivy-covered facade and twin front doors with the post office serving Washington, Virginia, 22747. The original Washington.

Recite last night's reading, boy.

Washington was a wilderness surveyor. Age 17. In July 1749, he laid out Little Wash —"

The First *Washington, boy. Do not demean it by calling it "little."*

He kept a journal. "I laid off a town." He sketched it with Main Street and Gay Street running parallel. Four cross streets, sir, from Middle to Jett.

You have a question, boy?

Why is it called Gay Street, sir?

As Tip returned with the papers, the post office door flew open with a bang. Clete Mahan, wearing his moth-eaten U.S. Postal Service sweater, held the door with one hand, the local newspaper in the other.

"I saw your pickup," he said, breeze mussing his comb-over. "The Lord bless you."

"Why, thanks, Clete. This's my daughter, Marley. You remember her?"

Cletus Mahan nodded. His day job was running Little Washington's post office. Concerns about his commingling of church and state regularly arose on the community listserv RappChat, but Reverend Clete liked to say he served The People 7 a.m. to 4 p.m., Monday through Friday, and The Lord 24/7.

"You are a literate man, Master Tyler. I grant you that," said Mahan, page turned to the opinions and letters. "I only hope you can be saved from the grips of your atheism."

"We'll see, Clete," said Tip, turning toward the bank of nickel-plated boxes. "You sure turned 'em out for the school board meeting."

"While you were by yourself, I noticed. 'The righteous chooses his friends carefully.' Proverbs."

"I'll keep that in mind," Tip said.

Tip checked P.O. Box 35. Rolled inside were *Science News, Sierra.* Nothing from France. He tossed a postcard from the American Petroleum Association with pastoral scenes touting natural gas — propaganda sent to members of the Society of Environmental Journalists. He walked out to the waiting Marley and pulled out his pocket watch: 6:45 a.m.

He glanced across the intersection to the white pillars of the Inn at Little Washington. A bellman packed Hartmann luggage in a crimson Bentley as a couple waited. The balding fellow wore a fawn cashmere sport coat and khakis, his companion a clingy leopard-print tunic, leggings and black leather boots up to here. They'd probably driven out the afternoon before from Georgetown or Great Falls to celebrate an anniversary or a Birthday with a Zero. They'd strolled the quaint village's streets, taking all of a half-hour. They'd poked into the galleries, lingered at R.R. Holland's emporium, then dropped a wad at the Inn's pumpkin-hued Shoppe.

No doubt they'd kicked off the Inn's five-diamond experience with cocktails in the Monkey Bar. The main event was a five-course dinner featuring the region's ranchers and growers. A shared Carpaccio of Baby Lamb with Caesar Salad Ice Cream (Wit's End Farm, Amissville). Medallions of Veal Shenandoah for the gentleman (Belle Ridge Farm, Woodville), Lobster Omelette for the lady, with the chilled beet pasta salad (Fairleigh, Hannah Run

Hollow). The sommelier would have gone with a crisp, slightly oaky 2008 Shafer chardonnay, followed by the '98 Chateau Palmer Margaux. Dessert featured Montmorency cherries from the Inn's own gardens across the street. They likely took the '73 Taylor's Crusted Port from the 80-page wine list up to the junior suite with fireplace for a good grunting shag in a canopied bed the size of a small state.

Embers likely still glowed in that suite this chill morning, as did the gentleman's memories of shaved truffles and Calvados cream sauce. Also burning was the hole in his pocket for the 18-hour bacchanalia: $2,515.45. At local fund-raisers, the from-heres say they can't afford to win the generously donated dinner-for-two at the Inn. Can't afford the tax and tip.

Tip hoped the couple hadn't missed the Inn's best offering: breakfast in the garden room. Local pork sausage, orange-yolk eggs, cinnamon croissant. A Limoges cup filled with 13 exotic fruits. In the bellman's hand, though, was the lagniappe for departing motorists: a boxed picnic lunch complete with half-bottle of the Inn's signature viognier.

For more than 30 years of acclaim, James Beard Awards and glossy cookbooks, the Inn and The Chef had put the village on the foodie map. As main employer and largest landowner in town, the Inn called the shots at City Hall, where The Chef also sat as vice mayor. He first ran and won in a futile attempt to scrub his tasteful street of B.O. Jenkins' scabrous junkyard just two doors down. Nowadays a constellation of galleries, shops and B&Bs rise and fall with the Inn's seasons. Locals smirk after meeting yet another newcomer initially wooed by the good country life during a visit to the Inn. A return visit later, the newbie has plunked down high six figures for a leaky farmhouse and 25 acres. "Where's my cut from all your closings?" The Chef often teased the village's real estate agents.

Everyone chuckled at the tabloid fascination — *Petraeus biographer texted at Inn while husband fumed. Hollywood honeymooners Ryan and Blake slip out Inn's side door*. Even the coffee-drinking, Red Man crowd outside Quicke Mart gabbed about The Chef's $17 million breakup with his longtime partner, the question being: Who got Sahara and Shaman, the Dalmatians inspiring the spotted togs sported by the kitchen staff? (The answer drew sniggers: "He did.")

Tip watched the bellman close the trunk.

"I need to set up a tasting over there," he said to Marley. "After all, I offer a local, artisan brandy!"

Dozens of the Inn's ex-sous chefs now served up agreeable dining experiences across the Piedmont. Agreeable everywhere but here, Tip rued, holding open the café's door.

"Hello, sugar," said Linda, a frost-tipped plus-size. She worked the register while her husband, Big Jim Jay, flipped home fries. He aimed a pointer finger at Tip, mock-firing with a wink.

"Morning," Tip nodded back. "Everyone remember Marley? My daughter."

Chairs snugged up to a dozen tables covered in brown and white tattersall. Tip and Marley took the middle table.

"Welcome back," said the waitress, bringing a silver pot and clean mugs. "Tip, she's a keeper."

"Thanks, Miz Michelle," Tip smiled as Walker loped in. "Marley, I apologize now for anything and everything you hear from us."

"What's said at the café stays at the café," Walker told Marley.

The county had long forgotten Walker Longwood's integration of the café with his father and Tip and Jeter Tyler.

Walker and Tip were just teens when they met in 1967, the year Jeter enrolled Tip and Ting in the all-black Scrabble School, the only white family fed up enough with Byrd Organization segregation to do so. Years later, Jeter admitted his "righteous" decision had unleashed a vicious whisper campaign from some "respectable" from-heres.

The other Scrabble students mocked Walker, a beanpole whose Angela Davis-worthy Afro added five inches to his frame. Everybody knew he was smart and got straight As. Nobody had ever heard him talk. They'd heard he'd nearly died from bee stings as a toddler when he got too close to the hives at the Longwood family's place, so they giggled every time they passed him in the hall. Stinger, they called him. Bee-man.

The next April, the day after Doctor King's assassination, a group of

Scrabble students approached the young Tylers and began to curse. Walker stepped in front of the pair with folded arms, wordlessly ending the confrontation. Tip gave Walker *To Kill a Mockingbird* from Fairleigh's library the following day to say thanks. The next day, Walker gave Tip a copy of Richard Wright's *Native Son.* That began a lifelong exchange of books on politics, nature and philosophy.

"My bees are settling down after their trip back from the California almond fields," Walker said, still standing. "It was a tight fit, getting six hives in that panel truck. Good news, though. They're all chardonnay Democrats."

"Who's *this* young un?"

Marley turned to see a drawling speaker grabbing Tip's shoulders.

"Off limits, my friend," said Walker. "She's family."

Provo Starke, nearly as tall as the beekeeper, extended a hand to Marley. Sandy hair and a Sam Elliott mustache set off his rancher's garb: tan Stetson, Levis, navy pocket T-shirt, short-sleeved despite the chill.

"You must be Marley. Those cows poopulating your pastures? They're my old reliables. You folks are good enough to give 'em shelter."

"Black Angus. My favorite," Marley said.

"Momma Starke, she read that editorial of yours," Starke told Tip. "Said to say sacrilegious fools burn eternally. I'm gonna start callin' you Torch."

"I thought *you* were the hunka-hunka burnin' love, Marlboro Man," said Gus Martini, popping through the door. A head shorter than Provo, he removed a purple Martini Vineyards cap, loosing a shock of jet-black hair.

"Are all grape growers humor-impaired, or is it just a Roaming Catholic thing?" said Starke.

"I heard it said you're a practicing Moron."

"Mormon, pal. At least our preachers don't diddle acolytes."

"At least the Kennedys won," Gus said. "Marley, we heard you were back. How are you?"

"Michelle, get these folks some of that miserable stuff you call coffee," said Starke.

"Provo's impersonating a comedian again," came another voice. The speaker, a blonde with taut ponytail, was hanging up a brown leather jacket and trooper's hat. "I can run you in for that."

Respectful nods all around. "Sheriff." "Fran." "Mornin', ma'am."

With a grace bespeaking an Olympic veteran, Fran McKinney swung into the seat next to Tip. She half-stood to look Marley in the eye across the table, clasping her good hand.

"Miss Albemarle Tyler. Haven't seen you since state finals."

"I still have our state champs trophy," said Marley, grinning as the others sat. "You were our rock back in goal. You haven't changed. Well, you *have* ..." she said, eyeing the uniform.

"Haven't we all," said Fran with an eye-rolling scan of the table. "Welcome to the Thursday Morning Irregulars. Closest thing we have to a chamber of commerce."

The sheriff snapped open the weekly *Reporter* and tapped the headline on Tip's guest editorial.

"You're rusty. There *is* such a thing as a Virginia gentleman," she said. "Did you forget religion's one of those First Amendment things, right there with press freedom?"

"Lots of us think the founders shoulda put the Second first," Provo said.

"The accident story's pretty accurate," said Fran. "They quoted Dub Anderson. Not even *he* had ever heard of *two* deer getting hit. He's older than dirt."

"I took that curve and BOOM!" Marley said. "Good thing Tip was following."

Fran McKinney leaned forward, nodding for the others to come closer. In two terms as the county's first female sheriff, she understood discretion.

"We thought something was off about those deer. I had my deputy take the big carcass, the doe, over to Frank Davies at the Ag Department lab."

Other tables were filling quickly with a mix of ex-hippies, bank staffers and wide-eyed hikers in Georgetown hoodies. Tip nodded to County Administrator Al German and Commonwealth's Attorney Dave Walton, both in jacket and tie. Paul Schaefer, the latest editor striving to make the *Reporter* readable, sat with the paper's publisher, Andrew Forster.

"Thanks for the piece," the publisher mouthed silently to Tip.

Conversation buzzed as plates stacked with biscuits and flapjacks arrived. The Irregulars talked Lions Club, grandkids, property taxes. Miles Massie, scion of one of the oldest from-here clans, left without a nod to anyone.

Marley studied Fran McKinney's ease among her peers.

Tip grabbed the check. "My treat, but we gotta go. Time to check on my barrels."

"Ditto," said Gus. "New shipment of bottles coming in."

"Nothing excitin' ever happens around here," said Provo, grabbing a toothpick.

Marley and Fran stood. "You could pick worse places to recuperate, Marley," the sheriff said. "Be careful, though. Tip and your aunt occasionally need a referee."

"Wish they had wireless," said Marley.

"Oh, how's Ting getting around? That Beemer needs work."

Marley looked at Tip. "Not sure yet."

"You OK to drive? An automatic?"

"I'm on painkillers," she said, lifting the cast. "They're legal. I think."

Fran smiled.

"Tip, she's coming with me. Marley, walk this way."

Marley grinned. "Talk this way ..."

"What?" Tip said.

"Girl thing," said Fran, putting on the trooper's hat.

CHAPTER SEVEN

Monday, Oct. 7, 9 a.m.

The fat clip file sat on Milton Smythe's oak desk, the one the folks at James Madison's Montpelier estate never could account for after the '03 inventory. The Mosby County supervisor, unopposed in next month's election for what would be an unprecedented 11th term, leaned back. The high-backed chair groaned beneath his girth. His scowl darkened.

Spread before him were maps of New York, Pennsylvania, Ohio, Virginia, Maryland and West Virginia. Thousands of neon-yellow XXs marked the locations of natural gas wells. Magic Marker orange snakes showed sinuous pipelines for liquefied natural gas. His computer screen glowed with a topographical map of Mosby, wedged between Shenandoah National Park to the west and Rappahannock County to the north and east. A dotted red line showed the boundaries of Burlwood, bordering on the Hughes River, 12 miles north of Mosbyville. A purple bull's eye was labeled "WELL SITE."

"Royal purple," he whispered.

Rich as a king.

He'd prided himself on masterminding what was already the acme of his public service career. No one else in Northern Virginia saw what he saw, knew what he knew. Not those smartass Chantilly technocrats. Not the bazillionaire K Street lobbyists. Not the Charlottesville tweedy-heads or the muddy-boots crew from Blacksburg. The Richmond dweebs who pass for bureaucrats? Ha! Not even that wet-behind-the-ears Jewish fella in Congress. Whatshisname ... Cantor. Never bothered to step foot here in Mosby County; too busy foiling the Socialist in the White House and his gay Hollywood liberal friends.

Milton Vincent Smythe had spent years measuring himself for greatness in governing, close by the homes of Jefferson, Madison and Monroe. Laboring in obscurity, benefitting from geographic isolation, gathering IOUs. Mosby's senior supervisor had a firm grasp on the controls here in the smallest of the

Old Dominion's 95 counties.

Smythe had spent his early years in Mineral Springs, Pennsylvania, a dot on the map southeast of Pittsburgh. That was before his father, a Fuller Brush salesman, died in a fiery turnpike collision with a flatbed carrying steel destined for a new Philly skyscraper. On the day of JFK's inauguration, Smythe's widowed mother moved her family back to her parents' home in the Mosby County hamlet of Bankston. Her eldest son fell under the spell of the Harry Byrd Organization and soon ran errands for the governor's Mosby flunky.

But Smythe had always kept an eye on his native Keystone State. Drilling in the Marcellus Shale Play had fueled Pennsylvania's economic boom in less than a decade. He liked how these pipe-smoking geologists used a word like *play* without irony, especially after the initial toxic spills into pristine creeks. Beneath Appalachia's hills sat more than 400 trillion — *TRILLION!* — cubic feet of gas, the feds said, just begging for a get-out-of-jail-free card. Enough cheap, affordable energy to heat and power U.S. homes and businesses for 40 years, according to the O'Bidens squatting in the White House. Bridge energy, they call it, but it is how America will break its dependence on the camel jocks' stash.

Too bad all that natural gas didn't avail itself earlier, Smythe thought, rising, needing a stretch. Might have saved U.S. military lives.

Drilling in the 7,000-foot-deep Marcellus had already recharged Pennsylvania coffers with $3.2 billion in 2009. The boom brought thousands of jobs to replace those lost when the steel mills shut down, courtesy of the damn unions; now those same mills were turning out miles of pipeline-perfect steel. And while the White House gave lip service to shovel-ready projects, the real job creators were punching holes in the ground and getting this great country moving again. Nearly 2,500 permits had been pulled to drill in Pennsylvania in 2010 alone, and a lame-duck administration in Harrisburg had given a green light to all of it with minimal regulation. There were 1,100 wells in Bradford County alone, northeast of Pittsburgh.

The gas flowed thanks to hydraulic fracturing, the nifty process of sending water, sand and chemicals more than a mile beneath the surface, then horizontally a mile in each direction into 400-million-year-old porous rock. Explosions precede the high-pressure flushing of millions of gallons down those wells, freeing trapped pockets of gas and bringing it right up. You might think fracking is the new F-word, something people do behind closed doors. Go ahead and think that, my friend. Meanwhile, we real economic developers appreciate the brilliance of Big Oil and the engineers who deploy these super techniques across the great United States.

He walked to a window and looked at the minuscule John Singleton Mosby Square. No grandeur. Not yet. For a cash-strapped county dependent on skinflint landowners who bridle at the mere mention of a property tax increase, the sprawling Marcellus promised *unfathomable* revenue. It would be enough to make the veteran public servant the envy of every pissant county administrator in Virginia. Enough to fund the future Milton V. Smythe Courthouse on this very square.

Smythe had tracked the Marcellus in his home state for years. He kept in touch with his Mineral Springs cousin, Henry Cody, and Henry's son, Hank. He saved articles in this very manila file, stuffed with items from *The Post-Gazette* (damn liberals!), the *Tribune-Review* (right-minded editorials), the *Plain-Dealer* (the Truth Stealer) and the *Inquirer* out of Philly — a pale shadow of its former self. The lamestream media was asleep at the switch when it came to big complex economic stories like the Marcellus. Those Fourth Estaters failed to see the epic possibilities. Too busy stalking Kardashians.

This New Industrial Renaissance was sweeping the nation, taking off like a rocket in natural gas patches in North Dakota and Texas, North Carolina and, soon, California. Still, the Marcellus was the king of 'em all.

Conditions were ripe to exploit the big basin even here in Mosby, which he'd controlled for four decades, outwitting or outliving his fellow supervisors. Child's play, really. No one showed up at the supervisors' meetings. He made sure the county administrator's office had a revolving door to keep any incumbent from getting too much experience. He gave cronies and cousins what few paying county jobs there were. And, of course, owning the weekly *Mosbyville Monitor,* the town's only media outlet, didn't hurt. People tend not to argue with a man who buys ink by the barrel, he'd observed to fawning supervisors at the annual Virginia Association of Counties conventions.

It wasn't natural gas that would provide the payoff here in this corner of Northern Virginia. It was too troublesome. Once freed, gas relied on spider webs of pipelines to travel from the wells to distant ports and refineries, crossing state and county lines. That meant regulation. Oversight.

No, Smythe's brilliant breakthrough was realizing that even little ol' Mosby County, way down on the Shale's southern fringe, could help Big Oil in its hour of need by taking off its hands fracking's dirty little secret: The 25 percent of the millions of injected gallons that came back *up* as toxic, salty wastewater. Hurled back up the wells, just like puke.

Produced water, oil execs called it in public. The tree huggers were less euphemistic: Frackwater.

From the get-go, the industry needed to find the wastewater a home. Somewhere. Anywhere. Once the millions of gallons completed their round trips through the geologic layers, they returned briny and gray with the same chemicals that went down in the first place, and then some. And you couldn't just ship frackwater off to a waste treatment plant.

The oil companies found temporary homes for the slop in hollowed-out containment ponds near their rigs, but the drillers — those wonderful Halliburtons and Shlumbergers — realized frackwater needed a permanent home. Kind of like that nuclear waste they ought to bury in the caves out there in Nevada.

Pennsylvania legislators acted quickly. Not here, pal.

Engineers being engineers, they went to work on a solution to fracking's biggest annoyance. We'll run a test; just shoot the stuff right back down an unused well. Same method, in reverse. And, wouldn't you know it, it stayed put. Got 'er done. At first.

The happy answer to the frackwater dilemma was right across the Keystone State line in eastern Ohio, with its Rust Belt legacy of blazing rivers and abandoned oil wells.

Ohio said: Sure, we'll take it. For a small fee.

Smythe had tracked the speed with which the drillers found willing recipients of frackwater, trucked over to the reopened Ohio wells and flushed right back down. The Buckeye State was quick to spot an opportunity, too, permitting nearly 200 *new* disposal wells in one year.

Here's where Smythe's expertise triumphed. As a slimmer youth, he had tromped every square foot of Mosby County, knew every farmer and rancher by name. Right there on the rolling grounds of Burlwood, the county's largest property at 2,600 acres, was an abandoned well. Mosby lore held that the well was drilled in 1941 by Burleson Spink Sr. That old man had gumption, far more than his two lazy sons.

The old patriot thought he might help the Allies beat the Nazis if he could strike oil. Spink Senior might have swung and missed on that dry hole, but he'd homered in other ways: logging, investments, commercial real estate. The old man was smart; he made sure he owned the mineral rights for *everything* beneath. He'd left quite a concern to his sons, and they hadn't managed to screw it up. Yet.

Smythe realized the old well was perfect for frackwater disposal. Taking the idea to Burl and Woody Spink had been simple. With their notoriously poor stewardship of the estate, they had been mere annoyances until America elected its first black president. Now the brothers were hosting weekly training sessions for something called the New Militia at Burlwood. Until recently, Smythe's only dealings with the Spinks were to bring neighbors' complaints to their attention. But the supervisor knew the brothers were suckers for anything with a nice payoff, especially if it had the added advantage of keeping state and federal regulators out of their lives.

Best of all, he had something on Woody that could send the closeted sibling to the pen for a long, long time. Before last November's elections, Woody had shown up at Smythe's office with a story idea for the *Monitor* — something about Obama taking his marching orders from the Trilateral Commission. When the meeting was over, Woody mistakenly left his iPad behind. Smythe, curious about the gadget, found that the Web browser was open. Woody was signed on to a gay porn chat room. His alias: HardWoodMosby.

The gist of the chat made it clear that Woodrow Spink had a predilection for underage boys. And now Smythe had photos to prove it, taken by a *Monitor* photo intern Smythe had assigned to follow Woody to a liaison at a Holiday Inn Express across the state line in Bridgeport.

Smythe had needed all his political guile to seal the deal with the Burlwood Boys. They were already the county's largest water consumers. Like 90 percent of their fellow residents, they got water from wells drilled into the aquifer. Burl, the elder brother, had gone on a recent pond-building spree. "I like frog legs," he explained. Their monthly water bill skyrocketed.

Smythe waited until the Spinks came to bitch about the bill. Let's negotiate. I'll discount what we're charging you for trucking in the pond water, plus sell you the millions of gallons a month you'll need for your *new* contribution to the nation's economy: Your very own frackwater well.

He'd reeled 'em in on a weekend trip to Pittsburgh, where he introduced the Spinks to the folks at Green Valley Resources, a scrappy drilling firm Smythe had carefully researched. They gave the brothers the full-court press. Wearing personalized gold hardhats emblazoned with GVR, the brothers watched a drilling operation in nearby Washington County, where dozens of tankers slurped up the salt-laden gray stuff from containment ponds, then rolled west to Ohio.

When Green Valley's flack started talking about chemicals and the environment, Smythe stopped her short. "Boys, there's a little thing called the Halliburton Loophole. Our former Vice President, Mr. Cheney, slipped it into his last big energy bill. It means Green Valley and other drillers can use whatever-the-hell chemicals they want in hydraulic fracturing, and they do not have to disclose." Who knew?

Smythe plopped in the leather chair again, mouth curling into a trace of grin.

The Cheney thing had hooked Burl. What the brothers didn't need to know is that Smythe effectively controlled every potable tap in the region. Had he wanted, Smythe could've regaled the brothers with the tale of his carefully crafted friendship with late West Virginia Sen. Robert Byrd, the doddering Prince of Pork, the Earl of Earmark. Byrd's soft spot was the U.S. Constitution; he carried a version in his breast pocket. Every Sept. 17, Constitution Day, Smythe drove to neighboring Orange County, where the Madison Foundation folks turned Montpelier into a red, white and blue celebration of the sacred document and its diminutive father. After the West Virginia senator's tearful remarks each year, Smythe would insinuate himself at the luncheon, ultimately sitting next to the octogenarian and mumbling when he said Mosby County, Virginia. After the ninth such affair (and after paying off the senator's legislative aide), Smythe had what he needed — an 11th hour Senate appropriation for a new water treatment plant. In Mosby County. *Virginia.*

Even with the steep discount for Burlwood, Mosby County would rake in 50 cents per gallon of water sold to flush the frackwater deep below. The amount of water needed would generate a heretofore-unthinkable amount of revenue for the county — such a bonanza that no one would notice when Smythe stashed half the take in his Swiss account.

"Gentlemen, you'll be doing a service, and Virginia will get a share of what's hers," he told the Spinks.

The deal was now done, out of the sunshine, of course, as Smythe himself wrote the supervisors' agenda and buried the item under Old Business. Green Valley had already started operations, with trucks coming in nightly from Pennsylvania to that purple bull's eye on Smythe's map.

But keeping a lid on was already a challenge. Atop the clip file was the guest editorial from *The Rappahannock Reporter*, the rag across the county line. That crusader Tippecanoe Tyler had resurfaced, seemingly intent on riling up both tree huggers *and* Bible thumpers.

The highlighted paragraph about fracking suggested Tyler knew plenty about the Shale's dip into Virginia, close enough to bring the natural gas debate into the Piedmont. Smythe envied *The Reporter's* devoted readership. Now, dammit, fracking could well be on the lips of scores of Rappahannock residents.

Trouble.

But he had a plan. Milton Vincent Smythe *always* had a plan.

He pulled out a newer clip file, labeled Green Valley Resources. On top was a color printout from the website's Civil Engineering Staff section featuring a smiling blonde in blazing lipstick.

Roxanna Raye Bleigh. Project Manager.

CHAPTER EIGHT

Monday, Oct. 7, 9:30 a.m.

Francis Thornton's name graces the Blue Ridge gap crossed by the Army of Northern Virginia in its retreat from Gettysburg in '63, as well giving the initials to FT Valley Road, also known as Route 231, the handsome byway snaking south from Sperryville to Mosby County.

As his pickup turned off the valley road and headed up Hannah Run Hollow, Tip enjoyed the commanding westerly view of early autumn.

Though the seasons of Rappahannock are distinct, autumn is the consensus rock star. Recent winters have been mild; two hard freezes and an occasional dusting. Spring arrives early, with the red serviceberry and flowering quince harbingers of thaw. Jonquils, dogwood and azaleas soon introduce a virginal white, dotted with hints of Impressionist color. Summer evenings pulse with hazy greens and a symphony of insects and amphibians. Autumn erupts in russets, oranges and yellows, wowing streams of motoring leaf-peepers and proud locals alike.

The Sports Junkies on 106.7 The Fan were rehashing the Nats' meltdown in last night's playoff thriller. "Strasburg was toast in the sixth. What was Davey thinking, leaving him in there?"

Tip passed the Baptist church sign, shaded by the Founder's Oak, in front of the historic Meeting House. The lettering in the top line posed a constant inquiry to all heading up the hollow.

Got Jesus?

Sunday's sermon topic filled the next two lines.

Faith v. Nature:

He Createth

Still doing battle.

Tip was trying to make sense of what his own eyes had seen. Purple deer. Marley'd confirmed it. Two sources.

As he zagged up Copperhead, he wondered if Marley was back. If not, he'd have to explain his solo return to his sister.

He took a right at the estate's entrance, decorated with seasonal squash and cornstalks. Ting had been keeping farm manager Sunday Lopez busy. Watering Provo's grazing cattle. Cutting hay, twice per season. Summer garden, winter canning. Fences and stone walls. When all that was done, helping with Tip's cider and brandy. It all generated enough income in advance of two Boomer retirements to make life, as Ting quipped, "Fairleigh comfortable."

He parked. The view from out front never failed to impress.

The manor house rested on the foundation of Jeremiah Spink's log cabin, finished in 1759. After Appomattox, Gen. Fletcher Spink added a stone kitchen and stables to its flanks, with steps leading up to a new main floor. Subsequent Tyler renovations by Tip's grandfather Taz added a second floor with four bedrooms on each corner opening to a balustrade at the top of the staircase. In the 1950s, Jeter added wide porches on three sides and a new kitchen in back.

Not sure what Ting might say.

Tip had never been sure when it came to the women in his family.

He and Rennie O'Keefe connected only after her brother's death, a pairing far more physical than emotional. The young couple committed to staying together after the high school pregnancy and miscarriage. Even in those awkward early days of discovery and gangly limbs, sadness darkened her mountain girl spirit.

Rennie was wary of the whole Missouri thing. Tip had gone from 14-year-old gofer for *Reporter* editor Louis Allbury to out-of-state scholarship winner at the nation's oldest J-school. The teenaged Virginians arrived in the Midwest fresh off their elopement, the same month five White House operatives were arrested breaking into the DNC's Watergate offices. Tip found work at the Broadway Diner; Rennie waited tables at the Paquin Street Café in the ground floor of their building.

He was thrilled and apprehensive when the twins were born. They arrived right as his make-or-break senior year began. Rennie carried most of the load of caring for the infants while Tip gained notice with his City Hall reporting. When Tip got a summer internship in Miami, Rennie refused to go to the big city and took the girls to Virginia. Her mother's depression had deepened, so Rennie turned to the only place she could: Fairleigh. The twins enjoyed Jeter's wacky wisdom; Ting was around to help babysit. From then on, it was summers in the country for the precocious toddlers.

Toddlers. Wow.

The Fan prattled with an ad for Just for Men. Tip switched the radio off and sat quietly.

Adults now. And one home.

Two nights before in the hospital room, he'd stood by as Ting caught up with his daughters. The women chatted comfortably, Maddie and Ting feeding sips to the patient. There's little left in my garden but squash, Ting had said. Remember Maddie's old Wakefield beau? He's tending bar at the Blue Rock. The Artists' Tour is coming up. Poor Mr. Hackley, killed by a speeding trooper out on Lee Highway.

Tip envied their bond, but understood it. Ting had wound up raising the girls at Fairleigh, pretty much on her own. After all, it was all his fault.

"Despite the circumstances, Marley," Ting had said, holding the juice container. "It means more time with me."

"I am kind of bunged up. I guess it's better to heal here than Colorado."

For all the drive Madison Tyler had from the beginning — valedictorian at Wakefield Country Day School, business degree and lacrosse at UVA, internships on Wall Street and K Street, White House Fellow, Senate staffer, now foundation exec — her identical twin, Albemarle, had a slower motor and a wandering spirit.

The week the twins graduated from Wakefield, Marley — Honor Society secretary, yearbook photographer, honors in Spanish and French, varsity letter in soccer — took her uke, her photo gear, an REI backpack and hit the road.

Adventure ensued: postcards from Santorini and Jakarta, a fling with a tapas bar owner in Barcelona, a gig with an all-girl band in Dún Laoghaire. The 15-month trek through Africa. Grinning photos atop Kilimanjaro. The jam session with Ladysmith Black Mambazo.

The year the twins turned 24, the small Tyler clan gathered in Indianapolis to attend Maddie's graduation — master of arts from the Center on Philanthropy. At the Thai restaurant afterwards, Marley had shown her cards. "I'm thinking about the Peace Corps. Interview's next month."

She spent five years in Chad working amid a dysentery epidemic. She returned to Fairleigh, dragging from a parasitic disease. After a quick recovery, she was off to Colorado to give snowboarding a try.

Carbondale, the valley village next to Aspen, became her place to explore the double black diamond trails. She rented a basement room from a nice engineer at the base of Mount Sopris. Marley sold occasional prints out of a gallery in Aspen, but paid her few bills shoveling mounds of snow off the expansive roofs of absentee Saudi princes and Palo Alto entrepreneurs.

At 38, Marley Tyler had avoided entanglements. Never brought a friend or lover home. "I snore," she joked.

Tip killed the engine, unaware how long he'd sat pondering. A black Lexus SUV came speeding up the drive.

Tip opened the pickup's door just as Ting came from around the corner in her garden boots, sipping from the old metal flagon she kept at the garden's well.

The driver's window of the Lexus slid down.

"Loaner from the sheriff!" Marley yelled to her aunt.

"I love that gal!" said Ting, draining the water in one last gulp.

"It has Florida plates," said Tip, walking up.

"It'd been sitting in impound for months," said Marley, closing the door. "Some drug trial."

"Come on in," Ting said. "You need rest. I'll make tea."

"Wait until I tell you about the deer, Aunt Ting."

Tip started up the steps after his daughter when Ting pointed to the cider house.

"Aren't you behind in your Stonewall schedule?"

He stopped. Marley turned at the top of the steps. "Well, um, thanks for breakfast, Tip. Interesting crowd. Every Thursday, huh? How'd that get started?"

"I needed to crawl out of my cave. I asked Walker to introduce me around. He brought Fran in. I invited Provo, who can't help but tease Gus. Others come and go."

"Hey, we need to figure out what's up with those deer. Crazy, huh? No one's gonna believe it."

"*National Enquirer* stuff."

"You're the pro."

"Was the pro," Tip said. "I gave it up. No computer, no TV, no wireless. No cellphone. I have my old email account and I check it every so often at the library. That's all I've needed."

"I thought Blackie was the old dog around here. You saying you're not up to new tricks?"

"Something hinky going on, that's certain."

"I gotta get my computer checked out." Marley said. "Come with. There are lots of new things on the market."

CHAPTER NINE

Thursday, Oct. 10, 5:45 p.m.

Roxx Bleigh assessed herself in the mirror. Fluffed the hair.

Need a new look. Holidays coming up.

She applied the Coral Crush. Pursed the lips.

The mirror does not lie.

She stretched and latched the 38C Bali in the front.

Rihanna sang on the iPod, one of Roxx's few connections to civilization these days.

"We found love in a hopeless place..."

She joined in, off key.

Love. Ha! Too friggin' busy.

Roxx was unsure what to wear to tonight's client dinner at the restaurant just down Sperryville's Main Street from her temporary quarters, the Hopkins Ordinary B&B. What with supervising two shifts at Burlwood and starting reinjection this week, she'd been busy.

Cheap bastards coulda taken me to that Little Inn.

They didn't teach dress-for-success at engineering school. The few women she'd seen around definitely dressed down. No single style seemed to dominate. Cashmere + jeans = the horsey set. Floral dresses + unlaced work boots = artists. Fleece vests + chambray shirts = ranchers and farmers. She hadn't seen one "professional" woman yet.

No one wore makeup. So much for her beauty pageant training. Lipstick was her one concession.

But it was nice to have a reason to wear something other than the Engineer Ensemble: Twill Dickies and jeans jacket over blue oxford cloth shirt.

An hour earlier, she'd settled on her own take on horsey: Cotton cowlneck sweater, black jeans, silver blazer. Nothing plunging. She didn't want her clothes to draw attention away from her concerns about the well.

Looking longingly at the Christian Louboutins, she opted for Chinese peasant loafers. The walk was short, but the sidewalks were friggin' uneven. And this was business, after all.

A final glance.

Screw it. Give these geezers a gander.

She returned the cowl to the dresser and slid into a lacy black square-top tank.

That's more me.

She grabbed a navy pashmina and donned the blazer. A sober assessment. Still professional.

By habit, she reached for her iPhone. No bars. Clockwise swirl.

Forgot! No friggin' signal in Crappahannock!!!

She locked the cottage door and headed out into the warm October night.

She walked in the Thornton River Grille at exactly 6 p.m. The open kitchen was already busy. She saw the Spink brothers and some jumbo dude at a table in the middle. They stood as the maître d' escorted her.

Eye contact. Shoulders back.

"Gentlemen! Woodrow, Burleson. Thank you for inviting me!"

"Evening, Miz Bleigh," Woody said. White hairs torqued from his ears. She'd met the Spink brothers once before, three weeks back when Bill Dinwiddie had introduced her as project manager. Bill expressed to them the firm's concerns about the nighttime work, but on the drive down he'd made it clear GVR saw Burlwood as a toehold in Virginia.

"Hi ya again," said Burl. "This is our Mosby County associate, Mr. Smythe."

More like Jabba the Hutt.

She shook the soft, damp hand.

"Please call me Milton. Is it Ms. or Mrs. Bleigh?"

"Ms." She threw them the pageant smile.

No one offered to help with her chair.

Gentlemen, my ass.

They opened menus.

"The guys at the well say you go by Roxy," said Burl. His rheumy eyes were locked, where else.

"Roxx, actually," she said, fiddling with the blazer's only button. "R-O-Double X. No Y."

Bill had drilled her on the importance of taking command. She sized up her dining companions.

Gaydar going on that *one. Burl's a letch. Jabba's the brains here.*

As they studied the menus, the maître d' seated two diners along the wall behind Roxx. She smiled their way, scooted forward and did a double take. *Morgan Freeman?*

"Woody, hand me that wine list," Smythe said brightly. "Perhaps they have something from Barboursville. My favorite tasting room, Barboursville. I'm a regular."

Burl was staring. Again.

The cowl might *have been better.*

The waitress spieled off the specials.

"I'll have the Caesar. And the sirloin, medium," said Roxx.

"Says here the beef's grass-fed from Mount Vernon Farms," said Burl. "They went off the organic deep end. Who gives a shit what the cows eat? I'll have the crab cakes."

Woody aped his brother.

Smythe appraised the waitress. "The Octagon. Is it the '08? I hope it's not the '09."

Jabba's showing off.

Assured, Smythe ordered the '08 and a lamb shank. Then he darted a glance at the brothers.

"Ms. Bleigh, I did not expect a little lady to head this assignment," he said. "But Burl here tells me we're off to a good start."

Sexist asshole. Down to business.

"That's true. We began this expedited … engagement … last month. My crew has hit every key metric. The nine-acre site was cleared of 300 trees in the first three days."

It looks like a war zone.

"Excavation for the chem — uhhh, containment impound and dump pad began immediately and has been completed in record time. Some 400,000 cubic yards of Portland cement."

"Yes. Mosby Cement. From Bankston," said Smythe, crooked smile playing above the jowls.

Bill was right. Emphasize the metrics.

The salads arrived. Burl cleared his throat. "Join me in the blessing."

Smythe grabbed her hand.

"Heavenly Father, bless this bounty from the land," Burl said. "We ask your continued blessings for Christian patriots and our unfettered rights and liberties."

Creepy.

Roxx picked up her fork. "We've taken the shortcuts you wanted. Tarps instead of a permanent cover for the pond. Two layers lining the pond instead of the recommended three."

"Please lower your voice," Smythe hissed. "Could you lean forward?"

She scooted her chair up. Full jostle. Burl's eyelids twitched.

"Our hydrology and materials teams analyzed the old well. They removed a permanent cap."

We pulled out the rotted stump.

"It was originally drilled to 4,000 feet and was in bad condition after nearly seven decades. We need to go twice that deep, the equivalent of a new Class II. We've repaired the visible casing. We're running diagnostics on the first 1,000 feet. We're proceeding cautiously."

"Meaning what?" Burl snapped.

Meaning it's older 'n dirt, jerk!

"Mr. Spink, we have to work with what we've been given here. The wells in Ohio used for reinjecting flowback are different. The Mosby well has to withstand the pressure of the return of millions of gallons of the, umm, the liquid assets. We had to spend five project days removing and replacing the existing casing before we could inject anything. It's a change order. I'll include it in my next report."

Burl blurted. "Milton, you said —"

"Hold on." The supervisor put up a hand as the waitress poured the wine.

"Do go on."

"Meanwhile, I was there when deliveries from the tanker company out of Mineral Springs began late last month. Early last week, we ramped up deliveries. And gentlemen, after an initial test with 50,000 gallons down the pipe, we began flowback reinjection Friday."

She sat back and smiled.

"Guess this calls for a toast," Burl said.

Roxx clinked her glass and looked all three in the eye to avoid the seven-year, bad-sex curse. She then turned serious.

"We *will* need to tighten controls on spillage at the dump pad. We've had some early … issues with containing all the recycled water and keeping … umm, foreign … bodies out."

Stupid deer.

"We like those truckers. You do know we own the trucking company," Woody said, winking.

Must tell Bill. Time to close.

"Despite delays and one episode I *should* mention, the Mosby engagement is on time," Roxx said. "We don't anticipate exceeding budget by more than 10 percent."

"Episode?" asked Smythe.

"We found a deer carcass at the bottom of the pond last week. Apparently they think they can walk out on the tarps. We disposed of it and took steps to prevent repeats."

One full-time guy with a rifle.

"Pains in the ass is what they are," said Woody.

"You could fence off the site," she ventured.

"Too costly," said Burl.

"Heck no," Woody said. "Just use a rifle."

"That's right!" said Burl. "We're environmentalists, not Bambi lovers!"

The brothers brayed with laughter.

The entrees arrived. The fat cats talked about the Redskins and the team's hated owner. Roxx mostly nodded. Decent steak. A bit chewy.

"Nice red wine," she said, trying to contribute.

"Remember the name," Smythe said loudly. "Octagon. From Barbours-ville."

Over warm apple pie and decaf, Smythe spoke again. "Ms. Bleigh, keep us posted. I'll remind you to exercise the utmost discretion."

"Right," Roxx said. "I'll turn my reporting over to EPA and DNR —"

"Leave that to us," Smythe interrupted, glancing the Spinks' way.

"But it's required," she said.

"I know all the proper authorities," Smythe said. "Submit your reports to me. My county administrator and I will be happy to review them and send them forward."

NO WAY. Gotta tell Bill!

Smythe smiled crookedly. "Meantime, your clients have something. Right, Burl?"

The elder Spink reached into his jacket and removed an envelope. "This is Smythe's idea."

"Give it to her, Burl."

"Ms. Bleigh," the supervisor said, "we believe it will be useful for you to find a classy place to stay while you're here, something long-term. With this … uh, package, you might find a pleasant rental. In Rappahannock County, please. Take a day off for that."

"Well, I —"

Burl handed her a hefty envelope.

"You're going be here for a while, so you should get to know the locals," Smythe said. "Keep your ears and eyes open. Your Green Valley boys can manage the overnight deliveries. But be careful; these Rappahannock folks tend to be rather involved."

"Damn tree huggers," Burl Spink belched. "Check!"

CHAPTER 10

Thursday, Oct. 17, 7:30 p.m.

Tip looked up from his new laptop. He'd been at it since lunch, getting the hang of the touchpad and right and left clicks. Already a dozen bookmarked websites spilled down the screen's left side, the bounty of a deep dive into hydraulic fracturing. He'd netted more information in one afternoon of Google searches than a week of shoe-leather reporting back in the '80s.

His head still spun from the Star Wars experience of the Apple Store at Fair Oaks Mall yesterday. He'd nearly done a 180 when he and Marley were sucked into the crush of customers, the pierced clerks in blue T-shirts, the iPads and iPhones and … ay yi yi! He hadn't seen this much eye-popping hardware since *The Herald's* art department. All that seemed like the Dark Ages.

An hour and a One to One session later, Tip walked out with something called a MacBook Air and an iPhone. A stop at RadioShack in Manassas for a wireless router gave them an excuse to indulge in burgers at Five Guys.

Tip realized getting the new gear was the only way he was going to scratch the itch of the deer mystery. Even if the spotty cell signals made calls and texts an adventure in Rappahannock, he now saw all sorts of ways the laptop would help in reporting. Not to mention his brandy-making business. He lost the rust quickly. Photos and video. Hot spot. Shortcuts. Downloading apps. He didn't quite get Twitter and all the @s and hashtags, but Facebook was cool, and he'd reconnected with a few former colleagues.

He stood, stretched and walked to the window. Mike Shannon was doing the pregame rundown on tonight's NLCS matchup. "The Nats owned the Cardinals in the regular season, but Wainwright's a tough cookie."

Two vehicles sat next to the Lexus. He recognized Fran's cruiser, but not the white Prius.

The iPhone buzzed. One of those text messages. From Marley.

<u>Want dessert?</u>

His stomach rumbled. "Ting OK with that?" he typed, thumbs unfamiliar with the compact keyboard.

She's OK.

Five minutes later, Tip walked in to Fairleigh's dining room with a bottle of Stonewall. His sister sat at the head of the mahogany table flanked by four others and the remains of a feast: lamb chops, risotto, pickled beets.

"I guess there's plenty left," his sister sighed. "Grab a plate."

That classic sigh. Sadness and bitterness.

Tip knew why. He'd been the central player in her drama.

Dolley Paine Madison Tyler was born in 1958 on a bitter cold February day. The *Reporter*'s obits would note the death of Sara Lincoln Tyler from complications of childbirth. When Jeter, bereft, brought the baby home, Tip begged to see. "She's a tiny little t'ing!" he shouted. Jeter laughed.

Ting. The nickname stuck.

Tip knew it had been hard for her being the only white girl at Scrabble School, but they were both better off for the experience. After he and Rennie left for Missouri, his sister finished high school and attended Mary Washington College, graduating with the Class of '80. She planned to use her English degree to teach "up north." She'd written her older brother a happy letter with her plans for Jeter's graduation present — a cruise of the eastern Mediterranean.

She returned that July, offers from a Main Line Philadelphia district and Wakefield Country Day lying in the foyer. But there her weeping brother sat on the kitchen floor at the center of a confusing scene: two bawling, sunburned 5-year-olds. No Rennie. Sketchy details. Dry Tortugas? Navy ruled it an accident.

She helped Jeter plan the funeral. When he left with the twins to return to the Miami newsroom, Tip too loudly doubted his ability to care for kindergarteners in a place like that. I did it, said Jeter. So can you.

They were back a month later; Tip a wreck, smoking and rambling and pleading. The same professional who'd boasted about Miami being a great news town now sounded like a frightened country boy, describing an urban hell overrun by loco Marielitos, Liberty City rioters and Cocaine Cowboys. He'd tried to combine profession and fatherhood, he insisted. He and the girls had found a cheap two-bedroom north of downtown. Hookers and pimps owned Biscayne Boulevard, he said. Coke was everywhere, even in the newsroom. He had to wear a bulletproof vest to report in Overtown. His feisty girls had been invited to leave two day-care centers already. The kicker was the Sunday afternoon he'd taken them to the Omni mall to ride the carousel. He'd been standing between their bobbing horses when he heard the pop-pop-pops and felt the whiz of a bullet. Another shootout between Colombian drug gangs.

So, yes, he'd counted on the whole thing going his way. He'd begged his father and his sister to keep Maddie and Marley. They love it here.

He'd been the agent of Ting's indentured servitude. He knew Jeter would side with him. It was a Virginia thing. Point blank, he told Jeter he *needed* Ting to remain at Fairleigh and be the proxy for the farm spouse he'd lacked since her mother's death. Later, Jeter told Ting: These little ladies need a mother figure. Just like you did.

Tip was impressed with the way she took it and the deal she negotiated. She'd care for the twins. Stay and teach at Wakefield. But every Christmas break from then on, Ting would travel solo to a far-away destination. Jeter would just have to manage. Tip left for Miami, promising to send checks and visit often. The checks continued, but the more his reputation grew, the less often he returned.

No surprise the twins imprinted on their aunt and picked up on her resentment.

Tip knew his return to Fairleigh galled his sister. He never challenged her supremacy and kept to the cider house. He earned an occasional spot at her table, often with Walker and Fran as guests.

Tonight it was the sheriff's turn. In full uniform, she sat beside Marley. Maddie Tyler stood, along with a tall, wire-rimmed Chinese-American in crisp dress shirt and purple tie.

"Hi, Tip," Maddie said. "We've come out to check up on the patient. Meet Les Leong."

"Her beau," Marley said. "He's an undersecretary at Energy in charge of enforcement."

"Mr. Undersecretary, it's a pleasure to meet you."

"Please. It's Les. Folks at Energy talk about your days at *The Herald*."

"Uh-oh," said Tip, shaking hands. "Just know I always pursued the facts, wherever they led."

"Your daughters are entertaining. Like Maddie times two. And I thought one was —"

"That's enough!" Maddie said with a reproving smack to the wrist.

"We don't see enough of you, Madison, dear," said Ting as Tip speared the last chop.

"Best part of the ride," Les said, "was entering … how'd you say it? Fock-year —?"

"FUCK-ya County!" four Tylers said in unison, laughing.

"Jeter always thought Faquier folk were snobs," Ting said.

"Les and I talked shop," said Maddie. "We're old UVA classmates."

"Madman here still drops UVA into every conversation," Marley said to Fran. "Lawnies!"

Tip watched the color rise in his daughters' cheeks.

"Need me to cut your bites?"

"Save the world yet?"

"Could if we weren't always bailing *you* out! Oughta call you Greece."

"Wonk."

"Be civil, ladies. Fran has handcuffs," Ting said. She coughed.

Though a carbon copy of her sister, Madison Lightfoot Lee Tyler exuded a confidence that comes from sharp-elbowed play on Wall Street and Capitol Hill. Jet-black, shoulder-length hair. Thin white band tucked behind petite ears. Hint of makeup.

"As a matter of fact," Maddie said, scanning the faces, "the foundation is going make me a vice president. Alvaro will recommend it at next week's board meeting."

"Vice President *and* Chief Program Officer," said Tip. "They couldn't pick a better person."

"Thank you," she said, blushing.

No one was surprised by Maddie Tyler's vertical blur at the Fairfax Grant Foundation, a $1 billion funder with a mission to "elevate the lives of all

Northern Virginians." She joined the foundation after her wild decade with the Senate Energy and Natural Resources Committee. Her take-no-prisoners style earned the nickname Mean Green Fighting Machine.

"Will you still get to do all that environmental stuff?" Ting asked.

"Of course. I'll just be more engaged with the executive committee and board."

She paused.

"You have the floor," Marley said.

"They like my direction on energy policy. We're bulking up thanks to some amazing grantees. There's so much going on. Uranium mining. Hydraulic fracturing. We need regs, like now."

"I'm glad to hear you mention fracking," said Tip, swallowing. "I see it's being considered over in the valley. Rockingham County. Lots of spills and blowouts in Pennsylvania."

"The administration understands the need for regulation," Les said. "We're working on it. EPA's issued air standards. Interior's got public lands. Justice *is* enforcing. But it's such an opportunity to break OPEC's hold."

"It's a finite resource," said Tip. "What happened to alternative energy?"

"In a word, Solyndra."

"Enough of this work stuff," Ting said, folding her napkin. "I think we need a walk before dessert. Up for it, Marley?"

"You bet."

"Fresh air," said Les. "Now you're talking."

Tip stood. "I'll just clear the table."

The twins glanced at each other.

"No, you should come," Marley said.

"Les was asking me about family history," said Maddie. "I'm fuzzy about some of the lore."

"Well, all right then, grab your coats," Ting said. "The cemetery. But first, please excuse me. The powder room." She stood, coughing as she left.

"I've got a flashlight," Fran said.

"I'll bring the Stonewall and some cups," said Tip.

Maddie circled to her sister's side, helping her up. "I love you like a sister."

"Only one you've got," Marley said with a hug.

Tip followed the two couples from the dining room into the wainscoted foyer. They took jackets and fleece vests from hooks. Tip reached for blankets from a hallway chest. As they stepped outside, Fran spoke.

"How is she?"

"Who, Ting?" Marley said. "She was really great when I was in the hospital."

"Have you noticed that cough?" she said.

CHAPTER 11

Thursday, Oct. 17, 9:30 p.m.

Tip turned on the floodlight at the back of the barn. The black walnut, guardian of the Tyler burial plot, cast spidery shadows.

Ting brushed the husks and leaves off a wrought-iron bench and gestured to Les and Maddie to sit beside her. Fran spread the blanket on a stone bench for herself and Marley. Tip squatted, opening the bottle.

"Is that your new stuff?" Fran asked.

"Yeah, second batch."

He poured an inch in six cups. "See what you think."

"Well it burns, burns, burns ..." Fran sang in faux bass.

"Nice finish," said Les. "I need to develop a palate for Calvados."

"I'm required to call it American apple brandy," Tip said. "Calvados applies only to the region. Like Champagne and sparkling wine. But you watch. One day all you'll have to say is *Stonewall*."

"To Virginia," Ting said, raising her cup.

"To Virginie," said Tip, a catch in his voice, mentioning his missing wife's given name.

The others waited.

"She introduced me to Normandy, and to cider, really," he said. "Her father taught me the art."

"Wherever she may be," said Fran, shining the flashlight on the stained gravestones.

Tip stood. At his feet were two small tablets at a slight remove from the others.

Slayton O'Keefe.

Rennie O'Keefe Tyler.

"Well then," Ting said. "These girls know *my* take on family history. What's yours?"

"Maddie said the O'Keefes were Scots Irish," said Les.

"I met the girls' mother and her brother, Slayton, the summer before I went to Rapp High," Tip said. "Slate was my age, Rennie a year younger. I was writing a feature on the families forced to leave the Blue Ridge lands by the government as they created Shenandoah National Park. They'd been moved to government-built cottages off Fodderstack. Unceremoniously called Resettlement Lane."

"Eminent domain," Maddie said. "We studied it at Wakefield."

"Happened 75 years ago," Fran said. "Lots of resentment."

"No kidding," Tip said. "Rennie opened the last door I knocked on. I'll never forget. 'Shenandoah National Disgrace,' she said. Slate joined her and asked me my business. When he reached for a shotgun, I took off!"

"On the first day of school, I ran into them in the hallway. I apologized. Rennie seemed to accept. Not Slate. He and I went out for football that afternoon. At the first practice, he knocked me silly. Next play, I retaliated. We went at it, wound up bloody and both got kicked off the team."

He paused for a sip.

"But then we became best friends. Bucked bales, swam at Rock Mills. Picked apples. Rennie joined us some, but she and I didn't really get together 'til after Slate's funeral."

Fran directed the beam at an imposing stump opposite the black walnut.

"Tell Les about the tree," Marley said.

Tip exhaled.

The first accident.

"It was July Fourth weekend. Slate and I were rising juniors. I wanted to ask him if he'd mind if I dated his sister. I dared him to drink some of Jeter's applejack. We climbed the black walnut, just as big as this one, high as we could, and passed the jar."

"Jeter would have tanned you," Ting said.

"The storm came up so fast. It's true what they say; you sense the bolt before it strikes."

Tip paused, then pointed. "The tree clipped the barn right up by the light. I came to on the barn floor. Jeter was looking down at me and told me to stay still. I knew why when I tried to move my arm. Broken. Told him it was my fault. I asked him where Slate was. He didn't answer. That's when I knew."

"Whew," said Marley. "What did our mom do when she found out?"

"She was cool toward me at the funeral. When school started, I went to her locker and started to say something. She slapped me. Hard. Then she hugged me. Grief, I guess. I hugged back. She smelled like lilac. I have to say I never felt anything that good."

"Jeter had it all wired for you to attend William & Mary," Ting said. "But she was pregnant by Christmas."

"Yeah, the whole from-here dream. He wanted me to go Greek, come back, work Fairleigh with him, run for delegate. But when he heard she was pregnant, he kicked me out. I stayed with Rennie and her mom until we eloped."

"Nasty old man Spink was behind your rejection by William & Mary," said Ting. "Then that bachelor editor came to the 'rescue.'"

"True. I was fortunate to have Louis Allbury believe in me," Tip said. "He covered what the Mizzou scholarship didn't."

"Too bad his gentility didn't rub off on you," said Ting.

"We had to get out of here. This is no place for teen pregnancy. And Missouri might as well have been the other side of the moon. She miscarried in January."

Fran trained the light on the newest stone in the ancestral lineup. "James Tazwell Randolph Tyler," she read.

"J-T-R," Les said. "I get it."

"Yeah, the family name thing," said Tip. "That all began when the President's son James Tazewell Tyler — he'd been a surgeon in the war — moved to California. Needed a new start away from the battlefield. When his son Taz, originally named Tazewell Randolph, returned to Rappahannock a generation later, he boasted of a fortune in gold. He was a bit shaky on his genealogy and didn't look like a Tyler. He'd dropped the *e*, making it Tazwell. But his wife was your great grandmother, Esperanza Obregon. Sonoran by way of Fresno. They were Jeter's parents. Of course, that's why we're considered come-here's to this day."

"So that's where the dark hair and good looks come from," said Fran.

"Ting is Dolley Paine Madison Tyler," Maddie said to Les. "Virginia to the max. Tip is Tippecanoe Tazwell Tyler."

"Made for a good byline."

Ting stood. "I put the pie in to warm. Let's go."

"Maddie, I want to pick your brain about fracking on the way back," said Tip.

The group rose.

"Rockingham's awfully close," Tip said. "What's happening in Pennsylvania is worrisome."

"Good jobs, I've read," Fran said.

"Yeah, it's rosy," said Maddie. "The economists always tamp those numbers down later. But we're taking a look at it at the foundation."

"Something about Marley's wreck has me curious," Tip said. "People have reported dozens of incidents related to drilling. 'Fraccidents.' Exploding compressors. Tainted creeks. Methane leaks. Dead animals."

"What do you know about the chemicals?" Maddie asked.

"The stuff they mix in with the water and sand to frack the wells? Bad stuff. Benzene. Toluene. Barium. Even arsenic."

"You're sounding like Tip the reporter," said Ting.

"Look," Tip said. "Apologies, Les, but we're talking Big Oil here, the industry that's so wired into politics and foreign policy."

"Powerful, yes," Les said. "We're trying to change that."

"Don't forget," said Tip. "They brought us Exxon Valdez and Deepwater Horizon."

CHAPTER 12

Saturday evening, Oct. 19

Gotta tell Bill. Monday.

Roxx looked in the rearview. Checked the outfit.

Dressed to impress.

From her spot in the long line of cars arriving at the old school in Little Washington, she admired the two-story Shaker structure. She parked as directed on the sloping front lawn.

Some fund-raiser for kids, Cindy Hanson had explained during the day with the real estate agent. "Please come. Everyone who's anyone in the county will be there. Rob will sign you up as our guest."

Looking at places in Rappahannock had been a hoot. Breathtaking views everywhere. They bought cider at an orchard. Met intriguing people. Roxx liked Cindy's kind nature. Her husband, Rob, was full of local gossip over lunch at the Blue Rock Inn on the highway.

But Roxx had been jangled since the dinner with Jabba and the Sphincters. The way they'd trampled her authority really pissed her off. She'd submitted the regulatory reports and sent them to Smythe. She'd summarized the dinner in her weekly report to Bill and closed saying reinjection had started in full at 0830 this morning.

She didn't mention the envelope.

Its heft shocked her. "It's an investment in your success," Smythe had oozed. Concern mounted as she stacked the Benjamins later on her bed. All 200 of 'em.

Friggit. They're the clients. They want to "pay" me to spy? Call it research.

But this *was* a long-term engagement, and having a comfy place here? Sweet. She'd bought her Pittsburgh condo near the hockey arena at the top of the market. Nice to have a cushion.

She started to slide out of the 2014 Jeep Grand Cherokee — a Green Valley perk, forest green. She'd debated about what to wear; it wasn't just men she wanted to impress tonight. She'd settled on skinny jeans, a black V-neck T-shirt and an ancient snakeskin jacket. A heavy gold link necklace completed the look: urban cowgirl.

The red-soled heel of her left Laboutin stabbed the sodden turf. She wobbled, grabbing the door.

"*Fuck* me!"

She pulled her leg back in and examined the pump. Inches of mud.

She closed the door and leaned into the passenger floorwell. Among several spare pairs piled there she found the cowboy boots she'd worn years back to the Charlottesville bars.

Tap tap on the window.

What! The! ...

A muffled voice.

"Didja mean that?"

Looking past her shoulder, Roxx saw a patch of navy and a black leather jacket. She straightened and moved to slide the window down. Didn't budge. Engine off.

Crap!

She opened the door, too fast and hard.

The Stetsoned stranger jumped, shaking a banged knuckle.

"Pardon my language! You scared me!"

"Medic!" he drawled. "Jus' kidding. Afraid I saw your struggles. I'm Provo. Provo Starke."

"So sorry!" said Roxx, getting an initial take as he doffed the hat. Tall, sandy hair, white at the temples. Bushy white eyebrows and mustache. Had 10 years on her, easy. She felt — *OMG*! She felt *flushed*.

"I keep forgetting I'm in the country," she said, slipping the pumps off. "Wrong shoes."

"It's muddy. I'd carry ya 'cross the lawn like in the movies, but looks like you're fully capable."

Roxx laughed, pulling a boot on. "Anyone ever say you sound like that actor? He does that commercial. 'Beef. It's what's fer dinner.'"

"I've heard it said. The least a gentleman can do is escort a lady inside. If I might ask, the lady is ..."

"Fine, I'm fine."

"Pleased to meet ya, Ms. Fine. Does that come with a first name?"

"Ha. Sorry. I'm Roxx. Roxanna, really. Roxanna Bleigh. I go by Roxx. R-O-Double X."

You're yapping!

"Lemme guess. Older brother Paper? Baby sister Scissors?"

"What?"

"Joke. I'm pleased to make your acquaintance. May I?"

He helped her from the Jeep.

"The Tony Lamas'll fit right in," he said. "Those heels *did* make a statement with that outfit."

Yessss! Urban cowgirl's working!

"Something I threw together," said Roxx, taking his arm.

Nice biceps.

They avoided puddles and walked up the drive.

"Where ya from, Roxx?"

"Anywhere. Everywhere. Army brat. Currently Pittsburgh."

"Long way to come for a party," he said.

"Oh, I'm working a project ... over in the next county."

They entered to see the happy distraction of a bustling registration table.

"Hello, Provo," said a bushy-haired redhead behind the table.

"Bleigh?" Roxx said tentatively. "With a B? Guest of Rob —"

"I *love* what you're wearing!" said the redhead. "The Hansons are inside."

"That's real pretty, too."

"Miz Claire Hargadon here's one talented painter," said Provo. "A work of art her own self."

"That's enough out of you, Provo."

Claire stage-whispered to Roxx, handing them drink tickets. "We ladies call him the Provocateur!"

"Red or white?" Starke asked.

"Me? Gosh. I like Oregon pinots."

Long way from Cold Duck.

"Let's see what Virginia can offer," said Starke, off with a gentlemanly bow.

"So good to meet you," said Claire. "Cindy said you all had fun."

Jeepers. My reputation precedes me.

"I did, too. This county is really charming."

"Locals say once you find it, it never leaves you. Just go right in there, and welcome!"

A stage was at the auditorium's far end. A bluegrass trio shared space on-stage with antique auction items. She saw the Hansons and waved. Starke returned, handing her a glass with a generous pour.

"Local dago red," he said. "See what ya think."

The Hansons took turns with introductions for the first hour. Tweedy gentlemen farmers. Gen Xers with chunky designer glasses. Boomers sporting gray ponytails. She was surprised by their ... *quality*. They weren't local yokel. More worldly. Urbane, that was the word. Like they could live anywhere.

She realized *she* was causing some of the buzz.

Rob's asides were helpful as he worked the room with Roxx at his side. She met a retired CIA director, a famed conductor ("must call him 'Maestro'"), an Olympic equestrienne, the sheriff ("Fran; never Frances"), a llama rancher ("helped start Google"), a former congressman who'd been on a corny sitcom, a CBS reporter ("did the fall of Saigon"), a college provost and his actress wife ("the Croatian Sensation"), winery owners and more than a few consultants. Rob nodded at one over-dressed couple. "Recognize them? They crashed the Obama state dinner."

Provo hovered. Not that she minded.

Roxx lost track of the names, but the partiers seemed to prize more *where* they lived, all using an approximation: close to Battle Mountain, near the Laurel Mills store, around Castleton View, past the gray stables, next to the azalea nursery. A patrician gent named Miles, off with a group Cindy called the "been-here-forevers," said his "family place" was on Old Massie Road.

Roxx took a breather at a pub table and glanced about.

They're checking me *out.*

Provo approached with a gent in corduroy sport coat and khaki. Gaunt. Dimples. Hazel eyes. Dark hair, with a white streak at the widow's peak.

"This's my thinkin' buddy. Tip Tyler," said Provo, placing a hand at the small of her back. "Tip, this's Roxx Bleigh. She opens doors with enthusiasm."

Game on.

She offered Tip a hand.

Handsome in a rugged way.

"He's the keeper of some of my herd, but watch what you say," said Provo. "Tip once scribed for *The Miami Herald.*"

"Pleasure, Roxx. I just work with apples now. What brings you to Rappahannock?"

"My Jeep Cherokee."

"I mean, what do you do?"

Third degree.

"I'm, uhh, a project manager … with clients, I mean. Next county over."

Gotta get my story straight.

"I looked at a cute place today on Long Mountain Road. I might just take it. Will you guys excuse me?" she said. "Ladies room."

Mirror space was tight. Mrs. Congressman stood shoulder to shoulder with the Maestro's wife.

"This year's Castleton Festival did get *won*derful reviews," the Maestro's wife was saying. "The young directors he's mentoring are *so* energetic. It's taken *years* off his shoulders."

"You know our Homespun Homecoming weekend drew 15,000 and the whole sitcom cast?" said Mrs. Congressman. "A little boost to the local economy."

Roxx touched up her own lipstick.

Getting hit on by the best-looking man here.

Roxx roamed the big room. She perused the live auction items on stage. A side room to the right overflowed with a silent auction. As she stepped down, she smiled at Provo as he filled a plate with hors d'oeuvres. Her pageant smile.

She peered into the packed silent auction room, anything but silent. She joined the fray, enjoying the easy eavesdropping. Bid sheets promised hot-air balloon rides, autumn watercolors, mountaintop dinners. Trophy wives dropped names and hobbies. The fellows talked of some hunt. In the crush, she felt a firm thump against her blue-jeaned hip. She spun, just as the CBS guy walked past. She wobbled for a second and reached out to catch her balance, grabbing a leather sleeve belonging to none other than Provo Starke.

"You OK, ma'am?" he asked, standing close. "Thought I'd invite you to join me for vittles."

"It's crowded, Mr. Starke. Believe I will."

They edged out. She headed to the food. She watched him as he returned to the bar.

She filled a plate with local cheeses and Virginia ham biscuits. Beet salad from Fairleigh. By the time she found the table, Starke was back with wine for her and a beer for himself.

"I saw a sheet in there offering firewood," she said. "Starke's Red Oak Ranch. That you?"

"Black angus cattle. Two hundred head. Landed there after a coupla tours in Iraq."

"I put a bid in on it."

"It's good oak, split by Momma Starke herself. Might come in handy up on Long Mountain."

"Yeah, the place has great views and a neat fireplace. Should be toasty, especially now that I have a woodpile."

"I like the views here plenty," he said.

Definitely hit on.

"Your mother must be a character."

"She's been accused of that."

Starke caught her eye as he pulled on the long neck.

"I ciphered you to be a D.C. socialite when I saw you parking."

"Actually, I'm an engineer."

"Haven't met many lady engineers."

"We git 'er done. More drilling than your dentist."

He snorted at the joke mid-sip.

"Sorry. Old grad school humor."

She took a napkin and wiped his mustache. His hand rested at the small of her back.

"Why would you hit on socialites, Mr. Starke?"

"I'm only bein' neighborly."

"Firming up your reputation?"

She sipped her wine and snuck a glance.

Firming up indeed.

"So, what's with the name Provo?"

"Momma didn't like her daddy's name. Horace. Named me after her hometown."

"Provo. Utah, right?"

"Didn't offer much, unless you're one of us."

He bent in, close.

"One of … ?"

"Mormon. Rare in these Eastern parts."

She bit into the ham biscuit, leaning in, décolletage in full view.

"Yum. Flaky and savory."

"The way I like my women."

"Mr. Starke! How often do you get away with *that*?"

"Only when it counts."

Tip Tyler and the tall sheriff, elegant in pressed uniform, approached. Fran McKinney stopped just short.

"Call me tomorrow," she said to Tip, loud enough for Roxx to hear. "Results came in on that … *venison* package. We need to talk."

Tip slapped Provo's shoulder as the quartet circled the table.

"Just how'd you and Miss Bleigh meet?"

"Roxx and her door make quite an impression." He raised skinned knuckles.

Talking about the Jeep. And me. Slick.

"First impressions, they say," said Tip. "I met someone tonight. Claire. Redhead at the door?"

"She hangs out mostly in her studio," Provo said. "I'm surprised you haven't met. She is rumored to be available."

"There's dancing after the auction," said Fran. "No one asks me."

"Might be the sidearm," Tip said.

"Polite as always, Tip. I thought Jeter raised you to be gentlemanly."

Provo looked at Roxx. "I just mighta found my pardner."

Here we go!

"Refill?" Provo asked Roxx. His hand had moved up her back.

"Actually, I could use some fresh air."

The auctioneer's amplified voice filled the room. "Ladies and gentlemennn … "

"Good timing."

They sauntered out as the crowd was drawn to the auctioneer, heading to the parking lawn. Provo led, holding her hand. They turned the corner outside of the spill of light.

Roxx pulled him back.

The kiss, immediate and soft, was salt and beer and tickly mustache.

"My kind of fresh air," she said.

"My kind of lady. Seen any stars like those lately?" he said, looking up.

"A few, right now."

He took her hand again. "Follow me?"

They hurried to a red F-150 parked a few yards from the Jeep, up against a hedge. The pickup's bed was packed with square bales. He let go long enough to drop the tailgate, and then startled her by grabbing her by the waist. He lifted her up and sprung up beside her.

"Good night for stars," he said, reaching for a blanket. He gave it a billowy snap atop the bales.

"Have a seat."

At first, she tried small talk, asking about family. He shared a few details about service in Iraq.

She leaned in, steered his cheek and kissed him gently.

"There at Qom —"

"Quiet, cowboy. Let's enjoy the darkness."

They kissed nonstop, first seated, then reclining. He slipped his jacket off, and he helped her out of the snakeskin.

"Thank goodness for the blanket. Chilly."

And wet.

"Getting warmer?" he said, drawing the blanket tight with one hand, the other fondling.

"On fire, buddy."

The party's muted din joined a chorus of frogs. The Milky Way was bright as Times Square.

They kissed as V-neck and T-shirt made way for heated skin.

Starke tickled her breasts with his mustache. Roxx pulled him closer, reaching for his zipper.

"Boxers or briefs?" she giggled, feeling first for the elastic, then lower. "No *wonder* they call you the Provocateur!"

He grinned, then propped himself up. "I find myself unprepared. How far, little lady?"

All in.

"Till I see stars. But let's pull out at the right moment."

They huddled, giggling and shushing, Provo on top. She guided him in with a gasp.

"Whoooeee! Been a while, sir. Outta practice."

"Me too. Like ridin' a bike."

Tight. Slow. Smoother. Faster. Urgent.

OH-rion. Cassi-OH-peia.

He mashed her to his chest. She bit his lower lip to keep from yelling.

In seconds, she knew.

Provo began to roll off. The truck swayed. He fell back.

"Hoooleee mamma!" said Provo.

And swayed again.

"You feel that?"

"Well, I haven't for quite some time," Roxx panted.

"Seriously. Didn't you feel that?"

Provo sat up.

"No pun intended, darlin', but I swear that was a damn earthquake."

CHAPTER 13

Saturday night, Oct. 19

Woodrow Spink waved from the porch.

Burl honked as the Escalade cruised down Burlwood's drive, off to lead a meeting of the Christian Patriot Society in Mosbyville. In years past, the brothers would have attended the charity auction up in Little Washington. That was before they'd taken sides.

The Spinks had embraced the Tea Party. Early on, they'd found themselves in thick with the boys of the Sovereign Citizen Movement. Some disavowed their "Socialist Security Number" and the government that issued it. While the Spinks didn't hold with radicals like Terry Nichols of Oklahoma City infamy, they collectively spoke of taking up arms rather than accepting any taxation.

That Mosby County would be a Sovereign hotbed made perfect sense to anyone up on the Civil War. John Singleton Mosby ranged the northern Piedmont, his shadowy guerillas daring Union cavalry to enter Rebel territory at their peril. His riders roamed from the banks of the Rappahannock up through Leesburg, seizing federal supply trains rich with armament, payroll and sides of Indiana pork. Mosby's Raiders thrilled readers of the Southern press, but each sortie put Robert E. Lee in a bind, given Mosby's propensity to keep the plunder after taking sanctuary on Piedmont farms. At the next opportunity to bedevil, Mosby's men would assemble in Upperville and ride off for the next skirmish.

In Mosby Territory, folks still slap a $5 bill on the counter with Abe Lincoln face-down.

Burl Spink had taken it upon himself to organize the passel of Woodchucks, pickup drivers and Rush Limburgers. Their monthly meetings began with a Pledge to the Second Amendment but usually devolved into discussions of the best way to field-dress roadkill.

Woody had begged off with a headache. He also chafed at the nickname

Chief Light in Loafers. The second Burl was out of the driveway, Woody bustled to the garage and started up the Gator.

"I want to meet me some *big* young truckers."

The four-wheeler bounced up hill and down before the lights at the well guided him closer.

He stopped, high above an impressive sight. A yellow tower with crosshatched girders soared 100 feet, swaying with effort, bathed in light, dwarfing workers bustling below. Plastic piping shimmied as it carried frackwater the color of milk chocolate from the containment pond into the well. Three tankers idled near the dump pad, the first backed up to the edge. A crew fiddled with equipment at the back of the truck.

Woody rolled downhill and parked in front of a trailer labeled Office.

He knocked. The door opened. Malcolm Jones's head poked out.

"Who the heck are you? Where's your hardhat?"

"I'm Woody. Woody Spink. I'm your owner."

"Say what?"

"I mean I own Burlwood," he said, louder. "And you are?"

"Sorry I didn't recognize you, sir. I'm Jones, deputy project supervisor. Catching up on my paperwork. What can I do you for?"

"You're black."

Jones snorted. A 25-year line veteran of Big Oil with experience across the Marcellus Play, Malcolm X Jones grew up in Pittsburgh's Hill District and attended Westinghouse High. Unlike Roxx with her P.E. degree, Jones was School of Hard Knocks, supplemented with night classes at Duquesne. The call this month promoting him to night project manager was long overdue.

"Born that way, my brother," Jones shouted.

"I have a brother. Burl. He's the owner, too."

"Seriously, Mr. Spinks, what do you want?"

"Well, we own the trucking company, and I'd like to ... umm ... meet my employees."

Jones hesitated.

"Well, then, let me fix you up."

Jones disappeared, reemerging with earplugs and a hardhat. He handed them to Woody.

"We take safety real serious, sir. My crew starts every day with the Safety Minute, just like Exxon. I'll walk you over, now, but then I gotta get back to the paperwork."

Woody's hat shimmied like a bobblehead. Jones motioned him to follow.

"Your first experience with hydraulic fracturing, Mr. Spinks?"

"I *love* saying it," said Woody. "Fracking. No fracking way. Frack you. No, I don't mean *you!*"

"Yeah, fracking, man. It's been goin' on for years. We're a lot better at it now."

"What's happening there?"

"So, Mister Spinks, we retrofitted your daddy's old well, sir. That well, from the Nineteen damn Forties? It wasn't up to standards, no way. But we are all about making it work. We shored up the casing through the aquifer best we could. We drilled much deeper and put new casing all the way down. Now put your earplugs in."

The din of the high-pressure pumps rose. Malcolm began to shout.

"We started pumpin' frackwater back full time this week."

"Is it dangerous?"

"Why you think we wear hardhats?"

"Can I meet the truckers?"

"Over there."

As they approached the pond, Malcolm pointed to the closest tanker and shouted.

"We get 27 to 30 trucks a day now. Watch that spill pad there. The crew attaches the hose. Hose siphons the load. It takes 20 minutes per truck. Each one carries 4,000 to 6,000 gallons. The empty trucks go back north for another load."

"Spill pad," said Woody. "Sounds like a dirty diaper."

"It's about three-quarters filled. That's a lotta frackwater. It's pumped down the well along with that water you all get us from the county. It comes in that pipe over there."

"We get a discount from Supervisor Smythe."

"Funny thing, though," Malcolm said. "We gotta keep one man all night shooing deer away."

Shouts came from the spill pad. A crewman coupling a hose to the containment pond valve had lost his grip. The hose flailed like a riled snake, gushing grayish liquid, soaking the crew.

"Shit, man!" yelled Malcolm, running to help. "Hit the cutoff!"

"Is that supposed —?" Woody said.

Ten seconds later, the crew found the cutoff switch and wrestled the spewing hose in place.

Woody stood helplessly as thousands of gallons of frackwater rushed around his ankles, trashed his velvet slippers and headed toward the Hughes River.

Soaked, Malcolm hustled back to Woody.

"That stinks!" said Woody. "Rotten eggs!"

"Saline. Those salts have been down below a looong time. I think you better go now, Mister Spinks."

"Is that going into the river?"

"'Fraid so, sir. But we are gonna clean this up! Safety first!"

Suddenly Woody lurched and landed on his butt, soaking his Dockers.

Malcolm braced his legs and threw his arms out to maintain balance.

The ground swayed like a bobbing canoe.

CHAPTER 14

Sunday, Oct. 20

Tip was awake well before Blackie licked his dangling arm.

He remained in bed above the cider house's living space, piecing the dream — no, nightmare — back together. It began well enough, holding hands with a redhead on a sunlit balcony. Running through a maze, chased by a purple deer. Sitting high up on a black walnut branch. It ended as always, same brutal jerk: Slate, sliding off the branch, just out of reach, staring back. Same with the others: Bump with Rennie. Jeter, sliding. Marley, out cold. Same recriminations.

The clock said 5:35 a.m. He rose, walked to the dresser and looked in the mirror. Bags beneath crusty eyes. The white streak amid the black seemed wider. The dimples were deeper.

He pulled his shoulders back, inhaled and spoke to the patient pup.

"Carpe diem, Blackie. Cider Sunday."

He dressed in khakis, gray Martino sweatshirt, green fleece vest, Stonewall cap.

He peered out the window at the top of the stairs.

Fog. Good.

He crossed the small living area — flagstone floors softened by area rugs, brown leather couch and club chair, one-butt galley kitchen. He took the can of Bustelo down and mixed the grounds with sugar. He filled the Moka pot and found the *cafecito* cup. He loved this ritual he'd brought up from Little Havana.

Staymans from the orchard filled a bowl on the counter. He took one and bit.

Tart. Good sweetness.

Tip flicked on the computer and opened Pandora. Amazing thing, this free music. Steely Dan.

"I never seen you looking so bad my funky one ..."

He clicked a local news link out of Charlottesville, scanning for an explanation for last night. Twenty minutes into the auction, Tip had felt it. A display case rattled. Bottles in the bar spilled. A worried buzz filled the room, but the fund-raiser continued.

AP Briefs. Slight temblor, 2.7 on the Richter scale, north of Charlottesville.

Wonky deer. Earthquakes.

Tip knocked back the Cuban coffee and walked into the yawning workspace. Chestnut 4x6 beams spanned the 15-foot ceiling and marched toward the barrel storage. Bins of applewood dried in a corner. The bulky copper still he called Adolf and its cooling coils took up space on the east. Bottle racks lined the west wall. An antique sorting table stamped Blue Ridge Fruit Growers Cooperative sat in the middle.

The wooden, hand-cranked cider press, cleaned and bleached by Sunday Lopez, stood ready for today's pressing. Tip had dragooned Walker and Provo. Marley was on board. He'd texted an invitation to Maddie.

Tip fed a couple logs to the potbellied stove and lighted it with newsprint. He couldn't wait for Provo to show up with the scoop on his evasive engineer.

"Let's go, Blackie."

They headed up past the burial plot to a fenced-off half-acre. Tip clambered over the rails, landing in the orchard's dwarf plot. Fog swirled in the branches, trees 8 feet tall, grafted five years ago with M9 stock, rows 12 feet apart, aisles separated by 20 feet.

Ting's cough. Doesn't add up.

He pruned branches withered by brown rot virus. Late-harvest fruit hung heavy and expectant.

Time to call Doc Freeman.

Up the knoll, the semi-dwarf Hewe's Crab. Just beyond, the orchard's oldest section, spread over two acres — full-sized trees, heirloom and commercial grade. Topping the crests where cool air descended beneath the boughs were 25 varieties, most acquired from downstate orchards.

For hard cider, Tip started with Albemarle Pippin, then blended for balance, sweetness, tartness, aroma. Arkansas Black. Stayman, of course. Rappahannock Beauty. Paradise Sweet, in honor of Jacques Paradis. The brandy blend added astringent Hewe's Crab for extra tartness. He was pleased to have cuttings of Parmar, the best brandy apple, from a ciderist down near Floyd.

Tip had returned to Fairleigh and a drought seven years ago. He'd inherited half the estate on Jeter's passing, but he was little more than an interloper. In the eyes of locals, Ting *was* Fairleigh.

Despite the paper's buyout check in his pocket, he had been at a low point. Embarrassed by the bungled awarding of the Pulitzer. Despairing of print's spiral. Ruing the collective inability to stop the pillaging of the planet. Regretting romantic failures. Shamed by his treatment of his sister, his daughters. Ting had met him with less than a hero's welcome. He shut himself in his boyhood bedroom and killed the better part of a bottle of Maker's Mark.

He refused to take any visitors, his Scrabble School friend included. Ting wouldn't stand for it. She threw the bedroom door open. Walker Longwood entered.

"Work it out!" she yelled.

At first, Tip just listened. The beekeeper described the deepening drought's effects on his hives. Talked about haying season and cattle prices. Joked of being an "avowed apiarist."

Hearing anew the details of country life awoke something in Tip, who had spent more than half a lifetime in urban journalism chasing every environmental Armageddon.

"All I know is I'm through with newspapers."

"It's like the Dalai Lama says," said Walker. "Everyone has a seed of good heart."

"But I saved lives! Exposed evil!" Tip shouted. "Everything's a shambles. Print is dead! My sister loathes me. My daughters barely tolerate me."

"There's a reason you feel like you're drowning," Walker said. "You latch on to no particular faith, my friend. That's not so easy for someone who views the world as black or white. You'd best start living for the good of the gray and the mystery of the in-between."

The beekeeper drew himself up.

"You need to thank your sister. She has been beyond reasonable to have you back. You were lucky Jeter allowed you half of this place, buster. Given your lifelong behavior toward women, you're fortunate to get that. I watched her raise those girls. She expected them to pull their weight. She'll hold you to the same. Put some gloves on those soft city hands. Walk that orchard. Your apple house, it's a rat hole."

He rose to leave.

"And quit moping."

Tip spent the next four sweltering days tromping the ravines and hillocks of Fairleigh. The Hughes was a trickle. The hardwood groves across from Burlwood droned with cicadas. Ting's still-tender beets sat wilting. The stunted grass didn't yield a second cutting that year.

The evening of the third day, Provo Starke, back from Iraq, swung by to talk with Ting about grazing 50 head on Tyler land. Afterward, he and Tip took beers to the orchard for sunset. The recovering journalist appreciated the depth beneath the ex-soldier's humor.

"You know this orchard was our morel mushroom patch?" Tip mused. "They popped out the day after a soft spring rain. Jeter had the knack of finding them. Ting has Sara's recipes. They still call 'em merkels?"

The next day, Tip studied the orchard, overgrown with tree-of-heaven and autumn olive. The trees showed damage from an unholy trinity of brown rot, tent caterpillar and black bears. Tip recalled driving the crates to the Front Royal rail spur in Jeter's old flatbed.

At week's end, Tip went to his sister with the first of many apologies and an idea. Let me turn the apple shed into my own place. Outfit it. Attack the orchard. Do cider. I need to learn more about distillation beyond what I learned in Normandy. But I'm going to make a go of brandy.

Weary of seeing her brother traipse about her house in boxers, Ting amended the plan.

"This isn't a B&B, Tipster. Sunday Lopez needs help with the fences and weeding. You'll do your share of the chores. The shed and the orchard are all yours."

Lopez served as contractor for the renovation, well-suited having spent winters in Manzanillo building his mother's casita. Tip was the labor. Walker and Provo provided strong backs, wisecracks and philosophy. In four months, Tip had his spartan cider house apartment. No TV, no computer.

The orchard was next, the plan, audacious. Organic. 100 percent. Virginia was in the early stages of a hard cider revival, and no one was taking up Calvados. Fairleigh's orchard hadn't gone through the Prohibition-era gutting of cider trees in favor of sweet eating fruit like Red Delicious. Tip and Sunday repaired fences and pruned the diseased trees. Over his first winter, Tip designed the orchard's semi-dwarf and dwarf additions and ordered rootstock.

Tip began experimenting with the distillation and barreling of apple brandy. He wrangled with the regulators, one generation removed from the revenuers. And he splurged on Adolf, the alembic copper pot made in Germany by Adolf Adrian. It gave his place the look of a Jules Verne novel. Between hard cider in the French style and brandy, he figured he'd find a market.

He and Blackie reentered the warmed cider house. Tip signed in to the Society of Environmental Journalists' site. He clicked on the listserv.

"Remember me? What can you fracking rascals near the shale plays tell me, stat?" he typed. Knowing what he'd provoke, he continued. "I'm about to drill down deep my own self."

CHAPTER 15

Sunday, Oct. 20, 9:30 a.m.

Blackie barked and scrambled out the door. Tip closed the computer.

Sunday Lopez let himself in with an *"Hola!"* He'd been part of Fairleigh ever since Jeter hired him away from the Frost Diner. He'd taught Tip everything from plumbing to mending stone fences to making taquitos.

"Your daughters, they are here. Where is your skillet?"

Marley was on the manor home's porch, greeting her sister and Les Leong in the drive.

"Glad you could make it," Tip said, walking out toward them. "Or is it just you doubt my ability to actually produce something?"

"I just had to prove to Les I come from rural roots," said Maddie, casual in jeans.

"You picked a good day to crush," said Leong, smiling, attired in Dockers and checked shirt.

"Tip, Les wants to see Adolf," Maddie said.

"Don't worry, Mr. Tyler. I'm not Treasury."

"Tip. Hey, you want to see licenses, I have licenses!"

"I need to say hi to Aunt Ting," said Maddie. "Les, stay here. I'll be right back."

Sunday Lopez cracked eggs into a glazed bowl as Tip showed Les inside.

"Another mouth to feed, amigo," he said. "Les, this is Sunday. Mas familia."

Blackie barked. More vehicles.

"Les, come meet the Rappahannock Debate and Cider Society," Tip said.

Walker was reaching for honey jars in his panel truck. Provo dropped the tailgate of his F-150, pointing to an odd wood and stainless-steel contraption rising above three apple crates.

"Like our new whimmy-diddle?" Provo asked. "Remember last year when we didn't like the grind we were getting? I postulated a garbage disposal might just do it. Well, here she is."

"Whaddya call her?"

"Little Miss Stonewall," said Provo.

A half-hour later, frittata and toast consumed, the twins joined the men to set up tables in the sun outside the cider house. They unloaded Starke's Staymans and carried them to the cooperative's sorter, where Albemarle Pippins and a half-dozen other varieties sat in bushels..

He handed a hose to Les. "Let us spray."

"It only goes downhill from here," Walker warned.

The twins set up to cut the sorted fruit. Despite her cast, Marley halved the apples, blemishes and all, trying to keep up with Maddie. As fast as they could fill a two-gallon bucket, Sunday Lopez fed the fruit into the maw of Tip's old-fashioned wooden press for a first, rough grind. Walker pulled that capture bucket and hiked it to Provo's whining contraption for a second mashing. Tip showed Les how to man the press, and before long the undersecretary was producing steady rivulets of sweet juice, employing an axe handle for the final press, leaving a pile of pulverized pomace. Tip poured the juice into 30-gallon plastic barrels, but he mostly supervised a la Tom Sawyer, listening to the comfortable chatter.

"Little Miss Stonewall, she makes quick work of the apples," said Sunday.

"And one hellacious racket," Walker shouted.

The cider house radio played the bluegrass hour from Charlottesville.

"Makes me feel like part of what Wendell Berry calls the producer class," said Tip.

"Any word on last night's little shimmy?" Walker asked. "My bees were cranky."

"Item out of AP," said Tip. "I plan to ask around."

"*El terremoto*," Sunday said.

"We heard about that at Energy," said Les. "We're looking into it. Eastern quakes are rare."

"You're a pretty good worker, Les," Walker said. "Don't muss those chinos, though."

"Reminds me of picking grapes in Sonoma," Les said. "What you expect to get this year?"

"Shooting for 40 to 50 gallons," said Tip, handing him a Rolling Rock. He pointed to four plastic barrels.

"Barrel one: Sweet cider; pure Stayman. Barrel two: Hard cider in the French style; mostly Albemarle Pippin. That'll ferment maybe eight weeks. Barrels three and four: The Stonewall blend, destined for five years aging in oak."

Tip handed out chilled green bottles all around.

"It's before noon," Provo needled Sunday. "Isn't imbibin' on your namesake day a mortal sin?"

Ting walked up from the house carrying a hamper.

"It's an army!" she yelled, smiling. "Where are you when I have beets to pick?"

"Alms for the weary?" Walker said.

"Ham and cheddar on sourdough."

"Much obliged, ma'am," said Provo, taking a sandwich.

"Say, Mr. Starke," said Tip, a tad casual, "you were being mighty courtly last night."

Provo's cheeks reddened.

"I take the Gentleman's Fifth."

"A certain blonde in cowgirl boots," Tip pressed.

Starke quickly took a bite, rolling his eyes in feigned helplessness.

"Ellen called," said Ting. "She and Gus have invited us for bocce Saturday."

Blackie barked.

They turned to see Fran McKinney's brown cruiser coming up the hill.

Marley put down her knife and smiled.

"Oh, hell. I was supposed to call her," Tip said.

The sheriff stepped out of the car with a swing of her ponytail. She was dressed in jeans, unzipped George Mason hoodie and a vintage Redskins jersey with Riggins's No. 44.

"Hey," she said, easily catching the apple Marley tossed. "You people have your priorities all wrong. Kickoff's coming right up."

"I forgot what you looked like outta uniform," Tip said. "Sorry I didn't call."

"Well I just thought you'd want to know. The results came back from Frank Davies. Deer autopsy?"

Fran pulled out a note pad. "Are you ready for this?"

Ting put a hand on Marley's shoulder.

"That deer had one ungodly mix of chemicals and salts in its system. Benzene. Acetone. Strontium. Barium. Arsenic. All higher than allowable levels."

"Arsenic?" said Marley.

"Sounds like a fracking cocktail," Tip mumbled.

"Watch your mouth," said Ting.

"No. The chemicals ..." Tip said, forehead creased.

"How would a deer ...?" Maddie asked, trailing off.

"That's not all," the sheriff said. "It had ingested so much bromide, it was purple. Cyanotic."

"Where do you find bromide around here?" Tip wondered aloud.

"Have a sandwich, Fran," said Ting.

"Thanks. How can I help? I hope you ladies are limiting the knife work to apples."

A short time later, the Debate and Cider Society finished the day's task with 45 gallons in storage. As Sunday began to clean up, Tip described how they would later barrel, bottle and label the products as winter set in.

The crew walked past Ting's garden, its neat rows spent after a productive summer. Blistered tomatoes littered the vines and carpeted the ground.

Marley bent to snatch a cracked tomato. Her sister talked up ahead with Les, back turned.

Marley hauled back and threw. The *splat* on her sister's jeans sounded like the first salvo at Fort Sumter.

Ting hiccupped in shock. "Albemarle Tyler!"

"Lordy!" said Provo.

Maddie assessed the damage. She stared poker-faced at her twin. In a blink, she grabbed two heirlooms from the nearest cage and fired.

Marley deflected the first with her cast. The second sailed, landing between the Riggins's Fours.

The sheriff frowned.

The garden went silent.

Fran looked down, slowly removed her hoodie and stepped in front of Marley. "We call that assaulting an officer, but ...." Without looking she hurled a tomato softball style. The undersecretary's chinos exploded at the knee.

Another whizzed past Tip and smacked Ting's shoulder, dislodging the basket. Tip turned to see Walker's grin.

Pow! Tip looked down at the spreading glop on the Martini logo. *Pow!* Upside his head. He wiped and looked at his hand.

"Hey! That's —"

"Zucchini!" said Provo, aiming his next at Fran.

The twins, gulping in laughter, racked up direct hits on each other. Ting turned toward Tip. With an overhand worthy of Double A, she hurled a juicy Rowdy Red.

"Take *that*, brother!"

It exploded belt-high. Marley's next caught his bicep. Maddie scored with a hard one to his hip.

Tip took cover behind a cage, peals of laughter in his ears. He grabbed the closest tomato.

"You started this!" he whooped, missing Marley. He grabbed another as her zuke splotched his sneaker.

The Tyler women advanced, shouting gleefully, pelting the kneeling Tip.

The others halted, watching the scene unfold as the trio closed in.

Ting's last toss knocked his cap off. Tip fell to all fours, laughing hard, blinded by seeds and blistered skins and tears.

The others watched, quiet now. Tip's laugh subsided, sides heaving, tears now coming from a deeper place.

After a couple seconds, he stood. He was dazed. Panting. His daughters tentatively approached.

"Tip?," said Maddie. "Are you —?"

He caught their wrists before they could react and pulled them into a sodden bear hug. He waddled them, all laughing now, toward his sister. Ting backed away, wary.

Tip and the twins wobbled.

"Timberrrr!" said Provo as they toppled, laughing, into the compost pile.

Tip stayed on his back, coated in Technicolor glop, laughing daughters at his side.

"Gonna have to call you Heinz 57," Walker said.

CHAPTER 16

Saturday, Oct. 26

"Is this the last box?"

"Yessir!" Roxx yelled through the front door to Rob Hanson, who was standing behind her Jeep in the drive below. "You all were *really* nice to help me get settled."

"Pretty clothes," said Cindy, closing the armoire.

"For an engineer," Roxx said.

"I'm sure UVA was hard," Cindy said. "It's almost on par with Tech." She caught herself. "I mean, that's what they say."

"Not so bad I couldn't manage," said Roxx. "Truth is it's hard in the field. Older guys don't know how to act around us 'gals.' Their brains are located elsewhere."

Cindy blushed. "I think you'll like this place. Long Mountain Road has the best views in Rapp."

Rob joined them in the converted garage. A tan couch and tufted Queen Anne chair faced the flagstone fireplace. Roxx had discovered a bottle of Veuve Clicquot in the kitchenette with a note from the owners upstairs, Sean and Martin O'Connell. A card above the embossed name Twin Rocks said, "Welcome!"

They stood at the glass sliders and looked west to Thornton Gap, some four miles distant. Autumn-flamed ridges rode in waves toward the higher peaks. A Holstein herd grazed below.

"She can see Old Rag," Rob said.

"Sorry to go, Roxx, but we have one more appointment in Woodville," said Cindy. "Nice older couple from Fairfax. They've looked at Stan Bronson's place six times now."

"So we'll see you later for bocce?" Rob asked.

"Sounds like fun."

He'll be there.

Roxx had thought plenty about Provo Starke since the truck-bed romp. And herself. She wasn't looking for an entanglement. Not here in the boonies. Had his number. Didn't call.

"Just behind the school," said Cindy. "Bye!"

Roxx picked up a box and put it on the queen-sized sleigh bed. She'd used a Sharpie to label it STUFF. She removed a framed photo of Ralph and Barb. Next out was a box of Trojans.

Too late for these.

She slid it into the drawer of the bedside table with a sigh.

What was I thinking!? Heavenly sex ... but, Jeepers, there at the end ...

She didn't know a thing about bocce. She grabbed her iPhone, forgetting the Crappahannock Curse.

She saw two bars and yelled. "4G! I love this place!"

She sat and pecked in the search. Bocce. Lawn bowling. Old Italian men.

Can't believe I get a signal!

She grabbed another picture and placed it on the oak dresser. Mont Blanc loomed behind two sunglassed faces: Ralph and an angelic Roxx. Family weekend in the Wiesbaden days.

She opened the hard case of her Lenovo laptop to finish her weekly report.

"Malcolm Jones began stint as nighttime PM on site," she typed.

Management is not what it's cracked up to be.

"Reinjection paused to assess well casing. Two more change orders on the casing issues. Well integrity remains a concern."

Still a piece of shit.

"Containment nearing 75 percent capacity. Monitoring leaks at the dump pad."

Gallons, not ounces.

"Workers recommended by the owners joined second shift Wednesday."

Buncha right-wing nutjobs.

"Other unskilled are reliable."

Migrants. Solid.

Roxx paused. How would she explain the ... payment?

PMs don't get OT. Gittin' 'er done.

She looked around her new digs.

Almost as nice as my condo.

Roxx saved the draft. The Wings tune on her Nano was ending when she caught the lyric.

"So what's all the fuss? There ain't nobody got spies like us."

She showered in the compact bathroom and dried fast in the chill. Quick makeup session.

Go light. Sunday picnic.

She found the retro Keds and the pink hoodie she'd worn to Wahoo games at Scott Stadium. Another box held a ball-cap collection. She put the Green Valley cap on the dresser, opting for the blue and orange V with the crossed sabers.

Let's go, Mata Hari.

It took eight minutes to reach Lee Highway. The gun shop had a line out the door and a big sign: WELCOME OPEN CARRIERS! She turned at the elementary school. A large wine barrel soon announced the entrance to Martini Cellars.

Blues music wafted from the tasting room's deck. Day-trippers from D.C. sat at picnic tables.

Through the glass doors, Roxx saw a slim man in a St. Louis Cardinals cap. Tip Tyler. She started to duck away.

Provo's pal. Danger.

Tip saw her and waved.

Caught.

She smiled and walked in.

"Roxanna, right?" said Tip, offering a hand. "We met —"

"Of course! The fund-raiser. Call me Roxx. R-O-double X."

"I'm grabbing a bottle of Martini's finest here from Shelly. Shelly, Roxx."

"Welcome to the Cellars," said a smiling brunette behind the counter, a large crucifix dangling over her Martini polo. "This is our Moonrise. Real drinkable on such a nice afternoon."

"Roxx is new 'round here," said Tip. "A civil engineer."

Did that ever come up? Civil? Or even engineer?

"Welcome to God's County," Shelly said. "Sign here, Mr. Tyler. Hey, the pastor and I missed you again."

"Slipped my mind again. But do say hi to Clete. Hey, ask him how the dinosaurs might have gone and gotten themselves extinct when homo erectus wasn't around to bag 'em for dinner."

"Mr. Tyler, that's —"

"Grilled T. rex. Goes nicely with a Bordeaux blend."

Shelly ignored him and shifted attention to a newly arrived couple.

Tip, grinning, turned to Roxx. "Follow me."

They took a side door, Roxx hanging back a step. Orderly grapevines sloped toward the western horizon. Down below sat a pair of slim rectangles paved with pebbles. A group gathered beneath a spectral sycamore.

"Those are the courts," said Tip, turning. "Ever play before?"

"No sir."

Never said civil engineer ... to anyone.

"It's fun. Have you met the Martinis?"

"No, sir."

"It's Tip. The last person who called me *sir* was my dad. When he said it, it meant I was in trouble."

"OK. Tip it is."

"You'll like Gus and Ellen. I'll introduce my daughter. She's down there. She's more your age, maybe a bit older? I can never tell. She's the one with Provo."

Roxx looked quickly. A woman with a cast on her arm chatted with Provo, who turned. Roxx waved, timidly. He saluted.

People were pulling dishes out of coolers and setting up lawn chairs.

Crap. Didn't bring a damn thing.

"Hey, Roxx!" said Cindy Hanson. "You all, this is Roxx Bleigh."

A chorus of hellos.

"Hey there, Cap'n Bleigh," said Starke, touching her arm.

"Hello again."

"How are you?" he asked quietly.

"Like Elvis said: All shook up."

"Hey, welcome to the Cellars," said Gus, grinning, offering an all-encompassing sweep. Broad as a fireplug. Nice black hair. "Call me Gus. It's easier than Guglielmo."

Looks military. Like Dad?

"My wife, Ellen."

Sophia Loren.

"So good to meet you!" Ellen said. "We hear you're all but moved in!"

"Just about," said Roxx. "Cindy and Rob helped a lot. I met the sheriff last week."

"Wahoo, huh?" said Fran. "Go, Patriots!"

"Help yourself to snacks," Ellen said. "What can I pour you?"

"I'm Marley," said the woman with the cast, waving.

"Did you say —"

"Marley. You missed my sister and her friend. They had to get back. This is my aunt, Ting."

"My long-suffering sister," Tip said. "And this fellow, Walker Longwood, is a keeper of bees."

Morgan Freeman lookalike. Seems ... familiar.

"Pleasure. Walker, is it?"

"Have I seen you before?" he asked. "Thornton River Grille, maybe?"

Oh crap!

Roxx rewound to the business dinner. "Anything's possible."

Maybe. Jabba blocked my view.

"Ellen, my usual bocce partner, I am about to forsake you," said Provo, unzipping a bag and pulling out a smooth green ball. "I educate rookies. Roxx, care to hook up?"

Gawd!

She blushed and took the ball. "Wow! That's heavy!"

"Cindy, let's give 'em a match," said Gus.

Soon, two doubles matches ran in parallel as green and red balls arced toward a small white ball. ("The pallino," said Gus.) Shouts of joy mixed with whoops of competition. The players balanced wine glasses as they stepped into their shots.

"You're a festive bunch," Roxx said.

Him, most of all.

The game came surprisingly easy. Roxx enjoyed the wine — fruity, light. The music from the deck was great. She liked the camaraderie. When she knocked two red balls away from the white thingy, she and Provo celebrated with a hug.

Old Spice. So nice.

The players soon squinted into the setting sun. Conversation lulled around the food and the quickly disappearing wine. Ellen and Ting gabbed about beets and goat cheese recipes. The vintner took an accordion out and played *Funiculi Funicula.*

Roxx and Marley found they had Key West pasts in common, and Roxx wondered if there might be a friendship in the making. Tip's daughter was definitely grooving on the sheriff, though.

"What happened?" Roxx asked, nodding at the cast.

"Fatal encounter with a purple deer."

Purple. Like the containment carcass. Uh-oh.

"Yikes! Where'd it happen?"

"We live south of here, on the county line, up against the park."

Near Burlwood.

"Silver Cloud saved her," said Ting, coughing. "What are we to make of that deer?"

"Scientists say bromide causes certain animals to turn cyanotic … go purple," said Tip from behind, quietly. "Like the victims of Spanish flu in World War I. I read about a purple squirrel in Pennsylvania state park. Near some drilling?"

Did he just look at me?

"A squirrel?" Walker said. "That's nothing like the deer Marley hit."

"The deer that *hit* Marley, we're thinking," the sheriff said.

"How could a deer get full of bromide?" Ellen asked.

"Or go postal on me?" asked Marley.

"Not from eating rotten tomatoes," Walker said.

They laughed. All but Tip.

"Bromide, and the chemicals they found in the deer?" he said, gazing steadily at Roxx. "They're used in hydraulic fracturing."

Spider sense.

"Fracking," Walker said. "Going on just north of us."

"I've read about it," Gus said. "Domestic source of natural gas. Lots of jobs."

"But that's up in Pennsylvania," Rob said. "It isn't happening here."

"Oil from the home team," said Provo. "Could be how we keep soldiers like me out of the desert some day."

"The Marcellus Shale," Roxx blurted, surprising herself. "Trillions of gallons."

SHUT UP.

Heads turned.

"Trapped in striations," Roxx continued. "Miles below."

Am I blushing?

She saw Tip starting to ask a question.

Danger, Will Robinson!

"You wouldn't know anything about the impact on the aqui —"

Get OUT!!!

Roxx cut him off. "Wow! This has been soooo nice, but I am woofed! Moving day and all."

She bolted past Provo and headed uphill. Halfway, she turned, blushing.

Too fast!

"Thanks!" she said, walking backward. "Next time I'll bring deviled eggs or something!"

She stopped, too late to regain her composure.

"Gus, Ellen, thank you so much. Bye!"

"I'll see you to your car," said Provo, throwing Tip a worried look.

Even with long strides, Starke couldn't catch Roxx until she chirped her key to unlock the Jeep.

"Don't need to do that around here," Provo said.

Do what? Blow up the fucking party?

"I'm sorry. Wait —"

"Lock your car. Or your apartment, for that matter. Not in Rappahannock."

"Oh. OK. Listen, I'm sorry."

"What was that about?"

"What was what?" she said, opening the door. "I dunno. Too buzzed, maybe? I *am* tired. Nice crowd, but I don't know if I fit in. Big workday tomorrow…"

"I saw you weren't snacking. I'd say you need somethin' in your belly."

"What, now?"

"Your hasty departure deprived me of the opportunity to ask."

She hesitated. He looked on, sheepish.

Recoup. Now.

"I could use a burger. Haven't really eaten all day."

"Griffin Tavern. Flint Hill; on the left. I'll follow. Better yet, let me drive you."

By the time Tip reached the lot, the Cherokee was trailing dust. He was just able to read the Pennsylvania plate.

GIT R DUN.

CHAPTER 17

Sunday, Oct. 27

Tip and Blackie had been up since before dawn. He'd walked the orchard, marked a couple of the semi-dwarfs for grafting and checked out the Parmars, now old enough to yield fruit. The apples were destined for his next batch, a job his daily punch list suggested he start right now.

Instead, *cafecito* made, his computer glowed with the home page of Green Valley Resources.

He'd bookmarked it yesterday before heading to the vineyard when, with as much guilt as curiosity, he'd Googled Roxx Bleigh. Details were easy to come by. Fifth link down, Roxanna Raye Bleigh appeared in the same line as the company's name. In a click, he was on the Staff page. Project manager, Civil Engineering Division, Oil and Gas Exploration Department. A portrait had Roxx standing at a window in GVR cap, the yellow seats of Heinz Field in the background. Her bio mentioned hydraulic fracturing projects in New York and Ohio.

The personal stuff was easy, too: 82 Facebook friends, pictures with Tri Delts. The Facebook profile: Project manager at Green Valley Resources. Studied at University of Virginia. Lives in Pittsburgh, Pa. Relationship: It's Complicated.

But Roxx's abrupt departure had fired Tip's circuits just like in the old days when an anonymous envelope would land on his desk at *The Miami Herald*.

Journalism degree freshly framed, intern Tip Tyler had been assigned to the Florida Keys bureau, working for the State Desk when *Herald* bureaus lined both coasts.

Rennie and the twins crammed into a tiny Old Town Key West apartment on Grunt Bone Alley. His wife despised Florida, its sandy terrain and fetid humidity from the get-go. "I *hate* these no-see-ums. You're always gone. What am I gonna to do with these two all day?"

Interns worked 14-hour days, cranked out two stories per edition, took pictures and got their film on a plane by 5 p.m. each day to be couriered to the photo desk in Miami. Reporting in the 104-mile long Keys meant broiling drives up U.S. 1 to Key Largo, Islamorada, Tavernier, Marathon, then back to Key West through interminable stoplights. Monroe County was a licentious mix of sun-crisped hustlers, outlaw shrimpers and ethically impaired public servants.

Late for the airport film run, Tip was leaving a backgrounder with a county zoning official in Marathon, having begged her to explain the indecipherable Zoning Board agenda. He asked about a fat file on the corner of her desk. It's nothing, she said.

Later that night, she called him at home. Meet me at the Lorelei. Mile Marker 92. Sunset.

Over Heinekens and conch fritters, the source walked Tip through the file. In a remote stretch of pristine mangrove swamp on Card Sound Road north of Key Largo, eight developers' projects were moving rapidly toward approval. Once built out, the developments could bring as many as 45,000 new residents to a county already strained to provide water, roads and utilities. Greased palms, she implied. One behemoth 2,800-unit condo complex called Port Bougainville would soon dredge 35 acres — fragile saltwater, breeding grounds of spoonbill, snapper and shrimp. The desecration would roil the waters bathing the snorkelers' paradise of Pennekamp State Park.

"The bulldozers are lined up," she said, crying. "Can't stomach it."

He sped back to get his editor on the phone and work up a memo to the brass. The next day, Tip flew to Miami to meet the I-Team editor and a veteran reporter. They spent long weeks interviewing sources, reviewing county documents and tromping the properties. A month in, Tip found a seagull hanging on his picket fence, its neck snapped. Rennie went into a panic.

The four-day series fueled a grand jury investigation and resulted in criminal charges against sitting county commissioners. Investment bankers pulled millions in development funding, effectively shutting off the dozer engines. In Tallahassee, the Cabinet overtook the tainted county zoning process. A full-time offer in his pocket for $315 a week, Tip traveled to the state capital over

Rennie's protests to cover the meetings. Within a year, he was named bureau chief.

Meanwhile, Rennie was getting worse. Bacardi was cheap in the Keys. Her depression, dating to the miscarriage, had been diagnosed. Bipolar. She shunned her medications. Tip often got home to find the twin toddlers alone, crying.

One August, Tip met a team of professors who banded sooty and noddy terns near Fort Jefferson, 40 miles west in the Dry Tortugas. They invited the Tylers along.

"Let's go," Tip urged Rennie. "Girls will enjoy it. I pitched a story to Tropic. They'll pay."

After a boozy Friday dinner at A&B Lobster House, the ornithologists' group left Key West in two U.S. Navy boats. They arrived at the Civil War fort and soon got the hang of banding the cranky birds' pencil-thin legs. They camped that night beneath the Milky Way on the fort's grassy terreplein.

The terreplein. At his computer, remembering the night, Tip closed his eyes.

Waking. Rennie gone. Eyes adjusting to the black. Calling her name. Stumbling over Maddie.

"Where's your mamma, sweetie?"

"There, Daddy."

Not seeing Rennie in the intense dark until she was *rightthere*, at the edge, looking back at him. He reached out and found her cheek. Tears. Fresh rum on her breath.

"What's wrong, Mountain Girl?"

"You. Me. Florida. Everything."

"Take my hand. Here."

The bump. The silence. The sickening crack below.

Tip's wail woke the professors. Flashlight beams found the body below.

The choppy ride back to Key West began a miserable stretch. The flurry of Park Service questions. The morgue. The inquest. Embarrassing headlines in his own newspaper. Initial finding: Accidental death. Doubts shadowed the plane carrying Tip, the twins and the coffin to Virginia. Widower at 25. Clueless around his daughters.

"Your sister will always resent this," his father had said after Tip arrived later that summer to leave the twins.

Jeter nailed it. The tomato pasting might signal a thaw with his daughters, but Ting wasn't about to let up. Tip had sworn to her after leaving the newsroom he'd never return. In the intervening years, he'd grown to love his native Rappahannock all over again.

But once ink gets in your blood, it never stops pumping. Tip clicked on a new page.

FracFocus.org. — "The Chemical Disclosure Registry, a joint project of the Groundwater Protection Council and the Interstate Oil and Gas Compact Commission."

He tapped on the blue "Find a Well" superimposed over a green map of America. Typed "Virginia."

The Old Dominion's flattened triangle popped up. Tip zoomed in.

Rockingham County, two wells (proposed). Elsewhere: ***No activity.***

CHAPTER 18

Friday, Nov. 1, evening

Josefina and Sunday Lopez had been easy to spot last night on the fringes of the Halloween crowd. Marley Tyler recalled the kids' holiday as she drove to Sperryville.

She had watched as Rappahannock families streamed down Gay Street past merchants' sidewalk tables topped with overflowing bowls of processed-sugar bombs. Scores of My Little Ponies and Luke Skywalkers grabbed and ran to the next stand. Their brimming pails would keep them on overdrive for much of the next week.

"Were we like that, Tip?" she'd asked, straightening her Alice in Wonderland dress.

"How would he know?" said Ting, done up as the White Rabbit.

"Hey, we did some trick or treating in Key West," said Tip, ill-disguised as the Cheshire Cat.

"Thank God we talked him out of going as a purple deer," Ting whispered to Rob Hanson.

The Wonderland ensemble was about as organized as it got for Rob and Cindy's friends, sufficient to land a feature photo in the *Reporter*. Cindy and Rob were Tweedledum and Tweedledee. Gus Martini made a decent March Hare. Rob kept their teacups filled with chardonnay from a stash inside the office.

The content of the cups was visible when the Baptists' contingent passed by. Clete scowled, steering his tiny angels away.

Marley had gone reluctantly. Fran McKinney was on 24-hour duty, this being Halloween.

Marley'd waved to familiar faces among a clot of adults beyond the river of candy grubbers. Sunday Lopez had waved back, timidly.

"Ting, I'll be gone a sec."

Marley reached Sunday and a group in dusty jean jackets, knee-high boots and Yankees caps.

"*Hola* Domingo, *hola*, Josefina, how are you?"

"*Bien, senorita*. Ms. Marley, have you met Jose from Waterpenny? This is Jorge from Roy's Orchard. Guillermo is Mount Vernon's stone mason."

She shook hands. "*Mi nombre es Marley*. Good to meet you, amigos."

Jose and Jorge smiled shyly. Guillermo fiddled with a cellphone, then handed it to Jose.

"Happy Halloween!" said Marley. "Where are your costumes?"

The exchanged glances were more bemused than embarrassed.

"Most of us, you know, we have just come from work," Josefina said.

"Guillermo, can you get a signal here in town?" Marley asked.

"*Si, senorita*. We all get signals."

"How is that possible?"

"Signals, they are not a problem for us," Sunday said. "Not anywhere in the county. Guillermo is talented with electronics. He gets us signals."

"Please, you must come tomorrow to our church," said Josefina. "*Un gran fiesta*."

"Of course! *Dia de la Muerte*!"

"We would be honored."

Sunday Lopez smiled. "Look at these hombres tonight. Tomorrow you will not recognize them."

Marley thought back to the Halloween encounter as she entered Sperryville.

Most residents couldn't tell you the name of the artisan who built their neighbor's stone wall or cooked Griffin Tavern's great fish 'n' chips. Chances are it was someone born in Hermosillo or Veracruz, part of the county's invisible 3 percent. Conservative RappChat posters might battle liberals on border fences, but they'll praise "the guys" who bush-hogged their 45 acres.

Marley had spent hours tending Ting's garden with Sunday Lopez, speaking Spanish. She knew his pride that a given name, Domingo, had morphed into a U.S. nickname. Josefina had gone from early babysitter for Marley and her sister to pastry chef at the Inn at Kelly's Ford. Now their boys were at Wakefield, no small feat even with tuition assistance. The couple had been instrumental in founding the Iglesias de San Tomas on Sperryville's Main Street.

Marley parked, eager to glimpse their lives away from the fields and kitchens.

She saw skeletons as she walked in and heard the music. *Streets of Laredo*. Black banners with grinning skulls and red swatches hung above the church door. Pews had been pulled aside for a dance floor. Tables in the nave steamed with food.

She spotted Josefina and walked her way. Sunday approached and gave her a hug.

Marley handed him the bottle.

"Ribera del duero," said Josefina, reading the label. "*Gracias, senorita.*"

"You have not seen these fellows recently," said Sunday, motioning over two strapping lads. "Enrique, Ricardo, remember Senorita Marley Tyler?"

"Good lord, you guys have grown! Your father won't stop talking about your lacrosse talents!"

"Ricardo, he's the goalie," said Sunday "Enrique is captain. Both all-conference."

"And Duke has been calling," Josefina said. "Full scholarships."

"ACC lacrosse is tough," Sunday said.

"The toughest," said Ricardo, smiling.

"I know you from the trophy case," Enrique said to Marley. "The famous soccer team."

"Be careful, guys. I might ask you to sing the Wakefield alma mater."

A guitarist, violinist and trumpeter in gilt costumes and sombreros sauntered over, playing a *cancion*. They bowed.

"Guillermo! That was beautiful. Where did you learn to play?"

"Jalisco."

"Of course. Still getting a good signal?"

"This fellow," said Sunday, leaning in, "he is good. Like the man on the television. MacGyver. This church steeple? He and his friends, they work on the weekends. Now it is a cellphone repeater. He made signal boosters for us with coffee cans and copper wire."

"That is amazing. I must tell Tip."

Jose smiled. The trio began playing a *valse mexicano* in three-four time.

Couples stepped to the dance floor. Laughing children chased each other around the floor. Josefina brought Marley a steaming bowl of *pozole*.

"Mmmm," she said, spooning a mouthful of pork and hominy. "Like I remember when we were girls. Sunday says you're thinking of opening your own place."

"It is possible," Josefina said. "With scholarships, we might be able to use our savings. I have my eye on the Café Indigo in the River District."

"I heard it never really got off the ground." Marley closed her eyes and listened to the next song.

"You keep showing up in all the right places."

The familiar voice and light touch on her shoulder felt … right. Marley opened her eyes. Fran McKinney, wearing jeans jacket over uniform blouse, smiled back.

"What are you …?"

"Oh, come on! These are my voters. Others will be soon enough. Domingo, Josefina, good to see you. Those fellas are excellent."

"Sheriff, thank you for coming," said Josefina. "Please have some food."

"Thought you'd never ask, Josefina."

"*Pozole*'s great," Marley said.

"I believe I'm speaking at your next citizenship class, right, Domingo?" said Fran.

"New class starts Wednesday night," Sunday said. "Six p.m."

"America's future, right here in this room," said Fran.

She and Marley saw the change in Sunday's expression.

"I have a question for you, Sheriff."

"*Que pasa, amigo?*"

"Do you hear anything of sickness?" he asked, sweeping a hand around the church. "My people? They have rashes. Headaches. Weak muscles. *Problemas* with teeth. Especially to the south."

"That's … alarming," Fran said.

"I believe it is bad water." To Marley, he said: "*Con quimicos.*"

"What's that, Sunday?" asked Fran.

Marley translated. "With chemicals."

CHAPTER 19

Saturday, Nov. 2, 11 a.m.

"Lots of farmers in Pennsylvania just an hour north swooned when the companies pitched those leases to drill. Landmen made offers. One family's making $3 million a month for 600 acres. Others saw their properties overrun by Big Oil 'n' Gas. Water supplies ruined."

"You're obsessed with this," said Ting, sitting shotgun as Tip drove through Five Corners.

"There's just something about that engineer friend of Provo's. Hope she's here. I have questions."

"You don't like the industry much," said Marley, sitting in the middle.

"Let's just say I have history with 'em."

"How does it work, fracking?"

"You drill a mile deep. Then you drill horizontally in both directions. Like a big T. The wells run through layers of shale where gas has been resting in pockets for eons. They set off explosions, and then flush millions of gallons of water and sand and these ungodly chemicals down. The pressure brings the gas, including methane, back up the pipe."

"Sounds like a waste of water," Ting said. Joni Mitchell sang on WMRA.

"They free the gas, but a quarter of the water, sometimes more, comes back, this time with unwanted passengers. Salts like bromides. Naturally occurring radioactive matter. Methane they have to burn off."

"Wouldn't that cause global warming?" Marley asked.

"All that used drilling water stinks like rotten eggs. It has to find a home or get recycled. So a big side economy of this Marcellus Shale boom is taking care of the frackwater."

They waved as they passed a farmer repairing a roadside fence.

"That's Ev Slocumb, Provo's neighbor," said Tip. "Even if your farm is a mile away from your neighbor's well, they're down below you, drilling horizontally."

"Doesn't that make it a property rights thing?" Marley said.

"OK, so it's a drill-baby-drill situation," Ting said, coughing. "I read too, or have you forgotten? Lots of jobs, and Pennsylvania and Ohio sure can use 'em."

"It was starting to get some coverage in Colorado," said Marley. "Longmont and Boulder banned it. Maybe it's good until we can figure out where alternatives take us."

"This boom happened so fast the states didn't have regulations in place," said Tip, getting irked. "Still don't. Very few studies on the health impacts."

"Here we are," Ting said. "Red Oak Ranch."

"You sure you're not up to the hike today?" Marley asked her aunt. "It's not like you."

"Touch of the *mal de mer*," she said.

The pickup crunched toward the Starke homestead and the mountain's scrim of scarlet, vermillion and Meyer lemon.

"Here's what else. Marley's deer, with the chemicals? No way those deer could have come down from Pennsylvania."

"Wonder if Claire's here yet," Ting said.

"Claire?"

"I asked Provo to invite her."

"*Good* day for a hike," Tip smiled as they approached parked cars beside the farmhouse.

"I see the Martinis ... Hansons."

"There's Claire. And Walker's coming."

The hike had become an annual chance to play hooky. Pick a brilliant weekday in peak color, ascend Red Oak, breathe in the unobstructed view, trek down at sunset, gather for Momma Starke's chili, and finish it off with a swig of Provo's homemade hooch.

"Hats for everyone, Tip," said Gus Martini.

"Pink for the ladies," Ellen said. "Purple for boys. Hi, Marley!"

"Thanks, Signore Martini," said Provo, trying on his cap. "Blessed by Pope Frank?"

"Hey, easy on my fellow Jesuit!"

"Roxx coming?" asked Tip.

"Some of us have day jobs," Provo said.

"She OK?" Cindy asked.

"Near as I can tell."

Claire sat on the grass, lacing up hiking boots.

"Hope those are broken in," Tip said, squatting beside her.

"Oh, hi!" She smiled, ponytail bushing out from the cap. "I've done Stony Man! A few others."

Provo cleared his throat to get attention as Walker parked.

"Claire here gets front-seat shotgun so I can impress her with our Private Idaho on the drive over. Momma and Ms. Ting are gonna meet us up top."

Provo and Claire soon returned in the F-150. The hikers piled in back, then held on as the pickup jounced across ruts and creek bottoms, stopping in the ranch's easternmost field.

"I like my cap," Tip said to Ellen as they hopped out, looking up the densely forested trail.

"Walk with me?" she asked. "My husband is already racing Provo to the top."

Walker fell in beside them, shortening his stride.

"Guys, I had such a fright the other morning," Ellen said.

"What happened?"

"I visit our urban distributors, you know. I drive in early for the 8 a.m. Acela to Penn Station. Can you believe I left the Cellars at 4 a.m.? I-66 is just so awful."

"Commute from hell," said Tip.

"I stopped for gas at Quicke Mart and was about to turn back on Lee Highway. Believe me, I looked first. I started to pull out when this huge tanker truck came *so* fast from my left. He hit his horn." She gestured with a hard right turn of a steering wheel.

"It shook me up. And just as I got *back* on the highway, *another* tanker truck sped past."

"You'd expect that on the interstate," said Tip.

"I don't recall tankers in Rappahannock before," she said.

"Randolph at the Corner Store was telling me about seeing a bunch of 'em taking that turn in Sperryville," said Walker. "Then head south to FT Valley Road."

"We tell our visitors to the cellars they shouldn't worry about traffic," she said. "Hope that isn't changing."

They ascended past rock outcroppings and copses of fir. The fast hikers waited at the Starke burial plot for the others to catch up.

"This is my kind of hike," Marley said, beaming. "Good cardio."

Around 1:30, the group broke into a grassy clearing and huffed a steep 200 yards to the top. A whitewashed Forest Service fire tower capped the hill. Ting awaited with plates of veggies, grapes and pimento cheese sandwiches spread on a blanket. A cooler held water.

Momma Starke rose stiffly from her folding lawn chair.

"I've been reading *People* magazine," she mumbled. "Those Kardashians are the devil's spawn."

"Mamma, you've met all these folks?"

"Is this redhead some new lady friend of the blasphemer's?"

Claire blushed. Tip cleared his throat. "Ms. Starke, this is Claire Hargadon. And she is a lady, all right."

"What a view!" exulted Gus. "I always forget."

They turned full circles. Clouds fringed the tips of the Blue Ridge, so close you could touch 'em.

"There's an unbroken view all the way east to the Washington Monument," said Longwood.

"Roxx might have enjoyed this," Tip said to Provo.

"You're mighty curious."

"She ever mention Green Valley Resources?"

"Momma Starke raised me not to pry."

Foiled, Tip unsnapped his binoculars. "Take a look, Ellen."

"Old Rag's so close, I can see hikers," Ellen said, focusing.

Ellen handed the binoculars back. Tip found Old Rag, then edged north. "There's Fairleigh," he said. Then he inched back, skipping over a ridge, and focused on Burlwood's garish portico.

Boy, who was the first Tyler to own our property?

Grampa Taz, sir.

How'd he come to acquire it?

Royal flush, sir. Beat Mr. Spink's full house.

Tip swept the glasses across the Spinks' property. The glint of a tall metal spire stopped him, and he swung back. A large oval glared. Refocusing, he saw trailers and Matchbox-sized rigs.

"Walker, take a gander," he said, handing Longwood the binoculars. "What do you make of that?"

"You know," Walker said, focusing, "I had dinner at the Grille a while back with a friend from Mary Washington. Sat next to Burl and Woody Spink and some big fella who turned out to be an official from Mosby. That young lady? She was with 'em."

"Roxx Bleigh, you mean."

"Talking business. She mentioned a containment pond."

Tip stood silently a full minute, peering through the binoculars, before dropping them.

They paved Paradise.

The hikers stretched and began to regroup. The women helped pack up.

Tip turned to his lanky friend.

"Up for some recon tonight?"

CHAPTER 20

Sunday, Nov. 3, 1 a.m.

Tip parked in the commuter lot at Massie's Corner. The vantage point allowed them to check the highways in all directions.

The pleasant descent from Red Oak had rewarded the hikers with a glowing Red Oak sunset. After chili and a hopeful conversation with Claire ("Ting has my number. Call."), Tip had returned to Fairleigh and set his alarm for midnight. He filled a thermos with good-old Folgers and drove to the Longwood place to pick up his fellow spy. They sat in Tip's truck, sipping and waiting.

"Quiet tonight," said Longwood.

"What's that?

They watched a tanker truck steam down 522 from Flint Hill and turn on Lee Highway. Ten seconds later, another. Tip hit his lights and pulled out about 30 seconds behind the trucks. He hung back as the second tanker passed Little Washington, downshifted its way through Sperryville, then turned right down the steep incline of FT Valley Road. Just past the Mosby County line, the tanker's brake lights flashed, and the truck slowed. Tip slowed.

They looked at each other as the tanker turned right through a farm gate just past Burlwood's entrance. A guard watched the tanker head uphill.

"Think he saw us?" Tip asked.

"Don't believe so."

"Something's hinky," Tip said as they passed the farm gate.

"The Dalai Lama always counsels patience."

Tip drove a quarter-mile south on FT Valley, then stopped. He steered into a three-point turn and slowly headed back north. They pulled to the shoulder. Both trained binoculars on the guard. "Bluetooth earpiece," said Walker. "Rifle on right shoulder."

Five minutes later, another tanker made the turn at the farm gate. Tip could read its placard: RESIDUAL WASTE.

Three minutes later, another. The guard waved it in. That made four tankers in the time they'd been watching.

"What next?" asked Longwood.

"Gotta think. Believe I've seen enough for one night."

Tip was about to crank the engine when a set of lights came from the north.

A Jeep Cherokee approached the entrance and stopped. The guard walked up.

Tip raised the binoculars. Pennsylvania plate.

GIT R DUN.

The window slid down. Overhead light glinted off Roxx Bleigh's hardhat and liquid lips.

PART II

CHAPTER 21

Monday, Nov. 11, 1 p.m.

From the GVR boardroom on the 29th floor, Roxx Bleigh watched traffic cross the yellow bridges straddling the Allegheny, not far from its marriage with the Monongahela. Heinz Field loomed on the left, done up in Steelers black and gold. The sweet green outfield of PNC Park sat upriver, the local shrine to baseball's frustration now shuttered in the off-season.

She was early. The four-hour morning drive to Pittsburgh from Rappahannock County had given her time to think. Today's presentation was important. Bill Dinwiddie had helped her by phone last night.

She spent much of the drive comparing her recent life in the Piedmont to the tumult of urban Pittsburgh. She didn't miss the bumper-to-bumper on I-376 through Squirrel Hill. Didn't miss construction that kept downtown in a constant snarl. She could have stayed over in her condo last night. Instead, she'd risen early on Long Mountain Road, watched the fog dissipate in the hollows, had a quiet cup of coffee and enjoyed the drive through fading fall vistas back to Pittsburgh's version of civilization.

Rappahannock County was growing on her. She loved the mountains, the cows in the field below and the sparrows visiting the birdhouse outside her window. She thrilled at nighttime's intense darkness. She reveled in gravel road driving. She didn't miss fast food on every corner.

She liked the people. Especially Provo Starke. Star of her own commercial.

Still, she mulled her next step. The scratchy first sexual encounter in his truck, supernova intense though it may have been, was just a notch above wham-bam-thank-ya-ma'am. Provo had insisted some sort of earthquake had happened. She guessed he was right, since Malcolm Jones had recounted a similar jolt at the job site.

Provo had been such a gentleman at the winery, calming her after her blowup, taking her to that tavern in Flint Hill. They'd scarfed down bacon cheeseburgers with fries, chased by cold Sam Adams on draft. Make that several Sams. He drawled his stories — part Roy Rogers, part Jeff Foxworthy. They'd sat side by side near the dartboard, smooching occasionally. By 8, *Football Night in America* lit the flat-screens. By halftime, Brenda the bartender flat-out told them to get a room. Both had been nicely buzzed when they returned to her place.

She played the night back. He'd made a fire. Champagne in plastic cups. Comforter on the floor. Flames licking the oak logs. Spent condoms. His hands, curious and leathered. His torso, scarred from shrapnel and run-ins with renegade bulls. She'd inventoried each scar. He explained them all, keeping the drawling yarns going as he rolled on top again and again. Laughter prolonged her climaxes. He'd fallen asleep in mid-sentence, and she'd had to wiggle out from under him.

He'd stirred as the sun hit the eastern top of the Pinnacle, and she'd dropped him back at Martini. Provo had laughed. "Darlin', you snore worse'n I do. But I *do* like the view."

Snore?

"Mornin', Roxx."

She turned as Dinwiddie entered Green Valley's boardroom with three other guys.

Deep breath. Shoulders back.

"How'd you sleep?" he asked, placing a laptop at the seat next to hers.

"Got a few hours."

I do not snore!

"My slides are all set at the podium, Bill. Made those changes last night."

She shook hands with her comrades and sat as others trickled in. She was surprised to see another woman enter. A Callista Gingrich clone.

"Good morning, people," said Dinwiddie, addressing a dozen colleagues. "Everyone have coffee? Hey, we're pleased to have APA's Melanie Pike-Stanton with us."

Holy shit. The American Petroleum Association. Big Oil.

"My pleasure," Melanie said. "We're eager to learn about GVR's work in the Piedmont Pike."

Roxx smiled to herself.

Piedmont Pike. My part of the Marcellus Shale.

"Let's get started," said Dinwiddie. "We'll hear reports on two aspects of our early work in Northern Virginia. First, Roxx Bleigh, our Mosby County P.M., will update us on that recycling beachhead. Then Bob Lock from Exploration will walk us through an update."

Recycling. Nice spin.

"Roxx, you ready?"

Showtime. Just like you rehearsed it.

She rose easily in the four-inch heels and approached the podium.

"We believe GVR is still quite below the radar in Mosby County," Dinwiddie said. "Roxx has been running our team on two shifts, assisted recently by Malcolm Jones. So far the trucking operation has proceeded without incident. Roxx, please."

Manage the butterflies. Eye contact.

Roxx brought up her first slide, showing a beautiful sunset taken from the deck above her Long Mountain Road apartment.

"Beautiful shot," said Melanie.

"Where the hell's Mosby County?" asked a Pitt intern.

Roxx showed an aerial of the well site before construction. "Virginia. We began in September to take advantage of an existing well at Burlwood."

"The Spink brothers," Melanie said. "Great allies."

"They definitely prefer as little regulatory ... involvement ... as possible," Dinwiddie added. "On the plus side, they bought our trucking affiliate."

Roxx smoothly clicked through the slides and summarized the details point by point.

"Our assessment of the preexisting well is complete. At first, we had concerns about the old casing holding up through the aquifer. It took us two weeks to dig out the top 150 yards to pour new casings for the deepened well. We had a couple of major safety issues to deal with, but we were successful in addressing them. This slide shows the lined containment facility and dump pad. Then we had early problems with the cover and wildlife. Those have been resolved.

The compressor installation is complete. As you can see here, we have smooth management of the tanker fleet to and from our base in Mineral Springs. Here you see the flowback reinjection, now well under way. One million gallons recycled so far, with only four-thousandths of a percent spillage."

She paused, knowing the engineers were doing the math in their heads.

That's right. Four thousand gallons spilled. A truck's worth.

"Minuscule runoff into the adjoining Hughes River. Two minor injuries: one worker with headaches, another with a rash. We're on time, and within 10 percent on budget."

No flubs so far.

"Here's video of the first tests to send the recycled assets back down." The video showed Roxx smiling, standing before a vibrating steel drill tower.

"We did experience some new cracking in the well casing and a small amount of ... loss ... into the aquifer. But we believe it will disperse quickly with little harm to the environment."

"Were you there for that little earthquake?" asked Melanie.

"Oh. Yes." Roxx blushed. "I hardly felt a thing."

Beef! I mean Provo!

"Registered 2.7 as reported by AP," Dinwiddie said. "No one's connected it to our work."

"Let's keep it that way," Melanie said.

Roxx made eye contact all around the table. "I'll close by saying we expect to complete the first phase of recycling deliveries the first week of December. We believe GVR can ramp up pumping of 11 million gallons of Pennsylvania flowback once we repair the minimal cracking."

She ended with a daylight still photo of a dozen workers and a handful of local security guards smiling in front of the well. Roxx was front and center, thumb's up.

"Great work, Roxx," said Dinwiddie. "Bob, you're up next."

"Thanks, Bill."

Glad I went first.

Lock's first slide showed a Google Earth image of Northern Virginia. Dotted lines in green outlined county boundaries.

"The Piedmont Pike is the southwest trending spur of the Marcellus Play that runs parallel to the Blue Ridge *here*," he said, using a laser pointer. "Hope you read the report from Government Relations on the favorable regulatory conditions in the Piedmont."

"We're not a player, but Halliburton's desperate to lease George Washington National Forest there on the west side of the Shenandoah," said Dinwiddie, pointing.

Lock continued. "You can see the five-county area, from north to south, Prince William, Loudoun, Fauquier, Rappahannock and, finally, Mosby, where Roxx and her team have been. We have two-man crews working each county doing early exploration of HF's potential."

Drilling? In Rappahannock?

"The Exploration Teams were joined by our crack Early Outreach squad conducting the quiet phase survey on landowner favorability. This table shows the results.

"I'll cut to the chase. The geologic drilling potential is marginal to favorable along the whole Piedmont Pike, increasing as you move south. While we are poised to be in first-mover position among our ... competitors," he said, glancing Melanie's way, "that's only part of the picture."

Lock pointed to two towns. Middleburg. The Plains.

"These three northern counties include some of the state's highest-income demographics. Horse Country. Owners include Mellons, Rockefellers and the Kluge family. Robert Duvall and his wife are local owners and activists. These counties are also home to the well-established PEC — sorry, the Piedmont Environmental Council. They're the activists who kicked Disney out of Manassas. Here are some headlines showing PEC's successful efforts to halt Dominion Power's request in '07 to run new lines through Loudoun and Fauquier. These are experienced activists. Our Early Outreach team has been quite careful."

Dinwiddie jumped in. "Given the high risks involved in the next phase — the mailbox drop of the proposed leases — GVR could be in for confrontation in those three."

"Right," said Lock. "But here in Rappahannock and Mosby to the south, the parcels are smaller, the economic demographics are more in line with our success in Pennsylvania, and the politics are more favorable. Here's where the power lines went."

The map showed lines traipsing through the tilted parallelogram of Rappahannock.

"Our Early Outreach team has concluded landowner lease favorability is much higher in Rappahannock. Some 56 percent of landowners responded favorably to the concept of lease arrangements. Only a quarter hold full mineral rights. The PEC is less organized here, though there are a few unaffiliated tree-hugger organizations that add risk. The politics are clearly favorable there. Our relationship in Mosby County puts us close to shovel-ready there."

The Sphincters. Jabba the Hutt.

"We've initiated the mailbox drops in Rappahannock and Mosby counties," said Dinwiddie. "Here's a map of the plan. The landmen come next."

The close-up showed pins near Long Mountain, Red Oak Mountain and Copperhead Road.

Near me. Near Provo's place.

"That's such a critical stage," Melanie said. "Hearts and minds."

Roxx glanced at her. Ash blonde coif. Gray suit. Red, white and blue silk scarf knotted at the neck. U.S. flag lapel pin. Roxx looked down at her own scarlet power suit and white blouse.

I can rock it, too!

"Thanks, Bob. Any comments?"

"Thank you for not using the F word," Melanie said.

The Pitt intern sniggered.

"*That* got your attention," said Melanie, standing, unsmiling. "People, we do hydraulic fracturing. Not fracking. That mainstream media invention must be stopped. *NOW!*

"People, our biggest challenge is putting an environmental focus on the superb potential of this technology. Let me be frank. Even our CEOs fail to capture America's imagination about clean natural gas. America could well attain energy independence and we are *NOT* going to *BLOW* it!"

She had the room's attention.

"Our early window on the policy front is closing quickly. The feds are trying to get into regulation. The longer Cuomo dithers in Albany, the worse for us. Ohio is getting shaky on recycling. North Carolina narrowly approved hydraulic fracturing in its last session in a fluke."

She locked on Bill Dinwiddie.

"With all the furor over regulation, do you think you can capitalize on your first-mover advantage in Virginia?"

"We do."

"And you ... Roxx, is it? Nice to see a female project manager. Well done. Stick around?"

"Why, yes, ma'am."

"Call me Melanie."

The meeting broke up. Melanie steered Roxx to the windows with a practiced smile.

"Nice suit. Tell me something about yourself."

Hooboy.

Roxx spilled details. Army brat. JMU. UVA. M.E./Civil.

She took a breath.

"GVR has been good to me," she said. "A few challenges, you know."

"Dontcha know, honey," Melanie said. "Men think with their dicks."

OMG!

"You have a pretty way about you," said Melanie. "Have you done any modeling?"

"Who me? Well, some pageant stuff. Why do you ask? I'm just —"

"Roxx, do you believe in what you're doing?"

Believe? What am I supposed to say?

"Well ... I'm ... passionate, if that's what you mean."

"Passionate. Yes. Our key talking point. Roxx, my main work at APA is in strategic communications. We've invested millions in lobbying. We're quite good at it, but we're getting pounded. Leftie documentaries. Negative mainstream media. Matt Damon movies. Yoko freaking Ono. We *must* put a better face on hydraulic fracturing."

They looked below. Traffic inched across the yellow bridges.

"We're implementing a $100 million campaign to put our best foot forward. Print. Heavy radio rotation. Social media. TV in Top 20 markets. I just hit up GVR for its share."

"Wow. You have such a exciting job!"

Where's this going?

"I'm here to work with an agency in Shadyside. Talent search. I meet with them in an hour."

"Getting started right away, then, " said Roxx.

Don't be an airhead.

Melanie hesitated, and then looked directly at Roxx. "Care to join me?"

"Let me just check with Bill ..."

"I'll handle that," said Melanie, turning to leave the boardroom. "Wait here. Green Valley may have a more important resource than they realize."

CHAPTER 22

Tuesday, Nov. 12, 8 a.m.

The silver-headed gent closing the post office box was one of Rappahannock's most recognizable figures. Tall, cut from Humphrey's liberal Democratic cloth, Senator Evan Prost had represented Minnesota for three terms. Famously courted to serve as Clinton's running mate and lap dog, he had balked, preferring to stay in Congress two more terms before retiring to a nice spread off FT Valley Road.

"Senator, good to see you," said Tip. "How are things?"

"Civil, Tip. Out here, of course. Back there," head bent eastward toward D.C., "not so much."

"Not enough statesmen like you."

"Thank you!"

"To think Cantor is such a symbol of stalemate."

The Senator looked around and leaned in.

"I'm kind of glad we got gerrymandered out of his district!"

"I call him Eric Can't," Tip cracked.

"Mr. Cantor, now *that* man embodies leadership," said a voice from behind the metal boxes.

Tip bent to look through P.O. Box 35. Cletus Mahan peered back.

"Clete."

"Hello, Senator," came Mahan's voice around the corner.

"Mornin', Pastor." The Senator and Tip rolled eyes, regretting the choice of venue.

"Blessed is the nation whose God is the Lord. Psalm 33:12. Remember that, Master Tyler."

"I'll be sure to share that with our Muslim citizens," Tip said.

Mahan shifted his attention to Prost.

"Senator, did you get one of those lease proposals from the Pittsburgh drilling company?"

"Lease?" said Tip, alarmed. He riffled through his mail stack, finding nothing matching the description, as he and the Senator stepped toward the worn counter.

"Can't wait to share the one that came to the Meeting House address with my flock," said Mahan, leaning on his elbows. "We've been praying for a way to pay for our new building out on the highway. And like a divine blessing, there it was. Here, take a look."

Mahan handed over a legal-looking sheaf. Without a glance, the politician gave it to Tip.

"Came today," said the Senator. "Seems they'd like to drill for natural gas on my land."

"Drill? Here?" said Tip, flipping quickly through pages of boilerplate.

"The terms are quite reasonable," Mahan said. "Intrusion should be minimal."

"Clete, this is *fracking*!"

"Master Tyler! This is a government building!"

"The church is such a beautiful property. You wouldn't —"

"We can't afford not to."

"This is serious," said Tip. "We hiked Red Oak last week. From there it appeared Burlwood's got something fishy going on. I think it's related. Can't confirm it officially. And the Spinks won't call back."

"The company talks about good jobs," Mahan said. "My flock is mostly out of work or underemployed. This could be the advent of our economic salvation."

"Clete, what I saw from Red Oak? It was a punch in the gut."

"We have room for what they propose. You'll never know it's there, neighbor."

"Take it as an article of faith, Clete. Fracking holds risks to the environment and our health."

"My ex-colleagues *are* working on the regulatory framework," said the Senator. "The administration supports it."

"But fracking consumes *millions* of gallons of water," Tip said, alarmed.

"For each and every well! They drill using cancer-causing chemicals! There's air and water pollution! Thousands of truck trips for each well!"

"Big Oil has a history of being on the right side," said the Senator. "And a lot of political clout."

"They hold the cue, and we're the eight ball," Tip said. "Clete, let's keep talking."

Two new postal patrons walked in.

"A blessing, I tell you," said Mahan, turning to the new customers.

"Say, Tip," said the Senator, "almost forgot. The Hunt Invitational is coming up. Please thank Ting for granting the Hunt rights to ride at Fairleigh. Can you find time to ride with us?"

Tip, still flabbergasted, scratched his head.

"Doesn't the Hunt's territory include Burlwood?"

"Sure, you bet. Burl Senior was a Master of the Hunt."

"In that case, I'm game. My daughter, Marley? She's still recouping from that smashup, but she rides. May I ask her along?"

"Please do. We'll get you set up. Let me know. Good to see you, Tip."

Tip looked at his mail. An envelope from the Kennedy School. Probably another begging letter to alumni. As if Harvard needed it.

The KSG crest, with its crimson and cream stripes, always reminded him of Jeter's reaction.

Why go to that liberal bastion, boy?

Mr. Allbury was a Nieman Fellow. Journalism's most highly regarded fellowship. He loved his time in Cambridge. But I'd like an advanced degree, maybe teach some day. I can get a master's and dabble in environmental stuff at the Kennedy School. Niemans don't get an advanced degree. Harvard might just reset my journalist's cynicism.

What's wrong with William & Mary?

Ever notice how they boast of being the Harvard ... of the South?

Tip loved the irony of how Harvard is so beholden to tarnished donors and corporations. The Business School had an institute named for inside trader Mike Milken. A Kennedy School benefactor was convicted of price-fixing. And its main public space? Where world changers and wonks meet for speeches and socials? Used to be called ARCO Forum after oil giant Atlantic Richfield, responsible for America's largest Superfund site. ARCO is now … British Petroleum. BP. As in Deepwater Horizon.

The Forum. Scene of the first social gathering for fellows and mid-careers beginning the fall semester. Professionals with serious chops. Testosterone and perfume.

He remembered it in crisp detail. Remembered *her*. Strawberry blonde curls. Dimples.

He eyed her name tag. France. Belfer Center for Science and International Affairs.

And his fateful foray into flirting.

"I come from a state with your name."

"There is a U.S. state called Paradis? Why has no one told me this?"

The adorable accent.

"Virginia. Your *first* name. Virginie."

"You must meet my sister, Louisianne. I am kidding. I do hope to see your country this year."

"What brings you?"

"We are a single Europe now, or so we would have you believe. The European Parliament is still sorting out its environmental powers. It appears my nation wishes for me to be involved."

"The environment. Good luck with that."

"I see you are Press, Politics and Public Policy. This explains your cynicism."

"Guilty, but I'm here to change that."

"*Bonne chance!*"

He felt the moment slipping away.

"I'm from a part of Virginia as beautiful as you are," he blurted. "I could show you some day."

"Goodness. You Americans *are* friendly."

She paused. Smiled.

"Virginie Marie Paradis. My friends call me Gini."

He took her hand. Slim fingers. Warm.

"Tippecanoe Tyler."

"And why are you named after a *bateau*?"

"Long story. They call me Tip."

"*L'addition.*"

The post office door banged open with an arctic gust, snapping his reverie.

"Hey, Tip. Sorry I'm late. Just dropped my daughter at school."

Reporter Editor Paul Schaefer juggled to shake hands. He had *The Washington Post*, a digital camera and a laptop. "Thanks for meeting me."

"Let's eat. I've just heard something new."

The Café bustled as they found a table.

"The usual, Michelle," said Tip. "What are you having, Paul?"

"Oh. Umm, egg-white omelet? With feta and mushroom? Wheat toast, dry."

"What's feta?" she said, offering mugs.

"Greek. Any goat cheese?"

"American. You want exotic. I'll give you Swiss."

The editor sighed.

"How's it going at the paper, Paul? I read every word. Front to back."

"Don't forget our Wednesday online preview."

"Different from *The Post*?"

"I thought I worked hard there, but we had seven editors in Features plus nine writers and reviewers. Here, I'm *it*. One reporter/photographer, Acey Youngblood. Asa's kid; one of the been-here Youngbloods. Plus I'm learning all this stuff for the Web."

"It was time for me to walk away from *The Herald*," Tip said.

"Congrats on the Pulitzer, I guess," Paul said. "What really happened?"

"The judges aren't supposed to divulge, but I had it confirmed from two former colleagues," said Tip. "I was a finalist in explanatory journalism for a series on the impact of sea-level rise on barrier islands. The judges initially picked me but made a late swap and gave it to that blogger."

"I remember now. Within the week, he had to recant major pieces of his story," Paul said. "Now it's the Pulitzer with an asterisk. But it's yours."

"It wasn't just that," said Tip. "It was a shock when Knight Ridder was bought out and disappeared, just like that. Now it's just a name in the corporate graveyard. None of the front office geniuses saw it coming. *The Herald's* bayfront building's been sold to a bunch of Malaysian casino kingpins who are tearing it down."

"Well, thanks for calling," Paul said. "We'd be thrilled to have your help, with your background and all. It's just ..."

"What?"

"Your letter. It was, like, typed."

"Yeah. I've been a Luddite. But my daughter's helping me. I got one of those," Tip said, pointing to Paul's laptop. "And one of these," pulling the iPhone out of his pocket.

"Cool. How's your signal?"

"Not bad at home. Poor elsewhere in the county."

"I had Acey make calls about the quake like you suggested. Didn't get much. There's rampant speculation on RappChat, of course. God's revenge kinda stuff."

"I plan to talk with an old prof of mine," Tip said. "Geologist."

"Here ya go," said Michelle. "Eggs over easy, home fries, bacon for Tip. Mister, your omelet."

"I don't think she likes my taste in breakfast," Paul said, once the waitress was out of earshot. "My wife's opening a coffee shop on Gay next week. *She'll* have feta. You said there's something new?"

"How much time did you spend backgrounding on fracking like I suggested?"

"All of five minutes. Big deal in Pennsylvania and New York. Lots of jobs. Cheap oil. Bridge energy. I called the Spinks and got Burl. No comment. I had to get back to page design."

"Did you look into the environmental consequences?"

"The industry swears it's safe."

"Paul, if your mother says she loves you —"

"I know, I know ... check it out."

Tip speared eggs and potatoes.

"That company I mentioned? Green Valley Resources? I just heard they're offering drilling leases. Here! In Rappahannock! Heard anything about that?"

Schaefer smiled and opened his Mac. "Acey went out to shoot photos. He came back with this."

The screen filled with a gorgeous shot of the massive Old Dominion power lines trooping toward Old Rag like Sherman's march to the sea. In the foreground, two surveyors bent over their work. Beside them was a logoed van.

"See what it says there? Green Valley Resources."

"This is here in Rappahannock? When?"

"Amissville. Yesterday. What do you think it means?"

Tip squinched his eyes shut and rubbed his temples.

"It means it's the bottom of the first, and we're already down by five. Look, this is a big story."

"I know. I need to think like a newsman. Investigate. Not my forte."

"I could lend a hand. Rusty as I am. "

"Your reporting chops are nothing but Grade A Prime."

"I can give you a lead or two. Some sources. My worry is you all don't have the bandwidth."

"Well, we do have this new partnership with VirginiaWatch."

"Tell me more," said Tip.

"It's the digital startup funded by the foundations. Harry Warren's running it out of Fairfax."

"I know of Harry from his *Journal* days. He should be good at getting records, finding minutes of public meetings, regulatory reports, that sort of thing."

"That'll take time," Schaefer said.

"You need to start somewhere. Here's a lead. The deer my daughter hit? It was poisoned by drinking too much barium. Turned it *purple*. That may explain its weird behavior. It's still a mystery how a local whitetail could consume that much barium. Coincidentally, that's what's in the frackwater up in Pennsylvania. And there were other nasty bits in the autopsy."

"You're saying this is related to fracking?"

"They use the same chemicals. They bring up those same salts. It might have something to do with Burlwood. Walker Longwood and I saw several tankers turn in there the other night."

"You know, other people have reported tankers. Al German said it's messin' with our roads but bad. But what's that got to do with drilling for natural gas?"

Tip leaned in closer. "This is just a guess. There's another side of fracking, the part where they dispose of the wastewater. Comes back up with no place to go. Think of it as fracking's vomit."

Schaefer put his fork down.

"Sorry. TMI."

"I read something about that. It's all going to Ohio, right?"

"Most of it. I did some Googling the other day. Watched a video or two. I think it's possible the Spinks are running a frackwater reinjection thing. Trucking it in. Can't say I understand the motivation just yet. Or what regulators have to say about it."

"I've never met the Spinks, but their reputations are, like, bizarre," said Paul, pushing his plate away. "Burl's some kind of zealot. Woody's ... Woody."

"Hard to believe they're acting alone. There must be government records somewhere."

"I'll talk to Harry, set up a meeting. If it involves Mosby County, though, good luck. Tight lid on that place."

"OK. Next. You need to interview a certain Ms. Roxx Bleigh. Works for Green Valley."

"Why are you so hot on this story?"

Tip paused. Sipped his coffee.

"You know what? I did years of objective reporting. Kept it balanced. Gave the corporate jerks the benefit of the doubt. Let the facts speak for themselves. Let the people decide. The whole watchdog role of the Fourth Estate. You know what else? The people can't decide, if they don't know. No one's stepped up to tell them how this fracking business slipped its nose under the tent. All these fraccidents. The industry is just using that to double down."

"Could be a boost to the economy," Paul said.

"Yeah," said Tip, standing. "That's exactly what they want you to think."

CHAPTER 23

Tuesday, Nov. 12, 10 a.m.

Marley dropped the rake and mopped her brow, moist despite the morning's chill.

"Phew! Sweating!"

"We Southern women don't sweat, dearie," said Ting, sitting on her haunches between rows of spent bean plants. "We *glow*."

Glow. Yes.

"Three hard frosts come in a row, you're done for the year," said Ting. "Glad you showed up when you did. How's that arm feel out of the cast?"

Glow. Described Fran.

"Great. Fran was nice to take me over."

The sheriff had insisted they take the loaner to the hospital follow-up in Warrenton. When Marley picked her up at the Gay Street office, Fran wore civvies. Marley understood why after they had removed her cast.

They parked behind the Black Bear Bistro on Main. "Easier to keep a low profile out of town," said Fran, smiling for the first time.

They took a booth in back and shared a bean cassoulet and the apple horseradish salmon. Each had a glass of California pinot as the fireplace sizzled. Marley listened, sensing Fran's need to unload out of uniform. Just so hard to recruit trained officers. Woodchucks never stop testing my authority. Fleet's breaking down. Can't compete with bigger counties and their tax bases. Supervisors already warning of budget wars.

But Fran surprised her with the change of subject. Tell me about Africa.

They demolished the bread pudding. The light touch on Marley's hand told her all she needed to know about what was next.

On the way to the Rip Van Winkle Motel, Fran told a story about a Fairfax commissioner who'd been forced to resign for sexual indiscretion. She told Marley to check in under the name Shirley Temple. "Here's cash. Let me in five minutes after you get the room."

When they left at 4 a.m., Fran went first. They'd joked about the walk of shame as they dressed. Marley watched Fran head to the car from behind the curtain. The powerful arms and shoulders hardly seemed capable of such tenderness.

No shame in that walk.

"Earth to Marley," Ting said.

"Oh. Sorry, Auntie. There's just so much you gotta do with a garden to get it ready for winter, right Sunday?" said Marley as the Tylers' farm manager returned with a wheelbarrow.

"You were a good helper 'til you fell in love with that camera," said Ting. "Check that debris in front of you. Anything looks diseased? Or might be all pesty? That goes in Sunday's burn pile."

"*El infierno,*" Marley said, smiling as he swiveled the wheelbarrow in front of a knee-high pile. "Domingo, haven't you been hanging out with my aunt for 30 years?"

"*Mas or menos.*"

"And I still don't know a word of Spanish," said Ting, pulling up dried cornstalks. She coughed, first once, then three times.

"You OK there?"

"Can't shake it. Marley, leave those beets alone. They're aggressive self-sowers. They'll come back beautifully on their own."

"Maybe it's time we got flu shots."

"Let me get another drink."

Ting stood and walked to the spigot at the edge of her garden.

"What do you know about our well, Auntie?"

"Jeter drilled this one for the garden. Maybe 40 years ago," she said.

"How deep is it?"

"Deep enough."

"No, seriously."

"You drill until you hit water," said Ting, irritated. "Why do you care?"

"Just asking."

"The water table," said Sunday, "it is close to the surface."

Marley held the farmworker's eyes as she asked the next question.

"And how safe is our water?"

"I've never been sick a day in my life!" Ting said. "Enough. We have five more rows to do."

They all turned when Tip's pickup rumbled up the drive to park. Blackie bounded up, tail wagging.

"We're in the wrong line of work," Tip said, walking to the garden. "They just said on the radio each Cardinal player will get almost $400K for winning the Series."

"Where you coming from?" asked Marley. "Café?"

"Yup. Talked with Paul. There's more going on with this fracking thing than we realized. A lot more. I'm gonna start helping 'em."

Ting scowled. "You prom —"

"Look, do you want to see this place go to hell in a hand basket?"

"Easy, brother."

"Somebody's got to do it. They need help."

Ting sighed. Coughed.

"Make yourself useful," she said. "Those tomato cages need attention. Half of 'em are toppled over."

"Yes'm," said Tip, exchanging a wink with Sunday and taking off his jacket.

"Ting, I dropped by the Inn with a sample of Stonewall's second barreling. The Chef said he'd share it with his sommelier. Said to be sure to thank you for this year's beets. Best ever."

"Good! The new guys running the Public House in Flint Hill want to add my beets to the menu."

"So's this the day Marley helps you plan next year's garden?"

"Help?" said Ting, taking a gulp from her battered flagon. "She's got the whole thing sketched down to the inch."

"Might as well be useful," Marley said. "More beets there, where all that squash is. We want to move the heirloom tomatoes. More sweet potatoes. It's a blast, plotting out a garden. It's so much fun to get your hands into this good dirt."

Ting straightened with a wrinkled nose.

"Smells funny."

She sat on the stone bench near the spigot.

"You OK, Aunt Ting?"

"It'll pass."

Tip straightened the cage around the Black Crim tomatoes. "Ting, do you remember the discourse with Jeter about the environment?"

"Which one? It usually started with that gruff 'Girl, how do you best respect the land?'"

"Don't make fires you can't put out, sir," said Tip, channeling his youthful self.

"Pick up the trash and carry it out with you on a hike," said Ting, picking up the routine. "Leave only footprints."

Tip, chuckling: "Don't pee in the river, sir."

Marley laughed. "Bet that one got you extra chores."

"Boy," said Tip, sounding like Foghorn Leghorn. "Mr. Jefferson's grand purchase added the entyah drainage of the Mighty Mississip, the Great Missourah and its tributaries to this great nation, all the way to the Tetons. Those waters make everything we do on this land possible."

"And I would say 'Water is life, sir.' He'd call me a good girl and give me a cookie."

"I thought those chats were just for us twins," said Marley.

"Wrist OK?" Tip asked Marley. "I'm thinking of going to see your sister's office this week."

"I'm thrilled to be out of the cast. What's the occasion?"

"Dunno. I've been thinking," he said, untwisting more wire. "They do an awful lot to like there. Oh, by the way, I saw the Senator today. We talked about the Hunt Invitational coming up. Said to ring him if we wanted to join in. And it happens to include Burlwood. Think you're up to it?"

"I do miss riding. We about done here, Auntie? I need a nap."

"I will shut down the garden well spigot," said Sunday.

"Not before my ceremonial last quaff of the year," Ting said.

Tip picked up Marley's tools and walked with her to the garden shed. Ting coughed again.

"You need to talk to Sunday later," Marley said. "He told us a couple things the other night you'll want to hear. Cellphone stuff. Something else about bad water down this way."

"Bad water?"

CHAPTER 24

Wednesday, Nov. 13, 8:45 a.m.

"We should be arrivin' at L Street in 10 minutes, miss," said the chauffeur, who had introduced himself as Hiram.

Roxx blinked awake.

The squat Jamaican steered the stretch limo with one finger as it cruised above the Potomac, crossing the Theodore Roosevelt Bridge in brilliant November sunshine.

The past two days had been a whirl. The visit to the agency, the stunning proposal from Melanie, the quick meeting with the GVR honchos. And now this. The car had arrived at the Long Mountain Road house at 6 a.m. Watching Hiram negotiate the hairpins had been an adventure. She snoozed the minute they hit Lee Highway.

"Remind me never to be a D.C. commuter," Roxx said, touching up her lips. Melanie said there'd be breakfast at APA headquarters for the first session of the "I'm a Natural" campaign.

Despite the excitement, Roxx's fuzzed mind was elsewhere.

Provo Starke.

What a blown opportunity last night was. A real date, she'd called it when she'd phoned the ranch. Provo Starke had accepted the dinner invitation happily. He brought wine and a huge bouquet.

"Zinnias from Momma Starke's garden," he'd said.

Instead of rehearsing her APA script, Roxx spent the late afternoon frantically readying dinner for two. She'd made a hasty two-hour round-trip to Culpeper to get dinner essentials: candles, cloth napkins and wine glasses at the Cameleer. Then Safeway for rib eyes, salad-in-a-bag, *Martha Stewart Living* and the makings of Martha's pièce de résistance, ratatouille ("So simple! So colorful!").

Simple my ass.

The kitchen was not Roxx's natural habitat. Following Martha's complicated directions, she sliced her onions, seeded the tomatoes, peeled the eggplant and dried the salted slices between layers of paper towels. She cut her finger dicing the herbs she'd snitched from the owner's deck.

Provo's wine was decent. "Jus' liked the name. Fat Bastard," he grinned, taking in the sunset.

Roxx joined him on the patio.

Screw Martha. A little food, a little wine and a whole lotta love...

She'd forgotten the canola oil heating on high in the cast-iron skillet. The flash from the kitchen made them turn. Flames toasted the cabinets above. Provo ran back in, grabbed a hot pad with his right hand and pulled the blazing pan from the heat. He stood in the middle of the kitchen. Roxx hurriedly poured a glass of water from the tap and turned.

His panicked "Nooooooo!" startled her as she dashed the water into the fire.

Hot oil sloshed his forearm and sizzled on the floor. He put the skillet down with a loud "Dang*nab*it!"

They spent three hours at the emergency room. When they left, Starke's arm was swathed in gauze. The bill for services was $2,576.95. They drove through Chic-fil-A for soggy sandwiches and fries. Starke awkwardly ate left-handed on the midnight drive back. He got out of the Jeep at her place, mumbling a goodbye and something about ObamaCare.

So much for a real date. Another lost opportunity to address what was *really* on her mind.

Earthquake sex and second-degree burns. Not exactly Love Story.

"Here we are, miss," said Hiram.

APA's sixth-floor foyer boasted wainscoted oak walls, thick carpeting, etched glass and brushed platinum. The biggest flat-screen Roxx had ever seen flashed gleaming images of sinuous pipelines and cozy homeowners watching snow fall.

Melanie Pike-Stanton's assistant whisked Roxx into a dark cubbyhole little more than a closet with a monitor, video camera, sound boom and hot lights. A stool sat in front of a dark blue cloth backdrop covered with the APA logo and small white Capitol domes. A world-weary cameraman nodded. A mousy makeup girl slouched in the corner, chewing gum.

"Let's get right to work," said Melanie from behind. "I lobby Senator Kaine in an hour."

Roxx turned.

No croissants?

The makeup girl walked over with powder and brush.

"This is Lilly. Caleb's behind the camera. Take that stool. Did you read the script?"

"Yes, of course. It … reads well! You have your own studio!"

"Our very own Hollywood."

Lilly tucked Kleenex around Roxx's collar. Caleb leaned in to attach a lapel mic.

"You'll see these folks when we do the location shoot," said Melanie. "OK. Your line is…???"

"Oh. My line. Could I use Roxx? —"

"No, dear. Your given name polled better. Line?"

"Hi, I'm Roxanna Raye Bleigh, and I'm a natural! And so is natural gas!"

"Very good. Then we go for the gut. Tell me if you recognize the voice."

Melanie picked up a remote and clicked a button. The monitor filled with a soaring bald eagle.

"Clean, efficient natural gas …"

"Is that James Earl Jones?" asked Roxx.

"Best voiceover in the biz."

"Wasn't he Darth Vader?"

"Just watch. I'll start again."

Images eased in and out. Iowa cornfield. Nuclear family, picnicking. Golden retriever chasing a ball. Barefoot toddler on a wood floor. Smiling execs — black, white, Hispanic and a leggy Asian — entering an elevator. Time-lapse sunrise over an offshore rig. Batter swinging. Fans cheering.

"Clean, affordable natural gas creates jobs in America," Darth boomed. "Vital to our homes and businesses. Bridge energy for an independent America."

Melanie hit pause. "Your lines from this studio shot go next. Look in the camera and run through them. That thing is a teleprompter. It'll scroll your lines, but try not to look at it. Ready, Caleb?"

"And, ready."

Roxx read from the teleprompter.

"As an engineer, I care about America's environment. Natural gas burns cleaner than coal, and there's plenty of it right here in the States! That's why I'm a natural!"

"A little wooden. You were reading," Melanie said.

"Is that supposed to mean I'm, like, a natural blonde? Because I am."

"Run through it again," Melanie said. "Say it like you believe it."

CHAPTER 25

Wednesday, Nov. 13, 10 a.m.

Seated at his computer with slices of Stayman and his second *cafecito*, Tip punched in the phone number from memory.

"Doc? Doc Freeman? Hey, it's Tip Tyler."

"Tip! My favorite Florida journalist! Or should I say favorite Virginia moonshiner?"

"Married to the orchard, Professor. But I'll always remember the geology field trip to the Keys you led my junior year at Mizzou. Windley Key fossils. It's how I got started."

"You did your part to keep the Keys weird and wonderful. Hey, that Stonewall of yours is mighty fine."

"I'll send a bottle from the new batch, Doc. How's Columbia?"

"Growing. You'd scarcely recognize it with all the development south of the stadium."

"Let me get right to it. You were always the first source on all things geologic. There's a situation here that concerns me. You know about the Marcellus Shale Play and all the natural gas drilling just to the north of me?"

"Fracking. It's all they talk about in my journals. There's a spur of it down your way."

"The drillers have set up shop here. Plus I'm worried about what might be happening with an old well next door. Could be a reinjection getup."

"The Marcellus got it started, but the Bakken? It's put a lot of people to work in North Dakota."

"There and lots of other places where they really need jobs. No doubt about it, professor. But it didn't take long for our mindset to change from holding it in reserve to drill, baby, drill."

Tip's door creaked open. Marley peeked in. He held thumb and pinkie to his ear. On a call.

"But, Doc, the downsides. The environment. People living beside the wells. Their animals."

"It does seem they're out ahead of the research, Tip. That's Big Oil for you. Wired that way."

Tip motioned Marley to take a seat.

"My daughter, Marley, just popped in. Marley, this is Tom Freeman. My geology guru from University of Missouri. Mind if I put you on speaker?"

"Not at all. Hello, Marley."

"Hi!" Marley smiled.

"I don't have many heroes, Marley, but Dr. Freeman is on the short list."

"I just play with rocks."

Tip finished his coffee. "Doc, can we lob some questions your way?"

"Fire at will."

"Let's start with the chemicals."

"Lubrication, pure and simple," said Freeman. "It's sorta like adding a squirt of dish soap to get the water and sand into the shale. That sand props up the cracks, lets the gas escape."

"The industry says the chemicals are there in minuscule amounts. Up to 1 percent. But you taught us to do the math."

"Right. If the average well uses eight million gallons, and 25 percent of it returns to be disposed of, then 1 percent of *that* equals 20,000 gallons. Enough to fill five tankers."

"Times thousands of wells," Tip said. "That's a lot of chemicals. They have to get from wherever they come from to those well sites. So they're trucked in."

"Did you say eight *million* gallons?" Marley asked. "For one well?

"Yep. Not so much of an issue where you are, young lady, but think about West Texas —"

"Or Colorado, where I've been living … until recently," Marley said. "Water's not exactly bountiful out there."

"Sixty percent of the U.S. faced drought conditions last year," Tip said.

"You got it. Now, the companies are quick to say their chemical cocktails are proprietary. It *is* cutthroat, Tip. Truth is, they don't have to talk about 'em because of Cheney's Halliburton Loophole. But a couple of lawsuits outed them."

"Do they really use arsenic?"

"Yes. Dangerous stuff. It all needs careful handling. Toluene. Barium. Hydrogen sulfide. Something called 2-BE ... and no, we're not talking *Hamlet*. I'll email you the contact info for Enrique Valenzuela. Fella I know who's been working on the chemical angle out of Duquesne."

"People should know more about that," Marley said.

"States are hung up on requiring disclosure in their new regs," said Tip. "Can't imagine what people would think if they really knew what kind of concoction the industry's using. What's worse is gas drillers are exempt from the Safe Drinking Water Act."

Freeman sighed. "The big boys and little fly-by-nighters are *all* into fracking."

"You gotta wonder who the EPA is really protecting."

"Never heard soapboxing out of the old Tip."

"Sorry." Tip blushed, looking at Marley. "Once you get to enjoy an unspoiled spot like Rappahannock County, you want to keep it that way. But on *that* topic, isn't the real threat fracking's impact on the aquifer?"

"The industry insists there are thousands of feet of impermeable rock between the deep drilling and the water table. That shale holds ancient salts. Deeper you go, the saltier it gets."

"Doc, your career was built on mapping faults everywhere, not just along the tectonic plates, right? What about that Duke study?"

"A classic. They brayed when it came out. Said it proved fracking isn't contaminating water."

"That was the headline, but the body of the report said otherwise."

"Exactly. Here's what we geologists took from that study. Briny water and frackwater from those deep layers can definitely find its way up via other avenues. What we call pathways."

"What you mean is faults and cracks."

"Precisely. Frackwater finds those naturally occurring pathways and can pollute the drinking supply. The Duke guys couldn't say if that would take a year or eons. But it does match up with some work a hydrogeologist did in New York. He found that a combination of those naturally occurring faults *and* the effects of hydraulic fracturing itself could help those chemicals and salts find their way to the surface, in just a few years. So, yeah, I'd worry."

"You mean those chemicals are poisoning our drinking supply?" asked Marley, incredulous. "And they just keep doing it?"

"There are other risks," the professor said. "You have drill casings leaking into the aquifer. You get ground-level spillage that can run off into the water supply. The tankers leak. Have you read about the 400-page study by that University of Texas center? Again, the headlines reported only that there's no impact on the aquifer. But it did note all those risks I just mentioned. Turns out the prof who wrote it was a paid Big Oil consultant. Really tarnishes academia."

"That's not the half of it," said Tip. "A lot of that frackwater comes right back up, carrying those same chemicals and bringing the old salts to the surface. Sodium and calcium salts, barium, strontium, iron. Heavy metals. Naturally occurring radiation. They use it to de-ice highways."

"Right, Tip. Some 20, 25 percent returns up the pipe along with the natural gas and methane. Needs a place to go."

"A quarter of eight million is … two million gallons!" Marley said. "What happens to it?"

Tip scrolled through bookmarked sites on his laptop, then showed Marley a cross-section of a well. Freeman continued.

"That frackwater, if it's ever gonna be reused, has to be recycled. It's cost-prohibitive. Some dump it illegally. The industry is reusing it to frack more wells. And they're pumping 90 percent of it down abandoned wells. Much of it in Ohio. That's standard practice."

"Abandoned wells," said Tip. "Just like Burlwood."

"You mentioned barium," Marley said. "Could there be enough barium to turn a deer purple?"

"Wow. Deer? Not my line of science. I did read about cyanotic squirrels. I can steer you to a biologist out your way. From Slippery Rock."

"Ha! Slippery Rock," Tip snorted. "How appropriate is that?"

"Now remember, I worked for Humble while finishing my doctorate. The companies say if the wells are drilled right, you don't have much more to worry about than minimally visible environmental degradation above ground."

"A growing track record says otherwise," said Tip. "Up to 10 percent of the new wells leak. Then there's the 200,000-gallon spill in Wyoming County, Pennsylvania. The nighttime light coming from the North Dakota flare pipes is brighter than all of Chicago."

"I saw that. Methane's 70 times worse than carbon dioxide for global warming."

"The industry just seems bulletproof," Tip groaned, "deflecting *every* concern about the environment or human health by calling it anecdotal."

"Until a conclusive study comes along that proves otherwise —"

"They're gonna keep saying their shit don't stink," said Tip. "It's all getting uncomfortably close, Doc. Lease proposals are appearing in my neighbors' mailboxes. Our talk here convinces me there's a rogue flowback setup, all trucked in, right next door. And yet there's no record."

"The industry likes gaps. The states are slow to develop regulations. Or don't want to."

"Doc, we haven't even gotten to the real question for the geologist. Did you read about our recent earthquake here? Quakes are rare around here."

"Sure are. There's no major fault line there like the New Madrid near me. I hope you saw that study in Ohio, the one that confirmed the reinjection wells were causing earthquakes. And another out of Washington State says fracking itself causes small quakes."

"Manmade earthquakes?" asked Marley.

"You've got it, Ms. Tyler," the professor said.

"Talk about messin' with Mother Nature," said Tip.

"Take that Oklahoma quake last year. It registered 5.7. No small potatoes. Damaged 200 buildings. Caused by fracking. So far, these manmade quakes have been small. But my life's work was all about proving quakes are strange animals. At day's end, it isn't wise to induce seismic activity on purpose."

"So here's my last question, Doc. Does anyone keep long-term records of seismic activity here in the Piedmont? Seems to me if a company planned to drill, or even just reinject, due diligence would require that they study past quake activity and probability before starting."

"Absolutely. One of my former students teaches up at Carnegie Mellon. Name's Anna Grace. She's mapped the Marcellus Shale. I'll put her in touch."

"Much obliged, Doc. It's time we ring off. I've taken a few notes I want to share with a journalist named Harry Warren. Could I have him call you and go over some of this on the record?"

"Sure. By the way, Tip and Marley, I don't mean to give the health impacts of the Marcellus Shale drilling short shrift. But the industry will keep on keepin' on until someone produces irrefutable evidence. That might just have to be you and your journalist pals."

"Thanks, Doc. Be well. Look for some Stonewall coming your way."

"M-I-Z!!!" the professor shouted.

"Z-O-U!!!" said Tip, laughing as he hung up.

He looked at his notes, then Marley.

The smile faded.

CHAPTER 26

Wednesday, Nov. 13, 2 p.m.

"You'll regret this, Woodrow!"

Milton Smythe waddled down the steps of the Spinks' portico. The weekly update with the Burlwood Boys had not gone well.

Smythe turned for a last word, but the door slammed.

He stood, taking in the yellow-brick monstrosity with its long south wing and foreshortened north wing. Burl inhabited the former, Woody the latter. A life-sized cross in white neon hung between the columns.

Gaudy. Charmless. Just like the proprietors.

Worse, the house, built well above the ridge line, violated the local comprehensive plan preference for nocturnal darkness. Day and night, it was visible from miles away.

"Idiots!" Smythe shouted, wheezing up into the cockpit of the black Hummer H3. It started with a roar, spewing a gray cloud. "A Jesus Christ PR spot!"

He didn't return the wave of the guards flanking the estate's entrance, part of the Spinks' growing security force. At least they'd consented to that.

Seated in Burl's library, cocktails in hand, the Spinks had informed him with oozing smarm that they'd agreed to Big Oil's asinine request to shoot a TV spot at the project site. Tomorrow! Camera crews and helicopters and everything coming to Mosby County! No permits requested, no public safety needs outlined, no time to sap the visiting crews' wallets to the benefit of county coffers and his own pockets. And the featured talent? That lipsticked engineer!

Don't you realize this will expose the whole operation, put it squarely in the sunshine, he'd cried? The project will be on the radar of every Tom, Dick and friggin' hairy-ass regulator from D.C. to Richmond. And the lamestream media too.

"First thing those out-of-town feature writers will do is man-on-the-street interviews with my constituents. They'll write about them 'tucking into the pulled pork special' at the BarBeeQ Barn," Smythe predicted. "They'll describe us all smirky-like. A hick-backwater-forgotten-by-time-one-horse burg 'nestled in the bosom of the Shenandoah National Park.' Same old crap. They won't have the decency to quote me and note my unblemished service."

Far worse, Smythe had added, would be if *The Washington Post* or *The New York Times* were to commission another investigative magazine story like the one *The Times* had done: *The Fracturing of Pennsylvania.* That piece held the top spot in his growing clip file. It wasn't a win for our side. It enumerated the health risks, the sick children, the dead cows, the smelly water. They'd interviewed pissed-off farmers who'd bought into fracking by leasing for a pittance only to see the drillers devastate their properties and kill their dogs. So they claimed. Big Oil denied all. Anecdotal.

"And those interviews will be an entirely different matter. They'll probe for details. Ask for records. Barge into to our meetings. Pry into *your* politics. I've covered my trail pretty damn well, but we're talking *BobfuckingWoodward*! Let me remind you: You may not give a shit about permits and approvals and regulations, but this state does."

The Spinks remained unconcerned. They told Smythe they got all the news they needed by reading his very own *Mosbyville Monitor*, watching Fox and listening to WGTS, the Contemporary Christian radio station. Burl had said he was proud that their SuperPac, Leave Americans Alone, had continued underwriting Limbaugh even after he'd called that Georgetown law student a whore.

"You fail to see the risk involved!" Smythe had thrown back his Manhattan and stormed out.

Smythe was doing 45 now, through a school zone, when he realized he was back in Mosbyville. He slowed to 40 and saw a scrawny backpacked tween dive out of the way. The few pedestrians on downtown's crumbling sidewalks cringed as the Hummer zoomed past.

The supervisor normally waved to these muppets. Not today. He needed a strategy. Stat.

He slammed the brakes in midblock. A white panel truck from Hickman Twins Painting honked and swerved.

Smythe did a five-point turn right in the middle of Main. He gave the cursing painter the finger and headed toward *The Monitor's* cinderblock office a block away.

A yellow and black Smart Car sat in the "Reserved for Publisher" space on Main Street.

Smythe rolled forward and nudged the Hummer's bumper against the encroacher. He gunned the engine slightly, pushing the vehicle forward with ease. A spider web of cracks appeared on the tiny car's windshield.

A shrieking woman ran out. Smythe realized she was his new receptionist/ production manager.

"OMG! Supervisor Smythe!? My Bumblebee!"

"If you *were* publisher, you could afford a real car. No one parks in my space."

He threw her a twenty. "Here's something for the windshield. Where's Kelso?"

Before becoming *The Monitor's* editor, Kelso Arbuckle had flacked at King's Dominion amusement park north of Richmond. He took pride in spelling "Clydesdale" correctly in a news release when the hoofed Bud shillsters showed up one Fourth of July.

The triumph was short-lived. The AB folks had Kelso kicked curbside when Spottswood, the beer wagon's prized Dalmatian, died after eating a batter-fried Snickers from Kelso's hand.

Arbuckle had waited tables at an Olive Garden in Newport News for two years before landing the $1,900-a-month gig as the weekly's editor, no benefits. He made acquaintances in the small town easily, if you counted among his buddies Jack Daniels and the St. Pauli Girl.

Smythe burst into the tiny newsroom, catching Arbuckle as he gnawed a BarBeeQ rib.

"Supervisor! Hi! Rare appearance!" Arbuckle stood, wiping sauce on his chinos. "To which do we owe the honor?"

"What. To what."

"What?" said Arbuckle, eyebrows knitting.

"Forget it. What do you have planned for this week's front?"

"Well, boss," said Arbuckle, smiling nervously, "it's an advance on the dried-flower show by the John Singleton Mosby Baptist Ladies Auxiliary. Twenty inches and three color photos."

"Rip it up. I have an assignment. A *big* one, assuming you can draft it. I'll do the polishing. Where's that photographer?"

"King. Jeff King. Shooting a Lyme disease feature."

"Whatsyourname. Bumblebee Girl."

"Elissa Landsberg, sir. You hired me last month! I've brought in two new accounts —"

"Well, Elaine, here's another twenty. So I bumped it. Increase the press run by 500 copies."

"Must be some kind of story!" said Arbuckle.

"A Special Edition. And rehire that driver. Some of these copies are going to Rappahannock."

Elissa raised a hand.

"We … *The Monitor* doesn't have outlets in Rappahannock."

"Get some. Start with that grocery store in Sperryville."

Smythe reviewed his decisions. "Let's see. Story, photos, print run. Send it to AP."

"We're not part of The Associated Press, sir," said Arbuckle.

"Put it on the PR wires, dammit."

"What else? Who's running our online edition?"

"We don't have one," Arbuckle mumbled. "You never authorized it."

CHAPTER 27

Wednesday, Nov. 13, 3 p.m.

Tip's old pickup turned heads as he inched down King Street. The two-hour trip to Old Town Alexandria featured the permanent rush hour stretch of I-66 at the Beltway.

Dappled sunlight on the last sugar maples gave the afternoon a Zen quality. Old Town's mash-up of gilt-edge history and trophy-wife fashion made it a prime people-watching spot.

Tip turned right on Fairfax Street.

Boy, you turn 16 soon. Tell me about the Fairfax Swindle.

Sir, which version?

The Virginia version, of course.

The sixth Lord Fairfax inherited a land grant from King Charles II in 1719. The Fairfax Grant, sir. Five million acres, from the Potomac to West Virginia.

Go on.

Fairfax claimed it all. It was big enough that the House of Burgesses said it belonged to them.

It was Virginia land, boy. Not some bauble for Lord FancyPants.

Fairfax negotiated. Kept some. Wasn't 'til the American Revolution that Virginia got it all back.

Why is this relevant, boy?

Because Lord FancyPants was 16?

Tip found the parking garage. Minutes later, wearing his blazer, yellow and blue D.C. grid tie, white button-down shirt, Dockers and Topsiders, Tip arrived at the fourth-floor lobby of the Fairfax Grant Foundation, brown bag in one hand, laptop in the other. As he approached the receptionist, he doffed the beige cap with the crimson H.

"Here to see Madison Tyler."

"You must be her father," said the receptionist. "Tip, right? Let me get her."

Tip scanned the foyer. On the wall, protected by a clear glass capsule, hung a George Washington sketch of the proposed town of Alexandria. Tip leaned in and found the date. 1748.

"It's an original," said a voice from behind. He turned and smiled.

"Madison Lightfoot Lee Tyler. I always imagined saying that in a setting like this."

"Hi, Tip," said Maddie. "Haven't seen you since —"

"The garden. I'm still finding seeds in places they'll never grow."

"Hey, that's the tie I got you for Christmas!"

Warming.

"Figured I'd barge in sometime."

"Of course! Your first time here. Is that what I think it is?"

"The bottle? A small tribute."

"No! I mean that laptop! Is that yours?"

"Just another digital dude."

"Welcome to the world of Grumpy Cat and the Kardashians. Come with me. I'll see if Alvaro can join us."

Maddie's corner office featured a mahogany desk from 1850 backing up to a credenza housing three 17-inch monitors. Plush armchairs in rich damask faced the desk. Oak bookshelves held leather-bound Virginia titles. A quartet of upholstered chairs circled a conference table.

She entered, trailed by a three-piece gent with a Michael Douglas hairline.

"Alvaro Verdeja. Good to see you again, Mr. Tyler."

"Please call me Tip. I brought you this."

Verdeja removed the bottle from the brown bag and beheld the label.

"Ah, your Stonewall," he said. "Many seek to bribe us in exchange for a grant. We will record the gift at year's end and enjoy it before then. *Gracias.*"

"Did I hear you correctly? We've met?"

"I don't blame you for not remembering. I was at the law school. You were a lordly Kennedy School Fellow. A couple of us crashed a mixer you guys held at that dive across from the Charles Hotel."

"Charlie's Kitchen! So you met the Political Junkies!"

"Not John Harvard's idea of a student interest group. But I later saw you introduce Tip O'Neill at the Forum. Tip and Tip."

"The Junkies. We were more notorious than effective."

"Figures," said Maddie. "My father, tied in with a rogue group at Harvard. Shall we sit?"

"I am happy to take this meeting," said Verdeja, sitting. "You are famed for your environmental reporting. Thank you for that. Wish we had more of it. What brings you?"

"I know very little about how to approach a foundation, even one employing my daughter."

"Of course. Don't call us, we'll call you. Oz-like grant-making. We *are* trying to be more open and transparent. We even publish our phone number now."

"I'm aware the environment is one of your funding interests. I'll get right to it. Have you followed the fracking boom?"

The execs exchanged glances. "As it happens, yes," Verdeja said. "There's little happening in Fairfax Grant's geographic area of interest for now, but we *have* been in conversations about collaborating with several place-based funders up north. Pennsylvania. New York. Ohio."

"That's the purview of Les's work at Energy," said Maddie, shifting uncomfortably.

"Yes, and that's a related thrust."

Tip leaned in. "I fear fracking is getting uncomfortably close. I have reason to believe a property in Mosby County has some sort of frackwater reinjection operation going on. Trucking it in, likely from Pennsylvania. In full disclosure, it adjoins our family's farm. And there's evidence that drilling for new fracked wells isn't far behind for Rappahannock County. All without so much as a whisper of permits or regulation."

"Natural gas drilling is being proposed in Rockingham County, over in the Shenandoah Valley," said Verdeja. "Part of our turf, yes. And the national forest is at risk."

"Stop me if this isn't what you do here at Fairfax Grant, but I have some suggestions."

"Some?" Maddie asked, her discomfort growing.

"First, the national drilling boom has taken every jurisdiction by surprise. Statehouses are scrambling, from Albany to Sacramento. Until the feds move in, it's left to the states to regulate."

"The administration is reviewing extensive new regulations," said Maddie.

"Good, but they're saying maybe next year? Meanwhile it's a Wild West out there. As far as I can tell, Richmond hasn't gotten off the dime. Our county administrator wants to act but can't. The industry plows ahead. It doesn't have a sterling record of self-regulation."

"That's an understatement," said Verdeja, unbuttoning his suit coat.

"It just cries out for an objective and well-publicized study on the regulatory climate, something that might include recommendations for how to sort it out, ensure public safety, penalize bad actors," said Tip. "Isn't that the kind of thing you do?"

Alvaro and Maddie looked at each other. Maddie smiled.

"Interesting you say that, Tip," she said. "Alvaro, I don't talk shop with my father. Do you mind if we tell him what's up?"

"Certainly. Tip, we pooled resources to do just that six months ago with other foundations," said Verdeja. "Hired some Philadelphia consultants. Sage. We expect a final version this week."

"May I share the draft with my father?"

"Don't see why not. Just wait for the official release. Is that it?"

"Health concerns. There's been little mainstream media coverage about the water and air issues. ProPublica, of course. I'll bet you've read about poisoned water supplies, headaches, lesions near fracked wells. Livestock with stunted tails. There's got to be a connection with the chemicals. But every time an academic study comes out, the industry insists it's all anecdotal."

"And you think …?"

"Maddie's twin was driving near our place and hit two deer. They were purple."

"Purple?"

"Cyanotic. It's possible they came into contact with barium-loaded frackwater. If it affects animals that way, what about us?"

"I see where you're going," Verdeja said.

"No one has pulled together a comprehensive, research- and clinical-trial based study. Something that could prove what's happening beyond anecdote."

Alvaro smiled. "We have been talking with the Robert Wood Johnson Foundation folks. They're on top of that in Pennsylvania with several major academic partners."

"Could you coattail on that work, maybe get the study extended down into our territory?"

"Tip, you know more about us than you let on," said Verdeja. "That is in our wheelhouse. I'll see RWJ's boss next week at the Non-Group. I'd planned on asking her just that."

"Non-Group?"

"Oh, sorry. The heads of *all* the big foundations — Ford, Gates, Knight, RWJ, MacArthur, Hewlett, Packard, Carnegie. We get together, usually at the Willard. It started informally. Thus the inelegant name. We share updates on what we're doing and where we're heading."

Verdeja stood and stretched. "I must get to my 3:30. Mr. Tyler, you've done your homework. Madison and I will discuss this. We need to go through due diligence, and we must consider the family connection carefully. Fully divulge any potential conflict of interest. Your daughter is about to become an officer here."

"We're proud," Tip said, standing, opening the laptop. "I was hoping you'd consider funding a journalism —"

"Tip ..." Maddie warned.

"You're a place-based foundation. You qualify as a partner for that matching program for digital start-ups. Here's VirginiaWatch's home page. We've got an idea involving your funding a regional FracWatch."

He handed it to Verdeja, who perused it.

"We're familiar with what Harry's doing," said Verdeja. "Send this to me by email. I cannot promise anything, but you brought some interesting prospects today. Maddie, walk with me."

"Thanks, Alvaro. Thank you, Madison Tyler," said Tip, bowing formally to each.

"Meet me at the elevator in five, Tip," Maddie said.

Tip waited, peering again at the Washington survey, watching the foundation's young staffers come and go with purpose. His pocket watch said 4:30. Maddie walked up, poker-faced, holding a fat binder.

"You were pushing it, especially with the VirginiaWatch thing."

She broke into a grin. "But he's impressed. Here's the draft. You didn't get it from us."

"Thanks. I've gotta head back. Lions Club meets tonight."

"Take 50 West. It's faster. Give Ting a hug and my sister a slug for me."

CHAPTER 28

Wednesday, Nov. 13, 6:15 p.m.

Hiram had dropped Roxx back at Long Mountain by midafternoon. A girl could get used to this.

Provo had left a message, offering to pick her up for the Lions Club meeting.

But Project Manager Roxx Bleigh had wanted GVR to know she took her responsibilities seriously, even with the distraction of the "I'm a Natural" campaign. She'd left a message at Red Oak saying she'd drive herself to the meeting.

She reviewed the day as she drove to Sperryville, hoping she wasn't late.

In the brief stop at Long Mountain, she'd had just enough time to change into the Engineer Ensemble — and be reminded by the still-slippery kitchen floor of the Skillet Inferno — before speeding off to Mosby to deal with a hornet's nest of management issues.

The Lions thing had come up the night of the flaming disaster. Two hours waiting for a nurse to bandage his burns gave Provo time for questions. Personal. Professional. At first, she'd minimized her gig at Burlwood. ("Just a big infrastructure project involving recycling.") She didn't mention the commercial or the "I'm a Natural" campaign. She *had* told him she wanted to get around, meet people. Which was sorta true.

Spy. For Jabba and the Sphincters.

He'd offered Lions as a way to meet the locals. They were reaching out to "lady professionals."

But these were real problems at the site. Even with the dazzle and distraction of becoming the Face of Fracking, with a national tour ahead of her, the situation at Burlwood could blow up if she didn't address every item on her list. Bill had OK'd her involvement in the campaign but asked her to tidy up affairs at the well site first. They'd been vague as to whether she'd return, post-campaign. But he'd also said the honchos were thrilled to have the exposure.

Priceless.

Her afternoon had been all about putting out fires. For starters, she and Malcolm Jones were worried about the integrity of the newly deepened casing. In every well site she'd worked on, the new drill hole was clean from the get-go, lined all the way through the shallow aquifer. This old piece o' shit was showing signs of stress in the first 500 feet. Their tests yesterday showed "some leakage," Jones said.

"Define *some*," she said.

"Hard to say. Maybe 600 gallons."

Any officially reported leakage, she knew, might lead to an immediate shutdown. She'd OK'd reducing the pressure of the frackwater reinjection in hopes it would relieve the stress on the casings. We'll call it "seepage" in the report, she told Jones.

Then there was the dump pad. Jones recounted the soaking he'd gotten in the hose incident as they scrutinized its corroded threading. She'd pressed him for details. It sounded bad. *Real* bad. She saw evidence of soil erosion beyond the concrete apron straight down to the Hughes River. How much had they lost before it was contained? Jones couldn't give her an answer. Maybe 2,700 gallons? A number *that* big was a red flag for GVR. Must include it.

The health situation was worrisome. Two more guys had complained about migraines. A third had nosebleeds. And she'd squirmed while talking to that guy with the ungodly rash on his forehead.

That's gonna leave scars.

She'd told Jones to tap the local workforce to fill in. Jobs, after all; that's what the Shale Gale was all about. He'd sniffed that locals steered their way by the clients were hostile.

"Hostile how?"

Roxx read Jones's silent glare.

"Oh. I get it."

She herself had seen the resentment the Sovereignists held toward the hard-working Mexicans. Racist, testosterone-fueled, trigger-happy, careless — a winning combination. But she'd triaged it, filling this last report to GVR with enough detail to say the problems had been fixed. Message: Gittin' 'er done.

And I am outta this Doofusville. I'm the Face.

As she drove past Rappahannock's postcard fields, still green halfway into November, she imagined what fracking wells would do to this landscape. She'd seen enough damage at sites in New York and Pennsylvania to know that when fracking arrives, there is no turning back.

Kiss these views goodbye. Hello, industrialization.

Roxx parked next to a phalanx of pickups and SUVs outside the fire hall. She freshened the Ruby Sensation and coached herself on her objectives.

Don't be smug. *Even though I'm about to be FAAAAAmous.*

Don't condescend. *Though most of these Gomers probably didn't graduate high school.*

Don't spill. *Melanie said be discreet.*

Most important, wait until the end of the night before telling Beef I need a break.

She'd come to this conclusion easily.

I like him, the sex has been fine, and he's weirdly gentlemanly. But he lives with his mother. *Seems injury-prone. And we still haven't addressed the whole first fuck. What was I thinking?*

But, hey, once they see The Face ... who knows? Broadway? Hollywood? Partner?

She caught a movement to her left.

The door swung open.

"Don't make any sudden moves. Only have one workin' hand left," said Starke, leaning in with a peck on the cheek.

"Ohmigod! Provo! You scared me!"

"I have that effect on women."

"How're the blisters?" she said, sliding out of the Jeep.

"Momma Starke's pickle juice is helpin'. Ready to meet some Lions?"

They walked into the expansive fire hall and saw two clots of members. To the left, jolly men and women bellied up to a bar. Roxx saw familiar faces — Rob Hanson, the Martini winery owner, the beekeeper. Provo had said he thought Tyler might be here, but she didn't see him. At right, solemn men gathered around a coffee urn.

"Teetotalers," whispered Provo. "That's Pastor Mahan. A quaff before introductions?"

"Water, please," Roxx said, surprising herself. "Would you introduce me as a project manager with a Pittsburgh engineering firm, living for now in Rappahannock? That would be sweet."

"May I say you are a prospective member?"

"We'll see."

Roxx met some surprisingly urbane types: A graphic designer for the World Bank, a former pilot for Eastern Airlines, a GOP bundler, a defense contractor, a CIA analyst, a British restaurateur and two county supervisors. The women included a llama rancher and a publicist from D.C.

They seem smarter than the Sphincters.

Roxx found the folks to be warm, the conversations wide-ranging and genuine.

OK, maybe not such Gomers.

She changed her mind about that quaff and approached the bar. Gus Martini poured a red from a bottle with his name on it. "My cabernet franc, Roxy," he said. "Guests drink free." She sipped.

"Thank you! Very nice! It's Roxx. R-O-double-X."

Roxx was surprised when the winemaker himself gaveled the meeting to order with the Lord's Prayer. Members recited the Pledge of Allegiance. Two or three eyes welled up. A guitarist hit an A major chord, and the troops mumbled the opening verse of *Blue Suede Shoes*.

"Time to introduce guests," Martini said. "Lion Provo, I know you've brought someone."

"Ms. Roxx Bleigh condoned my invitation to sample tonight's feast and meet you scoundrels," Starke said. "She's taken up temporary residence on Long Mountain Road."

A chorus of "welcomes."

"What brings you here?" asked the publicist.

Time for the game face.

"I'm a … civil engineer … out of Pittsburgh."

"Where ya working at locally?" asked a supervisor.

"I manage a … a project in the next county over. Infrastructure project."

"At the Spink place. Burlwood."

She turned and blanched. The voice belonged to Walker Longwood.

"There's been a fleet of tanker trucks going through our county," he said. "On the way to your project. What are they carrying?"

Ohhhshit.

She looked at Starke. His shrug said: You're on your own, kiddo.

"As a matter of fact, they carry … recycled fluids."

"Where they coming from?" the beekeeper pressed.

No turning back. I do know my lines.

"Pennsylvania. It's coming from Pennsylvania. We're doing our part for the environment by responsibly disposing of an inconsequential byproduct of the job-creating Marcellus Shale."

The smattering of applause stunned her.

"Clean natural gas," said Provo, surprising Roxx. "We need it to wean ourselves off OPEC's teat. And it may keep America's fightin' fellas like me off the battlefields of the Middle East."

"Don't need to convince most of us how important *that* is," said the defense contractor.

"We pioneered hydrologic fracturing for LNG in Oklahoma when I was with Exxon Mobil," said the restaurateur. "Great technology. Who are you with?"

"Green Valley Resources."

"That's the company on my lease proposal," said Clete Mahan. "We're ready to sign."

"I found one in *my* mailbox," said the analyst. "Should I put one of your wells on my property?"

"I could use the income," said the restaurant owner.

"Me too," said Provo, winking at Roxx.

Well, I'll be!

"We have a couple supervisors here," Walker Longwood said. "What's the county's position?"

Roxx opened her mouth to answer.

"Time and a place, people," Gus said, gaveling the discussion closed. "Before we get down to business, let's eat! Oh, hey, let's give a hand to Michelle and Linda from the Café for tonight's feast. What lurks?"

"We want to put y'all in the Thanksgiving mood," said Linda. "Open-faced turkey sandwiches on Holsum. White gravy over mashed. Peas. Punkin pie and *Cool Whip.*"

"Lions grub," Starke said as a line formed. "The sustainable fare for which we are famous."

Roxx exhaled.

"Darlin', that went well. Grab a plate. Guests get to cut in line."

CHAPTER 29

Wednesday, Nov. 13, 8:30 p.m.

The slog back from Alexandria was one for the record books.

Rush hour, as only D.C. can concoct it. Highway 50 through Fairfax was stoplight hell. Tip detoured to I-66 — bad idea — and had to pull off at a Manassas Starbucks for a bio break and a pumpkin latte. He sat in a 90-minute backup in Gainesville caused by a broken-down logging truck. By the time he'd crossed the welcoming threshold of Rappahannock, the Lions meeting had ended.

As he turned up Copperhead Road, Tip spotted Clete Mahan's plates up ahead: IPRAY4U.

Time for amends.

Tip turned in behind the pastor at the Meeting House. His pickup's lights briefly held Clete in silhouette against the ghostly, whitewashed walls.

"Master Tyler. I'm guessing you're not early for Sunday services."

"Clete, I've been thinking about our recent exchanges," said Tip, eyes adjusting to the dark. "I'm not sure what your Bible says about bygones. I imagine you have something at the ready."

"Colossians 3:13. 'Bear with each other and forgive whatever grievances you may have against each other.'"

"That works."

"Why now, may I ask why?"

"Something along the lines of 'good fences make good neighbors.'"

"I thought we'd see you at Lions."

"I'm just back from the big city. Traffic conspired against me."

"I left some papers here," Clete said. "Are you coming in?"

"Well, umm, OK."

The pastor climbed the slate steps, opened the plank door and turned on a single light.

Tip entered. Spare pews. White railing up front. Simple pulpit. A plain crucifix hung in the apse. He realized that outside the rare funeral, he hadn't darkened a church door since college.

He closed his eyes to see Sara Tyler, clutching a rosary. Languid Sunday mornings with Jeter at the Cathedral of *The Washington Post*, listening to Copland. Guitar mass at Mizzou ending with *Blowin' in the Wind*. Bawling twins in parents' arms earning parishioners' glares.

"You've never been here, have you?" said Clete from the pulpit.

"Miracles never cease."

"You are always welcome in the House of the Lord."

"Religion and me? Don't mix."

"Weren't you raised in faith?"

"My mother was Catholic. Died young."

"And Jeter?"

"More a man of nature. He'd say a good hike to Stony Man refreshed his soul."

"A fine spot to praise Jesus and thank Him for creating such natural beauty."

"Put me down as unaffiliated."

"I don't know how one can live outside the embrace of faith and risk damnation."

"Clete, it's a matter of perspective. There's a reason why newsrooms are lousy with skeptics. The more time I spent in journalism, reporting on the natural world, watching some dopes do their utmost to destroy it, often in the name of religion, the more I saw it as the problem."

"Some say journalism's the problem."

"As I'm aware. Before we demonize the scribes, pastor, look at the facts. If there'd been a wisp of a chance I'd favor the Catholics, the priest abuse scandal scotched the deal. Thanks, by the way, to *The Boston Globe*. The Vatican could teach the Stasi a thing or two about conspiracy. It's all about power over the powerless. My mother's religion enabled the Borgias, sanctioned the Spanish Inquisition and looked the other way during the Holocaust."

"Let he who is without sin …"

"True, all religions have dark sides, not to mention the capacity to start war in the name of their preferred deity. Let's talk about the Middle East."

"If only I had time," the pastor said. "Ah, here it is. The lease agreement from Pennsylvania."

"Oh, Christ!"

"Master Tyler! Remember where you are."

"Sorry. May I see? I'd like to study the section about mineral rights."

Mahan hesitated, and then handed down the fat manila envelope.

"It's quite generous," said Mahan, watching Tip riffle through the papers. "Offers $45,000 a year for five years. By the way, most of the Lions seemed supportive of this hydraulic fracturing."

"The Lions talked about this? How'd it come up?"

"Your friend Provo brought an impressive young lady. An engineer. She says if it's done safely, it's a good thing. My congregation has voted unanimously in favor of the lease. I meet with the company tomorrow."

"Listen, Clete. Before you commence any drilling, you probably have to give notice to your neighbors. That would be us, and unless there's something in the mailbox, I haven't seen it. And you'll have to file a plan with some state agency. That's due diligence."

"The drilling company said they'd take care of everything."

"I hope it's not too late, Clete. Because if you knew some of the environmental problems associated with fracking … the risk to groundwater from chemicals … the air quality … sick animals."

"Green Valley's fact sheet mentions none of that."

"Of course not. Does that surprise you? Here's a fact: Each fracked well brings with it 2,000 tanker trips. Can you see tankers right out there on Copperhead Road?"

Clete blinked. "Master Tyler, I have faith they would not steer us wrong."

"That's the problem! You have *faith*, in an industry run by imperfect humans, with a track record of epic failures, driven to maximize profit. Same faith you fall back on praying to Jesus."

"You are turning my words around."

"Pardon me if I stick to facts. Exxon Mobil. Deepwater Horizon. Poisoned creeks. The fact is, if fracking comes here, we can kiss the river goodbye."

"Take their information sheet."

"I will. Clete, at least have your lawyer look at this. Does the church own the mineral rights?"

The pastor's eyes darted. "I must get home. My wife and I TiVo Pat and Terry on *The 700 Club*."

"Please, Clete. Please find out. For your sake."

"I will pray on it," said Mahan, turning out the light.

CHAPTER 30

Thursday, Nov. 14, 4:30 a.m.

Tip jolted at the sound of the alarm.

He'd slept fitfully. The Meeting House conversation had segued into hours of self-examination about faith. It's impossible to be a person of faith in the fact business. Spiritual, perhaps. But his belief in the goodness of mankind would be shaken anew whenever he had to wrest a version of the truth from some golden-parachuted Wharton School CEO. What made that next to impossible was the barricade of guileless flacks, propagandists and protective admins.

Objectivity — the facts and only the facts — had steered him from revealing the plain truth: Corporate greed sanctioned inhumanity. It enabled soulless companies to victimize infants, endanger species and despoil rare habitats with impunity.

He'd had to leave opinion to the editorial writers, swearing each time they wimped out and retreated to mealy-mouthed positions. Kicked the can down the road. Moved on to the distractions of the next deadline and the latest hot story. Just like politicians and bureaucrats whose sole focus is self-preservation, not We the People.

Clerics. CEOs. Politicians. The condo board of the fourth circle of hell.

He'd made small steps toward a life in balance since his return to Rappahannock. Shunning technology had forced him to adapt to the cycles and rhythms of the land. Walking in the orchard's morning mists shielded him from the headlines and talking points. Here in the country, he found genuine friends and engaged in real conversations. He'd joined the Lions and advised the environmentalists for free. He'd put campaign signs backing Fran's runs for office along Copperhead Road and contributed cider to her fund-raisers. He became a member of the noble class of producers, not just consuming goods but growing and making them. So what if his contribution was apple brandy, a venial product he'd imbibed freely to wash down the peanut butter sandwich before bedtime?

He raised himself to his elbows. What really ate at him was the unending futility of it all. For all he'd done in service of Mother Nature, her Green Earth was in danger. Thanks to diddling clerics. Corporate greed. Cartoon pols. Couch-potato citizens. And the present threat: Frackers.

My new job description. Gentleman watchdog.

Blackie's licks brought him to his elbows.

"You stay home today, girl. Wrong kinda hound."

The mirror passed cruel judgment. Purpled half-moons. Bloodshot whites.

Tip had returned to the cider house to find a frock coat, rust britches and a bowler hat lying on his bed. A note from Marley urged him to read up on Hunt etiquette.

He was adjusting the bowler when Marley walked in down below. He caught a look from the top of the stairs. Black frock coat. Black buttons. Plain white shirt safety-pinned at the collar. Canary vest. Twill breeches. Leather boots. Brown velvet hunting cap. Leather crop and gloves.

"I say, looks as if you've stepped from a woodcut."

"Looks like you need *un cafecito.*"

"Will you get it started while I dress?"

"Hey, renting this stuff set us back a pretty penny," she shouted. "I've got my camera. And the vials. You sure this plan of yours will work?"

Tip grabbed the frock coat and headed downstairs.

"Look. We can't connect with Roxx. The Spinks aren't talking. They've got armed guards. It wouldn't surprise me if they were shoot-now-ask-later types. It might not be the most ethical way to get into Burlwood, but they *did* grant the Rappahannock Hunt permission to ride."

"Tip Tyler. Man on a mission."

"We are quite the pair."

"Like dude, like dudette," laughed Marley, swatting him with the crop. "Shall we?"

Fifteen minutes later, FT Valley Road was lined with F-250s, Silverados and horse trailers, parked at the side of the road.

Tip and Marley drove through a grove of new American chestnuts to park near the Senator's green-tinned stable. A yellow spill of light pierced the pre-dawn black. They doffed their bowlers to approach their host, elegant in scarlet coat trimmed in brass.

"Tip, looks like you came from a Halloween party," the Senator laughed.

"Just don't tell the press corps," said Tip, handing him a bottle of Stone-wall. "For your flask."

"Ah, the noble spirit. My thanks. Meet my lead hound, Bosco. Direct descendant of the Bywaters hounds that helped get this club started in '26."

The Senator appraised Marley.

Now, your daughter, Marley, is it? Welcome to the Hunt. You look born to the saddle, ma'am."

"I did my share of riding in Colorado, sir," she said. "I understand you are Joint Hunt Master."

"Glad you both could join us. You'll be riding with the Third Field. This is my daughter-in-law Margaret," he said, nodding to an approaching huntswoman. "She's your Field Leader this morning. Margaret, can you show them to their mounts?"

As Prost left, Tip wondered if he should have given him a head's up.

Margaret introduced Tip to a roan named Tin Whistle, Marley to the mare Ebony Esther. Soon they were cantering with a half-dozen others toward the starting point at the property's Pond House. On the way, Margaret explained how Tip and Marley would be positioned in the pod of riders known as the field.

They crested a knoll at dim first light and took in the Hunt's cinematic gathering below: three-score riders on breath-steaming mounts, others dismounted, working on tack. White hounds and mottled bitches schooled like fish. Riders in red, black and tan greeted each other in hushed whispers with air kisses, low chortles and pumping handshakes.

The Senator's arrival signaled the riders to mount up. The Huntsmen from each club took their disciplined packs, tails wagging, into a large pen. Astride his chestnut gelding, the Senator quietly welcomed the Masters from the visiting clubs and led the Lord's Prayer. Even Tip mumbled along.

The Senator signaled Miles Massie, the Rappahannock Hunt Club's other Master. Massie held what looked like a French horn to his lips and blew a startlingly loud note. The Whippers set out at a gallop.

Prost nodded to the leader of the First Field, and 20 riders headed to the right. A minute later, the Second Field went left. Prost cantered straight ahead, followed by his pack of hounds, Bosco in the lead. Margaret signaled her group to start.

"Halloo!" Tip said.

"Quiet, Tip!" Marley hissed.

The rising sun helped them orient to the course as Marley and Tip were introduced to the others. The Third Field fanned into a broad V, Margaret at the point, heading south. They traversed frost-tipped fields, through sagging gates, across frigid creeks, up ridges with breathtaking vistas.

As the frost melted, they rode east of the valley road on the Senator's property and two adjoining ranches. Just after 8 a.m., the riders crossed the scenic byway and headed toward Old Rag, aloof in the morning mist. They turned north and approached Burlwood's orderly white fences. A Hunt volunteer, watched by an armed guard, held a gate open as the riders passed.

At the top of a bald hill, Tip spotted the scar of felled trees and exposed earth a quarter-mile in the distance. The girdered yellow tower was taller than he'd estimated from the distance of Red Oak. A huge blue box, likely a compressor, was the size of a cabin. The gray oval next to it covered an acre. The site resembled a West Virginia strip mine — scattered trailers, tankers and workers.

The Field moved west toward Redmans Mountain, away from the wounded land. Tip gave Marley a silent nod, and then approached Margaret.

"Tin Whistle is hesitating. Looks like he threw a shoe. Should I walk him down to the highway?"

"He's a good horse, Mr. Tyler. Thanks for your caution. We'll go on without you."

"Permission to have my daughter stay with me? It's quite a walk."

"Of course," said Margaret. "Hope to see you both later at the Pond House."

Tip and Marley dismounted and waved as the riders disappeared, sun at their backs.

"Ready for some recon?" Tip asked his daughter.

"Lead on, Macduff!"

They trotted back, finding a vantage point above the well.

They dismounted and surveyed the scene. Workers milled like soldier ants. Tip saw a green Cherokee parked among other vehicles. Marley snapped photos with a telephoto lens, getting clear views of the tankers' Pennsylvania plates and the placards indicating the contents.

Tip focused on an eroded gully running from the dump pad toward the river. He pulled out his iPhone and began shooting video.

"Looks like the tanker driver hooks up a hose from his rig," he narrated. "Dumps his load. The drill tower is vibrating, likely from the force of sending frackwater back down."

The breeze carried an unnatural odor. "Rotten eggs," Marley whispered.

"Methane," said Tip.

She pointed to a cluster of a dozen people off to the side. Light standards made the scene unnaturally bright. Two figures hovered near a camera on a tripod. Another moved a glinting silver oval. All attention seemed focused on a figure in khakis and jeans jacket. Blonde hair spilled out beneath a hardhat.

"I'll be," said Tip. "That's Roxx Bleigh."

"Looks like they're making a movie," said Marley, using the telephoto.

Tip put the iPhone away.

"Here's what we do. I'll tie these horses up. You take one vial and get a sample where that gulley spills into the river. I'll take the other, go around the back and try to get a sample from the containment pond. You cross the river to our place, get a sample there and walk home. I'll take the horses back."

She looked at the activity around Roxx.

"Good thing they're distracted. Be careful."

CHAPTER 31

Thursday, Nov. 14, 10:18 a.m.

"Take Number Five. Action!"

"We're here in beautiful Mosby County, Virginia —"

"Cut!" said Melanie Pike-Stanton. "Try again, Roxx. You forgot to move toward the camera."

So cold. Breathe. Shoulders back.

"Get that rig shut down," Melanie barked, setting off a scramble by the pack of workers watching the scene. "How are we supposed to work with that racket?"

"I need one of those director's chairs," said Woody Spink, watching from the rear, hugging a Styrofoam cup. "All this standing around."

Burl stood beside him, nose wrinkling. "I'm gonna need nose plugs before long."

The compressor whirred to a stop.

"Quiet on the set," said Caleb Kinney, the cameraman. "Take Number Six. Action!"

"Here in Mosby County, we do our part for the American environment by sending responsibly —"

"Cut!" shouted Melanie. "Who's got the script?"

"Soundperson!" Caleb said. "Script!"

Melanie snatched the binder and read quickly. "I knew it. Roxx, honey, it's 'responsibly sending.' Let's take five," she said.

"Break, people!" Caleb shouted.

"Caleb, get the shoulder-mount," said Melanie. "I want cinéma vérité on a few takes. Can we get some mountains in the background? Instead of this clattertrap?"

Melanie spun on high heels and tottered in the gravel to the food truck. Roxx caught up.

"I'm so sorry! It's just —"

"Just read through your lines again! Again!"

Roxx welled up. She didn't want anyone to know she'd been feeling like crap. Tossed her cookies this morning. Probably the vile white gravy from the Lions.

Just nerves.

Bill Dinwiddie approached, wearing a green GVR baseball cap. "What's the problem, Roxx?"

"This is harder than it looks."

He angled forward and spoke quietly. "Roxx, we need to talk about this project site. I have concerns. We accepted the black ops conditions, and we're working on getting permits after the fact, but the conditions here ..." He trailed off. "They'll ask for the project manager."

Tears gushed as Bill walked away.

"Makeup!" yelled Melanie.

"This is quite intriguing, Ms. Pike-Stanton."

Melanie and Roxx turned and took in Milton V. Smythe.

Jabba.

In his fur-lined white parka, Smythe looked like the Michelin Man balloon in the Macy's Parade.

"I'm Supervisor Smythe. We're so pleased to have professionals of your ilk here in Mosby County. Might my man here, Kelso Arbuckle, ask a few questions?"

"Make it quick," Melanie snapped. "We were supposed to wrap an hour ago. I have a fund-raiser for Ted Cruz 2016 at 7."

Smythe shoved Arbuckle forward with a hiss. "Well, interview!"

"G-g-good morning," the editor stammered. "Could you spell your name? Is there a hyphen?"

"Back in one, people!" shouted Caleb.

Melanie pulled an American Petroleum Association news release and a glossy 8x10 of Roxx from her purse.

"Look. Kelso, is it? You seem familiar."

"Ever been to King's Dominion?"

"Maybe. Look, Kelso. We're behind. This is costing a fortune. Here's the dope on the campaign with my contact deets. It has APA talking points. Bio on our lovely engineer here. I'd email it, but I can't get a freakin' signal here. Use my quotes from the talking points. Email your story. I'll fluff it. *Before* you publish and post. Got it?"

"Post?" Arbuckle, said, puzzled.

She turned. "Caleb!"

The cameraman hurried over.

"Next time I use *real* actors," she hissed. "Let's do this thing."

"Quiet on the set. Take Number Six! Action!"

"Here in Mosby County, we're doing our part for America's environment by responsibly sending hydraulic frac —"

"Hold it!" said the soundperson. "Some weird sound …"

Lilting across the hills came the toot of a horn and the baying of hounds.

"The Hunt!" said Woody. "Darn! I knew there was something else today!"

"Another fox in Burlwood's henhouse," smirked Burl, nodding toward Roxx.

Melanie squared up Roxx's shoulders as the makeup artist dabbed the reddened eyes. Suddenly Melanie freed the top button, spreading the blue oxford to display cleavage.

"But I'm —" blurted Roxx.

"Working for *me!*" Melanie interrupted. "This time, Roxx, walk to your right and look back into Caleb's camera. Smile."

"Take Seven! Action!"

"Here in beautiful Mosby County, Virginia …"

Walk. Smile. Natural gesture.

"… we're doing our part for America's environment by responsibly sending hydraulic fracturing's byproducts back home."

A pause.

"Cut!" said Caleb. "I think we've got it."

Finally! No fuckups! Gotta puke!

Applause died as Roxx bent, hardhat clattering, to retch a thin stream of yellow.

"My sentiments exactly," muttered Melanie Pike-Stanton.

CHAPTER 32

Monday, Nov. 18, 11:45 a.m.

"Virginia's only Farm Use BMW," said the mechanic, handing Ting the key as Marley watched. "Good as new. Body work … bumper … new fluids … new windshield."

"Sunday will bring by those pickled beets tomorrow in payment, plus some of my brother's cider and brandy. After this, Silver Cloud and I are going for 400,000 miles."

"See you soon," said the mechanic, wiping his hands on his overalls. "I mean, hope not to see you!"

Ting's Beemer started with a satisfying rumble. She backed out to Gay Street. Marley followed in the loaner. They passed City Hall, crossed Middle Street and waved to the Episcopal priest blowing leaves from his churchyard.

They parked in front of a little café across from the theater. Britt's, the sign said.

"Remember when this was our grocery?" said Ting, coughing, closing her door. "After that, a video store, then antiques, later a bakery. I hear they have a table big enough for us ladies."

She cleared her throat and coughed. "Darn these allergies!"

"Just who are these Ladies Who Lunch?" Marley asked.

"You'll know some of 'em. It started back in the day when gals didn't serve at City Hall except to make coffee. We just needed a way to talk, once a month or so."

They entered and saw several women at the counter. Britt Schaefer, the owner, smiled as she wrote each order. A girl, maybe 8, sat at a stool wearing a blue hoodie, humming to herself.

"What's your name?" Marley asked.

"Leigh."

"My daughter," Britt said. "Today's soup is pumpkin ginger."

"Hey, Arva," said Ting. "You know my niece, Marley Tyler. Arva Jones."

"The photographer," said Arva. "I have one of your black and whites in my den."

"Really? Which one?"

"An emaciated child."

"Taken in Chad."

"Indeed. Striking. Do you have a gallery in mind here in the village?"

"Hmm. Hadn't thought of that."

"I'll introduce you to Jaye, then."

"Got anything like chicken noodle?" Ting asked at the counter.

"Everything is locally sourced from the Piedmont foodshed," said Ellen Martini. "Hello, Tylers. Marley, have you met Heather Mack, the mayor's wife?"

Marley shook hands.

"Arva, can I rearrange your name cards?" said Fran McKinney, removing her hat as the front door closed. "I'd like to sit next to our newbie."

Marley's eyes crinkled. "Am I in trouble, Officer?"

"You might be, getting mixed up with *this* crowd. Ting, I see Silver Cloud."

"We need to return the loaner, with our thanks. Those Florida plates got us some weird looks."

"Ladies, thanks so much for your patronage," Britt announced. "Leigh's here because it's Teacher's Work Day. Her daddy's out reporting. We'll bring your orders shortly."

In minutes, a dozen of the county's leading lights filled the table in the Gay Street picture window. Jaye Holland from the emporium. The Inn's sous chef, Ann Schneider. Cindy Hanson. Caroline Comer, the "Big Doings in Little Washington" columnist. Claire Hargadon, the artist. Across the table sat the mayor's wife, once a House staffer. Beth Hinson, the conservationist. Marley sat between the sheriff and Margaret Prost, the Senator's daughter-in-law.

"Did you enjoy the Hunt?" Margaret asked. "Missed you at the Pond House."

Arva sat at the head as the table filled with talk of nematodes, visiting grandchildren, the wine harvest. Claire mentioned how much Rappahannock reminded her of Santa Fe, only better. Britt and Leigh Schaefer brought plates and bowls. Young Leigh surprised them by singing grace in a clear soprano. The women clapped and laughed.

"No agenda, ladies," Arva said. "Busy week. Thanksgiving's coming. We have a guest."

"Not all of you have met my niece, Marley," said Ting. "Nearly healed from the accident."

A round of hellos.

"We heard it was quite an unusual bang-up," said the sous chef.

"If you call hitting *two* deer turned purple from chemical poisoning, unusual, then yeah," said Fran, patting Marley on the back.

Fran caught herself and looked at Caroline. "That's on background. Not attributed to me, OK?"

"OK, Sheriff. Purple deer?"

"You must be joking," said Jaye Holland, the emporium owner.

"Turned blue from oxygen starvation. We believe it consumed an excess of barium. Plus some other trace chemicals that are unbelievably scary."

"Consumed, as in drank?" Claire asked. "Where?"

"Not sure. The Tylers live up Hannah Run Hollow, you know. Near the Hughes River."

"We've had so many odd incidents lately," said Claire.

"Those frightening tankers," Ellen said.

"Poisoned deer," said Fran. "Ailing farmworkers."

"An earthquake," said the sous chef. "Our soufflés fell."

"What about those lease agreements in our mailboxes?" Cindy Hanson said. "Drilling for natural gas. Rob said a lot of Lions were interested."

"All of a sudden ..." said Marley.

"You didn't hear it from me," said the columnist, "but Paul Schaefer and our partners at VirginiaWatch are working on something big. Tip Tyler's in on it."

"My husband hasn't said a thing about this drilling," said Heather Mack. "Usually something like that needs public hearings."

"Permits," Ting rasped. "Regional impact."

The table fell silent for a minute, the women mulling what they'd just heard. Leigh hovered.

"Say, any of you have connections with Burlwood?" asked the Sheriff. "The Spink brothers?"

"My father-in-law does," Margaret said. "Why?"

"They're out of my jurisdiction, but they're running some sort of reinjection operation. We heard about it at Lions from their project manager, a young woman. Frackwater down the pipe. Everyone know what I'm talking about, fracking?"

Marley sat listening. She'd edited her photos. Good ones. The well. The gathered crowd at Burlwood. The filming. The containment pond. She'd given them to Tip, who'd cautioned her to keep quiet about their reconnaissance until the newspaper could publish them.

So many risks, all at once. The clandestine journalism had been a new thrill for an art photographer. She'd breeched Hunt etiquette; gotten away with it. The water samples were due back this week, on the QT. But the real frisson came from Fran McKinney's thigh next to hers.

Ever since Tip's interview with the professor, Marley had been bothered by the litany of fracking's health threats. Scary incidents dismissed by the industry as anecdotal. They made it seem so hypothetical. Now, not so much. The evidence was starting to be overwhelming.

She started to speak up when her aunt stood.

"I need to rest," Ting said. "It must be the excitement of getting Silver Cloud back again!"

Marley rose. "I'll get a lift," nodding Fran's way.

The women all waved and watched Ting leave.

Cindy turned to Marley. "Is she OK?"

"I've been worried."

"What are we going to do about this fracking business, ladies?" Arva asked.

"Well, for starters —" Marley began.

"I don't *want* fracking!" said a small voice. The women looked at the little girl.

"Why do you say that, dear?" asked Cindy.

"My cousin? He's in Pennsylvania. They have one of those wells. His puppy died."

"Ladies, I'm sorry," said Britt Schaefer. "Leigh, you know better than to interrupt!"

"No. Tell us more," said the mayor's wife.

"My sister's boy," Britt said. "Their cows *have* been sick. Two were born without tails."

"Sounds like we have an agenda item for next month, right ladies?" said Arva, standing. "In the meantime, have a wonderful Thanksgiving!"

Chairs scraped as the women grabbed their coats. Fran adjusted her hat.

"What are you doing on Thanksgiving?" Marley asked. "I suppose you must be working."

Fran gazed at her.

"Early shift. My folks moved to Great Falls. They spend Thanksgiving working in a D.C. soup kitchen. If this is an invitation to the Tyler table, why, I'd be honored."

Marley blushed. "Great. The Power Couple will be there. The way Ting's feeling, we could use an extra hand."

"What can I bring?"

"Wine maybe?"

"I've always liked the Tylers. Serious question, though."

"What's that?"

"Would you like me in uniform? Or holiday dressy?"

"Either. Both." Marley said. "I like you in both."

CHAPTER 33

Wednesday, Nov. 20, 8 a.m.

Up late last night working in *The Reporter's* small newsroom, chilled to the bone by the morning's orchard trek, Tip had driven into the village for breakfast with Provo.

No response in Box 35 to the four open-records requests. Nothing from France, as always. Tom Freeman had sent a hefty package of academic studies, and there was a big envelope from the Fairfax Grant Foundation. Almost lost in the stack was a plain envelope, unstamped, no return address: Master Tyler & Co., Fairleigh, Hannah Run Hollow.

Clete.

Inside:

> To Whom It May Concern:
> Please be advised we are proceeding with Green Valley Resources of Pittsburgh, Pa., on a job-creating, natural resources project on church property. Direct all inquiries to Green Valley.
> May God be with you in our Season of Good Will.

It was signed:

> The congregation of Hannah Run Meeting House

Penciled in below, a postscript:

> Thank you for your guidance!

Guidance? Crap! Aiding the enemy!

Tip peered around the corner. No postmaster/pastor.

He fed four quarters into *The Post's* news rack and grabbed the last copy, scanning headlines. One caught his eye. Front page, below the fold: *Fracking studies disagree on water concerns.*

Mainstream coverage. Must show Provo.

"Morning everyone," Tip said, looking around the Café.

Two Woodchucks in camo Carhartts sprawled at the big middle table. Tip took a four-top on the side, quickly scanning the fracking piece. It reprised the discredited Texas study and detailed the Duke report he'd discussed with the professor warning of imminent seepage of deep-injection frackwater into aquifers via "pathways." Both studies had been in the public domain for months, further evidence to Tip of *The Post's* slide.

Otherwise, the paper was filled with pre-Thanksgiving turkey features, GOP dysfunction and Hot Juicy News from Kardashistan. Even Doonesbury was in flashback mode.

What will *Bezos do?*

"Hi, Tip darlin'," said Michelle. Then, loud enough for the clueless squatters, "I'll get your *usual* table ready right quick."

"No worries, Michelle. I'll have the farm breakfast. Over easy. Grits. Ask Big Jim to have mercy on my sausage patties."

"Hockey pucks is what they are," said Provo Starke as the door clanged. He gingerly removed his jeans jacket. "Same provenance as that alleged coffee."

"Heard about your hand. How is it?"

"Except for shiftin' into third, I believe I'll live. Missed you at Lions."

"That's what I want to talk about."

The waitress slid two mugs on the table.

"You know what, Michelle? The gentleman and I are gonna be just fine, right here."

Starke squirmed. "Well, OK then. Michelle, eggs scrambled with cheese. If Big Jim can crisp up my bacon, I'll have a rasher. Huh. Rasher. That's one you don't hear much anymore, even from you word personages."

"You're edgy."

"Figure I'm about to be waterboarded."

"What exactly *is* going on with you and your project manager? And her company? Green Valley Resources. Mid-sized drilling outfit out of Pittsburgh. I saw her flowback operation at Burlwood. Now they're moving in with drilling leases. *The Reporter* needs to talk with her."

"Well, Mister Spanish Inquisition, Miz Bleigh and I have been keepin' company." Provo saw Tip glance at his gauzed hand. "I don't believe she's deliberately out to get me. She charmed the Lions, by the way."

"I was afraid of that. Has she told you what she's up to?"

Starke sat back, eyes narrowing. "She's boss lady of a recycling operation. Lady engineers are rare as honest lawyers and well-paid journalists."

"Have you seen what they're doing there?"

"All I know is they put a well back into operation. For hydrofractions."

"Hydraulic fracturing. Fracking."

"What the frack," said Starke, backbone up.

"And did you get one of those drilling lease proposals?"

"Yessir. We are for it, me and Momma. It's expensive, runnin' a ranch, just the two of us. Plus it might give our little county here an actual economy. Your man, Mr. Hope and Change? He's for it. This gas boom might just keep Jarheads like me away from Heaven's Gate, and thank you for your sympathy."

Starke started to rise. Tip put up both hands.

"Look, you know I appreciate your deployments."

"You like busting my chops."

Tip leaned in, quieter now. He pointed to the headline. "You are my friend. But have you seen those tankers on Lee Highway? You want 'em 20 times a day coming through Five Corners? Aren't you concerned about your water? Did you know livestock near North Dakota wells are being born without tails? You want that at Red Oak? Have you read anything about flaming water taps in Wyoming? About methane poisoning aquifers in Pennsylvania?"

Starke picked up his spoon and spun it. "They say it will be a minimal presence at Red Oak."

"Do we want drilling of *any* kind here in Rappahannock?"

"We can use the cash, Tip. It's $5,000 an acre they're offerin'."

"How many acres you and Momma Starke have total there at Red Oak?"

"There's the 155 on the one side, 45 on the other. Starke land for five generations."

"I'm not so quick at math but that's —"

"A million."

"Whoa."

"I need a new tedder. I gotta replace that water wagon for the herd on your place. I was gonna wait until Christmas to tell you."

"'Provo, I know that seems like a lot. But —"

"Momma's never seen that kinda money."

"That's peanuts over the long term. Especially if they take your acreage out of production. Have you calculated any of that?"

"Nossir."

"Have they brought up mineral rights? Do you know if you own your mineral rights? Have you looked at your deed? Talked with your lawyer?"

"You're mighty good at 20 Questions."

"Professional hazard. Did they tell you about the chemicals they'll bring onto your property?"

"Proprietary, they say. Only used as a necessary component of their technique."

"Guess what's commonly associated with fracking. Barium. Remember that wacked-out deer Marley hit? Too much barium. Imagine one of your bulls getting into that."

Tip pulled out a file as the plates arrived.

"It's proprietary because Mr. Dick Cheney got a little exception written into an energy bill back in 2005. Your drilling companies, like Green Valley and Chesapeake, are exempt from the Clean Water Act. They don't have to tell you what they plan to slip down their wells. But after one of 'em blew out in Pennsylvania, know what happened? Tens of thousands of gallons of toxic liquid spilled over their fields and into a nearby creek. Court records listed the chemicals."

"I 'spect they would. So what?"

"Here. Read."

"Not while I'm eating."

"OK, Provo. I will."

Tip opened the file. "The EPA documents showed that, quote, the fluid Chesapeake used in operations at the well contained more than two dozen chemicals, including methanol, glutaraldehyde, formaldehyde, 2-butoxyethanol and hydrochloric acid."

Provo cleared his throat. "Formaldehyde?"

"Yup."

Provo sipped from his mug. Pushed his plate away. "Not as hungry as

I thought." He spun his spoon and eyed his friend. "What makes you think there's a connection between fracking and some purple deer?"

"Burlwood's next door to me … has that big ugly containment pond. Oh, and by the way, think about how close that is to where your future steaks are grazing. How else do you explain it?"

Provo squared his shoulders. "What with the prices I'm getting for my herd? And the cost of cutting hay? And taxes, come due in January?"

"We didn't get one of those letters. Probably on purpose. Could I look at the lease proposal?"

"I guess. After all, that's what *friends* do."

"Just make sure you know where you stand with your mineral rights. Ask your lawyer. Who do you have? Miles Massie?"

Provo wiped his lips.

"That's not all," Tip said. "Did Roxx say anything about shooting a movie?"

"She's been busy. Traveling. Pittsburgh. Washington. All's I know is she came back all excited about the American Petroleum Association."

"Look," Tip whispered. "*I've* seen what's going on over there. All of us should worry. They chopped the top clean off the ridge. Big ol' tower. Compressor station. Containment pond the size of a small lake."

"So? Least the Spinks can go ice skating come January."

"Can't you take this seriously?" sighed Tip, just as Paul Schaefer approached, carrying a copy of *The Mosbyville Monitor*. He took a seat.

"Listen, Provo, could we get Roxx's number?" Tip asked. "We've been doing some … homework, and *The Reporter* is working up a story. Paul needs to interview her. Today."

"Go to her job site, Provo," Tip continued. "See for yourself. Imagine what it'll look like outside Momma Starke's window."

Fran McKinney walked in and waved from the register. "Takeout," she said, nodding to her friends.

Her two-way shoulder-mount chirped. She listened, her face draining.

"Cancel that, Big Jim!"

She quick-stepped to the table.

"That call? Randolph at the Corner Store. Bad accident at the Sperryville bridge. Fireball. Tanker truck. Gotta go!"

CHAPTER 34

Wednesday, Nov. 20, 9 a.m.

Milton Smythe smirked. There were perks to being a press baron.

Wednesday's *Monitor* stretched before him, right off the press. Arbuckle might not be the sharpest tool, but he followed directions.

The headline was Smythe's contribution. *Breaking News! Mosby in National Gas Headlights!*

Smythe reread with satisfaction, starting with Kelso Arbuckle's byline.

> MOSBYVILLE – In what is perhaps *the* most exciting local development in decades, our county's citizens can add national prominence to this week's list of things to be thankful for, courtesy of prominent patriots Burleson and Woodrow Spink of Burlwood and one very dedicated public servant.

Smythe reached for a red pen, circled "for" and began scribbling margin notes. "Dangling preposition?"

> First, Virginia is securely on the leading edge of our nation's exciting clean energy efforts to pump up the U.S. economy through oil and gas exploration to break American oil dependency and all-important job creation. For Burlwood in the northwest part of our county is a hive of activity as a hardworking crew from Green Valley Resources out of Pittsburgh, utilizing the latest new technology available and with an enthusiastic local workforce in shiny new jobs, is recycling the useless byproduct of hydrological fractioning via a refurbished, World War II-vintage well. The project is led by first-time Project Manager Roxanna Raye Bleigh, ME (Mistress of Engineering, from our very own University of Virginia), seen to the right in the *Monitor* photograph. (Isn't she just darling?)

Smythed scratched out "utilize," added a caret and penned in "use." And then: "Hydraulic fracturing, you turd."

Next time, he thought, I might just have to write it myself.

> Second of all, and in a *Monitor EXCLUSIVE*, we can now tell you that, debuting Thanksgiving Day, during the halftime of the Green Bay Packers and Detroit Bears NFL telecast, Ms. Bleigh will be *prominently* featured in a well-produced and expensive Public Relations image campaign in behalf of the prestigious American Petroleum Association, via a television commercial shot right <u>here</u> in Mosby County! Dial in! (WTTG, Fox5).

More red. "Detroit Lions, dipshit."

Could have used a second read, Smythe sighed. Christ, what must I do to keep this place going?

> Celebrities were in our county this week, including Melanie Pike-Stanton, Senior Vice President/Communications at APA, along with a talented film crew from Pandemonium Productions of K Street. (And we might as well add Roxx Bleigh, because after tomorrow night, she'll be a celeb, too! Our own Kardashian!)

"Good," read the next scribble.

Smythe smiled at his editorial orchestration. Everyone loves those Arabnosed beauties. Kara. Katie. Kitty. Whatever. House of big booties.

> All of this activity to the betterment of the lives of Mosby Countians is made possible via the tireless economic development efforts of 11-term Mosby County Superviser Milton V. Smythe, who recently won his eleventh term on our board of supervisers. He sponsored the unanimous proclamation this week at Mosby County Hall renaming Burlwood's well site as Freedom from Oil Dependence Hill.

More red. "Run spell check. It's 'supervisor.'"

> The superviser said the refracturing operation was ap-
> proved months ago in public hearings before the Mosby Coun-
> ty Board of Supervisers.

Smythe had doctored up an August agenda to create a paper trail, just in case pantywaist regulators came snooping.

> "I estimate the economic benefit to Mosby County to be
> north of six figures this year," said Mr. Smythe. (Full disclosure:
> Mr. Smythe is owner and publisher of *The Monitor*.) "Discount-
> ed color display opportunities are better than ever for potential
> Monitor advertisers wishing to cash in on this exciting oppor-
> tunity," said Mr. Smythe. Call Accounts for rates and details.

Smythe had adopted the disclosure statement anytime the *Monitor* quoted him. Transparency. Best practices, they call it. But the ad plug? Only a publisher would know how to word it.

> County employment numbers will likely rise on this good
> news, and next week we will interview the economist George
> Mason once he returns from the holiday break.

"OOPS!!!" Smythe's all-caps meant business. "Economist FROM George Mason, idiot!"

> "Clean, inexpensive natural gas is good for America-
> QUOTE GOES HERE," said Ms. Pike-Stanton, an attractive
> woman with vast experience said to have frequent hookups
> with the D.C. elite. She was away from the office at deadline.

The place-holding QUOTE gaffe had Smythe rolling his eyes. "Where did you learn to EDIT?" he wrote. "I'm docking your pay! Again."

> An unnamed APA spokeswoman would not confirm
> the specific dollar amount, but Melanie did say earlier our
> very own U.S. Congressman Eric Cantor, R-Virginia, and
> upcoming Speaker of the House, is being encouraged by
> large oil industry officials to pass a resolution in the House
> supporting hydrological fractioning and banning the "F-word"

(i.e., "fracking") from the English language.

The political plug had been another superb Smythe suggestion.

"I'm a natural!" said Ms. Bleigh. (And she sure is!)

The rest was all Arbuckle.

Efforts to get the Spink brothers on record about their self-less contribution to our county's fame were unsuccessful. "Call my attorney," said one Mr. Spink by telephone.

Unconfirmed rumors that prominent Afro-American actor James Earl Ray was present at the shooting procedures could not be confirmed. His voice is prominently scripted in the commercial, we have learned. We did hear a rumor that Kortney Kardashian planned to celebrate her second divorce (second this year!) at the Inn at Little Washington, but the *Monitor* takes pains not to grovel in gossip.

Smythe leaned back, satisfied. Citizen Kane could not have done it better.

CHAPTER 35

Thursday, Nov. 21, 10:10 a.m.

From the banks of the Thornton River, Acey Youngblood shot frames looking up at the buckled girders of the Sperryville bridge. The crumpled orca of a blackened Peterbilt lay wedged on its side across the molten pavement.

"Get the hell back from there!" yelled a HazMat-suited EMT.

Youngblood, looking like a mutant grasshopper in antique gas mask and floppy mane, hopped back over the yellow crime scene tape.

The orange medevac helicopter from Faquier Health rose with a staccato roar, teetering before gaining its bearings, pausing over the scene like an archangel before taking a tangent east. Its cargo: two Flint Hill volunteer firefighters gasping for life, lungs collapsing after a toxic whiff inhaled through paper face masks.

Paul Schaefer's plastic press credentials flapped in the copter's wake as he closed his reporter's notebook after a roadside interview with County Administrator Al German.

The editor headed toward the cordon where Tip and Sheriff McKinney stood. They watched as EMTs placed the bagged body of the last of three victims in the Virginia Chief Medical Examiner's van. As if an official inquest in Fairfax would yield findings other than death by incineration. Behind the EMTs sat the charred hulk of a 2013 Can-Am Spyder Roadster, 38 miles into her inaugural ride, all three tires melted by the 900-degree inferno.

Paul caught Tip's eye, then shouted to his photographer. "Let's sort this out."

Tip hurried over, tapping on his iPhone's notes app. Youngblood joined them, reviewing images in the viewfinder.

"I've phoned in a lead paragraph to Harry already," said Paul. "So we're already up online."

"Good," Tip said.

"I've got three DOA," said the editor. "Tanker driver is Hank Cody, Mineral Springs, Pa. *Was* Hank Cody. The motorcyclists on that three-wheeler were Charles and Phyllis Wellborne. Retirees from Manassas. Did Fran speculate on cause?"

"She thinks Cody nodded off, clipped the trike," Tip said.

"Looks like most of the contents spilled onto the bridge and below," said Youngblood, removing the mask. "Not sure what it was carrying, but from the looks of those HazMat suits, it's toxic. You can see it frothing down there, heading east."

"These rigs carry 4,000 gallons," said Tip. "The DOT placard was charred beyond recognition. I don't think briny frackwater would foam like that. Acey, could you check with the company to see what its waybill might say? Fran says until they know, they're treating it as an unknown hazard. Paul, shouldn't we call the governor's office? German says they're waffling on when to call the state of emergency."

"They've started to evacuate Main Street and the River District," said Paul. "They can't use the Schoolhouse," he said, nodding toward the building next door. "That's the county's normal emergency shelter. This is too close. They're going to take evacuees to the old school in Little Washington. I'll send Caroline Comer over."

"Fran says Lee Highway's a mess from Luray to Warrenton," Tip jumped in. "Zach Taylor's backed up to Culpeper. FT Valley's diverted back to Mosbyville. These motorists are pissed."

"Andy Forster's talked to a few of 'em," said Schaefer. "And he started on the editorial."

"Fran ran the tanker's plates," said Tip, looking at his notes. "Leased to Liberty Land LLC out of Mineral Springs, Pa. One of the Spink brothers' holding companies. So it was probably on its way to Burlwood. Let's at least try to confirm. The real concern is if it was a 'hot' tanker."

"What's that mean?" Acey asked.

"A fracking tanker carrying full-strength chemicals, not just the diluted flowback. That team over there from Virginia DEQ, taking samples? They happened to be on their way to Rixeyville when they heard the call. I have their numbers."

"I need to get back, start writing this up," said Paul. "Deadline's in an hour. Andy's in a sweat. The editions leading up to Thanksgiving are always fat with ad inserts."

"Get him to move press time back!" Tip urged. "You need to open up at least two extra pages for expanded coverage. And he should bump the press run big time."

"Right. OK. I'll try. Harry's gonna scramble to get everything we crank out posted and updated."

"Paul, all of this supersedes what my daughter and I turned in on Burl-wood and its well. Even if they *are* running an unpermitted operation, that moves *way* down in the main story. I'll rewrite it as a sidebar."

"I'd say we've got one main story, with me and Acey combining on it," said Schaefer. "You and Caroline can feed us details, Tip. Along with the pub-lisher's quotes from motorists."

"Right. And there are three, four, maybe five sidebars," Tip said. "I'll do the scene-setter from here with quotes from eyewitnesses. Redo the Burlwood piece, but all of this validates what we saw there. We need the official reaction. Richmond is silent so far, and the county says fracking's out of its jurisdiction. We need to ask how all this could happen without regs in place from Rich-mond. Can Caroline handle the evacuation?"

"Sure. What else?"

"I'll follow on water quality and the environmental hazard," said Tip. "I can rework the explainer on how fracking works. Paul, can Acey swing by the shelter, get some shots? I have one more interview here. I see Beth Hinson over there. Need a quote on the impact on the river and folks downstream."

"Caroline's column mentions purple deer. That's connected, right?"

"It is now," said Tip.

"What else do we need?" said Schaefer.

"You and Acey need to coordinate on a time line. See that ponytailed dude? That's William August. Graphic artist. I saw him sketching the scene, and he agreed to help on an infographic. Have Caroline call the hospital, check on the condition of those firefighters. See you back at the office. Oh, and do you think Harry can crank up an interactive map based on reports and emails and texts from county residents who've seen these tankers, when and where?"

"Whew! This breaking news stuff?" said Paul, eyes gleaming. "Wow."

"The ultimate reality show," Tip said.

"We're just a little weekly."

"Welcome to the digital age," said Tip.

CHAPTER 36

Thanksgiving, Nov. 28, 3 p.m.

Candles flickered in the middle of the dining room table, stretched to full holiday length. The orange and crimson Jacquard tablecloth barely covered end to end. Heirloom china and steaming platters of Thanksgiving fare covered every available spot.

Tip poured the Martini claret into the last of the long-stemmed glasses as everyone settled in to their places.

Ting rose from the head of the table. "With all the excitement of these past days… it's not *like* me to punk out. You all were so kind to come to my rescue! Look at this meal!"

"No worries, Auntie," said Maddie. "A toast to our matriarch, Dolley Paine Madison Tyler!"

"To your health," said Gus Martini.

"To the turkey," said Fran McKinney, in horse country elegant, next to Walker Longwood.

"You'll get better, Aunt Ting," said Marley, on Walker's right.

Ting sat with an effort.

"We usually say grace at the holidays," she said, scanning the concerned faces. "With such an ecumenical crowd, let's just offer a moment of silence to the higher power of your choice."

Mother Nature, thought Tip. *Sorely tested this week.*

Heads bowed. Ten seconds ticked off the grandfather clock behind Les Leong.

"Thirteen is a small number for the Tylers," said Ellen Martini, breaking the silence. "Years past, you've had two dozen."

"No need for a junior table," Tip said. "Unless you include exchange students."

"Tip! Be kind," said Claire Hargadon, smacking his hand. "Ahmet, dear, you must miss your family in Istanbul, but we're so glad you're here."

"I am most grateful to Miss Claire for hosting me," said the dark-haired teen. "This is my first American Thanksgiving!"

"I hear you have twin lacrosse players, right?" Leong said to Josefina Lopez, seated to his right.

"They are in a tournament. They will have Thanksgiving with teammates in Charlottesville."

"We'd have needed a spare turkey to feed them!" said Marley. She winked at Fran.

"Look at this bounty!" said Gus, seated across from Tip.

"*Dios mio*," said Sunday Lopez. "Where I come from this would be enough —"

"For a whole month!" Josefina said.

"I feel so bad for the families that were evacuated," Claire said. "Sheriff, is there timetable for getting them back home?"

"Call me Fran. Not sure. Saturday? I spent my morning with HazMat folks."

Marley picked up a serving spoon and began to scoop yams.

"Tip, you were kind to bring that ham and Ting's beets to the shelter this morning," said Gus. "The Lions were well-represented in the serving line by you folks. Thank you, Ahmet. Claire. Tip. Les, you must have dished out a ton of mashed potatoes."

"My humble county thanks you, Mr. Undersecretary," said Maddie, tipping a glass in her beau's direction.

"I stood next to the Senator!" Les said. "Someone took our picture."

"I can get you a copy," said Marley. "That casserole in front of Ahmet? Oysters Pettibone."

"I saw Provo and Momma Starke there," Martini said.

"Any Roxx Bleigh sightings?" said Tip with eyebrow raised.

"Marley, are you TiVo-ing the game?" asked Walker. "We've gotta watch that commercial."

"Anyone read that article in *The Monitor*? The New Face of Fracking," said Tip.

"Some of these dishes are new to me," said Les, eyeing the table.

"Maddie and Marley are the top chefs," Ting rasped. "What did you all manage in my absence?"

"Don't ever let my highfalutin' sister tell you she can't cook," Marley said. "Maddie was amazing at logistics. Ellen and Josefina helped in the kitchen. Fran set the table. Gus carved."

"Tip, will you serve the turkey?" Ting asked. "What else do we have?"

"Well, Walker's pheasant. Smoked ham from Belle Ridge," said Maddie. "Dressing. Two kinds of potato. Those are Fran's creamy garlic mashed. How you find time to cook I don't know! There's Josefina's jalapeno cheese creation. Yams with praline sauce; your recipe. I did Jeter's famous winter roots with your beets."

"Tip did his usual Oysters Pettibone in the cider house," Marley said. "Les, that's a creamed spinach dish with bacon. Old family recipe. Claire's roast brussels sprouts. Maddie's cranberry orange relish, of course. Ellen did the green bean casserole. Josefina also did two apple pies. And Les, how'd you know we'd need pumpkin pie?"

"Gus, your claret is exceptional," said Tip. "You brought the good stuff."

"Bottled water preapproved by the EPA," Leong said.

Silence fell.

"When do we get our wells back?" Claire asked. "Cooking without tap water's a challenge. What on Earth is our governor waiting for? The downstream population must be close to a million people."

"Our global-warming-denying governor," Marley said.

"I stopped in at the shelters, too," said Fran, pouring gravy. "It's been a frustrating week. Lots of unhappy people. They do have water, though. Lots of volunteers."

"I was impressed," Ahmet said. "I mean, to volunteer time on this holiday."

"Fran, any update from Al?" asked Tip. "Who wants dark?"

"He actually drove to the governor's mansion today to make our case for a state of emergency," said Fran, dropping her professional demeanor. "You know what Al thinks, off the record? The governor didn't win Rappahannock in the election, so ..."

"The Dalai Lama would say the governor's next life will not be easy," said Walker.

"Well," Ting sighed. "Bon appetit!"

The diners picked up their forks.

"Tip, I read *The Reporter*," said Ellen. "*Every* word. First, online. Then in print today. It made me feel like I was there. Really comprehensive. And just shocking."

"Marley's pictures, too. Unbelievable how they destroyed that hill," said Claire.

"I can tell you the secretary is concerned, if it's any consolation," Les said. "It's been a battle royal to get any regulations reviewed on fracking before the industry's lobbyists descend."

"Then partisans water them down more," Ting said. She choked on the last word, face reddening as she shook.

She put down her fork. "Folks, will you excuse me?"

Blackie barked from the front porch.

Ting stood and wobbled.

And fell.

The grandfather clock swayed and toppled with a crash.

The wine carafe slid from the sideboard and shattered.

The holiday table surfed atop a Jell-O'd floor.

CHAPTER 37

Thanksgiving, Nov. 28, 3:15 p.m.

Roxx sat in the 24-hour clinic's empty waiting room, filling out seven pages of forms. Awful place to be on Thanksgiving afternoon.

Can't wait to hunker down with Ralph and Barb. I feel like crap.

"I hope you don't mind," said the receptionist, an elfin Goth. "You look familiar. You on TV?"

"Not ... yet."

How'd she know?

"Wait! *The Monitor!* I'm from Mosbyville. I saw your picture in the paper! You're The Natural!"

Roxx planned to watch the game as soon as she could curl up at her parent's home in Great Falls. After the topsy-turvy week, she craved the familiar. Dad. Food. Football.

She'd spent the morning at Burlwood, addressing the project site's ongoing woes. She'd turned down Provo's invitation to Red Oak Ranch. Before heading to Great Falls, she needed to figure out why she felt so freakin' awful. The clinic was on the way.

For the past week, every call, every email brought new drama. And trauma.

First it was *The Reporter* guy. She'd tried her best to duck that by hanging up. She'd read that silly article in *The Monitor*. Then came the horrible news about the wreck on the bridge. She guessed that poor trucker, Hank, had dozed off. His run must have been delayed.

GVR's top PR honcho called to tell her to zip it. Bad enough she'd gotten the detailed email from Bill, asking her to explain conditions at the site and the numerous safety breaches he'd seen. But then Green Valley's CEO had emailed the entire company the next day with a link to the commercial embedded. "Our own Face of Fracking!" he'd written.

Melanie Pike-Stanton had called repeatedly, cursing a blue streak, second-guessing the decision to launch during the NFL game, worrying that Jon Stewart would rake APA over the coals for starting a campaign on the heels of a fatal inferno and spill. She did manage to cancel Roxx's appearance on Colbert.

An hour later, as Roxx was leaving Long Mountain, Melanie had called again to say APA execs who'd previewed the spot were ecstatic.

A real yoyo. Roxx had never been more conflicted.

Elated over the campaign.

Shocked by the disaster.

Scared by Bill's concerns.

Buffeted by Melanie.

Charmed by Provo.

Concerned she wasn't a True Believer.

Worried that fracking would ruin Rappahannock.

Sick as a dog.

She sat, sniffling, hoping this Doc in a Box could give her a prescription or something. She felt like she was leaving the scene of an accident. At least she was halfway home.

"Sign here," said Goth Girl, reviewing the insurance forms. "And here." "And here."

Goth Girl held *The Monitor* front page.

"What's that for?"

"Autograph? For my girlfriend? She'll freak! Oh, and the doctor will see you now."

Roxx struggled to keep the paper gown closed as she described her symptoms to the doctor. Headaches, worsening. Can't hold down breakfast. Losing sense of smell.

He took her vitals. Blood pressure. Temperature.

"How long?" he asked.

"A week or so. I'm sure it's stress-related," she said. "I'm under a lot of stress."

"The headaches I'm not so sure about," said the doctor. "The other stuff ...? Here. I'm gonna ask you to multitask. Take this cup in there and give me a urine sample. But first, pee on this wand. When you're done, give it back to me."

"It looks like a … a …"

"Pregnancy test," he smiled. "We'll know in seconds."

OHHHMYGODDDDDD.

She did as told, a cascade of thoughts tumbling. Provo. Bill. Fracking. Ralph.

She handed the wand to the doctor. He nodded.

"I'm surprised you didn't do this yourself. If I had to guess, I'd say you're about a month along."

HOLY SHIT.

Roxx stood.

Wobbly.

"I feel shaky and —"

"Me too," said the doctor, rising, ducking a falling tray. "Hold on to something! Quick!"

CHAPTER 38

Thanksgiving, Nov. 28, 3:16 p.m.

Ting tumbled. Fairleigh's solid walls groaned.

Tip felt an oyster slide down the wrong pipe. He gagged and coughed. Through watery eyes, he watched Rockwell morph into Dalí.

Ahmet's chair collapsed. Candles and wine glasses toppled. The flat-panel TV fell with a crash. Marley rose to help her fallen aunt, and then fell atop her. Shards from the shattered carafe sliced Claire's knee. The gravy boat hit the floor, spewing in *Dexter*-worthy fashion. Photos skittered from the piano. The refrigerator flew open, jars colliding, eggs cracking on the floor. George Winston's *Thanksgiving* stopped in the CD player. Lights flickered. Darkness. Silence.

Six seconds took an eternity.

Gus pounded Tip's back to relieve the blockage. Tip fell to all fours to catch his breath.

"Quake. Bigger than that other one," said Walker.

Fran ran to Marley for a quick assurance, helped Ting stand, and then sprinted out to her cruiser. The twins took their aunt upstairs. Gus Martini excused himself and his wife to check on their vineyard. Sunday used a napkin to stanch Claire's bleeding leg.

Blackie licked at the gravy spill.

Josefina looked at the train wreck on the table. She began triage, picking broken pieces of china and glassware out of the shattered bowls, deciding which dishes were unsafe.

Walker stepped out to make a visual inspection of Fairleigh's exterior. Tip followed.

Stunned, quiet, no longer hungry, the remaining guests followed Josefina's lead and cleared the table, saving what they could.

Tip and Walker returned to report that cracks spider-webbed all the way to the roofline.

The twins returned from upstairs to prepare take-home packages for each guest, quadrupling the portions for the Lopez family.

Sunday picked up fallen furniture and trinkets in each room, returning the interior to a semblance of order. Tip went out again to check on Provo's herd.

Les filled the sink from plastic bottles and washed dishes, his gravy-stained tie thrown over one shoulder. Ahmet dried and replayed the quake in video-game detail. The twins silently put away the unbroken china and silver.

Tip returned and picked up the landline. He called neighbors first, including Clete Mahan, asking if they were all right. He reached Paul. The coverage plan for *The Reporter* was solid.

An hour later, the somber twins escorted their guests to the front door, doggie bags in hand.

The house, eerily silent, was left to a sleeping Ting, her rattled brother, his exhausted twins and a concerned undersecretary of energy. Power returned. The men tuned in the Packers-Lions game on the small kitchen TV and watched the commercial. Before retiring, Tip and the twins agreed someone should take Ting to see Doc Rose Zimmer first thing.

Blackie followed Tip to the cider house. Before heading to bed, he opened his computer. AP reported 5.8 on the Richter scale, epicenter Northern Virginia, damage reported from West Virginia to Maryland's Eastern Shore.

His article on the Burlwood operation, rewritten after the calamity at the bridge, had left a key geologic aspect of the reinjection process awaiting proof. He looked again at the bookmarked sites recommended by Prof. Freeman. Reports of new fault lines in the Netherlands. Stories out of Youngstown halting reinjection until studies were concluded.

Atop his inbox sat his daily Google alert on fracking. First link: "New study in *Geology* magazine directly ties fracking to Oklahoma quakes."

Now he was certain.

"A *frack*ing earthquake!" he said, the epithet echoing into the dark interior.

He was surprised by Marley's voice from the front door.

"You're saying it's one of those … fraccidents?"

Tip stood.

"A *motherFRACKing* earthquake!"

Part III

CHAPTER 39

The Rappahannock Reporter,
Wednesday, Dec. 4

Editorial: A time for faith, a time for action

A momentous fortnight has passed.

Bad enough that our community was rocked to its ribs by the fire and toxic spill at Thornton River Bridge and the evacuation of Sperryville.

Then the strongest earthquake in a century rattled Thanksgiving Day throughout the Piedmont.

We are left displaced, distrustful. Despite what some insist, the causes are not yet fully known.

As you will see elsewhere in this week's edition, Rappahannock County has risen to the occasion in many ways. Heroism. Resolve. Resilience.

We face grave challenges. Let us do so together, as good neighbors do.

Such events can also split this community, as recent postings on RappChat suggest. Please keep your comments civil. But keep 'em coming.

The human toll — three deaths, two volunteer firefighters clinging to their lives, a dozen quake-related injuries — saddens us. Our hearts and prayers go out to the victims' families. We mourn the loss of our Commissioner of Revenue.

We are blessed with the underpinning of a faith community thriving in every hill and hollow. The power of their prayer will help us get through.

Our packed emergency shelter was a rock star, providing comfort until this week's all clear. Our grandchildren will have Thanksgiving stories to share for a lifetime!

It's too soon to tell what the economic toll will be as we sort through the shattered pieces, assessing damage to foundations, fields and fences.

There is visible damage — the scorched bridge, the fallen steeple at Washington Baptist, the shuttered Inn, the sundered roadbed at Slate Mills. All of that can and will be repaired. Reports of damaged wells are more worrisome.

Harder to repair is our faith in government. Our pleas to Richmond and Washington have gone unheard. We deplore the governor's reluctance to declare a state of emergency in the face of our travail. We fear for untold thousands of fellow Virginians south and east of us, imperiled by the swirl of frackwater in the Rappahannock River watershed.

The week did bring an economic boost when supervisors fast-tracked testing in Rappahannock for natural gas drilling. While reasonable people will disagree and the health risks do give pause, we should remain open to new technologies capable of tapping our nation's domestic energy supply and bringing new jobs.

The back-to-normal decree from Richmond might have emptied the shelter, but it will take time for normalcy, and trust, to return.

Until then, work together and keep the faith.

— *Andrew Forster, Publisher, and Paul Schaefer, Editor*

CHAPTER 40

Wednesday, Dec. 4, 6:25 a.m.

Packing in the predawn gloom, Roxx Bleigh smiled. It was the right answer. She peered out the window of her room at the Hyatt Regency on East Wacker in Chicago. Far below she could see the first glint from the Frank Gehry bandshell in Millennium Park. From the 18th floor, Cloud Gate, aka "the Bean," was the size of a lima.

Halfway through the tour.

The East Coast media markets and the bumpiest interviews in the "I'm a Natural" blitzkrieg were behind her. Watching herself on *Today* had been a trip. Philly had been a nightmare; all that rude blogger really wanted was her phone number. Split verdict in Pittsburgh — the *Post-Gazette* labeled her a shill; the *Tribune-Review* called her "a breath of fresh air for corporate America's stuffiest cloakroom." She hated the snide gossip columnists in Washington. Miami ate her up, and for a day she'd kicked Khloé and Kourtney to the *kurb*, baby.

Last night's A-List social at the Chicago Club was a chance to go glam with her new designer wardrobe, courtesy of the APA line of credit. But the tour's punishing pace and the monotony of the events were exacting a toll. The worst were the meet and greets, with ever-present Melanie Pike-Stanton whispering names of tuxedoed fat cats and their Botoxed wives. Roxx could easily predict which Texas-bred member would grope her backside while posing.

She'd mastered the talking points for the distracted media. Jobs. Bridge energy. Domestic source. Reliable technology. At the first mention of chemicals, Melanie cut off the interviews.

But from APA's perspective, it was working. The public wanted Roxx's autographs, and Melanie had even asked if she could sing, intimating a record deal in the works. The boos coming from the Turner Field fans after her *The Star-Spangled Banner* put that to rest.

"Doesn't matter if you can carry a tune," Ralph told her when she'd called, depressed, "so long as you carry your own weight."

Airport. Town car. Studios. Newsrooms. Reception. Repeat. Next city. No time to work out or eat properly. The minibar was off limits, especially the Cheez-Its.

The whole airport drill just sucked. Her name had somehow appeared on the suspected terrorists list. TSA fascists pulled her aside for the full pat-down every time. It slowed the process for all passengers, as the male agents always stopped to leer after the familiar cry of "Female assist!" Then, of course, Melanie flew first class; Roxx in coach.

As she packed, Roxx mused about having a day off in the Windy City.

Shop Michigan Avenue. Visit the Frank Lloyd Wright home. Get a deep-dish pizza.

Not a chance. Now it was off to O'Hare to continue the brutal, three-day western swing. First stop: Omaha (Melanie: "We have so much support for the XL pipeline there."). Dallas ("Smack dab atop the Barnett Shale."). Denver ("Watch out for the Boulder hippies."). Phoenix ("Thank God for red states."). Vegas, San Fran. L.A.! Then ... who knows?

Hollywood! I'm a Natural!

The capper: Melanie had added to the tour a holiday party back at Burlwood. ("The Spinks insist ... or they'll withhold their SuperPAC cash. APA's corporate jet will get you there in time.")

Roxx raced through the makeup drill. Mascara. Base. Blush. Revlon ColorStay Top Tomato.

Still rockin' it.

But the Face of Fracking was cracking.

Losing my religion.

The tour had been a great excuse to escape the clusterfuck in Virginia. In the minutes after the earthquake at the doctor's office, she'd made the tough — *hell, heroic!* — decision to forgo Thanksgiving with Ralph and Barb and return to the project site. Someone, after all, needed to oversee damage assessment and initiate the operation's shutdown. That new concrete sheath on the well casing certainly would have cracked. But when she arrived at Burlwood, some Bruce Willis type in a blue Grange Partners cap stopped her at the site's entrance. Didn't even allow her to get out of the Jeep. "We've got it handled. You are invited to leave. Now."

Stunned, she'd had to wait until she was nearing Warrenton for a phone signal to call Bill Dinwiddie. He was pissed. And scared; she could tell. GVR was backpedaling away from Mosby County, and fast. Grange Partners was out front now. Triage.

"Mosby's in the lawyers' hands, Roxx," he'd sighed. "We're doubling down on Rappahannock."

"You can't blame *ME* for an earthquake!" she'd whimpered.

"Do the tour. We'll reassess when you get back."

Reassess, my ass. Shit list.

It was appalling how the big-city media so easily bought into the APA campaign. They'd send a boozy business writer or a blogging intern with an eyebrow stud. Fracking was a big deal story, right? Huge upside, lots of jobs, but real consequences for the environment and for people living with drilling in their backyards. Where was the media on that?

They couldn't see past her looks.

I'm an engineer! With a master's!

She found herself mouthing the words. *Blah blah* clean natural gas *blah blah* safe *blah blah.*

Thank God no one had connected her or Green Valley Resources to Burlwood; no one except for *The Reporter* back in Rappahannock County. They'd called right after the tanker explosion. She'd ducked their requests for an interview and background about the reinjection process.

That poor Hank fella.

And yet with a day to prep for the tour, all she could think about was what she'd leave behind. That well had to be compromised. The workers and their health complaints. That briny crap and those chemicals swirling into that pretty river. Some legacy.

Don't be drinking that water any time soon.

She constantly replayed the dust-up with Provo. He'd shown up just as she was locking the door.

"Don't have to do that," he'd said, surprising her once more.

"Do what?"

"Lock the door, darlin'. This is Rappahannock. We trust each other."

"Well, I'm going away. Road trip. Who knows *what* kind of creep … a bush-hogger, maybe … a reporter … might just walk in and snoop in my panties drawer."

"Why are you crying, darlin'?"

"Town car's coming in a minute."

"Talk to me, sweetheart."

"I'm *pregnant!*"

Provo took a step back.

"That's what I get for going into battle without my armor."

"Oh, that's just charming."

"I, uhh, guess you're thinking it's mine."

"Well of *COURSE!*" she screamed. "You think I'm some *slut?*"

"Roxx, please, I mean no harm. Just a shock is all."

His immediate change of demeanor surprised her.

"When did you find out? When is it due? What do you want to do?"

"Provo, I don't have time for this."

And then the one that just might save his ass.

"What should *we* do, Roxanna Raye?"

The town car turned up the drive.

"I don't know, cowboy. Gotta go to work. I'm the friggin' Face of Fracking."

"Call me," he said, grabbing her bags. "Any time. How long ya gone?"

He'd left a zillion messages. She hadn't called back once.

But she'd spent plenty of time thinking about *IT*. To and from the airports, ignoring Melanie's corporate crap, uttering her scripted lines, smiling into the camera, checking into the hotels, meeting the Big Oily Dudes, thinking about *IT*.

Her. Him. It. Growing inside. Teensy little heart and lungs.

Big dilemma.

Roxx hadn't even changed her Facebook status past "It's Complicated."

Her so-called relationship with Provo had been little more than a series of disasters and some deserved sex. And all the time she'd used him to spy on the good people of Rappahannock.

She'd taken out a notepad to scribble the pros and cons.

Plus:

Romantic. Chivalrous. Funny. Boxers. Well-read. Heroic (Iraq). Good sex.

Minus:

Older. Lives with his momma in the sticks. Cow poop.

And yet she'd loved the antiques and solitude of the old Starke home when she visited. He seemed to know what he was doing around the ranch. He was proud of his '55 Harley. He talked about Red Oak a lot and gave her a bumpy ride to the mountaintop. The place had a psychic hold on him. She imagined Ralph would like Provo.

That was just looking at things through *his* filter. She felt *she* was the catch: Educated, attractive, professional. A 10. But her life list of Dudes Dated had only two guys a notch north of 7. Somewhere out there was Mr. 10 — the Whole Package. Provo was ... well, he was trending.

Minus: They hadn't even been to the movies. No B&B weekenders to, say, Annapolis. No chilly Wahoo games at Scott Stadium. Hadn't sat around in jammies together eating Häagen-Dazs watching *Homeland*. Did he even *get* Showtime? Where did he stand on the DH?

There'd been no chance for the *real* acid test — the catch of the day sandwich at the 7 Mile Grill in Marathon. Grilled? Or fried?

Until now, her work traveling from one GVR site to another had allowed her to avoid the settle-down, baby-booties thing. Who knew what was next after the Burlwood debacle-in-the-making? Or the tour? "Git 'er done" served as a motto, but it hardly encouraged commitment.

Roxx's own political views were still forming. Per Ralph, she'd voted for the kind of moderate Democrat that Virginia and Pennsylvania favored. She saw through the GOP's phony "Drill, Baby, Drill" crap, even though it advanced her industry. The Republican women's Reproductive Rights crusade was a load of horseshit. Even she knew *THE* best Supreme Court decision ever was Roe v. Wade. My body, my choice. Get your morality out of my reality, buster. End of argument.

My choice.

What about *It*? I choose … to think on it some more.

The tour had offered distance. Roxx knew enough about the consequences of hanging around fracking sites during pregnancy. Her sense of smell, gone missing for a while, was coming back. Her own health was one thing; she could tolerate the occasional headache. But she'd finally learned in the last project manager update about GVR's proprietary chemical package. Christ, it included enough arsenic and 2-BE and volatile organic compounds to scare 10 lives out of a cat. She couldn't see any good coming from exposing Rappahannock or anywhere *that* green and beautiful to such crazy crap.

Much less exposing *It* to it.

The naming thing has been rattling in her head. She was certain it was a boy.

She'd always dismissed names from her family as too bland, including Ralph. And Roxx might have worked for her, but a Flintstoneish Pebbles/Bam-Bam thing? Flint? Nah.

Something playing off Provo? Utah? Uh-uh. Starkey? Nope.

Small piece of Beef. Slider?

Ahh, but the *finest* cut of beef…

She'd awakened this morning with the dead solid perfect answer.

As she got to the Hyatt lobby to meet Melanie, Roxx Bleigh felt good for the first time in days.

Kobe.

Kobe Bleigh.

Kobe Bleigh Starke.

Booya!

CHAPTER 41

Wednesday, Dec. 4, 8:15 a.m.

Tip Tyler stared dully at the online headline: *Supervisors OK fast-track drilling exploration.*

A testament to failure. His failure.

He'd reread the draft of the editorial. Paul Schaefer had done his best to give it more heft, but the publisher's namby-pamby fingerprints were all over it.

He looked at the rest of the coverage. Had it only been a week since the earthquake? So much had happened. Everything, and everyone, seemed stacked against him.

Ting remained hospitalized, complaining of headaches, vertigo and that mysterious cough. The doctors didn't know the cause. Tests showed something wrong with her liver.

Marley spent days at her aunt's side, returning to Fairleigh only to sleep, then heading back to Warrenton in Silver Cloud. Maddie was consumed with her foundation's upcoming board meeting. The twins, it seemed, had reverted to blaming *him* for their aunt's health.

He and Sunday Lopez were carrying the brunt of maintaining Fairleigh. Little time for cider house duties, much less investigative reporting.

He had only himself to blame for the frosty reception at the newspaper office. You can push a small-town publisher only so far.

He'd helped the newspaper last week with some of the post-earthquake reporting, checking out and phoning in damage reports. The paper's team did fine on most of the breaking news aspects. But it had been tough sledding. Reliable sources were scarce. Roxx Bleigh had all but disappeared. The TV commercial had struck a chord with the major media, though. Her picture was showing up next to Brangelina and the Real Housewives.

He was floored by the weekly paper's reticence to dive deep into a big, developing story. He'd pushed. They'd pushed back: No reports so far of sickness downstream from the frackwater spill. Too soon to link the quake to fracking. Cut the governor some slack. Beyond our expertise. VirginiaWatch was diverted to a story about the boom in McMansion construction in Leesburg.

They'd fallen into the anecdote-only trap set by Big Oil. Tip saw evidence of APA's lobbying visit in Forster's office — a huge gift basket from Trader Joe's.

The timing could not have been worse. Just when he thought he had a leg up on moving *beyond* anecdote with samples taken from Burlwood's containment pond, he'd heard from the lab. He and Marley had sent the vials to Luray, along with water taken from the banks of the Hughes. The vials had shattered in the quake before testing.

Mosbyville, Richmond and K Street were in full denial. No one could establish clearly what the destroyed tanker was carrying. Liberty Land wasn't saying. No one knew what sort of damage the earthquakes had caused to the Burlwood well. Green Valley Resources was gone. The Spinks were laying low.

Since the bridge inferno, Tip had attempted something unfamiliar: mobilizing the tree-hugger community and enlisting them to act on the consequences. No one had a sense of urgency. They all seemed siloed, beating a single-issue cause, bound by geography, locked into their own opinions. Water this. Conservation easement that. Global warming. Deer ticks and Lyme disease. Year-end fund-raising. Somebody else's business. He understood Facebook was the way to reach the masses but that took time and required a redefinition of the word "friend." He had 23.

He'd asked the theater manager to show *Gasland*. No space on the schedule. Anyone aware of the documentary seemed predisposed to discount its findings. Liberal. Anecdotal.

The real sign of the apocalypse was the voice message from Paul Schaefer on Tip's answering machine after a day out stringing barbed wire. Item from Piedmont District Supervisor Jenkins on the agenda. Proposal for exploration. Public hearing tonight. Big turnout expected.

By the time Tip arrived at the courthouse, the hearing was well under way in front of a packed house. He saw Paul up front, head down, scribbling notes.

In the middle of five aging white men — the Rappahannock County Board of Supervisors — sat Leroy Jenkins, the ultraconservative Baptist from Revercombs Corner. Tip knew he was one of the chaw-spitting, coffee-swilling crew huddled mornings outside Quicke Mart. Al German, the administrator, sat at their right, squirming. At the podium some guy in a three-piece suit concluded a PowerPoint presentation. The crowd applauded.

The scope of the disaster was clear when the chairman spoke.

"Mr. Dinwiddie, quite impressive," said Jenkins. "Green Valley has done its homework. The economic benefits are clear. Mr. German, any more speakers in the public hearing phase?"

"Last speaker, Mr. Chairman, is Pastor Mahan."

Tip paled as the scene played out. Clete Mahan preened in front of the stacked audience as he detailed the done deal: An agreement in principle with GVR for exploration on church property. Congregation unanimous in support. Willing to start ASAP as a test case.

When Jenkins gaveled the public hearing closed, Tip hustled to the podium.

"Mr. Chairman. Mr. German. Was there public notice about this hearing?"

"Why, yes, Mr. Tyler," said Jenkins. "The usual channels."

"Aren't multiple public hearings required?"

"The chairman has invoked the special circumstance clause," said German.

"I'm an adjoining landowner."

"Proper notice was given, I believe," said Clete Mahan.

"Has anyone spoken against this proposal?" Tip asked, desperate.

"Why would they?" Jenkins asked.

"Has anyone from the medical community testified? People are getting sick."

"That's anecdotal," Dinwiddie said.

"Fracking causes earthquakes," said Tip. "Scientists have proved it. Has your company done due diligence?"

"We're only running a test," said Dinwiddie.

"But, folks," said Tip, "this technology is fraught —"

From the back, a shout. "Hearing's over!"

"Mr. Tyler, please take your seat," said Jenkins.

"But you must have read about the purple deer!"

The loudest laugh came from Dinwiddie, who led the guffaws reverberating in the courthouse.

Tip stepped back as Clete returned to the podium, covering the microphone with his hand.

"That's your science, Master Tyler?"

It played out in reliable fashion. A 4-0 vote, with Hampton District supervisor Malcolm Martin, the B&B owner, abstaining.

Thus, with stunning speed, a huge environmental problem of the type Tip once hopped on jets to cover now had a toehold in his own backyard.

On *two* fronts.

On *his* watch.

CHAPTER 42

Wednesday, Dec. 4, 11:15 a.m.

"Please say you're here to spring me. Breakfast here puts the blah in bland."

"It's not *that* bad, Auntie," said Albemarle Randolph Tyler, walking in to the sun-splashed room at Faquier Health. "I've got some of your pickled beets here in the backpack."

"Bless you. I'm all Jell-O'd out."

"Also brought you your favorite pillow. Fran, too."

"Our very own sheriff. You look tired, dear. Appears you're on duty."

"Always, these days," said Fran McKinney, watching as Marley helped her aunt raise her head.

"How ya feeling, Auntie?"

"Temperature's under control. Cough's better. I'm just itching to get back home. It's time to decorate!"

"Don't even think about that. You are here to get better."

"Ironic, isn't it? Not so long ago *I* was standing there and you had the broken wrist."

"Ting, you look better than last time I saw you," said the sheriff. "Can it have been a week?"

"Seems like it's been a month. They still can't tell me what's wrong."

"I was hoping we could get an update from Doc Rose while we're here," said Marley.

"She does rounds, usually about now. Have a seat, ladies, and tell me what all I've missed."

"Wow! Where to start? Fran?"

"Well, let's see. We brought you the paper. Lots there. The water situation … wells and all … that's the big thing."

"It's all so shocking," said Ting, buttoning her sweater.

"We're still trying to get full reports from around the county on quake damage," said Fran. "The biggest pain is having Slate Mills Road out for a month. Detours for miles north and south. Oh, and it seems your brother pissed off his journalism buddies a bit."

"No surprise there," Ting said.

"Let me tell you something about my father," said Marley. "Much as you might hate to admit it, Ting, I've seen him come alive working on his 'big story.' That man needs his journalism."

Fran changed the subject. "The Inn reopened."

"I'll bet the Chef lost a fortune. Week after Thanksgiving's always big," said Ting.

"We're AWOL from Ladies Who Lunch," said Fran. "Arva said they were going to talk about this fracking business. And the Christmas parade."

"Speaking of fracking, Ting. I'm not sure *what* to make of it. It happened last night."

"What? I don't need any more bad news. Something happen to Walker?"

"No, no. He's fine. But the supervisors had a public meeting last night. Your neighbor Pastor Mahan and his crowd were all there."

"The board voted to let that drilling company do a test well for natural gas," said the sheriff. "I wasn't there, but Malcolm Martin told me this morning."

"On the church property," said Marley. "Hannah Run Meeting House."

"Malcolm said Tip got there too late. Missed the public hearing. He tried to get a word in edgewise. Might have done himself more harm than good."

Ting sighed. "Always tilting at windmills."

"Yeah, but Tip's a quick study on his new high-tech toys," said Marley. "He and I have been researching those chemicals used in fracking. The stuff they suspect was in that tanker on the bridge. We think it's related to the stuff they flush down the well at Burlwood."

"It's a shame the quake destroyed those samples you got at the lab," Fran said.

Marley blushed. "You know about that?"

"The perks of law enforcement," said the sheriff. "I talk to the lab all the time. They call me any time something sourced in Rappahannock comes in. I'm glad *someone* got into Burlwood."

"What samples?" said Ting.

Marley grabbed her backpack, unzipped it and withdrew an empty jar.

"Tip and I are worried about these fracking chemicals being so near. We share the Hughes with Burlwood, after all, and it's all the same aquifer. We took some samples during the Hunt, but they all got smashed up in the quake."

"Sunday's people are complaining, too," said Fran. "About the water."

"Bosh. I've been drinking that water my whole life."

"Auntie, I have here printouts about what's happening in Pennsylvania to share with Doc Rose. The companies don't have to disclose what kind of chemicals they use in fracking. An environmental group filed one of those Freedom of Information Act requests — the same thing Tip filed after the tanker crash — and forced the EPA to make the records public."

"Read it to me."

"Umm. Let's see. It says Chesapeake pumped, quote, more than 14 million gallons of fluid to a depth of more than two miles ... before a blowout sent tens of thousands of gallons of the toxic liquid coursing over fertile farmland and into nearby Towanda Creek, unquote. The EPA documents showed, quoting here: "The fluid Chesapeake used in operations at the well contained more than two dozen chemicals, including methanol, glutaraldehyde, formaldehyde, 2-butoxyethanol and hydrochloric acid."

"Formaldehyde? Isn't that ... ?"

"Embalming fluid," said Fran. "It has a lot of legitimate uses. New cars. Tampons."

"But, Auntie, Tip's also turned up other gases, chemicals and what they call volatile organic compounds tied to fracking," said Marley, flipping to another printout. "Some of it goes down to flush out the gas. Some of it comes back up. Here's a list I want to share with Doc Rose."

She handed it to her aunt.

"Print's small. Need my glasses. Let's see."

Ting began reading as Dr. Rose Zimmer walked in.

"Benzene. Carbon monoxide. Methane. Explodes if confined."

"What're you reading, Ms. Tyler?" said Dr. Zimmer.

"We thought you could tell us, Doc Rose," said Marley, walking the page to the doctor.

The doctor found the spot and picked up reading.

"Ethylene glycol. That's a destroyer of the nervous system, liver, lungs and heart. What is this list?"

"Chemicals used in fracking up in Pennsylvania."

"Fracking. Christ. Pardon my language. They're trying to shackle doctors up there. Keep 'em from sharing information about patient treatment with nondisclosure laws. It's abhorrent."

She looked up, then down at the list again.

"Naphthalene. Well, that decimates red blood cells. None of these things are very friendly to us. Or our pets or livestock."

She looked at Marley.

"Where on Earth did you get this list?"

"There's more where that came from," said Marley, handing the doctor the stack of printouts.

"And why are you sharing this with —?"

The question answered itself as three women turned to look at the puzzled Tyler matriarch.

CHAPTER 43

Thursday, Dec. 5, 7 a.m.

Blackie crunched ahead through the frost-burned grass, oblivious to the post-quake assessment of the orchard. The trees survived save one of the oldest Arkansas Blacks on the highest knoll. The old tree's fall line was clean, respectful of its neighbors. Walker had offered to drop by early to help cut up the felled tree and cart the logs to the cider house. Tip had grabbed up three baskets this morning of late culls beneath the grafted Staymans and Parmars.

He and Walker would stack the apple logs and limbs for a season of drying. Some would go in the barrels to age Stonewall. Next winter, Tip would run the rest of it through a grinder to produce the wood chips that grillers crave for smoking game and poultry. Tip had muslin bags in storage with the Stonewall logo, and the Corner Store, R.R. Holland and Britt's had all agreed to sell another locally sourced product, one more proud part of Rappahannock's sustainable agriculture economy. One tree like this equaled 130 one-pound bags at $15.99 each.

The chips would be another Stonewall product to sell from his new website, once he got the kinks of the online payment system worked out.

Just call me Mr. Digital.

The website. Yet another project delayed. He'd get to such things later, once Ting and a semblance of normalcy had returned to Fairleigh. First things first. Priorities.

What happened when Madison took on the Brits, boy?

U.S. military was unequipped, sir. Poorly led. Couldn't stop the British from sailing up the Chesapeake. They marched on the new Federal City. Planned to torch the President's Mansion.

Not before Dolley Madison and the President's man Paul Jennings saved General Washington's portrait, right, boy?

Right, sir. The Brits, they still whipped us, sir.

But the Madisons, they got their priorities right, boy.

The season's chill was settling in for good now. Back inside, Tip removed his gloves and watch cap. He began the coffee-sugar combination for *cafecito* and breathed in the winter musk: fermentation, toasted apple, ash from the stove and a note of Blackie. The aromas so familiar from his first Normandy visit with Gini to Pays d'Auge and Bonnebosq.

Winter break, Harvard year. Gini served as interpreter and muse for her ciderist Papa. Tip scarcely recognized a word of their colloquial French. When Jacques Paradis used his daughter's name, it spoke of poetry and parfum.

Tip and Gini had become a couple at that first electric meeting in the Forum. She was equal parts Old World charm and modern sensibility, a devout Catholic who rose before dawn for a three-mile run and early Mass. She was Tip's first worldly woman, and it dawned on him she might show him the true path to being a gentleman. Where Rennie had been all tomboy elbows and urgency, Gini was soft, respectful, languid. By September, Tip had all but abandoned his Soldiers Field apartment for her flat at 18 Bank Street.

They fell in with a coterie of international mid-careers, Gini leading the European contingent and drawing in other ecotheorists, from Africa and Asia. Oddly, the Latino cadre from California, Texas, Spain and Costa Rica adopted Tip, the Miamian, lampooning his forays into Spanglish. Cambridge's fellowship ecosystem introduced the couple to other sabbatical journalists clustering around the Kennedy School and Walter Lippmann House, home of the Niemans.

The group moved amoeba-like, one night attending a high-profile speaker's campus visit, the next listening to Irish music at Plough and Stars in Central Square.

The relaxed class schedule — never on a Friday — gave the Virginian and the Frenchwoman a chance to explore Harvard Square, Back Bay and all of New England with their global posse. Hiking Mount Washington. Leaf-peeping in Lexington. Lobster rolls in Kennebunkport. He introduced her to baseball at Fenway. She found chocolat croissant in the Italian North End. He was thrilled by her intellect and alarmed by her vesuvial temper, flaring whenever the subject was his absent faith. When she set out alone to Sunday

Mass at the Basilica of Our Lady of Perpetual Help on Tremont, he stayed home with *The Globe*.

The long break between semesters presented a dilemma of where to spend the holidays. Ting Tyler sighed when Tip and Gini stayed at Fairleigh overnight before heading to Dulles the next day for an Air France flight. The Frenchwoman received a flinty reception from the teenaged twins. But Ting was proud to show her brother and his new friend two fine young women secure in their studies and extracurriculars. They laughed at Tip's reaction to hearing that his daughters had learner's permits.

The trip to Normandy opened his journalist's eyes. Virginie Paradis was an admired public figure, applauded as she walked through Charles de Gaulle. A light snow fell as they drove north to Normandy after an overnight in the Sixth Arrondissement. Jacques, a pipe-smoking widower, managed the Bonnebosq ciderie and Calvados operation alone with ease.

The stone farmhouse was cozy, devoid of Christmas commercialism. Gini was a devoted daughter, Jacques a mirthful and welcoming host. The gnarled trees and their tiny, bitter fruit were distant cousins to those in Fairleigh's nearly forgotten orchard.

Tip marveled at the ancient still Jacques employed for Calvados. The Frenchman used hand gestures and eyebrows to demonstrate each step of distillation. Tip and Gini helped bottle the Bonnebosq vintage that year.

Tip surprised Gini, and perhaps his newly romanticized self, with the proposal on Christmas Eve. The Cambridge marriage fed off the festiveness of June's graduation ceremonies, and even Ting felt comfortable with the packed reception's international ambience (upstairs, Charlie's Kitchen). Tip's only disappointment was the twins' resistance to Harvard Yard's charms.

Gini was athletic and always eager for another romp in the sheets. The sex, the tenderness, the closeness — that was never the problem. Nor was it language that drove the wedge. Gini's faith was inflexible. The pope is infallible. Jesus Christ died, was buried, and rose again. Saints perform documented miracles. Priests who abuse boys are flawed and can be rehabilitated, and besides, you do not talk of such things. Dominus vobiscum. Et cum spiritu tuo.

His blasé dismissal of all things religious banged against Gini's faith and stubbornness — the traits that drove her success in a government run by Frenchmen.

They tried to pull off an intercontinental commuter marriage, but aching absences and draining expenses took their toll. Tip returned to Miami, then served a Gulf War I tour as an embed with the Marines in Basra. Gini took a high-profile position with UNESCO. Perhaps it was inevitable that they grew apart. Never out of love, Tip wanted to believe. Just too many stretches out of each other's arms.

It came to a head during the Summit of the Americas in Miami in 1994, and for the stupidest of reasons, when Gini arrived as part of the blue-ribbon EU delegation seeking better relations with the U.S. and its Latin American neighbors.

The Europeans headquartered at Mayfair in the Grove, but after hurry-up sex in her room, Tip and Gini didn't see much of each other. She split off with her delegation; he co-anchored *The Herald's* coverage.

At a press conference on a natural resources pact Gini had been instrumental in crafting, she watched from the dais with rising anger as Herald Senior Correspondent Tip Tyler laughed from the back with the press corps at the Interior Secretary's lame joke about Freedom fries.

When he returned to her room, she slapped him.

"If that is the regard you hold for me, Monsieur Bateau, then remove yourself. *Au revoir.*"

She slammed the door.

They remained married, even cordial; her bishop ruled out annulment, and divorce was out of the question. Email and the arrival of cellphones encouraged occasional overseas communication. Her aid mission to Haiti after Hurricane Jeanne in 2004 put her somewhat closer. It was Tip's kneejerk idea to simply show up unannounced in Port-au-Prince as yet another tropical storm approached.

Her radioed response from the village to the south suggested she was open to a rapprochement. She told him to stay at the airport to await her helicopter.

It never arrived.

A week later, debris off the Dominican coast yielded five decomposing bodies. The flight manifest showed six passengers. Hers was missing.

Now each passing year widened the void. No remains. No letters to P.O. Box 35. No closure.

In two return visits to Bonnebosq during the marriage, Tip had crammed on the art of Calvados at the old man's knee. On his own at Fairleigh, his mistakes were legion but he was getting the hang of it.

Tip looked at his coffee, now cold, and heard a vehicle crunching up the drive.

Walker Longwood ducked into the dim cider house.

"Café cubano, sir?"

"I'll help myself. I went to see Ting last night."

"I'm going today. How is she?"

"Same. I'm worried about my bees. Something's not right. I've lost a quarter of my colonies —"

More car doors opening. Tip looked out. Paul Schaefer and Harry Warren got out.

"To be continued," said the beekeeper.

The editor removed his coat as Tip opened the door. "How's your sister?"

"On or off the record?" Tip snapped.

"Look, Tip. That was all the publisher's doing —"

"Lots on my plate. All this fracking crap. Walker and I have a tree to tend to."

"*The Reporter* needs you," said Paul.

"You're a small-town weekly. Very different realities. I push too hard."

"But you made all the difference these few weeks."

"My performance last night didn't embarrass you?"

"You were the only voice of reason. And, not to worry, you carry a lot of weight in this community. I talked to Forster. Time for another guest editorial. His idea."

Tip scuffed his toe along the floor, and then looked up.

"Had your coffee yet?"

The visitors walked into the tiny kitchen. Harry was itching to talk.

"Our interactive map showing the Rappahannock watershed will be a hit," he said. "That was a great idea, Tip. When those downstream folks see the risk they face ..."

"How did that supervisors' vote just happen like that and you — we — didn't know about it?"

"Trust me, Tip. I was shocked as anyone. Seems the drillers got to Jenkins. I'm looking into it."

"The next part of the story has to be a look at the Burlwood operation," said Harry, jumping in. "Who the Spink brothers are ... how they got that thing going."

"Out of the public eye," said Schaefer. "How did the supposed regulators *not* know?"

"You've filed the FOIA requests for the records with Energy? And the state folks?" asked Tip. "German says it's all state-regulated. But last night sure brought it right to our doorsteps."

"Tip," the editor said. "We need the Spinks on the record. We think we have a way in."

"What's that?"

"Tomorrow night. Burl and Woody Spink are having a holiday party."

"Not invited," said Tip.

"But Senator Prost is," said Schaefer. "We saw him today. And here's the interesting thing. He's looking for a fellow guest to don a tux. Wondered if you were available, Tip."

CHAPTER 44

Thursday, Dec. 5, 11 a.m.

If the clueless Spink brothers had known how badly they'd been ripped off, they'd have sent their armed Sovereignist pals to the supervisor's office. Charged 50 cents, when an average cost of a gallon was 15 cents. Even after a month, the number staring back at Milton Smythe from the Mosby County water department was obscene: 1.8 million gallons of pure water from the Mosbyville plant piped to Burlwood to flush frackwater. For the cash-poor county, $900,000. Extrapolated over just one year: $10.8 million. Eight figures in a county that has never *seen* eight figures. Enough to gold-plate the bathroom fixtures in the Milton V. Smythe Courthouse, even after Smythe had spirited away half.

Well, *had* been enough.

The supervisor's reading stack held evidence his scheme was unraveling.

On top sat Melanie Pike-Stanton's business card. He'd turned apples into applesauce with that TV commercial. He stapled the card to his Rolodex. Solid new contact with Big Oil. *The Monitor*'s front-page exclusive sold 39 additional copies.

Here was the damn *Rappahannock Reporter*, its so-called investigative journalism filling several open pages. (How *did* they get away with that generous news-to-advertising ratio?) Since it arrived, Smythe had been in triage mode.

It was bad enough his poor relative Hank had died. Smythe thought it best to avoid attending the funeral up in Mineral Springs for fear of drawing attention. He'd sent a sympathy note to the widow along with a Dunkin' Donuts gift card.

The accident and the spill, now of course they were quite unfortunate, but the Thornton River runs fast this time of year, right? Surely the payload had dispersed before doing harm. Besides, it happened in Rappahannock.

Smythe had been napping Thanksgiving afternoon in his Federal-style mansion on Main when the big quake struck. It threw him from his parlor chair to the floor with such violence his tabby never knew what hit her. Selfless public servant that he was, Smythe had driven to the courthouse within minutes to check in with his latest rookie county administrator on damage assessments. On the way, he tossed the late house cat in the dumpster. He balanced the possibility of an official disaster declaration (bringing millions in aid for the county's quake victims) against maintaining the status quo and its cloak of secrecy. Secrecy won.

He'd reached his feckless State Farm agent, making certain the company was on the hook for the damage to his mansion. It *was* sad to see cracks in those beautiful stained glass windows.

He awaited the financial reports from various county departments on quake damage. Truth is, only one property mattered.

Burlwood.

Things had gotten far more complicated when the Virginia Tech geologists pinpointed the epicenter in Mosby County minutes after the quake. How was he to know something unique in the Piedmont's geology made the region more susceptible to these manmade quakes? That's why they call them acts of God, for Christ's sake!

The national media had descended on Mosbyville, sending their third-team people, the ones stuck working holiday weekends. Smythe simply ducked. Courthouse closed for the holiday; no one available. Leaving the office he'd nearly clipped one of the satellite trucks.

His phone had rung off the hook, but he'd been able to screen the calls. It turned out those folks from Fox News were sweethearts. He'd done a sympathetic telephone interview with Gretchen Carlson, the one with the wonky eye. Others were left to do standups for their earthquake features from John Single-ton Mosby Square — sleepy town, holiday disrupted, rocked and shocked, yadda yadda. It sounded like a Kansas Jayhawk cheer.

Smythe shouldn't have been surprised by the next wave of tourists: quake peepers. The B&Bs in town reported an uptick of bored Baby Boomers will-ing to pay a pretty penny for helicopter flyovers, the only way to get access to

Burlwood and the quake epicenter.

Burlwood. Sticky wicket.

Smythe had printed the email from Green Valley Resources terminating the contract, pulling its team off the project site, saying the quake had compromised its position. Lots of whereases and therefores. Interesting that it was sent minutes after the quake. Well enough. That Roxcy whatshername didn't seem capable of running anything more than a red light.

Too bad. The GVR higher-ups seemed capable. Far more so than the replacement the Spink brothers presented to him — Grange Partners. With lightning speed, Grange had leapt to fill the void, offering the Spinks a favorable damage assessment, predicting they could get the well up and running ASAP. It mattered little to the Spinks that the Texas-based company was getting tattooed in Pennsylvania for desecrating state parks. The cost of doing business, said Burl.

For Smythe, it all boiled down to water. Grange Partners had suggested to the Burlwood Boys they look more closely at the water deal with Mosby County. He sweated when Burl told him they'd authorized Grange to negotiate with nearby counties to wrangle more favorable contracts. Grange had also provided a security crew to patrol Burlwood, hiring a bunch of Burl's out-of-work Sovereignists. Job creation!

Burl and Woody had rebuffed Smythe's counteroffer. He was certain he'd win it back once he played the trump card, exposing Woody's predilection for minors, at the holiday party.

If not? Those millions in his coffers would be turned off like a tap. The new courthouse? Toast.

Smythe had won one concession by showing the brothers the email from Virginia's Department of Mines, Minerals and Energy. *The Reporter's* coverage had finally put the whole well operation on regulators' radar, and the bureaucrats from Richmond had scheduled a visit next week. Smythe had convinced the Spinks to hit their delivery metrics before the window closed with a big final push.

The looming regulatory presence required the prudent destruction of his reading stack. The shredder at his feet was cooling; it had overheated as Smythe fed it county agendas and incriminating emails. He'd burned his desktop calendar and years of newspaper clips in the fireplace. He'd stuffed the Hummer with his personal bank records and anything else that might explain his occasional dipping into county reserves for kitchen remodeling and root canals. That stuff was going *home*.

Smythe sat here feeling he'd made himself bulletproof.

All he had to do now was let it die down. The satellite vans had left, off to chase Christmas tree-lighting stories in New York and the college football wind-down. His own *Monitor* was featuring the lead caroler from St. Lawrence Catholic — color photo, lots of poinsettias. A small roundup of quake damage would be part of the weekly police report.

But as he sat at the Madison desk, he knew he wasn't out of the woods.

All because of *The Reporter.* The scrappy weekly from Tree-hugger Town continued to shine light on news-darkened Mosby. Their unanswered requests for information on his answering machine made clear where they were going: Background on the Spinks. Regulations and permits. They were publishing illegally obtained photos, even calling for a state of emergency. Little did they know he'd helped parry the declaration with personal calls to the governor.

Smythe knew Andrew Forster well enough from statewide press meetings to believe the publisher wasn't calling the shots.

Had to be that Tyler fella. Tippecanoe. Smythe reached for the file with *Herald* clips and columns from long ago, the ones with the little pen-and-ink drawing of the writer at the top.

He sensed Tyler had a big-picture view, one that approached his own. Smythe could imagine the experienced environmental journalist orchestrating every word of coverage. A worthy adversary. He had to assume the *Reporter* would keep up the pressure.

Well, there are ways to deal with that.

Milton Smythe reached for the Rolodex and found the G tab. There. "Gobbler Buddies." His wild turkey season pals. He looked for the loosest cannon.

Leroy "Boomer" Smoot. 540-888-AMMO.

CHAPTER 45

Friday, Dec. 6, 6 a.m.

Tip rubbed his eyes and closed his laptop. He'd tried to get a start on the commissioned guest editorial. Back in the day, he could have polished off 750 words in 45 minutes.

The *facts* about fracking were all at hand. The science backed it up. Familiar ground.

But he only had to think back to the crowd at the public hearing, chubby visages nodding in support of Clete Mahan, to identify the challenge. He had to change hearts and minds. Hearts clogged like arteries with religious zeal. Minds made up by industry deception.

He had to make people care. Appeal to the Bible thumpers and gentlemen farmers alike.

It just wasn't coming.

Besides, he couldn't concentrate this morning.

The anniversary.

Walker Longwood was already up at the main house, poking around the attic.

Tip stood, drained his *cafecito* and grabbed the fleece vest. Blackie stretched and wagged.

"CD Day, girl. Let's go."

It was the Third Commandment of Ting Tyler. Without fail, through early snowfalls and late warm spells, through changes in fashion and taste, the First Friday of December at Fairleigh meant Christmas season. Thou Shalt Decorate.

His sister had started the tradition to engage the twins. Jeter was an eager accomplice and First Elf. Auxiliary Elf: Walker Longwood. Over the years, the decorating plan had evolved, but always to Ting's exacting standards. Fresh boughs from Old Rag's north side wrapped the porch and stair railings.

Miniature white lights popped on at dusk. Antique ornaments from Croatia hung like stalactites above the rockers on the front porch. The front door featured a grapevine wreath Ting brought back one January from Pienza. Fairleigh's wrought iron entry sign bore a massive red bow and more greenery.

Simple. Classic. Nothing religious or commercial.

Tip walked in to the main house and took the steps two at a time.

The same international scheme governed indoors. On the mantel, a blue-and-white porcelain Dutch village from Delft, a gift from Gini. Knit stockings from Norway. The Waterford punch bowl from Ting's month in Galway, destined to hold her eggnog.

Ting had always made a pot of white chicken chili to reward her Christmas elves after the long day of stringing lights.

Not this CD Day. Marley was with her now at the hospital. Maddie and Les had been invited to the Georgetown home of the new Energy Secretary, the one with the ridiculous mane. "Makes him look like Madalyn Murray O'Hair," Tip had observed.

No chicken chili.

Tip climbed the ladder and shouted.

"Grinch! You up here?"

"Unstringing lights, Ebenezer."

Tip stepped into attic, eyes adjusting to the dark. Walker sat in the Christmas corner.

"If you'd put 'em away better, I wouldn't have to go through this," the beekeeper said.

Tip scanned the attic's marginalia. Jeter's vacuum-tube RCA that once carried Cardinals' broadcasts from KMOX, 1200 on your AM dial. Correspondence Taz kept from his days in California. Esperanza's riding saddle. Trunks of Sara's clothing. Student desks bought at auction when Scrabble closed the two-room school. The twins' Easy-Bake Oven. Faded drapes, awaiting their Tara moment.

Anniversary. Just get through it.

"Just you and me, kid," said Tip.

"Don't take that as latitude, my friend."

Tip knew changing even one pine needle of Ting's decorating scheme would meet with a swift sanction from the experienced Elf.

"Let's do this thing," Tip said, grabbing the box marked "CROATIA."

An hour later, they stood at the base of the front steps, mopping brows. The weather was perfect for outdoor work: clear, sunny, high 40s.

Walker directed from the familiar script. Clockwise wrap on those lights. Hide that extension cord at the driveway. Careful with those ornaments; they don't make 'em anymore.

Jeter always said that.

"Careful with that ladder," Tip found himself saying, watching Walker carry the still-new aluminum extension ladder from the garden shed.

Six years ago.

Tip closed his eyes, remembering the whipping chill and horizontal snow.

Jeter had been animated as always. Clapping his gloved hands. Happy to have his son back from Miami, an Elf in Training. Drilling his offspring on Christmas at Monticello ("Mr. Jefferson called it 'The day of greatest mirth and jollity,' boy."). Gabbing about seeing nearly 100 Christmases now. Needling his daughter to play Elvis's holiday tunes. Ting refusing.

Despite gusts and age, Jeter had climbed the rickety wooden ladder resting on the central balcony. Ting, bundled up behind the open bedroom window, directed the proper way to anchor the evergreen ropery. Tip stayed below, tasked with steadying the ladder.

"*White Christmas*, boy. Name the cast."

"Bing. Danny Kaye. Rosemary Clooney and Vera-Ellen played sisters."

"Dean Jagger played the general," shouted Ting. "Be careful, there, Jeter."

"It was a remake of what?"

"*Holiday Inn.*"

They'd all heard the car coming up the drive. Walker had yelled from his decorating post at the entrance. "It's Maddie!"

Maddie, parking. Jumping out of the car. Opening the trunk.

Tip, letting go of the ladder to help.

Jeter, twisting to see his granddaughter.

Silent slide of wood on rail.

Ting, stifling a scream from the window.

Old man, gripping a rung, frozen in mid-fall. Smiling. Singing: "I'mmm… dreaming ... of a Whiiiite … Christmas …"

Final crunch of ladder on leaves.

Tears. Recriminations. Page One obit. A classic wake.

The aluminum *ping* against the railing interrupted Tip's reverie. He looked up to the lone black walnut, bare again, a sentinel protecting the newest family headstone.

My fault. Again.

"I know what you're thinking," said Walker. "It was his time. I could see that old coot's smile from down where I was."

"You may be right, but, dammit, I left my station."

"One of these days, George Bailey, you'll realize we all have life lists of near-misses and coulda shouldas. Yours is just a tad more epic."

"The Tyler curse."

"Accidents. Plain and simple."

"Everyone I've ever been close to. Now Ting …"

"You've known *me* a long time. I'm still here. So you haven't perfected your mojo."

Tip half-chuckled, half-snorted. "Sooner we get this done, the sooner we can take pictures to show Ting. And I have to prep for tomorrow's party. I have lots of questions for the Spinks."

"Meantime, how 'bout a little civil disobedience? Don't you have the Elvis Christmas CD?"

"As long as you never tell, my friend."

CHAPTER 46

Saturday, Dec. 6, 7 a.m.

Gauzy sunset. Pounding surf. A naked blond tot and a tall man wearing a Stetson are making a sand castle. The man looks up and starts to mouth something. "I lo —"

The flight attendant tapped Roxx. "Seat belts, hon. Landing at Hyde Field in five minutes."

When the means of transport is corporate jet, you can't exactly call it a re-deye. But after the final stop on the Face of Fracking Tour at the Santa Barbara Museum of Art, the Cessna CJ3 had taken off from John Wayne International well after dark.

Eight Days, 12 cities, 23 appearances. Seven TV shows, six radio spots. Four editorial board meetings where Melanie did all the talking.

A lifetime ago.

Roxx had allowed herself one glass of a sublime '98 Au Bon Climat Pinot Noir as she wandered the galleries after the requisite Fat Cat face time. Melanie had introduced her to Kelsey Grammer and Patricia Heaton, the actress from *Everybody Loves Raymond*. Red-meat Republicans. He reeked of cologne and gin. She was just plain rude. In fact, most of the "celebrities" she'd met on tour were vain or stupid. Or both.

Except Matt Damon. He created a stir by showing up at the Nokia Theatre presser with a couple of his kids. Everyone knew his movie about fracking had gone bust. He'd walked up to Roxx afterward to compliment her on the commercial.

Matt Damon saw my commercial.

Melanie was dismissive.

"Just another Hollywood socialist, Roxx," she said on the drive to Santa Barbara.

Roxx snuck a peek at the business card as she grabbed her purse. Matt

Damon. Pearl Street Films. *Call me!* penciled-in.

Matt Friggin' Damon.

She'd had no time to see Hollywood. L.A. was too big; too many cars. Smog. She liked Santa Barbara despite the GOP overtones. But as the jet hit the tarmac back East, she realized her interrupted dream wasn't about red carpets and Golden Globes. It was about *family.*

Beef and Kobe.

Some family.

She gathered her *Vanity Fair* and iPhone as tires screeched at the suburban Maryland airport.

The wan sun was hitting the low mountains to the west as they came to a stop. She gave Melanie — *Bitch!* — a parting air kiss and watched as the EVP for Big Oil jumped in one of the two waiting town cars, racing off to the District. Max Baucus needed help after another valiant vote against the anti-NRA legislation.

Roxx waved to Hiram as he grabbed her bags. The Jamaican driver was taking her to a quite different destination. Between touchdown and tonight's tour finale — the circle-jerk Christmas bash at Burlwood — she had one more difficult errand.

151 Potomac Way Road, Great Falls, Virginia. Home address of Ralph and Barb Bleigh.

Her parents had settled at last in a four-bedroom McMansion with a three-car garage — Barb's wish after dutifully trailing a husband engaged in intelligence around the world. Roxx liked visiting for some quality downtime: Naps, comfort food, eating popcorn while watching football with Ralph. Next week was the big one: Army-Navy.

This trip was different. Truth time. Ralph and Barb's little girl was knocked up.

And I'm keeping it.

In the chaos of the tour, once past the morning sickness, Roxx had sorted it all out. She knew she'd have to make her way back to Rappahannock to suss out Provo Starke's intentions. Somehow, she felt that was going to be the easy part.

She imagined Barb's harsh reaction. *My little girl. My (shouldabeen) Miss Monroe County. My best chance at grandkids. But not like this.*

Mommy or Barb the Bitch?

Much more important was her Officer and Gentleman of a father. He was the one who blew a gasket after the underage DUI and pageant disqualification. He was Proud Papa, though, thrilled to have a daughter with a master's from UV-fucking-A, and a salary-plus-benefits-plus-bonus engineering gig. He'd teased her. *You're the one who'll take care of doddering old dad.*

Daddy Dear or Ruthless Ralph?

"Nice neighborhood, Miss. Your folks, dey lucky."

Roxx had been so lost in thought she'd scarcely noticed Hiram. She tipped him a $100 as he rolled her bags to the front steps.

Ralph Bleigh opened the scrolled oak door and grabbed the bags from Hiram.

"My RoxxStar," he said, arms open for a hug. "How was Hollywood?"

Daddy.

Her eyes welled as she met her father's embrace.

"Well, I'm glad to see you, too! Why the waterworks?"

"Exhausted, I guess."

"We caught you on *Access Hollywood*. You *are* a Natural."

The Friggin' Face of Fracking.

"They're all jerks, Dad. And I'm not done yet."

The real tears began, trailing mascara.

"Something happen? Things OK with Green Valley?"

"Not really. My so-called life is a shambles."

"It can't be that bad."

"I'm scared, Daddy. Scared and hungry."

"That last one I can fix," he said. "Enter the mausoleum. That's what your mother has taken to calling this place. I'll make pancakes."

"The way you used to?" she snuffled.

"Bananas and bacon. Don't tell anyone, but I'm addicted to *Iron Chef*."

"This is the father who never let me watch *L.A. Law* or *21 Jump Street*?"

"The best is when Cat Cora smacks down Bobby Flay. He's a jerk."

"Where's Mom?"

"She volunteers at the homeless center in Leesburg."

"There are homeless people in Leesburg?"

Later, on a full stomach, Roxx had spilled the details as Ralph listened.

She began with the crazy black ops frackwater assignment. She described the breached containment pond. The horrors of retrofitting a legacy well hole. The drain pad spills. The creepazoid Spinks and Smythe. Her crew's health issues. Meeting the nice people in Rappahannock, including Provo Starke and even Tip Tyler. Spying on them. Her conflict over the "cash advance." The taping. The tour. That bitch Melanie. And tonight's Christmas party, a fund-raiser for the Spinks' PAC.

Then, after she'd showered and changed into comfy JMU sweats, she dropped the bombshell. Bombshells.

Pregnant.

Keeping it.

Due date: Early July.

Ralph took it all in, carefully and unemotionally. He asked a few questions about Green Valley and her career intentions. He seemed to size up Provo favorably. He drew her out about Rappahannock. He didn't judge. He smiled at the Damon story.

He spoke of her mother's unhappiness in Great Falls. The dream home was too impersonal. Unfriendly neighbors, except for the Asian couple next door.

Then Ralph told her something she'd never known about her mother: Her *real* dream had been to find a white farmhouse in the mountains. Room for grandkids. A book club. A big garden.

"I know a place like that," said Roxx.

Ralph asked a few more questions about Burlwood. They got online together and used Google Earth to zero in on Rappahannock and Mosby. He got on the phone ("If it's the same PAC, I think I can help there. I still have good contacts at Energy and down in Richmond," he'd said. "Time I use 'em."). He made a half-dozen calls to D.C. and the 540 area code. Roxx listened and filled in with new details, eyes widening with each call.

By the time Barb Bleigh returned home, father and daughter had plugged themselves into a plan. Roxx was pulled together and smiling. After a happy greeting, Ralph surprised his wife.

"Let's pack bags. Pick out a couple dressy things. Your celebrity daughter has invited us to join her in the country. Christmas formal tonight. We'll stay at Roxx's place. I've made a reservation for four at the place we saw on Travel Channel for tomorrow. The Inn at Little Washington. We'll leave after her appointment with that obstetrician from the club."

"Four?" Barb asked. "Obstetrician!?"

CHAPTER 47

Saturday, Dec. 7, 5:55 p.m.

Smythe downshifted the Hummer at Burlwood's entrance. Red and green lights bathed the entrance. The banner spanning the drive was crystal clear: "Keep CHRIST in CHRISTmas."

Smythe fell in with a snaking line of cars.

Took care of one bit of business.

He opened the window, handing a vellum invitation to a Ken and Barbie couple dressed as elves.

"The Spink brothers and the Leave Americans Alone SuperPAC welcome you," said Elf Barbie.

"Parking to the left," said Elf Ken, shivering in stretchy green tights.

"You aren't dressed for that front coming through," Smythe barked. "Winchester's getting hit hard."

Burlwood's garish manse topped the once-wooded hill. Smythe recalled the spat when the Spinks' father lopped the grove off the hill to begin construction. The resulting monstrosity was visible for miles around, a thumb to the eye of the scenic byway.

He parked and adjusted his bow tie in the mirror. He fell in with the tuxed and Botoxed swells heading up a path of cedar mulch lined by tiki torches. They headed toward a twinkling opening in a sprawling white tent with Leave Americans Alone pennants topping two central poles. The sides were taut, and the tent glowed from within. Holiday tunes from a small orchestra wafted into the night. Smythe entered and saw a Living Nativity at one end, complete with a squalling Baby Jesus. Aproned waiters dressed as reindeer offered flutes of bubbly.

Spink boys shelled out a mint. And they're busting my chops over a little water?

Smythe knocked back the champagne in one gulp and approached the registration table.

"Smythe. S-M-Y-T-H-E."

"Evening," said a Sarah Palin look-alike. "Milton, is it? Why, who is it you remind me of, sugah?"

"The Penguin," whispered her younger colleague.

They giggled.

"Here's your nametag. May I pin it to your lapel?"

"Where am I seated? I'm sure it's next to Burl."

"Hmmm. You've been assigned to Senator Prost's table. Table 18."

He looked. Waaaaay back to the left. Practically Siberia.

"And, if I may, Mr. Smythe, your check?"

Smythe reached in and pulled out the $1,500 check made out to Leave Americans Alone.

"Shameful, dunning a public servant like me. I need a real drink."

The woman pointed toward the bar. Smythe made a beeline. He spotted Burl Spink, wearing a Santa hat, arm around Robert Morris, the Tea Party congressman from North Carolina. Smythe knew Morris was a Cantor acolyte in charge of keeping the TeaPots in check.

Smythe bulled his way through the minglers.

"Oh, Milton. Glad ya made it. I was just telling the Congressman here about our recent interests in natural gas exploration. Congressman, Milton Smythe is the brains behind Mosby County."

"Where's Mosby County?" asked Morris. "Barkeep, another dirty martini, please. Three olives."

Smythe rolled his eyes. "Burl, what's with the seating?"

"Bartender, get this fella a drink. Milton, the PAC director's in charge of all that. If you want to talk bidness, Woody's over arguing with the caterer."

Burl steered his guest away. "Now Robert, are you as bullish on Ted Cruz as I am?"

Fucking blew me off!

Smythe ordered a double Maker's Mark and turned to assess the swelling crowd. One Percenters. Red-meat Reaganites. He counted three NRA board members. Couples down from Upperville, unnaturally tan for December. Bobby Duvall and his fourth wife, Luciana.

He watched as a middle-aged couple entered with ... that blonde! What-sername ... Roxx! She was stunning in a gown of forest green. He straightened his tie.

If I were 20 years younger ... or 200 pounds lighter ...

Smythe froze. Right behind Roxx Bleigh entered two mismatched gents. One was Evan Prost, the suave, tuxedoed former senator. The other, in blue blazer and khakis, was a fellow removing a ball cap. Black hair, white streak at widow's peak.

Tip Tyler. Older than his newspaper mug, but recognizable. Boomer Smoot's intended target.

Whatthehell's he doing here?

A sweat broke out as Smythe watched them head to the far bar. He scrambled back to the registration table.

"Hey, Palin. Who's that with Senator Prost?"

"Hold on, sugah. Let me see. A Mr. Tippecanoe T. Tyler."

"Where is he seated? Tyler?"

"Table 18. We just moved Woody Spink there at the Senator's request."

The orchestra played the final notes of *Adeste Fideles*, then a fanfare. The emcee took the mic. "Ladies and gentlemen, please find your tables. The salad course begins immediately. Speeches after the entrée."

Smythe panicked.

Got to find Woody.

Smythe spotted the younger Spink in red bowtie and cummerbund standing next to his brother and Rep. Morris. A photographer took grip 'n' grins.

As he moved toward the threesome, he saw Tip Tyler vectoring in the same direction.

Too late.

The crowd moved to find tables, clogging the tight spaces between. By the time Smythe arrived, Tyler was holding a smartphone to Woody's lips.

"Why, no regulation at all, nosirree," Woody was saying, smiling. "Not at *all* necessary to have the gummint —"

"Woodrow, please," said Smythe. But Burl Spink and Morris had already bent to hear Tip's next question.

"Have you continued operations at the well site?"

"Why, yes," said Burl. "Aren't you our neighbor from over there?" He pointed in Fairleigh's direction.

"Will you confirm your reinjection well is the cause of the quake?"

"Now waitaminit," Burl protested.

"Wouldn't the quake have damaged the well casing?"

"Oh you bet!" said Woody, fingering his tie. "My Negro friend, Mr. Jones, he was *quite* concerned —"

"Woody." Smythe tried squeezing between Tip and his now trembling subject.

"You and your brother own the tanker firm involved in the Sperryville spill, isn't that correct?"

"Burl thought it was a good investment —"

"Can you provide a list of the chemicals your tanker spilled into the Thornton River?"

"You know, when I saw formaldehyde, I —"

Smythe interrupted. "No media tonight, right Burl?"

Tip pressed on. "Don't you think property owners downstream in Richmond ought to know what they're drinking?"

"I'd like to know that myself, Burl," said the Senator, approaching from behind.

The sides of the tent began to luff like sails.

"That'll be quite enough," said Smythe, grabbing Woody's tux jacket, spinning him away.

"We're at the same table, Mr. Spink," said Tip. "We'll continue the conversation there."

Smythe flashed an obsequious smile.

"I don't believe we've had the pleasure. Mr. Tyler, is it?"

"I just have a few more questions about the reinjection well. And you are …?"

"How could you not …? I'm Milton Smythe! Mosby Supervisor."

"Good to meet you. You'd be quite knowledgeable, then, about the regulators' visit next week."

"The invitation clearly said no press."

"I'm the Senator's guest. And, by the way, I share a boundary with Burlwood. On the Hughes."

Tip thrust the iPhone toward Smythe's purpled lips.

"When were the required public hearings held? Can you show me the impact statement?"

"Well, I —"

"The state has no record of permits requested or granted. The EPA has no report of spillage from the containment pond; we have photographic evidence it happened at the site. Nor is there an environmental impact report on the dead wildlife loaded with the poisoning chemicals the pond holds."

"I'll have you know —"

"Wasn't the deceased driver a relative of yours?"

Smythe paled. "How did you find that out? I —"

Guests at nearby tables murmured uneasily. A chill wind rustled the centerpieces.

"We've made a Freedom of Information request, sir, for three years' worth of your county meeting records, but you could make it easy. Can you describe how this all came about?"

Smythe thumbed his upper lip.

"Mr. Tyler, I must take my seat," he croaked. "And all that was off the record."

"A bit late for that. Since you're interested in continuing on the record, here's my card. I'll come with a colleague from VirginiaWatch for the interview. How's tomorrow work for you?"

Smythe saw the concerned faces. "Sir, I am an upstanding public servant."

Clusterfuck.

Smythe did a 180, took half a step and stopped inches short of a pair of forest green globes, headlights prominent courtesy of the rapidly falling temperature.

"Supervisor Smythe. So good to see you."

"M-M-iss Bleigh!"

"Hi, Tip. Remember me? Roxx Bleigh. Gents, these are my folks, Ralph and Barbara Bleigh. Mom, Dad, meet our hosts and my former clients, the Spink brothers. This is Tip Tyler, one of my Rappahannock neighbors. This fellow is Supervisor Smythe of Mosby County."

"Where's Mosby County?" asked Barb.

"Mr. Smythe," Roxx said, "we have unfinished business. Tip, you might want this for the record."

With a smile, she turned to her father. Ralph Bleigh handed a fat envelope to a startled Smythe.

"This squares things up," Roxx said. "Want to count it? It's all there. All 20K."

Tip took photos. "Is this some form of payoff?" he asked.

Triple clusterfuck.

Fat raindrops began to hit the tent.

"No. Wait. I, uhh," Smythe began. "Ladies and gentlemen, if you'll excuse me."

He lurched to leave. His patent-leather shoe snagged on a chair. With an *oooph*, he face-planted into Table 11.

Barb Bleigh screamed.

The table buckled, broken glass and cutlery showering to the turf with Smythe, trapping a seated A&P Supermarket heiress.

The heiress shrieked. The crowd gasped.

And the heavens opened.

CHAPTER 48

Sunday, Dec. 8, 5:10 a.m.

Fairleigh's driveway glistened with rivulets from last night's chilly down-pour. Thank God it hadn't snowed. Marley Tyler parked Silver Cloud and gazed at the results of CD Day.

"Nice job, fellas," she said quietly, leaving the sedan's door ajar.

The cider house was dark. No barking from the black Lab.

Minutes later, Marley started a pot of coffee in Ting's empty kitchen. She opened her backpack, removed her laptop and a couple books. She grabbed her Nikon D800, checked its battery and screwed on her telephoto. She found her aunt's birding binoculars. She rifled through kitchen drawers, pulling out masking tape, a Sharpie, a battered turkey baster and four screw-top canning jars. She filled a jar from the tap, peeled off some tape and wrote KITCHEN. She tossed everything in the backpack.

She started to write Tip a text, then remembered how bad he was at checking for them, and how he kept his iPhone's ringer off. Instead, she jotted a note on a Post-it, pulled on hiking boots in the front hall and headed out. She stuck the note to the cider house door.

"Cancer. Adrenal. Can u believe?! Doc Rose to call. 2-BE. Scary. I'm on it. Marley."

She stopped at the garden spigot. Though Sunday'd shut it off for the winter, she gave it a try. The jar captured a trickle. She labeled it GARDEN.

She headed to the river.

Marley had formed the plan in the hospital room the night before, after a long talk with her sister. The vigil at her aunt's side had given her time to think. She'd read *The Post* and *USA Today* each day, but there'd been no new national coverage of the quake or the Thornton River spill. Walker brought last week's *Reporter* over, so she had a sense of local developments. And he'd brought a battered old paperback, *The Unsettling of America*, by Wendell Barry. Marley read it while Ting dozed. A prophet if there was one, Barry. Heed the land.

Then Doc Zimmer had come by with the latest labs, CTs and MRIs. She'd laid it out for Ting, least to worst, as her niece listened. Your headaches? And cough? Probably methane. It's been known to migrate into wells. Test your drinking water. Do you get yours from a well?

Biopsies of those lesions came back. Not cancer, but not normal. Sent back for more testing.

But the doctor had buried the lead. They'd found a dark mass on the adrenal gland. Potential tumor, she'd said. Small. Best option: Removal. Radiation. Chemo. Seven in 10 make it. Good chance of survival.

"Can you identify a cause?" Marley had asked.

She hesitated.

"We're running through that list you provided. We're isolating on something called 2-butoxethanol. It is used in fracking up in Pennsylvania."

"So fracking can cause this?"

"We don't know. Fully. The science is still new."

"This is *so* frustrating!" Marley'd cried. "I mean, my aunt's sick. They're running that illegal operation next door. I *saw* it." She reached into her backpack. "Here, want to see pictures?"

"Marley, it's not my forte, but what the investigators need is direct proof of a source of the chemicals. Proof those same chemicals are in the drinking supply."

"We *took* samples. But they were smashed in the lab by the quake."

"We need to be careful," Doc Rose said. "Correlation doesn't prove causation."

"Meantime, the industry says: 'No proof. Nothing beyond anecdote!' And just keeps on!"

Ting finally spoke. "Marley, dear, you're shouting."

"It's a good thing we're in Virginia," Doc Rose said. "There's a law in Pennsylvania saying if I ask drillers for the chemicals they use, I'd have to sign a nondisclosure statement and couldn't tell what we found. They're trying to silence doctors."

They discussed treatment options. Ting'd asked for something to help her sleep. The doctor left, promising to call Tip with an update.

Marley had opened her laptop to research fracking and water contamination. She boned up on the attractive engineer she'd met at bocce ball and wondered how she could be involved in the first place.

Marley stayed at it until the battery died. Her anger grew as she hopscotched: New wells popping up across America in a frenzy of drilling. Methane in water supplies near fracked wells, six times more often than elsewhere. Documented contamination with chemicals, gases, salts and radioactive materials. Farms and ranches ruined. Heavy salts. Arsenic. Benzene. Toluene. Stored openly in places like Burlwood's big concrete pond. Big Oil denied all but bought silence through nondisclosure statements with leaseholders.

She read of a case in Colorado scarily like Ting's. The drilling company admitted its fracking cocktail contained 2-butoxyethanol , nicknamed 2-BE. It was a known cause of adrenal cancer. 2-BE or not 2-BE? She'd snickered at the joke.

Marley had awakened in her hospital chair at 4 a.m., knowing what she had to do.

I *need* to know. The public needs to know! *Must* know. She understood that from watching her father's career. Democracy needs information to function. The truth. Not industry propaganda. Not political spin. You don't have to be a journalist to care. Or share.

Marley called her sister, woke her up. She was surprised, then excited, to hear what was about to go down on Maddie's end, how quickly the plan she and Les developed had come together. They synced on roles. She promised to fill Tip in. And Fran. But she had to leave. *Ahora.*

Fairleigh's forests were a familiar tangle of browned leaves and undergrowth. It took Marley mere minutes to reach the Hughes. She followed the river southeast as it curved and dipped, past pools and the Class 2 rapids where the twins had kayaked as teens. She passed the spot where she and Silver Cloud had taken the unexpected dip. Half a mile on, she crossed the stream just north of the Meeting House, stepping carefully on the mossy boulders to reach the Burlwood side. She gauged her location to be just below the well site.

She bent to collect a third sample. RIVER. She grabbed Ting's cell, called Tip and left a message. She headed uphill, trying to find the vantage point they'd used during the Hunt.

Halfway uphill, her right foot gooshed up to the knee in a deep hole and jammed against something hard. She cried out in shock and pain.

She pulled her sodden leg out and sat next to the hole, examining the skinned knee. She got up on hands and the good knee to take a closer look, shoveling away wet leaves. Her foot had struck a crumbly concrete basin, three feet wide, with a rusty cap like a manhole cover. She took pictures, and then resumed the climb.

Even early on a Sunday morning, the well site bustled. A tanker stood ready to pour its contents into the filling crater. Two others waited in line. Workers swarmed in the rigging above the well.

Marley lowered the backpack and removed her Nikon. Squatting awkwardly on her good knee, she trained the lens on the containment pond. Grayish liquid overran the crater's edge. She zoomed in on the pond's poly cover, half-submerged by standing pools left from the heavy rain. The top of a pine, likely a missile carried by last night's winds, had gashed the tarp. She snapped several images.

She surveyed the scene, trying to guess a roundabout path to the rear of the containment pond. A fourth sample, then home, a visit to the lab, and ... proof.

The crunch of leaves startled her. A pair of hands clenched her neck from behind. She gasped.

"I'll take that," said a raspy voice.

"DrillBit One," said a second voice. "We found our security breach. Over."

"Camera, please," said the first voice. "I don't know who you are, but it's called trespassing."

"No way."

The grip on her neck tightened. A knife zipped through the Nikon's strap. The grip relaxed around her neck, but she felt her arms pulled back. She cried out, mending wrist seared in pain.

"Easy, fellas! I just broke that wrist."

In seconds a zip tie bound her hands at the small of her back.

Marley craned to look. Anglos in their 20s. Muscled. Steroid heifers. Unsmiling. Ex-military, she guessed. Black watch caps, fleece gear. Grange Partners, the logo said.

"This way, ma'am."

"Where'd you serve? Afghanistan? Iraq?"

Silence.

"Linebacker at Nebraska?"

Steroid One poked Marley with a deadly looking automatic.

"Kansas. Nose tackle."

She stumbled downhill. By the time they reached the drill site, a small crowd had gathered.

An Ollie North clone stood with folded arms. The name stitched above his GP logo said "Trachtenberg."

"What are you doing?" she asked.

"Exactly *my* question, sweet thing," he drawled. "Unless you're one of Burl's pole-dancing playthings, looks like we have you dead to rights."

"She was taking pictures," said Steroid Two. "Here's her camera. And backpack."

Steroid One: "Shall we call Mr. Spink?"

"I'll take care of that."

They all turned as a bulbous figure in black waddled up. Bandaged forehead. Black eye. Purpled lips, recently stitched. Bow tie loosened around a bloodied tux shirt.

"You go 10 rounds with Mike Tyson?" asked Trachtenberg.

"Stow it. Tree hugger pushed me."

A doctor from Luray had treated Milton V. Smythe on Burlwood's porch after the storm passed. The table-smashing incident had set the party back a good hour. Just as well. The guests had been forced to huddle in the middle of the tent around portable heaters, vainly attempting to stay warm and dry. The Spink brothers refused to call an ambulance for the Table 11 heiress until the severity of her injuries — broken pelvis and right femur, not to mention the scowls of their guests — convinced them otherwise. Rep. Robert Morris had excused himself and fled.

"Who are you?" demanded Trachtenberg.

"I'm the government around here, and you are operating in my county."

"Sorry. Sir."

Smythe sized up Marley.

"By that nose of yours, I'd say you're a Tyler."

"By that gut of yours, I'd say you don't miss many meals."

"Like father like daughter. Why the camera, Ms. Tyler?"

"I'm a nature photographer. Working on my life list."

"This property's posted. These men here? They give badges to all visitors. Where's yours?"

Marley was silent.

Trachtenberg approached Smythe and leaned in.

"Serious breach of security," he whispered. "Caravan's coming. You know, right?"

"I know *every*thing," Smythe breathed. He poked Marley's backpack with his toe. The contents spilled. Mason jars with masking tape labels. Baster. Cellphone.

"Explain."

Marley remained silent.

"Madam, we have a judge here in Mosby County who takes a dim view of trespassing. I will recommend the owners press full charges."

"I'm a neighbor," said Marley. "And a Hunt rider."

"Well, there's a matter of personal risk. It's deer season, Ms. Tyler. You could have been shot."

"I'll bet your Swat Teamers aren't packing hunting licenses."

"Judge Joe Heitz. Fair man. Court convenes Tuesday mornings."

"Am I being charged? Who's charging me?"

"I'm an officer of the court," Smythe lied. "Have someone drive her to Mosbyville."

"Where's that?" asked Trachtenberg.

Steroid One shoved Marley.

"That way. Ten miles," Smythe said as she was led away. "Jail's on Main, next to the courthouse. I'll call ahead. Ask for Deputy Hopper."

The Grange crew angled Marley toward a white van.

"Grab that backpack," Smythe said to Steroid One. "Evidence."

Smythe mulled the damage this might cause his Scotch-taped operation.

"Check with me when they return," he said to Trachtenberg. "Now, then. I must go awaken our landowners. Big day here."

CHAPTER 49

Sunday, Dec. 8, 9:30 a.m.

Tip knew it was important to transcribe last night's interviews with the Spinks and Smythe. Knew that reporting would ultimately shed light. Knew Acey was coming.

But he sat at the computer after an hour of composition, reviewing something far more personal, more immediate. He *had* been invited to write it, after all. He gave it one last read:

An open letter to Rappahannock/DRAFT:

As I write I reel from the shock of not seeing something familiar and comforting, a thing so constant as to define forever. Before I could even talk, I knew about the Founder's Oak at the church next door. Oldest tree in our parts; reckoned to be 350 years young.

Gone.

I happened by late last evening on Copperhead Road, shocked to see a crew from Green Valley Resources equipped with chain saws and bucket truck and mulcher, already dropping the mighty limbs well into the night. It took mere hours. Left a hell of a mulch pile. All based on a signed contract, they said; all part of that test to see if we're sitting atop natural gas. I stood with Pastor Mahan, as shaken as he was. We hugged, mourning a mutual loss.

No more springtime rebirth as the old gal sprouts her buds on St. Patrick's Day. No more blanket of shade from August heat. No more timpani of autumn acorns pelting the tin roof.

Clete Mahan and his followers chose a path, dazzled by the almighty dollar, enabled by our elected officials, bulwarked by a blind faith in political rhetoric and corporate propaganda that ranks Job Creators as angelic, somewhere north of seraphim.

The congregation will suffer a bit, if only with higher air-conditioning costs. We have all suffered a collective loss, one as symbolic as it is real.

I write here as someone who has spent a life in the service of an ideal: The truth. Just the facts, ma'am. Documented and known. Witnessed with my own eyes. Head, not heart.

Just to get them on the record, here are a few undisputed facts about fracking, all sourced by science, the industry itself and, God love 'em, the EPA:

- Fracking's released methane hastens global warming.
- Its gases and chemicals poison aquifers and sicken us, our pets and livestock.
- It depletes water supplies and deepens draughts.
- Its frackwater byproduct causes manmade earthquakes.
- The drillers' leases screw landowners out of their royalties.

My focused pursuit of fact comes with its own blind spots. If you've met a journalist hot on a story, you know what I mean.

Leave opinion to others; that merely opens a Pandora's Box clogged with passion, judgment and doubt.

Those who know me best watch as I dwell on a lifetime of personal loss at close hand. In such circumstances, you Believers turn to your Lord (elevated by the upper case). As a man of science, I'm offered no such balm.

You Believers should know I envy your ability to give yourself over willingly to something powerful and unproven.

I've come to realize lately, with the help of a spiritual friend, that when Fate plays its hand with me at the table, it's gonna take the pot. So be it.

There's not such a big divide between us. There is something we share.

We have in common this place we love. Rappahannock County. We love its glades, its brooks and shrouded dawns. It anchors us. Nurtures us. Feeds us.

So I cross the divide and join you! Frack facts! Let me now speak from my heart.

We now see the "values" the frackers hold. Their Almighty is the Bottom Line. They are blind to suffering and humanity. The law sides with them. No wonder; they own our lawmakers, thanks to unrestricted corporate contributions to political campaigns.

If our county gives in, some of you will pocket Judas Iscariot's 30 pieces. But our loss will be forever. Already is. Founder's Oak.

No more unbroken vistas of fallow fields and blue-gray mountain mornings. Instead: Horizons pocked with rusting drill towers and leaking storage tanks.

No more silence, save the birds. Instead: Compressors and diesel engines.

No more clear streams, soon to run brown (as our Thornton does already).

No more fresh air. Get used to methane wafting in your windows, a stench so powerful you'll pass out. In months to come, you'll lose your sense of smell and taste. Some of you will visit doctors complaining of nosebleeds and open sores and shortness of breath. Some will see your livestock born without tails. Others will bury beloved pets.

As sure as little Ste. Bernadette's chats with the Virgin Mary at Lourdes, the Oil and Gas Industry (and Green Valley Resources, our very own Drill Corps) will look you in the eye and say: Not our fault. Anecdotal. They will ignore the facts and keep on drilling, baby. Drilling.

You will be silenced by their nondisclosures, barred from describing what you see and feel. You won't be able to sell your properties. No bank will give you a loan.

Some of you will stand around with your coffee and Red Man at Quicke Mart and pine for the Good Old Days. If only we hadn't succumbed to The Buck. If only our faith had been stronger.

Well, I too have faith, My Fellow Believers.

Oh, yes. I have faith that hydraulic fracturing IS the pestilent cause. Can be blamed for Pennsylvanians' health woes. Tied directly to water pollution in North Dakota. Found as the source of air degradation in Colorado. The facts back us up.

Keep the faith, Fellow Believers. But I'd keep your pens capped when Big Oil's landmen come knocking. For proof, there's that hole in the sky. Founder's Oak.

It is not too late. These *are* the Good Old Days. You can do something. Let us learn from their test at the Meeting House and see a future so ruinous as to open our eyes and move us to act.

Raise up your hands! Take to our roads and lanes! Rid nature's temple, our Rappahannock, of the moneychangers buying up your land and mineral rights!

Join me in shouting to the rafters: NIMBR!!

Not in MY Beautiful Rappahannock!

Tip saved the piece, scrolled to the top, deleted "DRAFT," signed the letter electronically and hit send. He figured chances were 50/50 Andy Forster would cave or severely edit the diatribe.

He rose from the laptop. Morning sun etched patterns into the barrels and glinted off the pot still. Blackie slumbered beside him. No wet-nosed demand for a walk in the orchard, likely due to Tip's late-night return to Fairleigh. Perhaps the dog had read Tip's excitement upon arriving home from the party.

She'd watched as her master quickly shed the coat and tie and took to his computer. She'd slept as he reviewed notes from the interviews, made several phone calls, downloaded photos and videos.

The overnight emails he'd read from Paul filled in a few blanks on the coverage plan for Thursday's *Reporter* they'd discussed before the holiday party. And Paul was sending Acey over to show Tip how to polish the video before posting.

Tip glanced at the landline beside the computer and saw "1 New Message." Then he looked at the time.

Later. Behind schedule. Parade Day.

Tip needed a shower and a shave. Needed to haul down the Stonewall banners stored in the rafters to drape on the sides of his pickup, then head into town.

On December's first Sunday, there is but one choice for how to spend the Lord's Day: the annual Christmas in Little Washington Holiday Parade. A make-or-breaker for the village's retailers and gallerists, the parade attracts families from Chester Gap and Scrabble and Amissville and even from over the mountain. It draws Log Cabin Republicans and Festive Progressives, Tea Partiers and Tree-huggers. Even RappChat's debate over The Death of Christmas vs. The Scourge of Happy Holidays hits pause for the parade.

Many were disgruntled by the postponement this year, but no one could argue with the delay's cause: the death and resultant funeral of the venerated Commissioner of Revenue Alyce Morton.

Tip had drawn the choice 18th spot in this year's parade lineup, sandwiched between the Rappahannock Elementary School Twirling Corps and Sherman Ranch's pack of llamas.

Blackie barked. He heard a knock. Acey poked in a shaggy head.

"Acey. Come in."

"This was stuck on the door," he said, lugging camera gear. He handed Tip the sticky.

Tip read Marley's scribble.

2-BE? On it?

"Is this your computer? A MacBook Air. No prob."

Tip clicked on the video. "Take a look at my raw stuff here. The envelope exchange is the key. Needs to be tightened. I gotta hit the shower."

In 12 minutes, Acey had edited the video of Roxx Bleigh's return of the bribe to a tight 0:26. Tip was dressed, Stonewall banners in one hand, red and green Santa's cap in the other.

"That's awesome, Acey! Go ahead, send it."

"I heard you used to type everything on, like, a typewriter," said Acey.

"Adapt or die, Ace," said Tip, putting the goofy cap on. "Hey, can you help me tie these banners on? I'm late. Blackie, come girl."

Acey grabbed his bag and followed. "Gotta get to the parade, too," he said as Tip opened the door. "Paul's promised an open page —"

BLAMMM!

Tip flinched as bits of stone exploded near his head.

WHATTHEHELL?!?!

BLAMMM! BLAMMM!

The cap flew off.

Blackie squealed.

"*ACEY!* Get down!"

Tip dove awkwardly to the frosted grass. The cap wound up beneath him, smelling of gunpowder, missing its snowball's puff.

Acey's camera bag crunched to the threshold. He grabbed his Nikon.

BLAMMM!

"*OWW!!*"

Tip rolled and covered his head. He lifted it to see the disappearing rear of a red pickup.

"Acey! You OK?"

"Think so ..."

"BLACKIE!"

CHAPTER 50

Sunday, Dec. 8, 10:45 a.m.

"Are you sure you're OK, Tip?"

Fran McKinney spoke into her shoulder-mount, patched through to Tip's landline. She stood on the county jail's deck on Porter Street, watching as Washington Baptist Church's doors opened, congregants spilling into the street. The chords of *Come, Thou Long Expected Jesus* soared in the morning breeze. She squinted and bent to hear. "You say Acey was just scratched?"

"Yeah," said Tip, juggling the phone while assessing the scene. "He was lucky. He's driving himself to the doctor, then the parade. He mighta gotten a frame or two."

"Your dog?"

"Bleeding. Not sure she's gonna make it."

"I'll call Bettie Miners for you at the clinic. Did you see the shooter?"

"Bastard had too much of a head start. I just caught the tail end of the pickup. Red. F-150. Gun rack. NRA sticker. Virginia plates, starting with a P, if that helps."

"Narrows it some. Listen, I have just one unassigned deputy roving the county. Everyone else is at the parade. I can send him over, take your statement. Set up a crime scene, send forensics later."

"Not yet. Gotta get to the vet. And the parade."

"Just don't touch anything. Hey, seen Marley? We'd planned to meet up hours ago."

"She left some kinda note. Oh, shit, and I got a phone message. Maybe from her. I'll have to play it."

"Go! Bettie will meet you."

Tip hung up, swore, and punched Play. Doc Zimmer's voice.

"Tip, we found a mass on her adrenal gland. It's cancer. Radiation, chemo, the whole nine yards. Could be caused by contact with the frackwater. Ever hear of 2-BE? Check with your daughter."

He took out his iPhone and saw a voice message from Ting's cell number. Marley's voice: "We've got something in the works. Don't worry. Oh, hey, guess I missed Decoration Day. Sorry. Nice job!"

Tip groaned.

Blackie, dying. Ting, cancer. Shooter on the loose.

He ran to the dog, lying on a bloodied blanket.

"Blackie! My Labradoubt!"

Tip's howl crashed down one side of Hannah Run Hollow and echoed back.

Let's go, girl!"

He dragged the blanket over and dropped the tailgate. He staggered to lift the 85-pounder.

Twenty minutes later, he turned up Christmas Tree Lane to Bettie Miner's veterinary office. She ran out to meet him with an intern and a gurney. They hustled the dog inside.

"You did good, Tip," she said.

"Should I come in?"

"You'll scare my pet owners away!"

Tip looked down. His jeans were torn. His shirt was bloodied. He pulled off the mangled Santa cap. He touched an eyebrow, then looked at the blood on his fingers.

"Ho, ho, ho," he said.

"New take on holiday garb?" said Walker Longwood, sauntering up.

"How'd you —?"

"Fran told me. At the jail. She said I'd find you here."

The beekeeper pulled out a bandanna.

"You're bleeding."

He dabbed at Tip's brow. "Looks like shrapnel. What happened?"

Tip gave his friend a quick download.

"Could be any number of peckerwoods," said Walker. "Anyone you have a beef with?"

"I'm not Mr. Popularity with the religious folks. I didn't exactly win hearts at the supervisors' meeting. Oh, and there'll be plenty more pissed off if they read my letter."

The vet came out.

"We're trying to get her stabilized. Gonna be awhile."

"Where can I wait?"

"There's nothing to do here," said Walker. "Besides," he said, pointing to the Stonewall banners in the truck bed, "don't you have to be someplace?"

"Go on, Tip," said the vet. "Come back this afternoon."

"A parade might seem kind of frivolous what with all that's going on, but trust me, it's the best thing for you right now," said the beekeeper. "Let's retie your banners. There's a spare shirt in my truck. Can I ride shotgun?"

Tip sagged. "All right. I need to fill you in about Ting anyway."

By the time Tip and Walker got under way, traffic on Lee Highway was backed up.

The village parade involved nearly everyone. If you weren't driving a vintage vehicle, pulling a float, marching with a fraternal organization, serving barbecue for Trinity Episcopal, staffing the City Hall art sale, herding Cub Scouts or directing traffic, you and your clan headed to town as spectators. Prime viewing locations along the six-block route went fast.

Tip and Walker turned in at Middle Street, staging area for parade units. Early parade-goers streamed past, hauling picnic baskets filled with ham biscuits and deviled eggs. Tip waved at a familiar face in clashing orange vest and yellow and blue Lions cap. He rolled down the window.

"Our Lion Sheriff told me about your incident, signore," said Gus Martini. "You OK?"

"Word travels fast. Yeah, I'm gonna live."

"We're about to put up the barricades. Your spot's up ahead."

Tip drove past motley units in various stages of readiness. Walker spotted the sign for Slot 18 — Stonewall Apple Brandy & Ting Tyler's Beets. They pulled in. Tip turned the engine off.

"Red pickup," said Walker. "Won't be so easy to find. Must be hundreds."

"Can't believe someone's out to shoot me! Coulda killed Acey! And he got my *dog*!"

"Sounds like you played some gotcha on the Spinks and that Mosby supervisor."

Tip exhaled and looked in the mirror. The maimed holiday cap sat askew on his head. A Snoopy Band-Aid from the glove box covered his eyebrow.

"'Tis the season," said Walker, opening his door.

They ambled toward the Inn, passing neighbors putting finishing touches on flatbed floats and festooned animals. A trombonist practiced scales. A group of farmworkers sat on a stone wall. Sunday Lopez waved at Tip.

Paul Schaefer stopped taking photos and waved. "Great letter!" he shouted. "Already posted!"

"What? Really?"

The noisiest unit, Slot 13, was the Rush River Motorcycle Club, members arranged in tight formation. Most complemented their black leathers with Santa hats or furred Santa jackets. Commonwealth Attorney Walton was among them, dressed head to toe in Grinch green. Tip waved to a smiling Ellen Martini, sitting astride a new Harley, clad as Mrs. Claus.

Provo Starke, in red Santa hat and Ray-Bans, sat on the rebuilt '55 Harley. He nodded at Tip with a grin as a troupe of gamine elves in sexy green felt tunics passed.

"Will that thing get you the length of the parade route?" shouted Tip.

"Runs like a greyhound. Heard about your set-to. How's Blackie?"

"Don't know," he said, closer. "I saw your gal last night. I think much more highly of her."

"Do tell."

"Let's just say she's on the side of the angels."

"I'll have you know we plan to dine in that august establishment tonight," Starke said, casually pointing at the Inn. "With Roxx and her parents. I've become a Foodist."

"Foodie. She here?"

"Off on some secret thing with her Pa. Ma's over there."

Tip and Walker carried on, passing a milling pack of hounds, Unit 9, Thornton Hills Hunt. Tip thought of Blackie.

Just past the hounds, he recognized some of the Ladies Who Lunch. A

young girl in front held a hand-drawn picket sign. It was hard to read until Tip
was right up on her.

I'M WITH TIP!

Stunned, he saw another placard and recognized Claire.

RAPP Big Oil's KNUCKLES.

A third, gripped by a smiling Arva.

BAN FRACKING!

A fourth, raised high by Jaye Holland: REMEMBER FOUNDER'S OAK!

"How!? What?!" he said to Claire.

"Are you OK? Fran told us."

"Yes, but how'd you pull this off?"

"That's Leigh Schaefer. Paul's daughter? *Her* idea. She read your letter
online and showed up with her sign. We all read it. Brilliant! Britt had extra
cardboard."

Tip knelt in front of Leigh. "Goodness, what can I say?"

"Thank you, I guess," she said. "I miss the tree, too."

"All great movements start with a brave act, and Leigh, you are one brave
girl. Thank you!"

He patted Leigh's head, stood and abruptly kissed Claire. A first, he realized.

"Thank you!," he blurted. "What are you doing after the parade?"

"Helping at Santa's Shed with the kids. Meet me there?"

"Sure. Oh, wait, Blackie! I'll have to go see her."

"Oh, of course."

Tip doffed the mangled cap and bowed. "Ladies, thank you all!"

They walked on, Tip's mood much brighter. As the numbers got smaller,
the units grew more important. Slot 5 belonged to the largest ensemble, the
Amissville NRA's precision rifle-twirling corps. The Maestro and his wife
sat shivering in a '38 Packard parked in the drive of B.O. Jenkins' Junkyard.
County Administrator German stood beside a replica of the Dukes of Haz-
zard's orange General Lee. Mr. Friskee, an award-winning Manx from Huntly,
held position No. 2, resplendent on a red cushion propped up on the back of a
'66 T-Bird ragtop.

Right in front of the elegant Inn entrance, awaiting the Grand Marshal, sat a black '59 Lincoln Continental convertible, banners boasting the presence of U.S. Rep. Wellington Harm. Few here knew Harm; redistricting had gerrymandered Rappahannock into his district. The first-term Tea Party congressman was off, probably glad-handing constituents in front of the Café.

The politician's pregnant wife, Courtney, shivered impatiently in the Lincoln. A clot of Harm's aides in D.C. suits stood by, all looking at PDAs, avoiding eye contact with the country folk.

Tip and Walker started toward the Episcopal Church lot when an unsmiling Fran McKinney waved them over, talking into her shoulder-mount.

"Trouble!" she said. She motioned to German to join her.

Tip turned to make eye contact with Provo. He dismounted and dropped his kickstand. Sunday Lopez came up quickly to join them.

"I was just on with the sheriff up in Warren County," said Fran. "Says two dozen or so tankers are in Front Royal. A friggin' caravan. They're about to head up Chester Gap."

"Tankers?"

"Like the one that spilled," said Fran. "All with the same CDL HazMat placard that says POISONOUS."

"More toxic waste," asked Tip.

Festive Parade Day parents pushed strollers past on either side of the sheriff's somber group.

"Any idea where they're headed?" said German.

"They ran the plates. Same Pennsylvania company that employed the late Mr. Hank Cody."

"Could be headed to Burlwood," said Tip. "Gotta go through Rappahannock first."

"Christ," said Starke, removing his Ray-Bans.

"I'm calling Jenkins, my rover," said Fran. "I'll dispatch him up to Flint Hill."

"That many trucks," said German. "More road damage. They should pay."

Fran signed off. "Jenkins is on his way from Amissville. He's our community college intern."

"Sheriff, my asshole neighbors have already put citizens at risk with their illegal operation," said Tip.

"They seem to be kicking it up a notch," Walker said.

"An act of defiance," said German. "They can't use our roads like some private turnpike."

Tip looked down Middle, where parade units made last-minute preparations. "Five minutes to go," he said.

"Can Jenkins intercept 'em in Flint Hill?" German asked.

"If he gets there in time."

"No hijinks, Fran. Just turn 'em around."

She scowled.

"One rookie. Two dozen tankers."

CHAPTER 51

Sunday, Dec. 8, 11:55 a.m.

Grange Partners had been only too happy to put out a call from Pittsburgh to Baltimore for tanker drivers with HazMat chops.

With what the Spinks were willing to pay, a flat $475 plus mileage, no wonder 103 men and 17 women clamored to join the tanker armada. A lucky 25 made the cut. Sweet gig: Round-trip from south of Pittsburgh to some backwater county in Virginia. Home in time to watch the hapless Dolphins get shellacked by the Steelers on TiVo.

Jamie Burnham, an Army reservist with three tours in Iraq, had made the short list by mentioning he'd been raised in Rappahannock County, right along the route. He'd clinched the job by warning them to move the armada from its originally scheduled date, Dec. 1, so it wouldn't conflict with some annual parade. Now he was heading the convoy, rolling south on the Zachary Taylor Highway on the winding downhill from Chester Gap. He picked up his CB.

"Home base, this is Burnham. Approaching Huntly."

"Lead Dog Burnham, this is Commander Ricky Love at home base. Call with any updates. Out."

Burnham puzzled why the buzz-cut bozo called himself commander, Grange being civilian.

He looked at the familiar terrain. Back in the day, he and his buddies from Rapp High had aimed many a spent Bud Light can at these very road signs.

He looked in the rearview. It was an impressive sight, all this sloshing cargo in 25 tankers on good old Akron rubber steaming down a country road in the early December sunshine. And one of 'em — they wouldn't say which — was "Cheney." Payload: Don't ask.

The caravan entered Flint Hill. He slowed to 35, then 25 as he passed Griffin Tavern. He recalled Fish 'n' Chips Thursdays there with Gramp.

Up ahead, Burnham saw a set of flashing blues. He grabbed the CB.

"Hey — I mean Commander — I see a roadblock ahead. One unit parked across both lanes of 522. Over. Wait. He's beyond the turn to Fodderstack."

"Lead Dog, Fodderwhat?"

"Fodderstack Lane. It's the back road to Little Washington. Looks like we could take it."

"I see it on the map. County Road Six Two Eight?"

"Yessir. Straight shot into town, then out to the highway."

"They are not — repeat, not — impeding your access to Six Two Eight?"

"No sir."

"Any violations you know of?"

"No sir."

"Proceed on Six Two Eight, Lead Dog."

Burnham slowed. The blue lights weren't on. He saw a slender deputy standing in front of the cruiser, Mountie hat in hand. No gesture, no signal, no nothing. Like a friendly detour.

Burnham signaled, turned right on Fodderstack and waved his thanks to the deputy.

Intern Jenkins blinked his eyes, fiddled with his hat and reached for his radio.

The second tanker followed. Then the third ...

CHAPTER 52

Sunday, Dec. 8, 12:10 p.m.

When it came to protecting the people and places she loved, the Mean Green Fighting Machine was not one to sit quietly.

Madison Lightfoot Lee Tyler and Les Leong had been shocked by the quake damage they witnessed on the drive back from the country on Thanksgiving. Pre-Revolutionary buildings with large cracks. Church spires in Warrenton, toppled. Shattered storefronts as far north as Manassas.

Maddie's anger had steeped for several days back at the foundation. She'd asked Tip and Marley to update her regularly via email. She'd hit the Internet, called old colleagues, began lobbying Alvaro and twisted her beau's arm.

She presented an emergency write-up to the Fairfax Grant Foundation board based on the health funders' report on fracking's negative impacts. They OK'd the plan to establish a regional clinic to treat residents living near fracked wells. She urged Alvaro to make a case to the leading environmental funders, urging them to draw the industry into a public-private, self-regulatory entity with higher standards for safety — something that would issue a Good Housekeeping-style seal of approval. That would be controversial, he said. But it's the right thing to do.

She and Les had sketched out a basic plan hours before Marley called from the hospital while Ting slept. We're doing this for *her*, they'd reasoned. For *them*.

Leong had been wary at first. This was a state matter; he had to keep his eye on the big picture. But, as Energy's lead appointee on writing fracking regulations, Leong knew the administration had been *thisclose* to new guidelines with protections and penalties. Then he'd watched his fellow bureaucrats, battered by Solyndra, cave to pressure from Big Oil's cuff-linked crew.

Maddie had worked on him nightly, wearing down his resistance. Regs or no regs, delays be damned, *some*one needed to stop that rogue Mosby operation. Stat.

She'd known enough about the cat's-feet arrival of fracking in Northern Virginia to hammer home one key point: Manmade quakes likely caused by frackwater reinjection already had despoiled the Piedmont's natural beauty. They were preventable. Continued activity threatened more damage and bodily harm. Wasn't *that* enough cause for Virginia's Department of Mines, Minerals and Energy to act? Even if Section 45.1-245, the imminent danger statute, applied only to coal surface mining? Close enough? Certainly, he'd agreed.

Together, they'd outlined an idea for Todd Quaday, DMME's top enforcement officer.

Leong briefed the secretary and his top enforcement guy, who quickly authorized Leong's request to team with Virginia. Something legal, obviously, but a clear action that would make a point: There *are* consequences for outliers who disdain government. After all, this *was* the administration that had gone to Abbottabad.

The plan lacked two final pieces: First, someone with insider dope on Burlwood. Interesting, then, when Leong told them of a call he'd received from his parents' next-door neighbor in Great Falls, an old source from Army intelligence: Capt. Ralph Bleigh. The captain and his daughter, turns out, had told her story and offered full cooperation in exchange for leniency. A couple Skypes and a conference call later, the plan and the players were set.

Second, samples from the drill site and a pair of eyes at the scene. Marley volunteered and had texted earlier she'd meet them there.

Now Les and Maddie sat in the back of the first of two DMME Crown Vics flying up FT Valley from Charlottesville. A state trooper with a SIG Sauer sidearm drove. A federal marshal with a .357 rode shotgun.

"We're five minutes away," said Maddie. "Can't raise my sister."

In the back of the second car: Todd Quaday and Roxx Bleigh. Beside another trooper up front, wearing headphones, sat U.S. Army Capt. Ralph Bleigh. "I know, I know," he'd said on meeting Leong. "Captain Bleigh. I get that a lot."

Leong was glad to have the Army intel veteran along. To keep Barb occupied, they'd arranged to have her watch some holiday parade up in Little

Washington.

"We should be a minute away from recon with BurlBird," said Maddie.

They pulled off in front of a country store. Maddie tried calling again. Nada. In seconds they heard their team's air support.

The 13-seat Bell Huey, with two more armed officers, zoomed in from the south. Capt. Bleigh's Army buddy Ken Norman, a beanpole nicknamed Fatboy after the Stock Island blimp, waved from the controls. His part of the mission: Ferry the Spinks and their Grange Partners goons to Charlottesville to face a boatload of state and federal charges, including violations of the U.S. Hazardous Materials Transportation Act, the National Environmental Policy Act, the Clean Water Act and the Toxic Substances Control Act.

As the copter landed, two deer hunters standing in front of the country store spewed coffee.

The raid participants huddled around Leong and reviewed their assignments. They were missing a critical member: Marley Tyler.

"We're just going to have to go ahead," said Leong, wearing an Energy Department shell over a bulletproof vest. "Could be a weak signal."

"Happens here a lot," said Roxx.

Seconds later, the sedans sped off, the Bleighs now in the lead. Destination: Burlwood.

It wasn't SEAL Team Six, but as they headed toward the estate, Maddie felt the rush of a righteous mission. She fiddled with her headphones and listened to the team's clipped chatter.

Leong patted his breast pocket, feeling for the warrants issued by U.S. District Judge Charity Perkins of the Western District of Virginia. They included an unrelated charge against Woodrow Spink for violating the Mann Act — Smythe wasn't the one who'd been monitoring Woody's love life. Thank you, NSA, he thought.

"Just over the next rise," Marley said.

The sedans crested the hill. Ralph sized up the scene at the entrance. One guard in a GP cap looked north expectantly. His weapon was leaning against the masonry entry.

"One target. We can take him. Let's go in side by side."

The cruisers zipped forward, screeching to a halt at Burlwood's entrance. The troopers drew on the guard before he could radio comrades. They secured him to the fence rail with zip ties.

"BurlBird, come on up," said Leong.

The sedans headed up the drive. Roxx's car aimed for the well, where they expected to find Marley Tyler.

The second car took a left to the mansion, stopping at the porch steps. Four doors flew open. Les and Maddie waited until the marshal and trooper signaled from the front door. Burl Spink opened the door wearing a bathrobe. Woody joined his brother, rubbing sleep from his eyes. Leong handed each of them a sheaf of warrants.

Two more zip ties and it was over. Capt. Bleigh radioed that they'd secured the well site.

A bone-shaking rumble announced the Huey's landing on the front lawn.

A boil of dust to the right diverted the attention of everyone on the front porch. They all watched as a black Hummer sped down the drive.

CHAPTER 53

Sunday, Dec. 8, 12:50 p.m.

Jamie Burnham encountered no traffic on twisty Fodderstack. Just as well; oncoming vehicles would have headed for the ditch on encountering the gleaming armada.

The tankers passed fields guarded by whitewashed fences, pocked by hulking bales. Weathered barns and apple crates snugged up to tidy stone walls. Slowing, Burnham passed Little Washington's town cemetery. The last driver, the one Commander Love called Caboose, reported that the cruiser from Flint Hill had fallen in behind the armada as it passed Moore Orchards. No flashing blues, though.

Burnham knew they were a quarter-mile from the village's main intersection and that frilly Inn at Little Washington that Gram despised. He saw cars parked on both sides and scratched his head.

A cruiser coming from town sped past, uncertain just what to do with a tanker armada.

He heard a marching band play the refrain from *Frosty the Snowman*.

Damn! The Christmas parade! Wasn't that was supposed to happen a week ago?

As a kid, the llamas had been his favorite part. By his teen years, it was the sexy elves.

He inched forward. One block. Two.

Nothing stood between the tanker and the village's main intersection. Burnham guessed that had been the second cruiser's post, abandoned to scope out the convoy.

A clot of parade watchers stood in the middle of Fodderstack. A couple in the back turned to behold a startling sight: a 4,000-gallon tanker at a standstill right between the Inn and its gift shop. Idling tankers stretched as far as the eye could see.

The pedestrians scattered, murmurs drowned by the bright tunes of the Rappahannock High School Marching Panthers. Burnham could see the natty blue and white tuba squad at the rear.

"Commander Love, this is Lead Dog. We have a situation. Over."

Burnham, sweating, described the scene.

"What the hell? A *parade*? Didn't we schedule this so we'd avoid their freakin' parade?" Love barked. "Can you proceed?"

"Well, Fodderstack becomes Main Street right in front of me. That's the parade route." He shook his head and added, "I don't know what happened — the parade's *always* on the first Sunday in December."

"Any idea how far along the parade is?"

"The band always leads off. I can see 'em."

"Lead Dog, we hear chatter on other channels. Units responding from three counties. You gotta get going."

"It's a Christmas parade, sir!"

"Lead Dog," said Love. "There's $1,000 more waiting for you if you proceed. *NOW*!"

Burham looked at the stacked-up tankers. He recalled boyhood weekends at the theaters on Gay Street, a block over. He tuned the CB so all drivers could hear.

"Follow me. Turn left here. Gay Street's the next right. Two more blocks, we take a left to Mount Salem, then out to the highway."

"Proceed," Love said. "Use extreme caution."

A grand, baby. Merry Christmas, Burnhams.

Burnham lowered his window, waved his Steelers cap out the window and let up on the clutch.

"'Scuse me, folks!" he yelled.

A tuba player turned and bleated a discordant note. *Winter Wonderland* tootled to a halt. The band parted like a blue and white sea. Three camels balked as their handlers pulled them aside.

Burnham kept waving his cap as he started the slow turn.

"Coming through! Won't take but a second!"

For folks standing three deep in front of the Café, the turning tanker blotted out the view of the Inn and the parade units they expected to see.

The sight of a tanker on the narrow streets platted by George Washington stunned the Lincoln convertible's driver. He spun the steering wheel and gave it too much gas, ramming the Inn's Relais & Chateaux flagpole. Courtney Harm screamed and fell back from her perch atop the white leather headrests. An aide, once backup point guard at George Mason, tossed his Blackberry, dove to the pavement and broke her fall.

Mr. Friskee bolted from the T-Bird, skittering toward the Inn. Two hounds from the Thornton Hunt bayed and gave chase. The cat zipped through the Inn's open front door, past the liveried doorman and up the stairs. The Manx scrambled into a junior suite occupied at that very moment by a startled Grover Norquist and Congressman Harm, in flagrante delicto.

General Lee gave the mayor's '38 Packard a nasty bump from the rear. The Packard went left, the '69 Charger right. General Lee's horn got stuck on the opening notes of *Dixie.*

The band director signaled *Cut!*

Spooked by the blaring horn, the remaining hounds scattered. A llama bolted. Three church ladies screamed from the Episcopal garden.

Lisa Smith, leader of the NRA rifle-twirlers, saw the commotion and dropped to a knee. She knew her replica 1903 Springfield rifle held no ammo but figured a feint might work.

"I order you to STOP!"

Lion Andy McLeod, an addled Woodville pig farmer manning a barricade, saw the rifle twirler take aim. The former Cavalier safety took two steps and tackled her straight into four other twirlers, toppling them like tenpins.

"Merry Christmas!" Burnham shouted, completing the turn on Gay in front of the Episcopal Church. Ahead, stunned volunteers selling pork sandwiches snatched chairs from the street's edge. The trailing tankers slowly made their turns.

Back down Middle Street and a curve away, Tip and Walker had returned to the pickup. They heard the commotion, and then saw Jaye Holland running in their direction, protest sign flapping.

They jumped from the cab and started running. They rounded the curve and spotted the tankers. As they ran past the farmworkers, Sunday Lopez jumped off the wall to follow.

Burnham slowly passed the granite obelisk commemorating Washington's 1749 survey work — the *original* Washington Monument. Up ahead, he knew, was the courthouse and jail, a left at the new Baptist Church, then Mount Salem Road.

Tip saw the fourth tanker turn in front of the Episcopal church's red door, just as Provo wheeled his Harley around.

"Provo!" Tip shouted. He managed to clamber aboard the moving bike, waving at the two riders right behind Starke with his Santa hat. "Let's find Fran!"

Provo gunned the engine and two other Harleys — Ellen Martini as Mrs. Claus and Commonwealth Attorney Dave Walton as the Grinch — maneuvered down Gay.

Ponytail swaying in the breeze, Sheriff Fran McKinney now stood in front of the courthouse as the first tanker passed by. She shouted orders into her hand speaker.

The Harleys rolled up and shut down.

"Slipped right down Fodderstack!" she said. "My guy had no idea what to do."

"We need a plan," said Tip.

"My cruiser's at the jail."

"Can we slow 'em down?" said Provo. "On the highway?"

"We've gotta stop 'em before Sperryville," said Walton, removing his Grinch hat. "That convoy can't cross the Thornton. The bridge is all messed up from the fire."

"How the heck are we going to stop them?" Ellen asked..

"You go!" Fran yelled, motioning to Mrs. Claus and the Grinch. "Take off after 'em!"

Two Harleys roared out.

Fran McKinney took a call on her shoulder unit. "Hopper? Long time, no hear. Say what?"

As the tankers lumbered past, she struggled to listen. Ten seconds lapsed.

She turned white. Closed her eyes.

"Got a ... situation," she said, quietly.

She waved over Lt. Joseph Elliot, ex-Rappahannock High soccer star. "I've gotta go! Take over!"

She sprinted off. Tip and Provo looked at each other, puzzled.

Sunday Lopez ran up from behind, excited, holding his cellphone.

"Josefina, she is at church," he told Tip. "My amigos, too. I tell them what happened."

"Who's there?" asked Tip.

"Manny from Sperryville. Alberto from Roy's. Juan and Guillermo from Mount Vernon. Francisco from Waterpenny. Jorge is from Kilby Farms."

"Josefina's on the line?"

"*Si.*"

Tip blinked. Rubbed the back of his neck. "Can you gather those fellas around Josefina?" he asked. "Put your call on speaker?"

"*Si, si.*"

"What in the world?" said Provo. "Hurry it up, Tip."

"OK, they are listening," Sunday said.

"Amigos, move quickly," Tip shouted. "Here's my idea ..."

CHAPTER 54

Sunday, Dec. 8, 1:10 p.m.

Jamie Burnham turned right on Lee Highway and saw the mountains. His mountains. He realized he hadn't felt this alive since Basra two decades ago.

"No, Commander," he said politely over the CB, "didn't look like anyone was hurt. Over."

Behind him was a vision of U.S. energy might — a glinting fleet hauling gas-liberating liquids through late autumn sunshine. Stunned parade-goers had cheered at first, thinking the tankers were part of the festivities, a variation of the heart-stopping Super Bowl flyovers.

His ballsy move had put them back on course.

"Lead Dog, keep it legal. See any police yet? Out."

"Nope." Burnham dropped the military formality.

"Lead Dog, imperative to get those trucks to Mosby County. Can you take up dual formation?"

"Yeah, until we hit the single lane entering Sperryville," said Burnham. "Then we take the left, go over the Thornton River Bridge."

"All units," yelled Love. "Odd-numbered units take to the left lane. Evens stay in the right lane."

Burnham eased left; the driver behind him pulled even. The driver gave a thumb's up. By now, Caboose had turned on to the highway. Burnham looked back. Damned impressive.

They approached St. Peter's ("Repent! It's Advent!") and the gun shop across the road ("Noon Today: Wayne LaPierre!"). Both lots were full.

Burnham relaxed.

"Keep it to 50, everyone," he said.

"Caboose here, Commander. We have bogeys. They just passed me. Over."

"Whaddya mean, Caboose?"

Burnham looked in his mirror. Coming up fast behind the caravan on the left was a Harley with a rider dressed like Mrs. Claus.

"Two bogeys, Lead Dog."

Popping out on the right shoulder came the Grinch on another Hog.

"No worries," said Burnham. He watched the bikers settle in front of his grille. "Holiday joyriders."

He winced as his speedometer fell to 45. He downshifted. Then 35.

"Shit, man! Hey, Lead Dog here! We have some enforcers. Bikers. Over." Then 30. 25. Downshift.

The lead trucks crested a rise at the Blue Rock Inn. Old Rag loomed ahead, squatting squarely over the highway, a hockey goalie defending the Shenandoah.

Now 20. 10. First gear.

"Dude, we're creeping along behind these Easy Riders. No way around 'em."

"It's *Commander* Love! Why the slowdown?"

"You tell me," said Burnham. "I ain't in charge of corporate relations." He heard cackles from the other drivers.

"You yahoos!" Love shouted. "Remember who's writing the paychecks! GPS tracking says you have two miles to Sperryville, 14 to final destination. Over!"

Inching along at 5 m.p.h., Burnham could see fields still aglitter with frost. They passed a Holstein herd hugging the fence row. A calf trotted beside him, then ambled ahead.

He rolled his passenger window down and shouted to the driver beside him.

"Gotta get rid of these Easy Riders!" he shouted. "Follow my lead!"

He tapped the gas pedal. The other tanker followed suit. The rigs inched forward.

Burnham was five feet behind the Grinch before he yipped. He gunned his way to the shoulder.

Ellen Martini eyed Burnham's tactic. When the other driver neared, she veered off, too.

"Yee haw!" Burnham said.

"Lead Dog, what's happening?" Love shouted.

"Smooth sailing!" said Burnham. "No lives were lost in the making of this trip."

A series of Burma Shave-style signs touted Roy's Orchard ("On the Right! Old Hollow! One Mile!"). Burnham had gone to Roy's with Gram and Gramp each week for fresh eggs, apples and an earful from Roy about the sorry state of the local economy. Old Hollow; the beginning of Sperryville's outskirts.

"Caboose," Burnham said, still poking. "Any signs of trouble?"

"Caboose here. One bike right behind me. Lotsa cars. Really starting to back up!"

"We ditched the enforcers," Burnham said. "Sperryville coming up. We'll speed up now."

Burnham flashed a thumb's up. The Blue Ridge was so close he could taste it.

He tapped the gas, then he leaned forward.

"What the *hell's* that?"

CHAPTER 55

Sunday, Dec. 8, 1:24 p.m.

The deputy stretched yellow crime scene tape across the porch banisters as Les watched. They'd grabbed files from an office cabinet labeled "Liberty Land" and the Spinks' laptops and iPads (one labeled "Woody's Treasures") for analysis. He'd return tomorrow with a forensics team for the rest.

"C'mon," urged Maddie. "Gotta find Marley."

They left the bound brothers with the trooper and headed toward the well site.

"That went OK," said Les. "No blood, no guts, all glory. Right?"

The Bleighs' sedan approached from the drill site. Roxx and Ralph Bleigh smiled.

"Bingo!" Roxx shouted. "Five of 'em were prepping the dump pad for a big delivery. We got 'em!"

"Already singing like canaries," said her father. "Director Quaday's waiting for his guys to arrive and shut it down. They'll wait for BurlBird's return trip. That's quite the deal they had going. Roxx had going."

"She made that clear in her statement," said Les. "It's all held up."

"I want to cooperate to the fullest," said Roxx.

"Did you see my sister?" asked Maddie.

"No."

"Did you ask 'em about her?"

"Todd was asking all the questions, and the deputy took notes. We did find this."

She held up a turkey baster with a yellow rubber squeeze top.

"Hey, I know that!" Maddie said. "It's from Ting's kitchen!"

"That's means —" Roxx began.

"She was here!"

Maddie pulled out her iPhone and found one bar. She redialed her sister.

Five rings. Message box full.

Les gave her a hug. "We'll find her." He leaned on the cruiser. "Good work here. Maddie and I will head to Little Washington to pick up Mrs. Bleigh for you as planned. You two will go with BurlBird back to Charlottesville. Hope you can still make your dinner plans!"

The Bleighs parked. The copter sat on the sloping lawn. Its cargo: two cursing Spinks.

Burl yelled through the open bay. "What kind of Gestapo deal is this? I am a sovereign citizen!"

"Your government, in action," said Maddie, walking closer. "Where's my sister?"

"We don't know," whined Woody. "Please give me back my iPad. Please."

"My lawyer is an NRA board member!" yelled Burl. "I demand to speak with him!"

"Plenty of time for that," said Les.

"Marley was supposed to fill Tip and Fran in. I should try to reach him, let him know how it went down," said Maddie, punching in the number. Same wait. No response. "I'll try texting."

"Dad's ready to rock 'n' roll, Maddie," said Roxx. "Hey, did I tell you I really liked your sister? She's cool. So are you. Does she, like, like the sheriff?"

Les Leong stuck out his hand. "Capt. Bleigh —"

"Ralph. Call me Ralph."

"Your nation thanks you."

Roxx turned to the reedy pilot. "Can we fly over Rappahannock first? Let's see it from the air."

Ralph helped Roxx into the passenger seat and jumped in. "Hit it, Fatboy."

Maddie and Les watched the chopper rise and swing north.

"Enjoy Leavenworth, assholes!" Maddie shouted into the roar. "Joliet! Shawshank! Whatever!"

She shed a tear. Les put an arm around her.

"I know better," she said. "With the lawyers these guys have? They'll be back for *60 Minutes*."

"Let's go get Roxx's mom, then find your sister."

In the Huey, Fatboy Norman motioned to the Bleighs to don their headsets.

"You two should feel good," he said.

Ralph patted his daughter's shoulder from the jump seat.

"Roxx, I hope you Green Valley people are more straight up than the Grange jerks."

"That coulda been me," she said. "I'm proud of you, Daddy."

"You and GVR aren't out of the woods yet," he said.

"I feel surprisingly good," said Roxx.

Good for someone who's a month along.

No boyfriend.

No job.

No date for New Year's.

Where's Provo?

The Huey swung over Burlwood's well and pond. She hoped it was the last time she'd have to see the place.

The Hughes River sparkled below. They saw a stucco church with a fallen tree and a new scar of industrial activity behind it. Next to it they saw a manor house with a white F on the roof and stone outbuildings. A herd of Angus grazed below.

"Is that Fairleigh?" Roxx yelled to Burl.

"Asshole Tylers stole it from us!" he shouted.

The copter skimmed atop the brown canopy broken by evergreens. Sere fields pocked with massive boulders and bales yawned beneath. Farmsteads with colorful metal roofs were framed by well-tended yards and trees now bare until spring.

"When we see the Thornton River," said Roxx, "that means Sperryville's near."

Wisps of chimney smoke and white steeples steered them toward the artist's village.

"I'm taking it to 1,000 feet," Fatboy said. "Hang on."

As they gained altitude, the national park and its solemn mountains loomed on the left. The tableau widened to take in Sperryville's random street grid and a tree-lined stream.

To the north, an unexpected scene unfolded as a dual train of two dozen shiny Matchbox tankers inched toward town.

"What do you make of that?" Ralph asked.

The slow-motion caravan began falling into single file as the road narrowed to one lane.

"Those look like the kind of tankers we emptied at the containment pond," Roxx said.

The armada began to pick up speed. Trailing it was a mile-long stream of traffic headed by an old Harley with two riders in Santa caps.

"Hey, that motorcycle!" said Roxx. "I could swear ... Daddy, it's Provo!"

Zooming down the empty northbound lane, driving against scant traffic, was a brown police cruiser with flashing blues and reds followed by two more motorcycles.

Ralph turned to the sullen brothers. "What do you know about this?"

"Our tanker boys —" Woody began.

"Shuddup!" said Burl. "We plead the First Amendment."

"Second!" corrected Woody.

"They'll have to make that left turn over there," said Roxx. "Cross that blackened bridge."

Fatboy settled into a controlled hover.

"Look!" Roxx shouted, pointing.

Ahead of the tanker fleet, careening down an orchard-lined road, a red combine traveling *much* faster than recommended swayed as it turned right on to the highway.

"Wow!" said Roxx, grabbing binoculars. "Must be coming from Roy's place. Old Hollow."

Right behind the combine sped another vehicle. Sped, if you can call a closed-cab John Deere pulling a flat mower going 20 fast. It hit the highway and followed.

On the opposite side, from the foot of Turkey Mountain, a purple half-ton towing a cattle trailer, unsafe at any speed, spewed a boiling plume. Covered in dust behind it chugged an Eisenhower-era tractor pulling a hay baler.

"Mount Vernon Farms," Burl muttered. "Free range nutbars."

Back on the right, an orange Kubota lugged a manure spreader, swaying violently, full load flying.

"Waterpenny Farms," Burl spat. "Organic zealots!"

The farm vehicles began merging into a semblance of single file on the highway.

"The drivers look alike," said Roxx. "Straw hats. Jean jackets. Ball caps. All grinning."

The farmland cavalry slowed and closed ranks, nearing the bridge.

The accelerating fleet of tankers rumbled near, now a mere 500 yards away. Their protesting air horns penetrated the helicopter's open bay.

"Head 'em off at the pass!" yelled Ralph.

"Look!" said Roxx. "The other side of the bridge!"

Massing on the village side of the Thornton River was a clot of blue front-end loaders, white horse trailers, red pickups and a Deere green ATV.

Roxx cringed as the police cruiser, lights flashing, jostled across the median before popping onto the southbound lane behind the string of farm vehicles. Right behind was Provo, his passenger holding on for dear life, Santa hat flapping.

Air brakes hissed in protest as the tankers slowed. Burnham swerved to avoid the manure wagon. A tanker in mid-pack tapped a bumper of the 15th truck. In seconds, 25 tankers came to a full halt, horns tooting, backed up all the way to Old Hollow. Behind them swelled a jam of hunters and Baptists going nowhere fast.

Fatboy kept the chopper steady. Roxx snapped pictures.

The combine stopped at the lip of the charred bridge. The cruiser spun, burning rubber, halting astride the highway between the disparate fleets.

Behind the tankers, the fantail of cursing motorists grew longer by the second.

A small helicopter zoomed overhead, startling Roxx. WTTG. Fox 5.

"There's another," said Fatboy, pointing to a blue ABC 7 copter. "I'm putting this baby down."

CHAPTER 56

Sunday, Dec. 8, 1:45 p.m.

Lt. Joseph Elliot flung the cruiser's door open and ran to the vintage Harley.

Tip let go of Provo Starke's torso and swung his leg off.

"Where's the sheriff?" Tip said.

"You are two crazy bastards!" Elliot shouted, his smirk a betrayal. "But until other units show up? You're my deputies. Raise your right hands real quick."

Two hands shot up.

"Santa One? Santa Two? You are Rappahannock County deputies."

"Fran sure shot off quick, Joe," said Tip.

"She got some call," said Elliot. "Last I saw, she was bolting in the other direction."

Elliot walked past a yellow diamond-shaped road sign bearing the silhouette of a tractor and a warning: NEXT 2 MILES.

Trailed by Tip and Provo, Elliot approached the lead tanker. "Engine off!" he yelled.

"Hey, it's Joey!" said Burnham, smiling. "Joey Elliot! Remember me? From high school?"

"Engines off," said Elliot. "*NOW!*"

Burnham's grin faded. He hesitated, and then relayed the message over the CB. The decibel level dropped except for the din of impatient traffic.

"License and registration," said Elliot. "Let me see your waybill, too."

"What for?" said Burnham. "It's only brackish water."

"Step down, please. Deputies, have the drivers bring license, registration and ICC docs over to the cruiser."

"Just heading to Mosby, Joey," said Burnham, sheepish.

"Not anymore. And it's Lieutenant Elliot."

Acey Youngblood sprinted from the direction of the traffic, gauze wrapping his shoulder.

"You charging us with something?" said Burnham.

"I want full cooperation," said Elliot. "Got it?"

The photographer climbed atop the tanker behind Burnham's to snap the scene: tanker in the foreground; the motley assortment of farm vehicles, their drivers cheering; charred girders of the bridge; the rusty jam-up on the other side. The focal point: an ironic yellow road sign.

"What'd we do anyway?" said Burnham, leaning on the cruiser's hood.

"That's up to the judge," Elliot said. "If you're carrying carcinogenic and radioactive materials without a Hazardous Materials Endorsement, that's a violation. Minimum civil penalty $5,000. Maximum up to $25,000. Failure to pay means a suspended license."

"License?" Burnham's voice trailed off.

"Oh, and speeding," said Elliot.

"Waitaminit!"

"My intern had you going 25 up in Flint Hill."

"Since when is 25 speeding?"

"Church Zones are 15 on Sunday. New law here in Rappahannock. You've been away."

The news copters hovered, their hopes of a live, O.J. Simpson-style chase dashed. The images showed a half-dozen farmworkers astride tractor seats, leaning out cab windows, whipping their ball caps. Two dozen people clustered around a police cruiser, hands on hood like contestants in a car-lot marathon, guarded by two men in Santa caps.

Acey sidled up to Tip to show him an image that would dominate VirginiaWatch and *The Reporter's* next front page. The AP version would appear in thousands of newspapers and websites around the globe. The following April, it would win the Pulitzer Prize for breaking-news photography.

Walker and Sunday Lopez walked up from the direction of the snarled traffic.

"Your truck's back a ways," Walker said. "Mighta lost one of your banners on Mount Salem."

"Josefina, she wants to know. Did it work?"

"See for yourself," said Tip, pointing to the phalanx of farmware. "*Muchas gracias!*"

Roxx and Ralph Bleigh hopped out of the Huey, rotors still swooshing, in front of the red schoolhouse. They spotted Maddie Tyler and Les Leong running across the bridge.

"We saw the whole thing!" Maddie shouted.

They jogged toward the cruiser. Maddie got there first and eyed her father's sorry-looking cap.

"I *thought* that was you," she said. "That was really something. How'd they manage all this?"

"My thinkin' buddy here!" said Provo, pounding Tip's shoulder. "His idea."

"Not bad for an old journalist," said Walker.

"Thank you." Tip turned to Maddie. "I checked texts waiting for the parade to start … you were on some … mission?"

"Burlwood's shut down," said Roxx. "We're headed to Charlottesville to book the Spink brothers and the Grange Partners crew."

"Any word on Smythe?" Tip asked.

"Smythe? Mosby supervisor?" said Walker.

"That's the one."

"Vamoosed," said Roxx.

Maddie hesitated, then took two strides toward Tip. She surprised him with a hug. "Know what?" she said. "This saved a lot of lives. That's no accident."

Provo walked up behind Roxx and her father. She turned as he removed his Santa hat.

"Pleased to see you again, ma'am. Sir, I'm Provo Starke. I've been squiring your daughter. If dinner up there at the Inn is still on, I promise to provide gentlemanly service and conversation."

"Pleased to meet you. May I call you Provo? Sounds like we have some active duty tales to swap."

"Look forward to it," Provo said. "Sir, a word with your daughter?"

Provo steered Roxx to the side. "This whole thing's got me thinking …"

"Provo. I … it's just … so much on my mind —"

"… about our developing situation," he said, glancing at her belly.

"I have so many questions. So much I don't know about you."

"Like what?" he said, pulling back.

"Here's one," she said. "A deal breaker."

"Ooo-K," Provo said. He removed the Ray-Bans.

"Fish sandwich, fresh caught. Grilled or fried?"

Starke stroked his mustache. "Grilled."

She smiled for the first time.

Provo grabbed her waist, serious.

"Got one for you. Boy or girl?"

She looked at her father. "I think it's time I tell him, Daddy."

"Your call, sweetheart."

"Well, Mr. Provo Starke, it's … both!"

"What?! How's that? You mean?"

"Twins! A cowboy and a little lady engineer!"

The mustache failed to hide the grin as Provo bent to kiss her.

"I was just getting used to callin' you Miss Natural Gas," he said. "But I've got a new 'un."

"You do?"

"Momma Fracker."

She slugged his bicep, indignant.

"That's just … that's so … that's kinda sweet!"

"What next, darlin'? How can I make right by this?"

"How about a proper date?" she said, undistracted by the swirl around them. "Or two or three?"

Jamie Burnham, watching from Elliot's hood, yelled above the horns and helicopters.

"What about our trucks?"

Elliot gave a steely look. "Volunteer fire departments are coming. They'll park 'em for now at this schoolhouse. We'll take samples of your cargo."

The lieutenant gestured to his freshly minted deputies.

"Thanks, fellas."

His shoulder-mount chirped. "Excuse me, folks," he said, stepping aside.

Tip grinned as the beaming farmworkers came up. "Amigos! You gentlemen saved our bacon!"

"They have names," said Sunday. "Guillermo. Juan. Alberto. Jorge. Francisco. Jose."

Tip shook their hands, looking them in the eye, repeating each name.

Elliot returned.

"That was the sheriff. She's leaving Mosbyville. That call she got? A former Rapp deputy at the jail there. Some brunette was being held as a person of interest. Said she was from up here."

"Marley!" Maddie gasped.

CHAPTER 57

Sunday, Dec. 8, 3:30 p.m.

"A winery?" Tip, panting, asked Walker as they reached the pickup, parked beyond Old Hollow. Sunday squeezed in beside the beekeeper on the cracked leather seat. "What about my dog? And I guess I have to track down Smythe."

"The vet will call," Walker said. "See if we can head in the direction of Orange County."

"Why Orange?" Tip asked.

"The Dalai Lama's favorite color," he said. "Let me tell you a story …"

Traffic on Lee Highway snaked single file around the tankers. Tip drove on the shoulder until they hit Water Street, the back road into Sperryville. The beekeeper reeled out his suspicions. He recounted the conversation among Roxx, Smythe and the Spink brothers that he'd overheard back in October at Thornton River Grille.

Tip and Walker dropped Sunday off at his church and watched him hug Josefina. They stopped at the Longwood home, trading the Studebaker for Walker's panel truck.

The half-hour drive took them through Rappahannock and Mosby counties to Highway 29, then over to Orange, past the entrance to Madison's Montpelier. Tip described the flying bullets at the cider house and the grass-roots fracking protest. They replayed the workers' flying wedge.

By the time the bee truck pulled into Barboursville, the sun was high in a bright December sky. They parked well away from the entrance, keeping a clear view. Mercedeses and Porsches bearing D.C.'s patriotic plates ("Taxation Without Representation") filled the lot. Conspicuous were two dusty vehicles side by side: A black Hummer and a faded red F-150.

"Hey!" said Tip. "I think —"

"You hang back," said Walker. "They might recognize you."

Tip studied the pickup as his friend entered the gabled tasting room. License plate started with P. NRA sticker. He took a photo with his iPhone and texted it to Fran McKinney.

Walker returned, poking his head in Tip's window.

"It's them."

"They see you?"

"Nope."

The beekeeper walked over to test the Hummer's passenger door. It opened. No alarm.

"Good. Come with me."

He opened the panel truck's rear and demonstrated how to secure the mesh over face and hands. Tip smiled hearing the next steps.

They were done in three minutes. Tip returned to the panel truck and waited as Longwood headed back to the tasting room.

Walker emerged in 10 minutes with a two-pack of wine. He sauntered to his truck and sat behind the wheel.

"They made me. Watch this."

The tasting room's doors flew open. Out stumbled Smythe. Behind him, a big-bellied sort in camo.

"Boomer Smoot," said Tip. "One of the Quicke Mart crowd."

Smythe jerked the Hummer's door open and climbed in. Smoot took the passenger's side. The Hummer roared to a start.

Walker Longwood smiled sideways.

The Hummer rolled in reverse for five feet. Stopped. It began rocking back and forth. With a screech and groan of asphalt, it lurched forward, crunching an XKE, setting off a car alarm.

"My bees, they don't like loud noises."

"Or sudden moves, apparently."

Even over the sound of the alarm, they could hear muffled cries behind the darkened windows.

"Each hive holds up to 30,000 in the winter," Walker said. "They are quiet until one gets angry. Then they *all* get angry."

An excerpt from the next novel in the series ...

CHAPTER 1 of *Along Came a Cider*

Tuesday, Dec. 24, 8:45 p.m.

That's when those blue memories start calling ...

The chime from Fairleigh's front door interrupted Elvis. *Blue Christmas.* Blackie barked from her bed in the foyer.

Dolley Paine Madison Tyler moved to rise from her wing chair beside the Rumford fireplace. "Who could that be? On Christmas Eve?"

"Aunt Ting, stay," said Marley Tyler. "You just came home yesterday! Let's go see, Mads."

Marley rose from the leather couch, hand leveraged on Fran McKinney's muscled thigh. Les Leong offered a hand to Madison Tyler, Marley's twin, at the fireplace bench. She refused it.

"We'll talk," she whispered.

"I swear, this place is Grand Central," said Ting, tartan blanket swaddling her lap and legs.

She watched as Walker Longwood, lost in thought, stood before the decorated Douglas fir. He reached easily to a high bough to straighten a delicate bulb.

"That one's from Uzbekistan," said Ting. "Nice to have a useful man around here."

"Hey, I resemble that remark," said her brother, raising a head from the Turkish rug where he'd plopped down to enjoy the blaze. "We fellas made dinner tonight."

"The cioppino *was* superb," said the matriarch. "Family recipe, Les?"

"All San Fran with a hint of Chinatown. Rappahannock County ingredients, though."

"Hey, how many guys *you* know can make sourdough? " said Tippecanoe Tazwell Tyler, a tad defensive. "From scratch? In my little kitchen?"

"I'm still cruising on the baklava from King Bee there," Fran said. She wore her blonde hair down, elegant in a red cabled sweater, leggings and long black boots.

"You were born to wear those," said Claire Hargadon, idly sketching the parlor scene.

"If I were still sheriff, I could make 'em mandatory," Fran said.

"The petitions make it clear," said Tip. "The people want you back."

"For the last time," Fran said. "I put personal matters ahead of professional when I went to spring Marley. The second I did, I'd made my choice."

Les read the shifting mood. "The snow's so beautiful. Bet that driveway's slippery by now."

"Marley and I are still going to Midnight Mass," said Fran. "My Subaru'll get there."

"I'd like to go, too," said Claire. "Dinner was grand. Maybe you could drop me off after Mass?"

"I'd forgotten you were Catholic," said Tip, swirling a Christmas mug of Stonewall, his artisanal apple brandy.

"Lapsed," said the redhead, closing her sketchpad. "But there's only one Midnight Mass."

"Say a prayer for me, Claire," said Ting.

"You are doing quite well for someone just out of surgery," said Walker.

"I just want to be healthy for my January swing. Then they'll start chemo. Only way I'd agree."

It had been a whirlwind two weeks since the Sunday everyone still talked about. The lead editorial in *The Reporter* had captured the community's joyous mood: *Rappahannock 1, Fracking 0*. The main section was devoted to the vanquished tanker fleet — *Showdown at Sperryville*. A second section was all about the parade.

The governor finally showed backbone, calling up the Virginia National Guard to drive the impounded tankers to reinjection wells in Akron. With the blessing of the Fairfax Grant Foundation board, Maddie Tyler had agreed to head a commission to draft legislation regulating hydraulic fracturing in the Old Dominion, complete with full transparency about the chemicals used.

Todd Quaday had calculated the cost of remediating the Rappahannock watershed, from the headwaters all the way to the sea, at north of $240 million. Fixing the torched bridge would take VDOT $12 million and nine years. It was VDOT, after all.

The Spink brothers were keeping three white-shoe law firms busy sorting through the raft of charges for running the outlaw well site at Burlwood, their adjacent Mosby County estate. Marley Tyler's stumbling discovery of the unknown second dry hole at Burlwood was a missing piece; turns out its abandoned shaft created the pathway the frackwater followed up to taint the Piedmont aquifer. State health officials now had a direct cause for the chemical poisonings, headaches and rashes suffered by Ting Tyler and others. The most damning evidence? The 80 percent dilute contents of Tanker 15, aka "Cheney."

Though it had agreed to provide fresh water to landowners in a 15-mile radius of Burlwood for two years, the American Petroleum Association was still touting fracking's safety. A new campaign ran nationwide. Melanie Pike-Stanton herself coined the tagline: "Trust Us, We Care."

The Bleighs were spending the holiday at Red Oak Ranch with their daughter and hosts Provo and Momma Starke. Roxx Bleigh and Provo sported tans from last week's trip to the Florida Keys, where Provo acquitted himself well — twice. First, at the 7 Mile Grill in Marathon. Fish sandwich. Grilled. Second, at Louie's Backyard on Waddell Street in Key West, where Roxx's Key Lime pie came dressed with an engagement diamond. Roxx was rethinking the name sh

Milton Smythe, swollen to twice his normal girth, was spending a solitary holiday in traction at Inova Fairfax Hospital, legs broken when his Hummer's airbags failed to deploy.

Boomer Smoot, who couldn't handle the shock of thousands of bee stings, would be buried up Gid Brown Hollow only after the serviceberries signaled spring's thaw. The assassin's service at Hannah Run Meeting House, Cletus Mahan presiding, drew two Woodchucks and Tip Tyler.

Tip Tyler, who'd fallen to his knees when Fran arrived home at Fairleigh well after the Parade Day hullaballoo with Marley Tyler safely sprung from the Mosby jail.

Tip Tyler, a name synonymous with fracking opposition. I'M WITH TIP signs pockmarked Rappahannock County byways. Green Valley Resources had swiftly called their landmen and drillers back home after the tanker debacle. Provo told Tip that the Bleigh family had anonymously donated the 18-foot oak newly planted in the Meeting House yard beside the yawning stump.

Tip Tyler, resolved to enter a new year free of the curse of His Accidency.

Tip Tyler, weighing feelings for Claire against the void of Gini Paradis's presumed death.

Tip Tyler, who wanted nothing more than to retreat to the must of his cider house. This gentleman watchdog stuff can get ugly.

"Tip, come quick!" It was Maddie, trembling. Not from the cold.

"What is it?" said Tip, hustling to rise.

Frigid air and fat flakes gusted past the open door. A stunning brunette in a tiny black cocktail dress stood at the threshold.

The Croatian Sensation, Tip thought. *The provost's wife.*

Mrs. Laurent Mazloff — native of Hvar, founder of the acclaimed camp for young thespians in Castleton View — teetered, jostling an opened bottle of Tip's Stonewall, her lips the color of merlot.

"Natalia!?" said Tip.

She staggered, sloshing Tip's corduroys with the artisanal brandy. Her black eyes bulged.

"*You! ... You!* ... You have *keeled* me!"

She collapsed, landing heavily on a very bandaged, very startled Labradoubt.

AFTERWORD

Mother Fracker is an act of fiction, a cautionary tale. It is inspired, in part, by a conversation with a respected foundation executive in Pennsylvania who introduced me one afternoon in 2010 to the rise of the Marcellus Shale and her unmitigated fear for the state's future.

Here in pristine Rappahannock County, Va., my neighbors can rest easy that the perfect storm of environmental horrors imagined in the preceding pages could not happen. For now. Local officials, some of Virginia's best, long ago had the foresight to enact a comprehensive plan that values agriculture, land conservation and natural resources above development and economic gain. That plan, frankly, remains only as good as the next challenge over the horizon.

Alas, our good fortune has not been shared by residents of Pennsylvania, North Dakota, Texas, Ohio, Wyoming and elsewhere in the United States who coexist daily with the environmental and health consequences of drilling for natural gas. Rappahannock and its fictitious neighbor, Mosby County, do not sit robustly athwart the Marcellus Shale, as does much of the Keystone State. I hope that means we are of no interest to Big Oil and Gas. Uncomfortably, that can't be said for the Shenandoah Valley and the George Washington National Forest to our west. Perish the thought of industrializing these natural gems with fracking towers and containment ponds. As a board member for a local environmental nonprofit, I work to keep it that way. Don't get any ideas, fellers. Git 'er done someplace else. Better yet, invest in alternative sources like the proposed wind field off the Virginia coast.

When I began this novel Jan. 1, 2012, I saw fracking as an isolated issue, below the radar and beneath the fold. Since then, it has spread like wildfire into statehouses in Albany, Raleigh and Sacramento, as America revels in the development of an energy source that *promises* jobs, cleaner air and reduced dependence on foreign sources of fossil fuels. But natural gas is not a limitless resource. In their support for the development of gas drilling, past and present administrations and the Environmental Protection Agency have not done enough to study the long-term consequences of hydrologic fracturing on our water supplies, surrounding lands and our health (two- and four-legged varieties included). The oil and gas industry must join in and learn from rigorous, unbiased studies and, at minimum, adopt self-regulation. Start with full transparency about the chemicals used in the process and an honest assessment of fracking's impact on the faults and fissures beneath us.

I have high regard for the journalists who strive to tell the story of fracking and its impact in the face of adversity, tilting at an industry with gilt pockets and sharp elbows. In particular, Pro Publica deserves my praise and your attention.

My friends and family network includes respected engineers, elected officials, administrators, lawyers, educators, ranchers, journalists, restaurateurs, real estate agents, strategic communicators and regular Joes and Janes. Rest assured, none of you are models for (or targets of) the kinds of salacious behaviors described in the preceding pages. Not one of you. And to my poker club pals, no, you won't get laid in the next book.

Larry *Bud* Meyer
Washington, Va.
Sept. 9, 2013

ACKNOWLEDGEMENTS

I've only just begun a love affair with Rappahannock County. Thanks go to those who've welcomed me: Kaye and Rick and Andrew Kohler, Jan and Ron and Josh Makela, Dave and Cathie Cody Shiff, Jim and Caroline Manwaring, Bill and Aleta Gadino, Jim and Liz Blubaugh, Larry and Kathy Grove, Jeff and Paula Christie, Roger Piantadosi, Walter Nicklin, Dennis Brack, Alex Sharp VIII, John McCarthy, Peter and Susan Hornboestel, good neighbors Mike and Bette Mahoney, Roger Welch, Spots Williams, Frank Raiter and Barb Kavanagh, Kate Wofford, Cole Johnson, Robert and Joan Ballard, Judy Tole.

Thank you to my friends and family readers. You all kicked my skinny little butt and made this work far more readable. Special props to Dr. Claire Meyer Waldron, whose Ph.D. should be in editing fiction.

Thanks and kudos, in no particular order, to:

Bob Morris, our spiritual advisor now plowing fertile fields as a Story Farmer. Mr. Morris brought out the True Floridian in me.

Doug Warren, who slogged through the earliest draft, then gave the kind of objective feedback I needed to take this thing seriously.

Doug Root, my kind of guy, who welcomed me to Pittsburgh where this all started.

Dave Lawrence, the most tireless champion ever. I'm a better man for having worked with him. And Florida's kids have a better future with him at the helm.

Scott Meyer, my grandfather, self-published author and gentleman farmer. His $25 loan fronted my first portable typewriter and launched a career. If there's an inspiration for Tip Tyler, it's Granddaddy.

My late parents, Bill and Joan Meyer, who gave a supportive push out the door.

My siblings. You inspire and motivate and challenge: Jennie McCafferty, Claire Waldron, Beth Meyer, Scott Meyer, Louis Meyer (I really do love engineers), Martin Meyer and rock star Jeanne Meyer. Also, for help and inspiration: Dr. Don Waldron. Ellie Meyer. Maddie Meyer. Art McCafferty. Jean Meyer. Alan Gerson. Cindy Meyer. Sean Meyer. Gabe Meyer. (Whole lotta Meyers!) And to all the others of the Clan: You're in here somewhere. Ditto for Alyce and Neil Robertson and their Morningside gals, Anne Marie and Kat.

Professional colleagues had their influence. To the journalists, thanks for all the nicknames you stuck on me in Hannibal, Columbia and Miami. To the foundation professionals, where's my grant? No, seriously, what a privilege it's been to work with you. Special shout out to the Communications Network.

To good friends everywhere, notably Mary and Dick Weden, Sheila and John Dunn, Patrick McCoy and Paul Advokaat, Barbara Dabney, Norah Schaefer, Pam Berry, Judy and Harry Warren, Ted Quaday, Lisa Smith and Andy McLeod.

On the road to writing: Mitchell Kaplan, Dave Barry, Judi Smith, Carl Hiaasen, Ken Wells, Randy Wayne White, Hodding Carter III, Alberto Ibargüen, Jose Zamora, Ron Sachs, Mike Capuzzo and Genevieve Gagne-Hawes.

Thanks to the pros' pros: Bill Pragluski of Critical Stages, Michael Huber of Millionth Monkey, Forrest Marquisee and Kaye Kohler. I don't need LinkedIn to offer the strongest recommendation for any of you.

Finally, to Anne Robertson: Muse, partner, inspiration and constant joy. I love you.